AWAKENED BY SIN

CRIME LORD SERIES, BOOK 4

MIA KNIGHT

COPYRIGHT

authormiaknight@gmail.com

DEDICATION

To Maile, my shadow who taught me my first lesson on heartbreak and loss and the true meaning of unconditional love.

1

SEVEN MONTHS AGO

FROM HER VANTAGE POINT IN THE VIP SECTION, CARMEN PYRE TOOK IN Incognito, the newest nightclub to open on the infamous Strip. The grand sweeping staircase and elegant chandeliers gave the club an upper-class feel, but the staff's uniform of leather and lace put off any notions that this was a run-of-the-mill club. An unholy crimson light set the mood and transformed the club into a decadent hell that encouraged them to indulge in their darkest fantasies. The atmosphere reeked of mystery and carnal delights, but she felt none of it.

Her nails dug into her leather clad thighs. It felt as if someone had picked up the blueprint for the dream house she planned with her late husband and invited her to do a walk-through without warning her that they used her discarded plans. Every detail was achingly familiar. She could feel it, those fucking tears just beneath the surface. The night she came up with the concept for Incognito played out in her mind in vivid detail. She'd always had a thing for costumes and had Vinny's full support in role playing. One night while 'serving' Vinny as a flight attendant, she came up with the idea of a club that would encourage people to conceal their identities and take advantage of the "What happens in Vegas, stays in Vegas" mentality. Incognito was her husband's last project, one he never finished before he was murdered.

You look beautiful, baby.

Her body locked as Vinny's familiar, reassuring voice drifted through her mind. She hung her head as memories cascaded through her. She spent a year and a half trying to outrun the memories of her husband. Now that she was back in Vegas, there was no escaping him. He was stamped into every square inch of this place. His voice whispered in her ears, stirring up a flurry of pain and loss that caused her chest to contract with the need to scream. She had been looking forward to attending this event, to let loose and forget her troubles. The Strip was her playground, an environment she had thrived in since she was sixteen. She'd hoped to be invigorated by the manic energy from the crowd, not be reminded of everything she had lost.

A striking couple made their way in her direction, distracting her before she lost her shit. The woman had honey blond hair, a slinky black halter dress, and a black lace mask with diamonds highlighting silver blue eyes. The man at her side was built like a linebacker and wore a dashing tux and black mask that made him seem even more dangerous than normal.

Lyla's eyes lit up as she rushed forward with a big smile. "You look great!"

Carmen hugged her cousin like a child in desperate need of reassurance. Lyla was the sister she never had and a beacon of hope in her otherwise dreary world. It had only been a few hours since they parted ways, but she wouldn't take anything for granted, not anymore. She pulled back and felt her pain recede as she took in Lyla's sparkling eyes. Her cousin was happy. No one looking at her would guess she'd been viciously attacked by a psychotic killer or that the high-necked gown she wore covered gruesome scars. The image of Lyla lying lifelessly in a hospital bed would be etched into her memory for all time.

She dredged up a smile and gave Lyla's ass a sharp smack. "You too."

She switched her gaze to Lyla's husband. Gavin Pyre, CEO of Pyre Casinos and former crime lord of Las Vegas, glowered at her. She had known Gavin for nearly a decade, long enough to see the good, the bad, and the downright evil in him. Gavin was on her shit list at the moment, despite Lyla's reassurances that her new husband wasn't abusing her.

Vinny's murder kicked off a series of bloody events, which left Uncle Manny dead, Lyla mutilated, and Gavin in prison. She spirited Lyla out of Las Vegas, and they went on the road. Four months ago, Gavin showed up in Montana and forced Lyla to marry him while also announcing that her father had died from a heart attack. They returned to Las Vegas, and she moved in with her grief-stricken mother. She hadn't recovered from losing Vinny and now had to cope with another staggering loss.

"Carmen," Gavin said, voice tight.

She gave him a cool look to show that he didn't intimidate her. "Gavin."

"Don't get into trouble tonight, Carmen."

Her temper, which had begun a slow burn the second she saw him, ignited. "Excuse me?"

"You look like—"

Lyla clapped a hand over her husband's mouth. "You look hot, and you're going to cause a commotion. He's nervous."

She flipped her hair and adjusted her boobs in her lace bustier. "He should be." There was a two-inch gap between the bottom of her top and the skintight leather pants. A glance in the mirror before she left the house told her that she looked sexy, confident, and in control. No one would see beneath the slutty exterior to her shredded insides. The white mask she'd been handed before she entered the club added just the right touch to her outfit.

Gavin yanked Lyla's hand from his mouth. "I just want to get through tonight without drama. Got me?"

His orders never failed to get on her nerves. Vinny had always deferred to him. How Lyla put up with his autocratic ass, she would never know. The only way she could handle him was to view him as an overbearing, annoying big brother. And like any irritating sister, she did her best to antagonize the hell out of him.

"I'm not making any promises," she said.

His eyes narrowed into slits. He opened his mouth to threaten her but was distracted when a man joined their group. The newcomer was dressed in a scarlet tux, cape, and red mask. He kissed Lyla on the cheek. Carmen glanced at Gavin, the possessive psycho. His jaw clenched, but he didn't go for the guy's throat, which piqued her interest. Vinny was the only man Gavin allowed to touch Lyla. Who was this guy?

"You look great," the stranger said to Lyla and turned toward her. "I don't think we've met."

Dark green eyes glittered through the slits of his mask. The man gave her a once-over that was curious rather than slimy. She was used to getting a reaction out of men, but he wasn't giving her one. Maybe her outfit wasn't slutty enough?

"This is Vinny's widow, Carmen," Gavin said.

Widow. The label smacked her in the face, causing a combination of pain and anger to tangle in her belly. Before she could snap at Gavin, the man in the red mask distracted her by taking her hand. Before she could pull away, he kissed her knuckles. It was a dignified, old-world gesture.

"My condolences," he said.

She shot Gavin an irritated glance before she focused on the mysterious stranger. "Thank you. And you are?"

"Marcus. I'm the new COO."

Gavin's new partner. "Vinny's replacement. Nice to meet you. You finished Incognito. It looks great."

"I'd like to talk to you if you don't mind."

She blinked. Talk to her about what? "I'm here to have fun and keep Lyla company. I don't want to discuss my husband."

"We don't have to discuss him. We can talk about something else," Marcus said.

Before she could think of something to say, Gavin interrupted. "Marcus, can I talk to you?"

"Sure." Marcus nodded to her. "I'll look for you later."

"For what?" she asked empty air since Marcus and Gavin had lost themselves in the crowd.

"Marcus is blunt and a bit strange, but I like him," Lyla said.

"But why would he want to talk to me? As Gavin said, I'm just a widow." God, she wanted to punch him, but that was nothing new. She slapped him the night she found out Vinny had been murdered, but she doubted he would let another assault pass without consequences. "As if that's all I am, a dead man's wife. Jesus, I'm a person, dammit."

"You know Gavin has no tact," Lyla said consolingly.

"And no manners."

"Let's get a drink."

Right. A drink. That's what she should have done the second she walked into the club.

"What's the special tonight?" she asked the well-endowed bartender.

"We have a drink called the Hookup that has tequila and—"

"I'll get two."

"You got it."

She watched the bartender's tits jiggle as she paraded along the bar. "Who's your doctor?"

"Dr. Hosen."

Carmen recognized the name and mentally filed it away for future reference. Years ago, she got a boob job to make her waist appear smaller, and now... now, she didn't give a crap about her waist. The Playboy look she'd favored since high school didn't do it for her anymore. On a recent trip to the salon, she dyed her platinum locks black, and now she was considering the unthinkable—going back to her natural breasts.

"Yours look amazing," the bartender said.

"They're okay, but they don't look as soft as yours. Let's see." She reached out, and the bartender did the same so they could compare.

The bartender nodded. "I'd say they feel about the same."

Carmen jumped when someone kicked her in the butt. She glanced over her shoulder and found Lyla glaring at her. "What?"

"Carmen, this is Alice, the community outreach coordinator." Lyla gestured to a woman standing nearby. "Alice, this is my cousin, Carmen. She's coming with us to the dog shelter next week to volunteer."

She was transfixed by the hideous, ill-fitted satin dress Alice wore. She looked like she just left an 80s high school prom. All that was missing were the braces and a metallic scrunchy in her hair. She looked as out of place in Incognito as a kindergartener at a strip club. Alice's mousy brown hair was pulled back in a halfhearted, messy twist, and her amber earrings didn't match her outfit.

"Nice to meet you," she said and shook Alice's hand. "You work for Pyre Casinos?"

"Yes. I just moved from Utah." Alice's eyes flicked over Carmen before she flushed and looked away.

"Mormon?" Carmen prodded, wondering if this woman was from a strict religious background that didn't allow modern clothing or makeup. It would explain her horrible fashion choices.

Alice frowned. "No. Why?"

"Just wondering." Surely, Alice owned a mirror.

Lyla shot her a repressive look. Carmen sipped her drink as she listened to them talk about the volunteer events that Alice was organizing. She didn't look tough enough to be in Las Vegas, much less working for Gavin.

"How long have you worked at Pyre Casinos?" she asked.

"A year. My position was created after..." Alice flushed and looked away.

"After Gavin went to jail and my husband and Manny Pyre were murdered?" Being politically correct had never interested her. It was a waste of time.

Her eyes flared with remorse. "Oh my gosh, I'm so sorry."

"It's okay, Alice," Lyla said, squeezing her hand. "I'm glad your position was created. It's great that Pyre Casinos created the Pyre Foundation and are giving back to the community."

"Yes," Alice said, clearly relieved. "Mr. Pyre has given me free rein really. I'm so excited that I get to make a difference through his generosity."

Alice's transparency was alarming. She was a goldfish among great white sharks. The men in this city would eat her alive. Alice wouldn't last long if she continued to broadcast her feelings on her face. She had to give this poor girl lessons on how to be a badass bitch.

"Here come the masses," Lyla said.

Carmen looked up as the VIPs descended into the club from the grand staircase with their entourage and a swarm of paparazzi. One figure stood out to her among the others. "Kody Singer's here?"

"The movie star?" Alice asked, going on tiptoe to get a better look.

"He better not come by me." She didn't need the drama tonight.

"Why?" Alice asked.

"He used to drunk call me all the time, that asshole. It used to piss Vinny off." Kody caused a shitload of problems in her marriage.

Alice's mouth dropped. "You used to date ...?"

"He was a week-long fling when Vinny and I were on a break."

"She broke his heart," Lyla said. "Kody is a pretty nice guy for a movie star. Come on, Carmen, he was really romantic."

"He doesn't know how to take no for an answer," she said sourly and switched her attention to the next VIP. "Douchebag in the house! Carter Raymond is here. Seriously, when's the last time he even played football? What a fucking show-off."

"You know him personally?" Alice asked.

"When your husband is COO of Pyre Casinos, you're obligated to go to a lot of events. You meet people." Before, it had been a game to acquire famous contacts. Now, she couldn't care less about who she brushed shoulders with.

"You stay around long enough; you'll know celebrities personally," Lyla said.

"Me? Celebrities?" Alice let out a nervous giggle-snort. "I don't think so."

Carmen signaled to the bartender with the great fake tits for another Hookup cocktail. "Getting celebrities involved in your community projects would be great publicity."

"I'm having a hard time recruiting volunteers, much less a celebrity."

To gain the media's attention, Alice needed celebrities to join her community events. Tonight, there was an exclusive pool to manipulate and exploit. Carmen eyed the crowd and decided it was time to call in some favors.

"I'll see what I can do," she said as she finished her drink.

She sauntered into the crowd and headed for the VIP tables. She nodded to the publicists, agents, and managers who recognized and waved her through. Unfortunately, the first celebrity who noticed her was Carter Raymond, a football player who retired in his prime and had been riding the sponsorship wave ever since.

"Yo, Carmen, you looking for me?"

He placed his hands on her hips as if he had every right to touch her.

"No, I'm not," she said flatly.

"Aw, girl, don't be so cold," he chided and flashed a smile that did nothing for her.

She patted his chest and gave him a patronizing smile. "Don't worry. I'm sure you won't be sleeping alone tonight. I can practically smell the hoes making their way to you right now."

"And if they aren't what I want?"

"That's your tough shit," she said and slapped his hands away.

"When you're ready, Carmen, you know where to find me!" he called after her.

She didn't acknowledge his statement. Men with money and power couldn't stand being denied something they wanted. Of course, once they acquired that something, they lost interest. That's how men of Carter's caliber worked. She wasn't interested in being someone's plaything. If anything, she wanted to be the one pulling strings and calling the shots. She was a fucking millionaire. She didn't have to dance to anyone's tune, especially not a selfish asshole with an ego.

The crowd erupted into excited screams as the stage lights flared, revealing a popular band. She tried to absorb the excitement emanating from the crowd. Tonight was about living in the moment. Drinks, superficial talk, and a good time. That was what she came for.

"Carmen!"

She kissed both cheeks of Bridgette Mackee, an up-and-coming actress. "Bridgette, it's been a long time!"

"It has! Where have you been?" Before Carmen could answer, Bridgette continued, "You know Gavin Pyre, right? Can you introduce me?"

Bridgette looked like a woman on a mission. Clearly, she was ready to take her career to the next level and was tired of her good girl image. Being seen with a notorious billionaire would give her the publicity boost she needed, but she chose the wrong target. Gavin was no one's fool, and despite the fact that she opposed Lyla's marriage, she wasn't going to allow Bridgette to sabotage it.

"He's married," Carmen said, and when Bridgette shrugged that off, she added, "to my cousin."

Bridgette blinked and drew back. "Oh."

"Why don't you try Carter?" Carmen suggested. She didn't fault Bridgette for her plan. If she had to play up to a man for a couple of hours to skyrocket her career, why not?

Bridgette glanced at Carter who was getting a lap dance. "I hope she isn't underage, or he'll get more publicity than all of us."

Carmen grinned and glanced around the VIP section. "How about The Punisher?"

Bridgette followed Carmen's line of sight to the hot UFC fighter. "You know him?" Bridgette breathed.

"Yup. Let's go." She hooked her arm through Bridgette's and made her way to The Punisher who stood when she approached. He gave her a peck on the cheek.

"Sorry about Vinny," he said.

"Thank you." She gave him a hug before she stepped back. "I want you to meet my friend, Bridgette. Bridgette, The Punisher."

The Punisher gave Bridgette a quick, appreciative once-over and then took her hand. "Hey."

"Hey," Bridgette said and gave Carmen a look that said I owe you.

Well, that was the point. She would let Bridgette's career mature before she called on the starlet. Carmen excused herself and moved onto the next celebrity, a young politician who could be president one day. For now, he was being a good boy and hanging with his crowd—businessmen, lawyers and the like, but she sensed his restlessness. He made a subtle play for her while the look in his eyes was anything but. She would bet money he was a regular at an exclusive gentlemen's club and had a discreet mistress.

She moved onto an old friend of Vinny's, an eccentric film director named Phoenix. She enjoyed his crazy hand movements and overzealous explanation of his current "art."

"The Pyre Foundation is doing some great things," she said when he paused to take a breath. "Would you mind talking to some kids about your art?"

"Kids?" Phoenix repeated as if she was asking him to talk to hyenas.

"You say you want to inspire people. Why not the next generation? Long after you're gone, they'll be talking about how you prodded their muse and dedicated their movies to you, the great one."

She could see that the idea appealed to him. She gained his tentative agreement and moved onto the next... and the next. Despite being on the road for over a year, her social skills hadn't suffered. She could bullshit with the best of them—flattering, tugging strings, and slapping down those who deserved it. This was her area of expertise and why she excelled on Vinny's arm.

At some point, she felt eyes on her. She glanced up and saw an attractive man watching her. He had the hot All-American thing going on. He had classic, pleasing features with dark hair, thick brows, and long lashes that framed big green eyes. He appeared to be in his early to mid-thirties. Everything was perfect from his styled hair to tailored slacks, black button up, and red silk tie. She had always been a sucker for a well-groomed gentleman.

"You're a pro," he said when he reached her.

"At what?" She waited for a sleazy line like, "Making me want you."

"Networking. You know how to handle difficult clients."

Okay, that was unexpected. She took a closer look at him and detected a gleam of amusement in his eyes. "Who says I was networking?"

"I do it for a living. I know another pro when I see her. What's your aim?"

"Aim?"

"What do you want from them?"

She inwardly bristled. She wasn't sure if he was accusing her of something. "Who are you?"

"Marcus Fletcher."

Her stomach clenched. The COO she met earlier. At some point, he ditched the red mask and cape for a spiffy suit. How could she have known he was hiding a handsome face under the mask? "Oh."

"What's your aim?" he asked again.

She considered ignoring him, but technically, they were his guests, so she admitted, "I'm helping Alice."

"Alice?"

"Your community outreach coordinator."

"I know who Alice is," he said patiently. "What are you helping her with?"

"Outreach."

"By talking to celebrities?"

"By asking them to attend events for better publicity."

Marcus smiled. It looked good on him—natural and genuine. She didn't want to like him and definitely didn't like the low curl of attraction that wriggled to life in her belly. She hadn't felt a thing for any man since Vinny died and didn't like that she felt a pull toward this man.

She took a step back and wasn't prepared when he took her hand.

"That's nice of you to help Alice," he said.

She looked pointedly at the hand clasping hers. "Yeah, well, I'm busy so—"

"What do you think of Incognito?"

She glanced at the dance floor, which was a writhing mass of beautiful people moving to the beat, and stated the obvious, "It looks like a success."

"Is it what you imagined?"

She looked back at him. "Excuse me?"

"You were involved in the initial concept. Is this what you imagined?"

She was nonplussed. "How do you know that?"

"Vinny had extensive notes."

Vinny had been a compulsive notetaker. He couldn't remember anything unless he jotted it down. What had Vinny included in his notes about Incognito? He wouldn't have mentioned her fondness for costumes, would he?

She searched his deep green eyes. "What kind of notes?"

"All kinds."

Something about his tone betrayed him. He knew about the costumes. She jerked her hand out of his and tipped her nose in the air. "You should give me any notes that aren't relative to your position as COO."

"They're extremely helpful," Marcus said. "And you came up with a great concept."

"It may have been a great concept, but you took it to the next level," she said with grudging admiration. A part of her resented the fact that Marcus had been able to execute Vinny's plans so flawlessly. "It came out better than I imagined. I'm glad you finished his project."

"If you have time, there are other projects I'd like your input on."

"Excuse me?"

"You're behind some of the most successful restaurants and nightclubs that Pyre Casinos has turned out in the past five years."

No one knew how heavily she had been involved in Pyre developments. She enjoyed playing the blonde bimbo. Only Vinny saw through her act and tapped her intellect, something she loved him all the more for. He talked to her about everything. She enjoyed helping him flesh out concepts. The fact that Marcus uncovered a piece of her that no one else knew about sent a streak of unease through her.

"I'm sure you'll do fine on your own," she said and took a step back.

"You aren't what I expected."

Even though she shouldn't take the bait, she stopped. "What did you expect?" Damn Vinny and his stupid notes.

"I've seen pictures of you, but you're more beautiful in person."

She was used to outrageous flattery, but the way he said it was more like a statement of fact rather than a come-on. What was Marcus Fletcher's deal? Why was he deliberately singling her out? He had Vinny's job, so what more did he want?

"I heard you went on the road with Lyla after her accident," Marcus continued. "I've wanted to meet you both."

"Why?"

"I wanted to meet the woman who could bring Gavin to his knees." He cocked his head to the side. "And I wanted to meet the woman Vincent Pyre worshipped."

The tears hit without warning. One moment, her eyes were clear, and the next, they were flooded. Her insides, which had been empty a moment before, were suddenly swamped with grief. She reached for an anchor. Her hand touched something solid, and she gripped out of blind instinct as she tried to control her pitching emotions.

"I'm sorry," Marcus said quietly.

How he closed the distance between them so quickly, she didn't know. She was too focused on trying to control her emotions that threatened to consume her. This was a nightmare.

"I heard about your father. That can't be easy after losing Manny and Vinny. I'm truly sorry for your losses."

None of the condolences she heard tonight affected her the way Marcus's did. It was the sincerity and sympathy in his words that made her feel as if he were slicing into her chest with a dull knife.

She twisted her hand in his shirt, threatening to rip buttons. He didn't try to stop her. He slid his hand beneath the fall of her hair and cupped the back of her neck with a familiarity that shocked her. She jerked her head up and stared at his blurry image through the tears.

He massaged her nape. "Are you okay? I didn't mean to—"

The intimacy of his touch and the way he addressed her as if he knew and cared about her felt wrong. He didn't know her, and she didn't want to know him. She pushed away and with great effort, stuffed her emotions into the empty, yawning pit to deal with later. Under normal circumstances, she would have sailed into Marcus, but she was barely holding herself together. Did he do it on purpose? Marcus might have earned Gavin and Lyla's approval, but he hadn't earned hers.

She stalked away. Within a matter of minutes, Marcus destroyed her composure and shoved her toward a precipice she'd been avoiding all night.

I'm still here, baby.

Pain threatened to bring her to her knees. He wasn't here, and she would never hear his voice again. She could feel the breakdown coming, like a freight train with no brakes careening toward the station. She scanned the crowd for Lyla, but it would be a miracle to find her in this crush. Her hands rose to grasp handfuls of her hair. She opened her mouth to scream—

"Carmen, I've been looking for… What's wrong, babe?"

Large, warm hands grasped her shoulders. She dropped her hands from her hair and stared into Kody Singer's soulful brown eyes.

"You okay?" Kody's hands smoothed down her arms, which were covered in cold sweat. "You're shaking. What's wrong?"

It's gonna be okay, baby.

She dropped her face on Kody's chest to hide the way her face crumpled. It wasn't going to be okay. It would never be okay. She took a shuddering breath and then another, trying to get a hold of herself.

"Did someone do something to you?" Kody asked in a low rumble.

She shook her head and couldn't hold back the hitch in her breath. The sound of the festive crowd clashed with her devastated state. Grief drowned out everything around her, filling her world with black loneliness.

Kody wrapped her close, and she let him. She wasn't sure how long they stood there, and she didn't care. He pressed a kiss to her temple.

"Vinny?"

Would there ever be a day when she would hear Vinny's name and not be affected by it? She nodded because there was no sense in denying it. Kody stroked the line of her spine.

"I'm sorry, Carmen."

For some reason, his condolences didn't have the same impact that Marcus's had, and for that, she was grateful. She ran a finger under her eye to brush away the last bit of wet and looked up. "Thanks. I'm—"

"Still hurting," Kody finished and trailed a finger over the curve of her chin. "Lucky bastard."

She let out a choked laugh, and he grinned. During a break with Vinny, she had hooked up with Kody after seeing Vinny in a club with some bitches. She decided to give Vinny a taste of his own medicine and went on a trip with Kody, which had been highly publicized. Even after she broke off the affair and got back with Vinny, Kody continued to call her and let her know how willing he was to replace Vinny.

The yearning in his eyes made her inwardly grimace. She'd known he wasn't the type for a wild weekend. He might be a Hollywood leading man, but he wasn't a playboy. He was a good Southern boy at heart and apparently, a one-woman man. Kody was a great guy and not for the likes of someone like her. She would drive him insane.

Belatedly, she realized what a spectacle she had made of them. Kody always had paparazzi following him. She glanced around and didn't see anyone snapping photos, but she spotted Marcus. He was still perched on the edge of a table, unabashedly staring. She resisted the urge to flip him off. That was probably what he wanted, the fucking bastard.

"I was hoping to see you tonight," Kody said, drawing her attention back to him. "It's been a long time."

"Yes. A lot has changed." Too much in too little time. She felt like life was giving her the beating of a lifetime. She got knocked down and managed to get on her hands and knees only to get kicked in the face. She brushed a hand over his bicep, which was definitely larger than the last time she saw him. "You're doing superhero movies now?"

"Yeah. You a fan?"

She hadn't indulged in a superhero movie, but maybe she was due. "I haven't seen your latest movies, but I've seen the posters. Your career is really taking off. Good for you, Kody."

"Do you want to get out of here?"

She was here to forget her reality for a few hours but hooking up with Kody would be a disaster. When she broke her self-imposed celibacy, it would be with a guy who knew the score. She didn't have anything to offer anyone, and Kody was a relationship man. That was the last thing she needed in her life. "No, I think I need to get drunk and dance."

"I'll come with you."

She cupped his cheek. "I don't want to see my face all over the internet tomorrow."

"Are you sure you're going to be okay?"

No. "Yes."

"If you need to talk, I'm here for you," he said seriously.

That warmed her shattered insides. She went on tiptoe and kissed his cheek. "I'll catch you later, okay?"

She eased out of his hold. She came here tonight to take a break from life, and that was what she would do. It was time to do what she did best—party her ass off and leave her troubles behind. Even though she didn't feel the beat in her bones, she lifted her arms in the air and shimmied through the crowd. She made her way to the bar by squeezing two men's asses, did two shots off a beautiful redhead, and downed two more before she headed to the dance floor.

She focused on the fist-pumping beat and let it fill her. The alcohol did its job. The pain in her chest evaporated, and she reveled in the smell of sweat, alcohol, and perfume. The press of people was comforting. Hands played over her sweat-slick body as she danced. A guy who couldn't be older than twenty-three grinded against her. She didn't discriminate. She wrapped an arm around his neck and swiveled her hips against his erection. His eyes went blind with need, and he kneaded her ass. His touch didn't evoke a spark of anticipation or excitement—nothing. Had Vinny ruined her for all men? The stranger's hands slid over her midriff and then traced the waistband of her leather pants.

"Hey."

Marcus stood in front of her, and he didn't look so smiley and easygoing now. He looked irritated, and for some reason, that made him more interesting than the guy grinding against her. The boy toy's hands stopped an inch from her breasts.

"She's married," Marcus bit out.

Her buzz disappeared. His words were as effective as a slap in the face. She was dimly aware of the boy toy backing off. Obviously, he thought Marcus was her husband.

"You can do better than that," Marcus said as he latched onto her wrist and tried to yank her off the dance floor.

She couldn't believe this guy! She caught sight of Alice watching with her mouth hanging open. She yanked away from Marcus and snatched Alice's hand, pulling her into the crowd with her. Fucking Marcus blew her high, so she needed a distraction, and Alice provided the perfect opportunity. She would spend the night showing Alice how to live it up on the glorious Strip.

"What's going on?" Alice hollered.

She stopped in the middle of the crush and faced Alice who looked rumpled and uneasy. "Marcus is being a dick."

Alice jerked. "A what?"

"Never mind. Dance with me."

She pulled Alice against her front and began to move.

"What are you doing?" Alice squeaked.

"Don't think. Just feel."

She wrapped her arms around Alice, who was as stiff as a mannequin. Carmen moved, encouraging the other woman to lose herself in the music and soak in the atmosphere. Alice did an odd two-step, and her eyes flicked from person to person. She grasped Alice's face and kissed her. Alice went rigid but didn't pull away. Carmen kissed her gently, seeking basic human connection and comfort when she felt so alone. She focused on the softness of her soft lips and... was that grape lip balm? Carmen swayed, and this time Alice moved with her, too distracted by the kiss to be uptight. When she pulled away, Alice's eyes were as big as saucers.

"I-I'm not... I mean, I don't swing that way," Alice stammered.

For the first time that night, Carmen grinned. "Me either."

"Then why—?"

"Look, now you can dance." She playfully swiveled her hips, and Alice copied before reason returned, and she went stiff again.

Alice stared at her as if she was an ax murderer. "I don't think this is appropriate."

"Appropriate?" She laughed and swung Alice around, making the skirt of her ugly dress flare. "You're in a club called Incognito. We encourage bad behavior." She gestured to the wall of mirrors surrounding the dance floor. "Behind the mirrors are private rooms you can rent by the minute."

"By the minute?" Alice echoed, and then her mouth sagged as it hit home. "Are you serious?"

"Of course, I am." Carmen accepted a kiss from a passing man without blinking.

Alice pushed the man away and tucked Carmen protectively against her. "You're drunk. You shouldn't... This isn't my scene."

"I know, but it's what you chose."

Alice frowned. "I didn't choose this."

"You chose Vegas, and you chose Pyre Casinos. This is an extension of your world, one you have to get used to."

Alice pursed her lips as she turned her words over in her mind before she gave a reluctant nod. "What do I need to do?"

Carmen leaned forward and whispered, "Live."

"I am living," Alice said.

"There's living and then living."

"I don't understand."

Carmen grabbed Alice's hand and led her off the dance floor.

"Where are we going?"

"Bar. You need liquid courage," Carmen said.

"For what?"

"To give you the balls you need to get what you want in life."

"I have what I want in life," Alice hollered over the sound of the crowd.

Carmen shamelessly used her body to make a space for them at the bar. "Two Hookups," she ordered.

"You can order a one-night stand at the bar?" Alice sounded scandalized.

Carmen laughed, pushed Alice onto a stool, and wrapped her arms around her. Alice was definitely a marshmallow and not ready to face the carnal sins that would come her way sooner or later. Innocence wasn't a part of her world. It had never been. She could spot a prostitute or stripper at a glance, had a breast consultation before she graduated from high school, and made out with her friends so they would be pros with their boyfriends. Nothing was out of bounds.

Alice quivered. Was she getting ready to bolt? Carmen ran her hands over the other woman in a bid to soothe and distract. Alice jerked as if she had been shot.

"What, are you a virgin?" she asked without thinking.

Alice's red face was all the answer she needed. Carmen stared at her. "Are you sure you're not a Mormon?" Mormon's were notorious for staying virgins until marriage.

Alice glared at her and didn't answer.

"Are you sure you aren't a lesbian?"

"Yes!"

"Then why are you—?"

"I'm focusing on my career."

Alice was clearly frazzled and reached out for the cocktail placed in front of her. She took a sip, and her eyes widened.

"This tastes good," she said, pleased.

Carmen didn't bother to warn her how potent it was. "Drink up."

It would be a long night.

2

FOUR MONTHS AGO

"YOU LIKE THAT, BABY?"

Carmen didn't respond to her dance partner. She had no idea what he looked like and didn't care. All she cared about was the relentless beat, the liquor flowing through her veins, and the bulge pressed against her ass.

Tonight was the night. She would exorcise Vinny once and for all. She couldn't take it anymore. She needed to feel something—need, excitement, anticipation, lust—anything but sorrow. Lyla was pregnant, content in her marriage, and making plans for the future. Her mother now had such a busy social life that she barely saw her anymore. Everyone had moved on except her. The fact that the monster who called the hit on Vinny was still on the loose enraged her, but like so many other things, there was nothing she could do. For a decade, she melded herself to the love of her life, and now, he was gone. Her broken heart left an invisible trail of blood in her wake. She was wasting away, but no one noticed. She lived in a world with muted tones, as if being in love with a dead man was killing her a little bit every day. The only way she could move forward was to cut out a piece of her soul and break her wedding vows by indulging in the oldest and most potent sin—sex.

"You want to take this somewhere else?"

She turned and looked up at her companion. He had been grinding against her for a good ten minutes now. She hooked her arms around his neck and surveyed him dispassionately. Hispanic, early twenties, very white teeth, and waxed brows so he was a bit on the metrosexual side. He had a nice body and would be labeled by most women as hot. None of that mattered to her.

"Lead the way," she said.

He tried to play it cool, but the colored lights showed dilated pupils and hard nipples through the thin material of his shirt.

"Okay," he said and clasped her hand before he began to lead the way through the crowd.

She briefly searched the crowd for Janice and Alice. She had met them for dinner at a Pyre Casinos restaurant to plan Lyla's baby shower. After, she bullied them into the club and lost track of them once she started doing shots at the bar.

When she realized her companion was heading toward the exit, she tugged on his hand. He turned and leaned close when she went on tiptoe.

"I want you to fuck me here," she said.

His Adam's apple bobbed. "Here?"

"Bathroom."

Fast and dirty was how she wanted it. She didn't want to go to this guy's apartment and act as if this was anything more than a random hookup. This was a slam, bam, thank you, ma'am, and she wanted it over before her conscience piped up, which was why she was nice and drunk. If she was going to be miserable, she wanted a damn good reason to be.

"Are you sure?" he asked.

Despite his question, she could see the excitement he tried to hide. What man didn't want a random hookup?

"Yes."

She started toward the bathroom and rolled her eyes when she saw the long lines. She veered toward the private lounge. The prospect pulled on her arm.

"That's for VIPs," he said.

She walked up to the bouncer who inclined his head and opened the door.

"Whoa, that was cool. You got connections, mama?"

She ignored his question and dragged him down a long hallway filled with private rooms for VIPs. He was thoroughly distracted now, which pissed her off. She made a beeline for the door at the end of the hall and yanked him into the women's bathroom. The bathroom was opulent and done in black and gold. A bright-eyed bathroom attendant sprung off her stool with a belt full of makeup brushes, perfume, pasties, glue, condoms, and more. She was ready to assist in any way.

"Scat for a couple of minutes. Watch the door," Carmen ordered and handed over two hundred dollars.

"Whoa, you're rich?" the prospect asked.

The bathroom attendant took the money and exited while the prospect started talking excitedly.

"Are you famous or—?" he began.

She pushed him against the wall and kissed him. He stopped talking and clamped his hands on her ass. She rubbed her crotch against his to entice her pussy. There was no spark of interest, nothing.

Carmen.

She stiffened as Vinny's voice tried to intrude. She should have taken another shot. She broke the kiss. "Go down on me."

He hesitated. "I don't—"

"If you don't go down on me, I won't go down on you."

He dropped so fast it would have been funny if she was in a laughing mood. She wasn't. She was beginning to panic. Was she destined to be a numb, celibate zombie for the rest of her life? A crazy woman who had one-sided conversations with her dead husband? The echo of his voice wasn't a source of comfort but one of immense pain. She couldn't do this any longer.

She was about to raise her dress when the bathroom door opened. She opened her mouth to tell them to get lost when Marcus walked in. He looked extremely fine in a navy suit that fit him like a glove. He let the door swing shut and looked down at the man on his knees in front of her, clearly about to eat her out. The fact that Vinny's replacement seemed determined to interrupt her from moving on was beyond annoying.

She crossed her arms. "Can I help you?"

"I thought I saw you," he said pleasantly as if they were at a cocktail party and not in the women's bathroom. "What are you doing, Carmen?"

"What does it look like?" she snapped.

"It looks like you're about to make a mistake." Marcus jerked his chin at the prospect. "Get lost."

"Hey, buddy, this isn't your business."

"It is," Marcus said, "and I run this place. Get out."

The prospect got to his feet and extended his hand to her. "Come on, mama, let's get out of here."

And go where? She wanted to be banged right here, right now in a public bathroom where it would be sordid and final. She didn't want to get a room for an hour. She examined the prospect objectively. Her sex radar told her he would be a lousy lay. He wouldn't bother to get her off, which would make her feel worse than she already did. The prospect wasn't old enough to move past jackrabbit sex.

She slumped against the wall in defeat. "Maybe next time."

The prospect was clearly bewildered. He looked back and forth between them before he shook his head and walked out.

She crossed her arms. "What do you want, Marcus?"

"You can do better than that, Carmen."

"I don't want better!" She stalked forward and prodded him in the chest. "This is the second time you've cock-blocked me. What's your problem?"

"I seem to have a problem with you trying to have sex in my clubs." When she opened her mouth to shout, he added, "And watching you sell yourself short."

"I can fuck whoever I want! I am gonna get laid tonight, even if I have to do it in the back alley."

"Why in a public place?"

He didn't sound shocked or appalled, merely curious. For some reason, this pissed her off even more. She'd run into him several times after Incognito's opening. He attended Lyla's baby gender party and two other functions. He always made a point to come up to her and chat as if they were old friends, which couldn't be further from the truth. Despite her one-word answers and subtle put-downs, he remained unfazed. She didn't want to like him, but he handled Lyla with genuine affection and effortlessly riled Gavin. This should have made him her partner in crime, but it felt wrong, almost like she was betraying Vinny by enjoying his company. No one could replace her husband, but that was what Marcus had done. He replaced Vinny as COO so well that Gavin had more free time than he'd ever had and business was booming. She didn't know how she felt about Marcus, so she avoided him to no avail. He popped up when she least expected him—like now. He was always well-groomed and annoyingly unruffled.

The urge to shock him made her say, "I need a fuck, and I don't want anyone to get the wrong idea. It's a hookup, nothing more."

She started for the door, but he stepped in front of her, eyes crinkled with concern.

"Carmen."

She held up a hand because she could hear what was coming. "I don't need you to tell me I'll get past this. It's been two years, and I'm not past it. It isn't going away. I need to snap myself out of this. I need to feel something..."

"Carmen," he began again with such gentleness that her alcohol-suppressed emotions began to stir.

"This is none of your business, Marcus. I know you have a big brother complex, but I can take care of myself."

She walked around him and reached for the door handle. His hand splayed over the shiny surface, keeping the door shut.

"Is that what you really want?" he asked.

"Move," she bit out.

He pressed against her back. The smell of his cologne wafted around her, and she stiffened as his body heat penetrated through the thin material of her slutty dress.

"I'm willing," he said.

Her hand tightened on the door handle. She couldn't have heard right.

"If that's what you want, I'll give it to you," he said.

She turned and examined him through a haze of alcohol and misery. "What?"

"Why are you so shocked? Don't most men want you?" he asked.

"Yes," she said without conceit. "But you're ..."

"I'm what?"

He was Gavin's COO. They would have to see one another after this. That defeated the purpose of a hookup. "I don't know ..."

He shifted her away from the door and placed her back against the wall. He cupped her cheek with that bold familiarity that freaked her out. This time, she didn't move away.

"Why are you so determined to waste yourself on boys who don't know what to do with you?" he asked.

"No one's ever going to measure up to Vinny," she said as his thumb rested against her bottom lip.

"No one will measure up if you're looking at the bottom of the barrel."

She shoved him, dislodging his hand from her face. "I'm not interested in a lecture. Hookups don't talk, Marcus, they fuck."

He slipped his hands into his pockets. "Do they?"

"Yes!"

His lips twitched. "It depends who you're hooking up with."

She bared her teeth. "I call the shots in this hookup, and I say no talking!"

He cocked his head to the side. "Is this what you've been doing since Vinny passed?"

She wanted to strangle him. "I haven't been with anyone since Vinny!"

He looked appalled. "And this is how you want your first time to be?"

"Yes!"

"Carmen—"

She held up a shaking finger. "Don't judge me! You have no idea what I've been through, no idea what it feels like to lose everything ..."

Alcohol suffocated her emotions, but she was losing her nerve. He was making her think, and that was the last thing she needed. Vinny's hold on her was so tight she couldn't breathe, couldn't function. If she didn't break his hold on her, she would be stuck in purgatory.

Marcus stared at her. Something was going on in his eyes, but she couldn't begin to decipher what that was. She felt very exposed under the bright lights, and this could only end in disaster. Even as the thought drifted through her mind, he nodded. He closed the distance between them and sank to his knees before her.

"If that's what you want, I'll give it to you," he said.

He leaned forward and nuzzled her crotch through her dress. She went rigid as a flash of heat shot from her breasts to her pussy. Adrenaline zipped through her veins as large hands slid beneath her dress and skimmed down the backs of her thighs, knees, and lower. He lifted her foot and kissed her ankle. She sucked in a breath that was amplified in the quiet bathroom. He looked up. Their eyes connected, and her body tightened. Despite his submissive position, there was nothing shy about the way he was looking at her. Green eyes glittered with the promise of carnal satisfaction. Warmth pooled low.

"Tell me what you want, Carmen," he murmured as he set her foot down and repeated the action with her other ankle.

He branded her knees with achingly sweet kisses and moved to her thighs.

"Your skin feels like silk. I can't believe you would waste yourself on that boy. It's sacrilege. You were meant to be cherished."

Once upon a time, she had been, but that felt like ages ago. There was no use searching for the perfect man because he wasn't out there. Vinny was her soulmate, and no one would ever fit her as well as he had. She had to learn to be satisfied with dirty, meaningless sex.

"What do you need?" he asked as his hands slipped beneath her dress and cupped her ass.

She thought he was a squeaky-clean, good boy, but he was ruining her image of him. He didn't seem the type to agree to a bathroom hookup. Obviously, he had a secret kink, so she would take advantage of it. She would probably regret this in the future, but she was too far gone to care. "I want it hard and rough."

"Mmmhmm." He pulled her dress up and examined her underwear. He grinned. "You came prepared."

"Of course." She squirmed as he stared at her. "We don't have all night, Fletcher."

He smiled. "Right."

He dipped his head, and his tongue slid over her. His hands on her ass gripped, and she angled her hips for him. The crotch less underwear she wore had been a calculated move on her part, and as his tongue slid inside her, she said a silent prayer of thanks. Pleasure unfurled inside her body, which had been in hibernation for too long. He grabbed one leg and slipped it over his shoulder, giving him better access. She closed her eyes and tipped her head back as she absorbed the feel of a man paying homage. Her body began to thaw, inch by slow inch, until the leg she was balancing on began to shake. Abruptly, she yanked his head back.

"Now," she ordered.

"So responsive," he crooned and kissed her quivering belly.

"Marcus," she snapped.

He laughed as he rose. He clasped her face between his hands and kissed her. His kiss was nothing like what she shared with the prospect. He tasted earthy, tempting, with a hint of spearmint. Her heart slammed against her rib cage so hard she was afraid he could feel it. Exultation raced through her. She wasn't sure why Marcus's touch evoked something in her, but at the moment, she didn't care. Desperate to feel more, she wrapped her arms around his neck and pulled him closer. He rubbed his erection against her while she clawed the back of his suit with her pointed fingernails.

"Now," she panted and undid his belt and pulled down his zipper in rapid succession.

"Mm," he hummed and cupped her breast.

She froze. She got breast implants at twenty-one. In Vegas, this was as common as getting braces. A couple of months ago, she took them out and was now back to a B cup. Holy fuck. No one told her how sensitive her breasts would be now that they were all natural again.

"Carmen?"

"Suck me," she whispered.

She didn't need to ask twice. He pulled down the top of her dress and pulled her breast into his mouth. When he flicked her nipple with his tongue, she nearly gave herself a concussion when her head kicked back against the wall.

"That's it," she declared as she pulled his cock out of his black briefs. He was hard and ready to go, just like her.

"I don't have a condom," he said.

She walked to the vanity where she left her clutch and retrieved one. He looked debauched in his spiffy suit with his dick out. She sank to her knees in front of him. She always believed in repaying a favor. She licked the tip, and he exhaled. She placed sloppy kisses on the underside of his penis without breaking eye contact.

"No," he growled.

He yanked her to her feet. He wasn't calm or controlled now. He pinned her against the wall and lifted one leg as he tried to fit himself to her.

"Wait," she said and showed him the condom.

"Put it on me."

She ripped the package with her teeth and smoothed the condom over him. She couldn't resist giving him a teasing stroke. He bared his teeth and shoved her hand away as he boosted her up with one arm. She closed her eyes. This was it. She held her breath.

"Look at me."

The growled order took a moment to penetrate. When she obeyed, she found herself looking at a man with one thing on his mind. The lust and need in his eyes amplified her own.

"Who's going to fuck you?" he demanded.

"Someone else if you don't hurry," she rasped.

He pressed against her, and she sucked in a breath. He tightened his hold on her waist when she squirmed. He wasn't even winded from holding her up. That added to her excitement. Every girl wanted to know a man could protect her... or fuck her against a wall without dropping her.

"Who's fucking you?" he asked again.

"You aren't fucking me, not yet." She closed her eyes and let out a low moan. "I can imagine that other guy fucking me just like this. I think he would—"

He embedded half his penis inside her. Her eyes flashed open as her body adjusted. Marcus stared at her, face pained as he tried to hold himself back. The force of his personality, normally concealed beneath a thick layer of civility was on full display. She was blinded by its primitive beauty.

"Marcus," she whispered.

The corner of his mouth quirked a second before he pushed until his pubic hair pressed against her smooth pussy. Carmen dropped her head back and panted as his cock, which stretched her just right, made itself at home. Vibrators and dildos did nothing for her. She needed a pulsing, warm cock, skin to skin contact, a man breathing against her neck, and hands digging into her hips. She needed the real deal. The slut who had been under lock and key for far too long urged her to cover his face with kisses. Instead, she wrapped a hand around his nape and tugged on his hair.

"Fuck me," she ordered.

He withdrew and slid home easily. She trembled with need. He closed his eyes. It was clear he was in ecstasy. The hands gripping her ass were going to leave bruises, but she didn't care.

He spread her thighs wide and began to move.

"Say my name," he ordered.

"Marcus." She would say whatever he wanted as long as he didn't stop. "Harder."

He obeyed and began to hammer her into the wall. She felt battered and dirty and loved it. She looked over his shoulder at a full-length mirror. Her inner muscles milked him. He grunted, dug his fingers into her flesh, and fucked her even faster.

Carmen examined their reflection. Her heels bounced with each thrust, and the image of her legs splayed wide for him was titillating. He buried his face against her neck, and she wrapped her arms around him and held on for dear life. Her gaze moved over his flexing ass, her nails clawing his back, and then her face, which was covered in tears. She released a handful of his suit to touch her cheek, not convinced the mirror was telling the truth. Her fingers came away wet.

She watched her face crumple in the mirror with dazed confusion. Grief flooded her, shutting down her senses one by one. Her limbs became heavy, and all that wonderful lust, excitement, and anticipation dried up in a nanosecond. The conscience she drowned in alcohol coughed up vodka and began to scream at her that this wasn't right—that she was still in love and cheating on Vinny's memory. She buried her face against Marcus's shoulder and hung on tight, willing his presence to banish the pain.

He stopped. "Carmen?"

She was trembling like a leaf in a storm. She clutched him desperately when he tried to draw back. "P-please."

"What's wrong? Did I hurt you?"

He was trying to draw away, and that was the last thing she wanted. A muffled sob escaped, and he went rigid. Despite her clutching limbs, he firmly extracted himself from her. She felt velvet beneath her butt as he settled her on a chaise in front of the vanity.

"Did I hurt you?"

She shook her head and tried to wipe away the tears. "I-I don't know what's wrong with me."

She wrapped her arms around herself as she began to rock. Her heart was being savaged by guilt and more pain than she could stand.

"I need alcohol," she said as her breath hitched. Oh, God. This couldn't be happening.

"I think you've had enough."

She reached out and clutched the lapels of his suit. "If you get me alcohol, we can finish. I can do this. I need to do this."

"You need to go home. Did you come with anyone?"

His detached tone told her he was done. The moment had passed. She bowed her head and clamped her thighs together. "Alice."

He moved away from her. She heard the rasp of clothing, the clink of his belt, and then a zipper. She bowed her head as mortification consumed her. Oh, God, she was an epic failure on so many levels.

"Alice, Carmen's in the VIP bathroom. Can you take her home? She's drunk and not feeling well. Yes. I'll meet you at the entrance."

There was a stark silence after he hung up. She cringed, waiting for the hail of insults or disparaging comments. She deserved them. She lured one man in here with the sole purpose of getting laid, only to have Marcus take his place and then cry all over him during what would have been spectacular sex. How pathetic was she? Her husband had been gone for two years and her first attempt to exorcise him ended in tears. She wished she could go back to feeling nothing. Shame wasn't better than grief.

"Is there anything I can do for you?" he asked.

Carmen shook her head.

"I'm sorry."

His polite apology made her flinch. This was her fault, not his. Even as she opened her mouth to reciprocate, she heard the soft snick of the door closing behind him. She buried her face in her hands as she drowned in humiliation and self-loathing.

"Carmen?"

The smell of fresh flowers reached her a second before Alice did. Desperate for human contact and a safe place, she wrapped her arms around her friend.

"Are you all right?" Alice asked as she rubbed her back.

Carmen nodded since she wasn't capable of speech at the moment.

"Can you walk?"

She nodded again.

"Good. Marcus says there's a back exit."

Alice helped her stand. She wobbled for a moment on her hooker heels and then steadied.

"Um ..." Alice brushed her dress down.

She didn't have the energy to be embarrassed over Alice seeing her crotch less underwear. Alice put an arm around her waist, which wasn't necessary, but it felt nice, so she leaned against her. Whey they exited, they came face to face with the bathroom attendant.

"Oh my gosh! What happened?" the bathroom attendant exclaimed.

"Aren't you supposed to be inside the bathroom, not outside?" Alice asked sharply.

"I paid her to stand outside," Carmen said wearily and directed Alice toward the exit for VIPs.

"Why would you do that?"

"I was being stupid."

"How?"

She didn't answer. They approached the exit, which was guarded by a bouncer. He took one look at Carmen's face and opened the door. Crying was bad for business, after all. They walked into the casino. Despite the late hour, it was brimming with people. Normally, crowds didn't blip on her radar, but right now facing a host of gawking strangers was the last thing she wanted.

As if Alice could read her mind, she said, "Here, let's go through the employee exit. Are you feeling sick?"

"No," she said and kept her head bowed as Alice navigated through the casino.

"I'm not going to let you drive. Where do you live?"

Her mother didn't need to see her looking a hot mess. "Can I crash at your place?"

"Of course."

Alice led her through the employee hallways to the parking garage and helped her into the passenger seat of a yellow VW Beetle. She clamped her legs together as the space between her legs pulsed.

"Why did you pay the bathroom attendant to stand outside?" Alice asked as she backed out of her stall. "For that matter, how did Marcus know you were in the bathroom in the first place?"

Those stupid tears were coming back. She hiccupped and covered her face with her hands.

Alice patted her knee. "Never mind. It doesn't matter. Just rest."

Carmen huddled against the car door and moaned as her conscience savaged her. By the time they reached Alice's apartment, she was crying uncontrollably. Alice spoke to her in a soothing tone reserved for children and helped her out of her shoes and dress and handed her a nightgown covered in rabbits. Alice wiped away her makeup and settled beside her on a flowery sofa.

"You shouldn't drink so much," Alice chided gently as she stroked her hair.

"I can't stand it," she whispered.

"Stand what?"

"The pain."

"Your husband?"

More tears fell. "I love him so much. I don't know how to go on without him."

"I'm sorry, Carmen."

An echo of Marcus's words and once more, unnecessary. "I'll get past it." She had to. There was no alternative.

3

PRESENT DAY

THE DAY VINCENT PYRE DIED, HER HEART STOPPED BEATING. IT LAY still and heavy in her chest for two years and eight months. She observed life passing her by with little interest. In her darkest hours, she wondered if the world would notice her absence.

Carmen sat on a rocking chair in her goddaughter's nursery with her heartbeat thudding in her ears. She was vibrantly, achingly alive. Her senses were so jacked that her skin tingled. She was very aware of her goddaughter's body heat seeping through her sweater, the luxurious wool carpet beneath her bare feet, and the gold clock on the wall, which was ticking ridiculously loud.

The monster who called the hit on her husband and brutally murdered Emmanuel Pyre was back with a vengeance. The trail of carnage he left in his wake would go down in underworld history. Lyla had been kidnapped from the hospital while visiting her mother who was in the ICU. Hours passed with no word of her whereabouts.

The monster had Lyla. She knew it. He would finish what he started. The knowledge of what he was capable of made her tremble. The ferocity of her emotions was so intense that she was afraid to move for fear of losing control. She tightened her hold on Nora who stared at her with her mother's eyes.

Her senses prickled a moment before she noticed Gavin standing in the doorway of the nursery. His impeccable suit, slick hair, and remote expression revealed nothing, but the wrath shining from his gold eyes told her all she needed to know. Lyla was still missing.

Carmen rose as he started forward. She already knew the answer, but she couldn't stop herself. "Did you find her?"

"I got a call from Lucifer," Gavin said.

"Lyla's in Hell?"

She was glad Gavin took Nora because her arms went lax with fear. She grew up hearing tales of what lurked in Hell, the taboo underbelly of Las Vegas that no one spoke of. Lucifer was the current king of Hell, and if the rumors were true, he was even more deranged and cruel than his father. Only one with no regard for their life dared venture into the notorious death club.

Gavin cradled his daughter close before burying his face against her. Nora grasped handfuls of his hair and tugged. Light bounced off the brass knuckles that adorned his hand. Carmen saw the glint of knives beneath his jacket instead of guns. The rumors must be true. No modern weapons were allowed in Hell. Panicked thoughts raced through her mind, but she didn't voice any of them.

Gavin raised his head and stared down at his daughter who waved her arms and kicked restlessly. The hands that held Nora trembled ever so slightly.

"Gavin," she whispered.

He may be an A-class asshole but witnessing him with his daughter had gone a long way to making up for his past sins. He stared at Nora for a long minute before he tipped the baby against his chest.

"Gavin," she said again, and his eyes flicked to her. "Bring her back."

He nodded and handed the baby over. "Take care of her."

"Gavin," she whispered.

"No matter what happens, you take care of Nora."

Fear grabbed her by the throat, and twin trails of wet slipped down her cheeks. "Gavin."

"Promise me," he snapped, eyes blazing.

"Gavin, you can't do this to me."

"Promise me, Carmen."

She grabbed a handful of his shirt and yanked him forward so they were face to face. He was a badass motherfucker. She had no doubt that he would do whatever was necessary to save Lyla, but if he was too late... She thrust that thought away before it could fully form. She glared at Gavin, a man she loved and loathed with equal passion. He had been her brother, enemy, and friend at different times in her life, but all of that faded away. Right here, right now, she had to believe he would come out of this whole with Lyla by his side. No other outcome was acceptable.

"You bring Lyla back to me," she said fiercely as the tears continued to fall. "And you make that motherfucker pay." For Vinny, for Manny, for all the hell he had put the Pyre clan through. The monster needed to pay for his sins.

He nodded, and she released him.

"You got this, Gavin," she said and willed both of them to believe it.

"You armed?" he asked.

She lifted her sweater to show the gold gun in the waistband of her pants. It didn't matter that the property was crawling with security. After what had occurred in the past forty-eight hours, she wouldn't be caught without a weapon.

Gavin strode away, head held high and back straight. An invisible cloak of violence clung to him. People would die tonight, she was sure of it. There was a trap lying in wait for him in Hell. Lyla was the bait, and Gavin was armed with only knives and brass knuckles.

"Be safe, Gavin," she called.

This was the finale, the last battle in a war that had been raging for almost three years. Vinny was the first victim the monster claimed. Tonight, it would end. Fragmented thoughts of encouragement, threats, and demands raced through her mind. She took a breath to call out one last time, but he was gone.

It took every ounce of control she possessed to stay behind. This was the second time in a matter of days that Nora's parents had asked her to look after their kid while they put their lives on the line. What the fuck? She was the one who should be charging into the bowels of hell. She was dispensable. She had no husband, kids, or responsibilities. Lyla and Gavin had a daughter, a future.

Nora's lip quivered before she burst into tears. Carmen felt like doing the same, but she reined it in and paced around the cream and gold nursery while she tried to soothe the distressed baby. Nora pounded her little fists against her chest in frustration. She brushed kisses over soft skin and cuddled the baby close.

"Shh, it's going to be okay."

She hoped Nora didn't notice the quaver in her voice or the fact that she was stiff as a board. She should put Nora in the crib since she was transferring her anxiety to the baby, but she couldn't let her go. Nora kept her sane. She breathed in that baby scent she couldn't get enough of and tried to shrug off the dread chilling her core. Lyla had to be alive. They would all get through this.

"Daddy will bring her back," she whispered.

Nora needed her mother, and she needed her best friend. Lyla had been through too much to die now.

It had been a hellish two days. She couldn't remember the last time she slept. The monster had been a step ahead of them this whole time, successfully concealing his identity and biding his time while he schemed and hunted. The future of the underworld rested on the tip of a knife. Her future depended on the outcome of what took place in Hell tonight.

The kickoff began when Lyla's father, Pat, showed up in the middle of the night, looking like a bloody extra from Pulp Fiction. He claimed his house had been broken into and Lyla's mother kidnapped. While they were trying to get the details from him, the fortress was attacked. It had been a marathon of terror—the race through the underground tunnel, the trek across the desert to the safe house, and Pat's betrayal. She would never forget Lyla's blank expression as she watched her father crumple beside the bed with blood pouring from the wound in his gut. Lyla's father had sold them out and led the monster's men straight to them. Even now, the foul taste of betrayal lingered on her tongue. The monster could manipulate anyone to do what he wished. If they couldn't trust family, who could they trust?

Carmen closed her eyes and whispered prayers into the yawning silence. The monster had been a step ahead of them for years. If Lyla's father was capable of killing his own daughter, anyone could be working for the monster, so she had to be on guard. Nora Pyre had been born to the most dangerous crime lord Las Vegas had ever seen, and for that, she would be hunted for the rest of her life. It was only a matter of time before he sent someone for Nora. If Gavin didn't make it... No. Something lethal and vicious unfurled in her gut. She brushed her hand over the warm metal pressed against her belly. They would have to get through her first.

A muffled sound behind her made her tense. She whirled, one arm holding Nora while the other brought up her gun. Her skittering senses came to a dead stop when she saw Marcus standing in the doorway. Even in the middle of the night, he was impeccably dressed in a tailored black suit with a handkerchief folded into a sharp triangle in his pocket. His perfect side part made him look like a sexy banker.

"What are you doing here?" she asked.

"Blade called me, and I wanted to make sure you're okay," Marcus said far too calmly for a man who faced a woman with a gun.

"I'm fine." She didn't lower the gun, didn't move a muscle. She couldn't afford to let her guard down, not after what she had been through. The monster exploited with a ruthlessness that made everyone a suspect.

"Carmen, put the gun down."

"I think you should leave," she said.

He didn't do as she suggested. Instead, he stayed put, stretching her already frayed nerves to the breaking point.

"What's going through your head right now?" he asked.

"You're too perfect," she whispered.

"What?"

"You filled Vinny's place so easily." Her overactive mind pieced together strange facts that made no sense. "Gavin put you, a former intern, as interim CEO while he was in jail. Gavin doesn't trust anyone, but he trusts you as much as he trusts Blade, and they've known each other for decades. Why?"

The gun wavered as Nora fussed. Logic and instinct battled within her. Two days ago, she wouldn't have questioned Marcus's loyalty, but witnessing Pat's betrayal changed everything. They were at war, which meant she couldn't assume anyone's loyalty was absolute. Her head throbbed as Marcus remained motionless in the doorway. This was just another scene in the nightmare that wouldn't end.

"You replaced Vinny in every way—at work and in the family. You're always there when everyone needs you. Gavin even made you Nora's godfather. You're the perfect agent—"

"I'm not working for him," Marcus snapped.

She tightened her hold on the gun. "How can I be sure?"

"You know me, Carmen."

She shook her head. "No, I don't."

She knew what he looked like during sex, that he was a money-making machine and dressed with the precision of a man who favored order above all else. She also knew that his acute concern and affection for Lyla didn't make sense.

"This is what he wants—for us to turn on each other. You can trust me. I'm not the enemy," Marcus said.

"I want to be alone." Last night, she killed her first man. When she saw the soldier outlined in the moonlight, something lethal and visceral took over. She stepped out of the shadows and pulled the trigger. It had been abrupt, gruesome, and final. She didn't regret it, but this was different. Marcus wasn't a heartless soldier hunting down a helpless baby. He was a man who kissed her ankles and touched her with gentleness and care.

She'd seen Marcus a handful of times since their disastrous hookup. The friendly familiarity he once treated her with was gone, and he spoke to her with the same polite reserve he used when speaking to a hotel guest. Even now, as she faced him across the room, his charming demeanor was absent.

"You're exhausted. Put the gun down," he said quietly.

"Why does Gavin trust you?"

"That's between Gavin and me."

She tensed. "He's not here to vouch for you."

Nora began to fuss, roused by her body language and voice. She jostled the baby with one arm and took another step back, eyes never leaving her target. Holy shit. Could she really do this? Could she shoot a man she had once hooked up with? What if she was wrong and killed an innocent man? But if she was right, her hesitation could be their death sentence.

"Just leave, Marcus." She didn't want to have to make a choice.

"You should put Nora down."

"Why aren't you leaving?" she demanded.

He took a step forward with one hand outstretched. "Calm down."

"Don't tell me what to do!"

Nora pitched forward. Carmen dropped the gun and caught the baby before she fell. Her heart stopped as the gun fired. She shut her eyes for a fraction of a second and when she opened them, Marcus stood before her. He picked up her gun, flipped on the safety, and tucked it in the back of his slacks.

"And that's why you shouldn't hold a baby and a gun at the same time," he said mildly. "Accidents happen."

"I didn't shoot you?" She wasn't sure if she was relieved or disappointed.

"No, which is fortunate since I wouldn't be much good to Gavin dead."

Nora's head whipped around at the sound of his voice. She made an urgent sound and reached for him as if she recognized him.

"Hey, baby," Marcus crooned. When Carmen backed up, he shot her a molten look. "Give her to me."

"No."

"You're not thinking clearly, and you're scaring her. Give her to me."

She rubbed Nora's quivering back, but the baby wouldn't be soothed. Nora's piercing screams sent ricochets of pain through her aching head.

"What happened?"

Two armed security stood in the doorway. They both had guns in hand and were staring at the bullet embedded in the wall. Marcus took advantage of her distraction to snatch Nora.

"Hey!" she shouted and balled her fists to fight for her but stopped at the sudden silence.

Marcus handled the baby like an experienced father as he settled Nora against him. The baby was quick to tuck her head under her godfather's chin and clutch a handful of his suit while she sucked her thumb.

Carmen whirled to face the guards. "Why did you let him on the property?"

The guards glanced at one another and then her.

"Who fired the shot?" the guard asked.

"I did."

They stared at her. "Why?"

"Why? Because we don't know who that fucker bribed, that's why!"

The guard's eyes flicked to Marcus and then back to her. "The boss didn't restrict Mr. Fletcher from the premises. Is there something we should know?"

"She's tired," Marcus said shortly. "I'll take care of her."

"Take care?" Carmen choked.

"Any word?" Marcus asked.

"No, sir."

"Inform us the minute you hear something. You're dismissed," Marcus said.

"Are you sure?" the guard asked with a wary glance in her direction.

"I'm armed," Marcus said, and they nodded and left.

"You're armed?" Carmen asked warily.

Marcus gave her a very steady look. "Of course."

He didn't seem the type to know what to do with a gun but looks were deceiving. He brushed his finger down Nora's cheek as he rocked her. The baby sighed contentedly against him.

Carmen felt bereft and a little crazed without Nora's solid weight against her. She had been welded to the baby for almost two days, and now, someone was taking over. "Why are you here, Marcus?"

Green eyes speared her. "No one should be alone on a night like this."

Her overstimulated senses fixated on the splash of red the handkerchief made against his suit. She took a breath to clear her head. His cologne drifted in the air between them, tantalizing and taunting her. It roused memories of their bathroom hookup. Her nails sank into her palms as a flash of heat sparked in her belly. She wasn't prepared for her womb to clench with need or the sudden slickness between her legs. What. The. Fuck.

"Carmen?"

She shook her head wildly. No. What was wrong with her? Her body went from unbearably cold to so heated she wanted to shave her head. She shuddered and paced away, trying to get herself under control.

"Carmen, are you okay?"

She was high on adrenaline, exhaustion, and fear. Her mind skittered in a dozen different directions. A geyser of emotions roiled in her chest, fighting to be freed. She adjusted her slouchy sweater and mopped up the lingering wet on her face with the large, droopy sleeve.

Everything jumped out at her—the color of a stuffed pink elephant on Nora's drawers, the prisms of light from the chandelier and the constant flow of air conditioning that felt like sandpaper against her sensitive skin. She tried to smother the urge to beat her fists against the wall or break something. Rage and fear collided in her chest. She wanted to throw her head back and scream at the top of her lungs. Instead, she scrubbed her hands over her face and tried to get herself together. She was overtired, overstressed and just... over it. It had been almost three years of pain, horror, and death. This had to end. She couldn't take much more.

"Carmen."

She whirled to find Marcus standing a few feet away, arms empty. Her heart leaped into her throat before she noticed the tiny mound stretched out in the crib.

"You're shaking," he observed.

She crossed her arms over her chest and tried to hold everything in. "You can go now."

"Save it. If being held at gunpoint didn't work, you should know I'm not going anywhere until we hear the verdict."

Her stomach lurched. "Verdict?"

"After Blade's call, I couldn't focus. I figured you were in worst shape than me, so I came by to check on you."

And she almost killed him. Even as shame crawled up her throat, she scowled at him. "I'm fine."

"You aren't."

She opened her mouth to make another heated denial.

"How could you be when Lyla's life is at stake?"

Her argument died in her throat. Dimly, she registered that she was in an oversized sweater, yoga pants, and didn't have on a lick of makeup. She was emotionally and physically stripped of all her normal shields and eons away from the vixen he encountered in the club bathroom. It shouldn't matter to her that she probably looked like shit since he wanted nothing to do with her after that disaster. She didn't blame him. She was a fucking mess.

"It's almost over," he said calmly.

"Over?" She let out a harsh laugh. "That's what I thought when Vinny died. Then he came for Manny and Lyla, and he's still coming for us."

"Gavin will bring her back."

"You don't know what he's capable of, and now, he's teamed up with Lucifer. You have no idea what they could do to her!" Scenarios she hadn't allowed herself to consider flashed through her mind. "Did you hear what he did to Lyla's mother?"

Marcus nodded.

Aunt Beatrice had been taken by the monster and tortured. Blade reported that her injuries were "horrific." Hearing Blade use that word sent a chill up her spine.

"Gavin won't let anything happen to her," Marcus said.

"You have no idea what he's walking into."

"I do know."

Something about the way he said that got her attention. "What do you know about Hell?"

Something was going in his veiled green eyes, something that put her on guard again. She took a step back and searched the room for a weapon. He released an aggravated growl.

"You can trust me, Carmen."

"How do I know that?"

"Because I'd never hurt you!" He ran his hands through his hair, mussing his slick do. "You and Lyla put me through hell this week. First, the attack at the hospital, and then, we lose contact with you for hours after they made the hit on this house."

"Why do you care so much?"

He stared at her. "What?"

"You don't know us. Why do you care so much?"

His eyes narrowed to slits. She sensed his energy change a moment before he started toward her. The hairs on the nape of her neck rose. He stopped less than a foot away and leaned down until their faces were mere inches apart.

A week ago, she could stare into his eyes with only a distant sense of discomfort. Now, the act of holding his gaze was so intimate it made her skin erupt in goose bumps. She lifted her chin. She would not be intimidated. This was Marcus, after all, and she was Carmen fucking Pyre. Once upon a time, she brought powerful men to their knees. She'd be damned if she got flustered over eye contact.

"I saw the surveillance tape. I know exactly what happened to Lyla and Emmanuel Pyre," he said.

4

SHE FELT AS IF THE BOTTOM DROPPED OUT FROM UNDER HER. HIS EYES bored into hers with an intensity that made her want to look away, but she refused.

"I didn't know Lyla before the attack, but I saw her after. I saw her smile and laugh. I saw her humanize Gavin and put him in his place. She's a walking miracle. I didn't think anyone could come back from something like that. That's why I care."

A tear trickled down her cheek, but she didn't look away.

"As for you, I wanted to meet the woman who put her life on hold to care for her cousin after she'd been attacked. I wanted to meet Vincent Pyre's backbone, the woman in his notes. He was a great man who taught me everything I wanted to know."

She held up a hand in a gesture of surrender, but he didn't stop. He was so close that his warm breath feathered over her chilled face.

"And you dare ask me why I care? How could I not care when you've all lost so much?"

His words and the mix of sympathy, bad temper, and need on his face made her stomach contract. It was all too much. She paced away as flashbacks of the night Vinny was murdered flashed through her mind. The familiar slap of grief was laced with terror, worry, and anxiety.

The opulent nursery faded away as memories of her desperate run across a moonlit desert with Nora in her arms obliterated her surroundings. With the monster's men on the way and no backup, Lyla had done the unthinkable.

"You run and don't stop, Carmen," Lyla said.

"Please." Carmen shook her head as tears streamed down her face. She was very aware of Nora crying against her chest. "Please don't leave me."

"I'll hold them off until Blade comes and distract them if I have to. Here." Lyla tucked a gun into the pocket of her robe. "Go."

Fear consumed her. "Lyla, you can't do this to me."

"I love you. Now, go!"

She made the impossible decision to save Nora and leave Lyla behind. She could still feel the merciless scrape of branches on her legs and the cold terror rushing through her as she ran. She suffered multiple strokes as she huddled against the canyon, listening to the deafening crack of gunshots echoing through the night.

"Talk to me, Carmen."

Her throat swelled with anxiety as she paced. "I don't want to talk about it."

"You have to."

"Why?" she snapped.

"Because you need to get it out. It's killing you."

She whirled to face him. Rage was better than worry, so she embraced it. A lethal combination of fury and panic collided in a vicious starburst in her chest. She felt as if she could breathe fire.

"What's killing me is that this isn't over," she said through clenched teeth. "What's *killing* me is that the motherfucker who killed my husband is still breathing. What's *killing* me is that Lyla's been kidnapped again, and Gavin is on his way to Hell!" She suppressed an angry roar. "It's been almost three motherfucking years since Vinny and Uncle Manny were murdered. If he touches one hair on her head, I'll rip his fucking heart out with my bare hands!"

"We're gonna get through this. Gavin will bring her home."

"Gavin told me he would take care of Vinny, and he's dead! Gavin can't stop him. No one can. He took everything from me! He took Lyla to finish what he started and I-I can't..."

He reached for her, but she backed away, shaking her head so viciously that she felt dizzy. Pain threatened to split her heart in two.

"She can't do this to me. I can't lose anyone else. My heart can't take it."

Bravado fled, leaving only fear. She was going to shatter into a million pieces. She wrapped her arms around herself and heard her teeth chatter from emotional overload and shock.

Two arms wrapped around her and drew her against a solid chest. The urge to burrow against him, to lean on another human being was so tempting, but she couldn't do that to him.

"Marcus, I'm fine," she said as she pushed against him.

He didn't budge. "You're not fine."

"I am—"

"Hush."

His hand slid beneath her hair and cupped the back of her head as he held her close. She was immediately engulfed in his scent and strength. For a moment, she held herself stiff within the circle of his embrace and made a valiant effort to save him from herself, but he didn't take the out she offered. He tucked her face into the hollow of his throat and hugged her tight.

"No matter what happens tonight, we'll get through this together."

Her attempt at keeping him at a distance crumbled. She was so fucking tired of being strong and holding everything inside. The need for human contact was stronger than her pride and mortification over her breakdown during their bathroom hookup. With a mewl of surrender, she collapsed against him.

He picked her up and carried her to the seating area on the other side of the nursery. He settled on the couch with her on his lap. She tucked her legs on either side of him and held on for dear life as her shields came crashing down. Fear had its talons lodged in her gut. She cried her heart out for Vinny, her father, Lyla and Gavin, and

Aunt Beatrice who was in a coma. It was too fucking much. She wasn't sure how long she cried, but when the storm passed, she slumped against his chest, and Marcus kissed her temple. It was a sexless, comforting gesture that made her feel coddled and safe.

"Gavin will bring Lyla back," he said as he ran his hand over her quivering back. "He's gonna end this. After tonight, it'll be over."

"How can you be so sure?" she whispered.

"Because I know Gavin. Besides, he doesn't want us raising Nora. That's reason enough for him to make sure he and Lyla make it through this."

For the first time in days, her lips lifted into a ghost of a smile. "I should have warned Gavin I'd teach Nora to dance on a stripper pole before she's seven if he doesn't come back."

She heard the rumble in his chest before he laughed. She tipped her head on his shoulder so she could watch. One hand stroked her back while the other sifted through her hair. The polite reserve was gone, and the easy affection was back. She soaked it in.

He looked down at her, green eyes filled with mirth. Heat unfurled in her stomach and spread. Memories of their hookup flashed through her mind—Marcus holding her against the wall, the feel of his cock stretching her, and the image of his ass flexing as he thrust into her... She breathed in his musk and that scent that made her mouth water with need.

Marcus ran his hand down her cheek. "You have a scratch here."

"Cactus."

Amusement faded. "You're safe now."

Her fear was morphing into something else, something she welcomed. For the first time in years, she felt a pang of hunger that had nothing to do with food. After being so close to death, the need to reassure herself that she was alive overrode everything else, even fear. Marcus was the only man who had been able to rouse an iota of passion in her since Vinny passed. On a night of uncertainty with death on the horizon, she needed this.

"Cold?" Marcus asked and looked around for a blanket.

"Not for long," she said.

"What?"

She kissed him. Marcus stiffened. She clasped his face, delighted by the simple pleasure of feeling his smooth skin beneath her tingling palms. Why hadn't she noticed before how soft his lips were? That they were perfectly shaped? He pulled back. She followed and gained access when he opened his mouth to speak. Her tongue swept in. Fuck. He tasted like... She rubbed her tongue against his to get a better sample.

Firm hands on her shoulders pushed her back until their mouths parted with a smack. She was panting as he held her away from him. One of her hands were locked in his hair, the other cupped the side of his face.

"Stop," he said in an unsteady voice.

"You taste like classy sin."

He blinked. "What?"

"I don't know why I didn't notice the first time."

His face closed down. "You don't know what you're doing."

She shifted and felt the hard ridge in his pants. He wanted her and didn't want a replay of their last hookup. Neither did she. Last night, when she killed that soldier, she made a decision. She decided to live. Vinny was gone, and he wasn't coming back. She could either live the rest of her days in misery or enjoy the pleasures life offered. Her eyes roved over Marcus Fletcher. He was definitely a pleasure to look at, but she would enjoy him even more if he was inside her. This was the longest she had been celibate since she was fourteen. She shut down after Vinny died, and now, she was awake and ravenous. She watched the hypnotizing rise and fall of his chest for a few seconds and savored the simple sight. Marcus was alive. She stroked her thumb over his bottom lip and had the pleasure of watching his pupils dilate. He was warm, responsive, and all male.

"You're drunk on adrenaline and fear," Marcus said in a gravelly voice and gripped her hips to push her away.

She rocked her hips on his erection, and his teeth came together with a snap.

He glared at her. "You don't know what you're doing."

She didn't care why Gavin trusted him. He'd had ample time to abduct Nora or kill her for holding a gun on him, but he didn't. He held her while she cried, and now, he was trying to save her from making a mistake he thought she would regret. She looped her arms around his neck and sucked on his earlobe.

"I'm sorry," she whispered.

"For what?"

She tasted the sharp line of his jaw. "For putting you in that position that night."

He tried to pull away, but she clasped his face and did what she wanted to do that night in the bathroom. She brushed gentle kisses over his face.

"When Vinny died, I did too," she whispered. "I've been taking care of other people, so I didn't focus on what I don't have." Words she couldn't have spoken a week ago were coming out of her mouth. She couldn't stop if she wanted to. "I've been a walking zombie. Not really tasting what I eat, not really feeling anything. I thought I'd be better off dead. I didn't want to live in a world without him."

"I shouldn't have—"

She slanted her mouth over his. He opened his mouth, and she took. Her hands dug into the back of his neck as his taste hit her starving senses. Classy sin. She moaned and shifted restlessly against him. He groaned into her mouth and leaned back.

"Carmen," he panted. "You... we can't..."

He tried to stand, but she couldn't allow that. She shoved him into the couch.

"Last night, when that guy came to execute Nora, I fought back." She stroked his face and stared into his eyes, trying to get through to him, to make him understand. "I want to live."

Her words hung in the air between them. He stared at her, lips parted as his lungs worked double time. His face was drawn with need, but his eyes were still calculating. She leaned forward, drawn to that delectable mouth and taste she couldn't get enough of.

"I've been sleepwalking," she said against his lips and looked into his eyes. "Wake me up, Marcus."

He stared at her, as still as a statue. The fact that he was resisting made her want him even more. He was trying to be honorable, and she liked it even though it was getting in her way. It was rare to find a man who would resist the chance to get laid.

"Don't you want me?" she whispered and kissed a line down his throat, unbuttoning his shirt along the way.

"Carmen." His voice sounded strangled, but he didn't stop her.

She nuzzled the hollow of his throat and ran her tongue along the smooth line of his throat. His shudder of pleasure and the feel of his hands digging into her hips made her smile. He wasn't going to make a move this time. This seduction was up to her. She mentally licked her lips in anticipation as she unbuttoned his shirt and viewed her gift in all its masculine glory. He was lean and cut just right.

"You've been training with Gavin in the ring?" she asked absently as she ran her hands over his abs.

Stomach muscles rippled. "Yeah."

"It looks good on you," she said as she ran her hands over his pecs and hard nipples.

He flinched. One of his hands moved from her hip to her ass, and she froze, waiting for a smack. His hand kneaded and then stopped. He closed his eyes as if searching for the strength to push her away.

The tables were turned, and now she would be the one to make the moves. Her conscience was curiously silent. There was a time for mourning, and hers officially ended last night. She was going after what she wanted, and the first thing on her list was Marcus Fletcher.

When she started to slip off his lap, his eyes opened. He didn't say a thing, but the hand on her ass flexed. He thought she was backing out. She saw reason and lust battle before his hand disappeared. He had more control than any man she had ever met, and she would enjoy breaking him. His eyes glowed with temper as she knelt in front of him. She sat there for a moment, staring at him. His hands flexed at his sides as he waited.

Her heart beat in time with the ticking clock. She savored the mix of elation, excitement, and anticipation rushing through her. She settled her hands on his knees and smiled when he tensed. She ran her hands up his thighs, and he jolted.

"Carmen."

Her name growled in that sexy voice was music to her ears. After running for her life, she was in the mood to play with fire, and Marcus was the perfect partner. She reached for his belt and kept eye contact as she unbuckled it and pulled down his zipper.

"What are you doing?"

He had Black Calvin Klein briefs with that white elastic band against a toned stomach. She had to take a breath to calm herself. The space between her legs begged to be filled.

"You went down on me. I think it's time I repaid the favor," she said and gripped his cock through his underwear.

A muscle jumped in his jaw. "Carmen, if you back out this time—"

"I won't," she promised.

She hooked her fingers into his slacks and briefs. He lifted his hips so she could drag them down and tossed the two guns to the side. He shuddered as she ran her nails down his muscled thighs. She teased him by panting over the engorged tip. He bared his teeth and shifted, brushing his dick against her lips. When she gripped the base of his cock, he bucked. She clucked her tongue and placed kisses all down the length of him to his balls and then licked delicately.

Marcus hissed through his teeth and sank his hand into her hair. "Suck me."

"Yes, sir," she said obediently and closed her mouth around him.

She kept eye contact as she played with him. His fist jerked in her hair, sending spikes of pain and pleasure through her. Watching Marcus lose control was one of the hottest things she had ever seen. His stomach muscles flexed as he resisted the urge to move. His breathing was ragged and labored, and his eyes... Those fucking eyes revved her up so much that one of her hands left his shaft and dropped between her own spread thighs.

Marcus yanked her back with a stinging grip in her hair and

pushed her. She toppled backward and couldn't hold back a delighted laugh as he ripped her leggings and sank two fingers inside her. She bucked and gasped when his thumb landed on her clit. She was trembling like a plucked bow. She felt fevered and frantic. Oh. My. God.

"Marcus," she gasped.

"You're soaked," he said harshly.

"I need—" she began but didn't have to finish.

His mouth landed on hers, and he pushed until she was flat on her back. He ran his penis along her folds, and she clawed his back. He grunted and then slid home all in one motion. She focused on the delicious stretch and sudden fullness. He buried his face in the crook of her neck for a moment.

"Do it," she panted, so turned on she thought she would die if he didn't fuck her right now.

"Give me a moment," he whispered.

She bucked beneath him, trying to begin the rhythm that would bring her the relief she needed.

"Behave," he growled into her hair.

"Make me," she challenged.

She wasn't in the mood to be placated. The need to savor was gone. She was shaking like a junkie in need of a fix. She needed him to finish the ritual so she could start anew. She needed to be fucked raw, needed a climax that was so mind-blowing that she passed out. She couldn't even get herself off anymore. It was unacceptable. This was it—the beginning of her new life, and Marcus was the key.

She grasped a handful of his slick hair, completely destroying his hairdo. She yanked his head down so their lips brushed as she spoke. "Fuck me hard." He opened his mouth, and she bit his bottom lip. "Fuck. Now."

For a moment, she wasn't sure he would comply. She could feel him pulsing inside her. Her muscles feathered around him, and his jaw clenched. He closed his eyes for a moment before he leaned down and gave her a gentle kiss.

"Marcus?"

He planted his fists above her shoulders a moment before he thrust. She collided with his wrists, which were caging her in. She grabbed his forearms, which felt like heated steel and braced herself, her mouth watering in anticipation.

Marcus fucked her. No finesse or fancy moves—it was fucking at its rawest and exactly what she needed. The slap of their flesh was loud and carnal, and she could feel ecstasy rushing toward her, but she needed more. She reached up and dragged his face down to hers. The taste of classy sin pushed her closer to the edge. Kissing wasn't allowed in hookups, but she didn't care about the rules. Marcus didn't push her away, so she drank deep. He spread her legs wide as she kissed him. She bucked as sensation upon sensation crashed around her.

Nora let out a mewling cry.

Reality ripped her climax from her grasp. Some semblance of rationality penetrated her desperate, lust hazed brain. She was fucking in Nora's nursery. She was the worst godmother in the world. She turned her face to the side, breaking their kiss.

"Nora," she huffed.

"She'll settle," he said and didn't budge. She shoved against his chest, and he went solid. "You said you wouldn't stop this time."

"It's not me; it's her." She was proud that she could string a coherent sentence together when her body was begging for release.

Marcus sat back on his heels, suit jacket and shirt spread wide, revealing a delectable body gleaming with sweat. She rolled on her hands and knees, then paused when his hand pressed on her lower back, keeping her in place.

"Marcus!"

She tried to scoot forward, but he gripped her hips and yanked her backward and tried to slip his cock inside her. She straightened and tried to get to her feet, but he wrapped his arms around her, keeping her on her knees. His hands slid beneath her oversized sweater. He stroked her quivering belly before one hand skated up her chest, and the other went to her pussy. He pressed two fingers against her clit, and she grabbed his wrist in a desperate bid for sanity.

"We can't—" She gasped and jerked as he squeezed her nipple, sending a thunderbolt of lust to her pussy.

"No backing out," he growled in her ear. "You promised."

"But she—"

His fingers slipped into her pussy. She gasped and tried to stand, but he wouldn't let her. His hand left her breast and collared her throat. It felt so good that she couldn't resist rocking against his wicked fingers.

"We're finishing this time."

"But Nora..." she began before his hand clamped over her mouth.

"She's fine. Look."

It was hard to focus on anything when her body was shaking with need, but she saw Nora in her crib, and she was silent once again. Still. They couldn't fuck in front of Nora. It was wrong—

Marcus maneuvered her so she was on all fours. Her heart leaped into her throat. Who knew he had a caveman lurking beneath the slick businessman façade? He reverently ran his hands down the length of her spine, and she arched into his touch like a cat in heat. Her body was on fire, and she was lightheaded with desire. He gripped her ass and kneaded again before he pressed his head against her entrance.

She rocked back to take his dick. He hissed and slapped her ass. The sting felt great. She laughed and rotated her hips. A hand clenched in her hair and tugged as he draped himself over her. One hand gripped her breast as he bit her ear.

"Ready?"

"Yes," she panted. She felt as if she had been waiting for this her whole life.

He planted his hands on the floor beside hers. His first hard thrust made her teeth slam together. She grasped the carpet as Marcus gave his beast free rein. She tipped her head down and held on for the ride. It was raw and elemental and everything she could have hoped. His teeth dug into her shoulder for three thrusts before he buried his face in her hair. His pants made her even hotter. She sacrificed one hand to jam it between her legs to massage her clit. His thrusts shoved her hand against her sweet spot, pushing her closer to the edge. She let out a loud moan. A moment later, his hand covered her mouth.

"Quiet."

She whimpered into his hand, which tightened over her mouth. She liked it hard and rough, and Marcus was delivering beautifully. She spoke urgently into his hand when she felt her climax coming.

"Do it. Come for me," he growled into her ear.

She erupted with a scream that would have been horror-movie worthy. He lost his rhythm as her vagina milked his dick.

"Oh, fuck," he moaned.

He dropped his hand from her mouth to wrap his arm around her waist and haul her tight against him as he came. He ground himself against her ass as the spasms passed. She collapsed face first onto the lush cream carpet as he folded on top of her and got his breath back. His head settled at the top of her spine, and everything in her settled. Yes, this was exactly what she needed.

"Okay?" Marcus huffed.

She nodded because she wasn't capable of speech. He tipped them on their side. He was still inside her and seemed content to stay there. Her heartbeat thudded in her ears while her body pulsed with vitality. He stroked his hand down her arm, side, and hip. He reversed and swept up until his hand gripped her breast. She mewled and arched.

"I didn't use anything," Marcus said.

Her eyes opened. She stared at the crib where Nora slept, blissfully unaware that her godparents hooked up ten feet away. "I have an implant in my arm."

"I figured, but I needed to ask," he said. "I'm clean."

"So am I."

"You sure?"

"Haven't been with anyone since Vinny."

He came up on one elbow, and she looked up at him.

"What about that celebrity Kody Singer?"

"Kody?" She frowned. "What about him?"

"You went on a date with him the day the hospital was attacked. You have a history."

"How do you know?"

"I saw you two at Incognito."

She forgot about that. That felt like years ago instead of mere months. "Nothing happened with him." She didn't mention that they had a heavy petting session in the bathroom at the hospital. She didn't actually sleep with him, so that was neither here nor there.

The sound of a ringing phone destroyed her serenity as effectively as a gunshot. She leaped to her feet as reality came back in a terrible rush. Lyla, Gavin, Hell. This was the call she'd been dreading. She snatched her ringing phone from the dresser and saw Blade's name on the screen. She fumbled with the simple mechanism to unlock the phone and closed her eyes as she put it to her ear.

"Blade?" she breathed.

"Carmen, it's me."

"Lyla?" She couldn't believe it. The breathy, feminine voice on the other end of the line was the last thing she expected. "Lyla?" she screamed and flapped her hand at Marcus who stood nearby, watching intently.

"It's me," Lyla said.

She clutched the phone with both hands. "Are you okay?"

"No."

"Are you hurt?"

"N-no. A-are you guys okay?"

She assessed Lyla's voice, which was shaky but clear. "Yes. Did Gavin get him?"

"Yes. It was Steven Vega."

"Vega? Rafael's brother? Are you sure?" Her mind conjured up an image of an emaciated, tiny creep. She could have strangled him with her bare hands. Her body flashed with heat that instantly faded when she heard a man's drawling voice. It wasn't Gavin. "Who's that?"

"Fucking Lucifer." Lyla sounded annoyed.

"Lucifer? Oh my God, Lyla. Get away from him."

"I'm trying." Lyla sounded out of breath, and there was someone laughing maniacally in the background. "Asshole."

Lyla just called Lucifer, the king of Hell, an asshole and didn't sound remotely afraid. Did she not know who he was? "Lyla, he's a sociopath. He runs Hell. You have to—"

"It's fine." Lyla sounded supremely unconcerned. "Are you okay? How's Nora?"

Now that she knew Lyla was fine, she was fantastic. "You took ten years off my life, but I'm okay. Nora's asleep. Are you coming home?"

"Yes."

Carmen squeezed her eyes tight, unable to believe that God had spared her cousin. "Lyla, is it really over?"

"Yes."

It was over. Vinny's killer was gone, and Lyla and Gavin were alive. "I love you."

"I love you too. I'll see you soon."

After they hung up, she clasped the phone to her chest and bowed her head. She took a long, deep breath as tears of gratitude and relief filled her eyes. It was over.

"Carmen?"

She blinked and brushed away a tear. "They're alive!"

His mouth quirked. "Yeah, I got that. They're all right?"

"Yes. I can't believe it."

She was lightheaded with relief. She swayed on her feet, and Marcus pulled her against him.

"Did I hear you say Vega?" he asked.

"Yeah. The nerdy brother. If I'd known, I would have killed him myself."

"Vega," he mused as he ran a hand down her back. "He tried to accomplish what his father never could... overthrow the Pyres. His family has the reputation and power to pull it off."

"How do you know this shit?" Her words slurred as exhaustion took over.

Marcus scooped her up in his arms. "I'll tell you another time."

"Where are you taking me?"

"You need to rest."

"I don't want to leave Nora."

"I'll wait with her until they get back. You're crashing. When's the last time you slept?"

"I don't know."

"Ate?"

"I ate marshmallows an hour ago."

He paused as he settled her in the guest bedroom. How did he know that this was the room she'd been staying in?

"Marshmallows?"

"Comfort food."

He smiled as he tucked her into bed as gently as if she was a toddler. "Your idea of comfort food is marshmallows?"

"What other kind is there?"

He chuckled as he leaned down and kissed her. It was slow, gentle, drugging. When he lifted his head, his eyes were heavy lidded and glittering.

"Do you feel alive?" he asked.

"Yes."

His thumb stroked her cheek. "I'm glad you're all right."

"Thank you," she said with as much sincerity as she could muster.

"The pleasure was all mine."

He kissed her again—a short, unsatisfying kiss—before he eased away.

"I still want to know why Gavin trusts you," she mumbled.

"The same reason you trust me," he said.

She fought sleep. "I don't trust you."

He chuckled. "Yes, you do."

Marcus said something else, but she couldn't make it out because she was crashing.

5

Carmen opened her eyes. She was flat on her back, covers pulled up to her chin, staring up at a shadowed ceiling. Her mind was a complete blank. She floated on a sea of nothingness and watched the play of sunlight dance across the ceiling as the sun rose.

Nature called. She stretched and suddenly became aware of the burning in her calves as if she went on a long-distance run. Simultaneously, her vagina throbbed, and her mind lurched into gear. Everything returned in a rush. Lyla was safe, the monster was dead, and she had been fucked by Marcus Fletcher. She threw back the covers and raced out of her room like a kid on Christmas morning.

She knocked on Lyla and Gavin's suite. No answer. That didn't stop her from opening the door. She peeked her head in and found Gavin lying in bed with a gun pointed at her. He lowered the gun as she tiptoed forward until she could see Lyla.

"She's asleep," Gavin rumbled.

Carmen hovered over Lyla who had Nora cradled close and listened to the sound of their synchronized breathing. She closed her eyes for a moment and said a silent prayer of thanks before she noticed Beau on his doggy bed. She gave him a pat before she rounded back to Gavin's side of the bed.

"You okay?" she whispered.

He grunted as he messed around with his phone. He'd never been the best communicator.

"Is it really over?"

"Yeah," Gavin said.

She gripped his arm. "You promise?" Lyla told her last night, but she needed to hear it again. She needed to hear it from him.

He looked up. The light from his phone illuminated a thin scratch on his cheek that hadn't been there the night before. He wasn't wearing his suit or brass knuckles now. He wore sweats and nothing else. His energy was quiet but still alert.

"He's dead? You're sure it was Vega?" she asked urgently.

"Yes."

Her voice was a bit hoarse as she asked, "Did you make him suffer?"

He stared at her for a long moment. "As much as I could. Lucifer cut off his head."

She wouldn't have been opposed to chopping off every limb with a chainsaw but being beheaded was okay. She only wished she could have witnessed it herself. "Why did he do it?"

He looked down, and she realized she was digging her nails into his arm. She released him and fanned her face, which felt hot.

"Vega wanted to prove to his father that he could do what he or Rafael had never been able to do."

Marcus was right. "He did all of this to prove a point?" It was unfathomable that someone would cause so much death and destruction to prove to his family that he wasn't weak. She lost Vinny over a fucker who had daddy issues? Her fingernails dug into her palms.

"Psychos don't need a reason to kill. They just do it."

"Right." She let out a breath and rolled her head on her shoulders. "But he's dead?"

"Yes."

She frowned. "Lucifer beheaded him? I thought they were working together."

"I cut a deal with Lucifer, and he handed Vega over."

"You cut a deal with the devil?"

He gave her a cold look. "I'll handle it."

Of course, he would. "It's really over?"

"Yeah."

No more combat training, running for their lives, or waiting for the next disaster. Vinny had been avenged and she could start anew.

She smacked his shoulder. "I'm glad you're still breathing."

His glare followed her as she exited. It wasn't until she closed the door behind her that she realized she still wore the oversized sweater from last night that rode high on her thighs and nothing else. She hightailed it to the nursery and searched for her leggings and thong but didn't see them. Gavin would shit a brick if he found out she fucked in Nora's nursery. She went back to her room and found her leggings folded on a chair with her thong tucked primly into the fold. Marcus. He was so fucking cute and never missed a thing.

She stripped and stepped into the shower, tilting her face up to the spray. Relief, joy, fear, and guilt tumbled inside her like clothes in a dryer. Tears slipped down her cheeks, but she didn't dwell on them. Moving on wasn't going to be easy, but she was fucking game.

She stepped out of the shower and surveyed herself in the mirror. There were dark shadows under her eyes, but they sparkled with zeal. She lost a piece of herself when Vinny died, but she'd been given a second chance, and she wasn't going to waste it. She would do whatever was required to push through the pain. Last night, Marcus helped her begin a new chapter. He awakened her body, which pulsed with life. That was the way to end this hellish ordeal—with a bang. She couldn't live in purgatory anymore, not when she had a taste of ecstasy.

Her body was covered in scratches from her run across the desert and her hair... She fingered the ink black strands. It was time for a change. Thanks to her workouts with Blade and Lyla's private martial arts instructor, she was in better shape than she'd been in years. She could do more lunges, but overall, not bad. She reached for her makeup bag and erased all traces of the past. The result was a fresh face, bright eyes, and a cheery peach lipstick that hadn't seen the light of day for years. The dark, heavy makeup she'd favored for the past two years slinked to the bottom of her bag. She completed today's look with white skinny jeans and a matching long-sleeve crop top.

When she passed the nursery, she found Gavin yawning as he changed Nora. Beau danced excitedly around him.

"Let me take her," Carmen said. "Get some sleep."

It was a measure of how exhausted he was that he didn't argue. She beamed at Nora who smiled back. She watched Gavin's retreating back before she gave Nora a mock serious look.

"You didn't see anything last night, did you?"

Nora flapped her arms.

"You're learning a little earlier than I planned, but you're going to take after me, so I guess it's not that bad. Aunty Carmen and Uncle Marcus got a little carried away," she whispered conspiratorially. "He was good. Better than good. He was fucking phenomenal if you want the truth."

A cherry-colored dress with a tutu skirt caught her eyes. She held up the tiny dress and was dazzled by the cheery color. She dressed Nora in the lace dress and clapped her hands.

"Who's the prettiest girl on the whole planet? That's you, baby." She picked up the grinning baby and put her on her hip. "Everything's going to be okay."

They made their way to the kitchen. She set Beau loose in the backyard and heated up a bottle. Her stomach yowled, so she stuffed a strawberry breakfast bar in her mouth as she fed Nora, who latched onto the bottle immediately.

Carmen finished her bar and looked around for something else to eat. She snatched a green apple from the basket on the table and stared at the shiny surface for a moment, mesmerized, before hunger won out and she bit. Taste burst on her tongue, and she hummed in delight. Nora stared up at her with wide eyes as she finished the apple in record time.

She tapped her feet restlessly. The gray blur dashing around the backyard caught her attention. Beau, a normally staid pit bull was going nuts. He ran full out, barking madly. Somehow, he too sensed it was over.

The rising sun lit a different world today—one that was new and full of possibilities. For years, she didn't recognize a new day as anything more than endless hours where she had to appear normal while her insides wept and bled. Vinny's death sent her into a tailspin of grief-stricken madness and guilt. She could finally tell Vinny that he had finally been avenged.

After Nora finished breakfast, she took her outside for a breath of fresh air. It was a beautiful day without a cloud in sight. Rust colored mountains rose above the wall that enclosed the fortress. The temperature wasn't hot or cold. It was just perfect. Her heart felt lighter than it had been in years. She was full of energy. Thanks, Marcus, she thought and couldn't hold back a satisfied smile. He definitely liked kink. Just thinking about his hand in her hair as she sucked him off or the way he forced her on her hands and knees was making her hot again.

"Your godfather is fine," she told Nora as she swayed to the sultry beat playing in her head. She couldn't stay still. "What do you think I should do about him, baby?"

She twirled and was rewarded with a delighted baby laugh. Beau's warning growl made her turn. A man she didn't know stood in the doorway that led into the house. Beau pressed against her side, and she gripped his collar as she took in the stranger. He was dressed casually in black jeans and tee with a worn leather jacket molded to broad shoulders.

The fact he was walking around unescorted was interesting. This guy would have been decorated with bullets if he wasn't supposed to be here. The stranger started toward her. Beau tensed at her side, but at her firm, "No," he sat on his haunches.

The sun highlighted the man's rich chocolate brown hair styled in a fauxhawk and his deep-set blue eyes. He was dripping sex appeal, but she wasn't fooled by his guileless smile. He had player written all over him.

"Please tell me you're the nanny," he said in a New York accent that made her insides clench.

Oh, hell yes. A smoking hot bad boy with a New York accent was an excellent way to jumpstart her day. "If I am?"

"Then, baby"—he paused for emphasis and looked her up and down—"you're going to make one of my fantasies come true."

She liked a man who had fantasies. "And if I'm not?"

"Then you can tell me one of yours, and I'll make both our fantasies come true."

She laughed. "I like that line. You don't mind if I use it, do you?"

"Feel free." His eyes switched to Nora, who eyed him curiously. "This is Gavin's kid?"

"Yes. Who are you?"

"Angel."

Carmen shook her head. "No."

"No?"

"Your name can't be Angel. It's a stage name, right?"

"Stage name?"

"You have to be a model or actor."

His eyes sparkled with humor. "I'll keep that in mind in case I need a backup career."

"Do you have a brother named Demon?"

He threw back his head and laughed. The sound was raspy and full of genuine mirth, which made him even more attractive.

"Roque has many nicknames. I think we'll have to add that one to the bunch," he said.

She froze. Roque wasn't a common name. She glanced at the gold eagle pendant lying contentedly in the vee of his shirt. The eagle's wings flared proudly on his chest, the symbol of ancient Rome. "You're Angel Roman?"

"So you aren't the nanny," he surmised and shook his head. "Damn."

"I'm Carmen."

His eyes narrowed. "Carmen... Vinny's wife?"

"Yes." She'd never met the Romans of New York, but she'd heard stories. Angel looked too friendly to be part of the notorious clan.

"Vinny was a good man," he said and inclined his head. "I'm sorry we didn't make it to the funeral."

She hadn't expected the Romans to attend. Vinny wasn't a blood relation to the Romans. Manny took him in after his parents died in a car accident. Vinny changed his name in his teens.

"What are you doing in Las Vegas?" she asked.

"I took Gavin's place."

She opened her mouth to ask as what, and then it hit her. "You're the new crime lord?"

He nodded.

"That's why Gavin went to New York," she said thoughtfully. Lyla must be relieved.

"You were with Lyla at the safe house?" When she nodded, he cocked his head to the side. "You look pretty happy for someone who was nearly gunned down two days ago."

"Vega's dead. That's all I care about."

Nora reached for him. He responded by moving closer, but he paused when Beau barked. She gave Beau a sharp command, and he quieted. Angel took Nora, but he stiffened when he rested the baby against his chest.

"What is it?" she asked.

He gritted his teeth and handed Nora back. "I got a scratch last night."

She put Nora on her hip. "A scratch?" His collar shifted, showing the edge of a bandage. "What happened to you?"

He gave her a piercing look. "I was with Gavin last night."

"In Hell?" She tugged on his shirt so she could see down the front.

"If you want to see me naked, all you have to do is ask."

She got a whiff of his cologne. It wasn't classy sin, but it was just as musky and seductive. His scent made her hand clutch the soft material of his warm shirt. Oh, shit. Had Marcus's initiation awakened her sex beast and now she would get hot for anything with a dick and pretty face?

"That's not a scratch." She forced herself to concentrate on the two huge gauze pads on his chest and not the color of his nipples. "What happened?"

"It's a whiplash. I'll be fine in a couple of days."

She looked up and was captured by hypnotic pale blue eyes mere inches from hers.

"About that fantasy ..." he drawled.

Nora let out a shrill scream, breaking the sexual tension. Carmen stepped back as Gavin approached. This was Angel freaking Roman. Beneath those stunning good looks was a man trained to be heartless and cruel, and besides, he was the new crime lord. He definitely wasn't a man she should be fooling around with.

Nora bounced excitedly as Gavin took her. Carmen slid sweaty palms over her jeans and focused on Gavin instead of his cousin.

"Lyla?" she asked.

"In the shower."

Nora pounded Gavin's chest and chattered as her father pressed a kiss to her temple. Both of Nora's parents were alive and well today. All was right in the world. She scanned Gavin, who still hadn't bothered to put on a shirt. In broad daylight, she could see that his knuckles were swollen, bruised, and full of nicks.

"Did you get hurt too?" She circled him and stopped dead when she saw the lash on his back. "What the fuck, Gavin!"

"What?"

The lash on his back was the length of her forearm and encrusted with dried blood. The skin around the wound was inflamed and must hurt like a bitch. "I hope you killed whoever did this."

"Of course," Gavin said.

"I think I got him with my trident," Angel said.

"No, I think I hacked his arm off with my sword," Gavin countered.

Whips, tridents, swords? Only in Hell.

"I hear we're not the only ones who got action," Gavin said casually.

Her heart leaped into her throat. "What?" Did Marcus say something?

"I heard you killed your first man."

She relaxed instantly. "Oh. Him. Yeah." She was giddy with relief.

"You killed a man?" Angel's expression was suddenly intense.

She folded her arms defensively across her chest. "I had to." Neither man said anything, so she snapped, "And I'd do it again."

Angel's mouth curved into a delighted grin. "Babe, you keep getting better and better."

Gavin looked at them and then declared, "Fuck, no."

"What? We're not related," Angel said.

Gavin looked so horrified that Carmen couldn't hold back a giggle. The devilish gleam in Angel's eyes promised that she had a new partner in crime to antagonize the fuck out of Gavin.

"Not fucking happening," Gavin decreed and pointed at the house. "Get out of here, Carmen. I need to talk to my cousin."

She sauntered toward Angel and trailed her hand down his arm and murmured loud enough for Gavin to hear, "We'll finish talking about fantasies later."

"Fantasies? What the fuck, Angel?" Gavin snapped.

She smothered a laugh as she ran upstairs and headed to the master suite. She found Lyla in the bathroom, brush in hand, ghost white. Her eyes were puffy, and her lips were nearly colorless. Despite her wan appearance, there was a hardness in her eyes that hadn't been there before. Lyla had come a long way from the fragile flower who ran from Gavin five years ago. Lyla morphed into a true crime lord's wife. Even though her hair was still wet from her shower, Lyla had a gun in the waistband of her jeans.

Carmen rushed toward her and wrapped her in a tight hug. "I fucking told you not to visit your mom in the hospital." She couldn't help herself. If Lyla hadn't gone to the hospital, she wouldn't have gone to Hell and endured whatever took place last night.

"Yeah."

Carmen examined her glassy, bloodshot eyes. "Are you okay?"

Lyla stared at her for a pregnant moment before she shook her head. "No, but I will be."

She braced her hands on her shoulders and squeezed. "Steven Vega?"

Lyla's eyes kindled with rage. "He was there the whole time. He was tired of being bullied by his brother, his dad, Gavin... He put on the mask and became the man he wanted to be. It's over now."

"Yes, it is. Sit. I'll do your hair."

She pushed Lyla onto a bench in front of the vanity and took the brush from her. Lyla stared straight ahead. It was clear she was still in shock. Lyla lived in her head and needed time to work it out on her own, but she would get through this. She always did.

"Mom's awake," Lyla said quietly.

"Aunt Beatrice woke from the coma? Is she okay? Is she talking?"

"We got a call last night. I went to see her. She asked about Dad."

Of course, Aunt Beatrice would ask about her worthless husband above everything else. Lyla wouldn't meet her eyes in the mirror. She could feel the silent pain radiating off her cousin. She wrapped her arms around her from behind.

"You did what you had to, Lyla. Your dad would've killed Nora—"

"I know," Lyla said and shook her head. "I couldn't tell her what I did. I just said he was dead. She didn't ask who killed him."

Lyla couldn't catch a break to save her life. She survived Hell and now had to deal with her mother who woke from a coma, asking for her husband who Lyla killed in self-defense. She gave Lyla another squeeze and kiss on the cheek before she resumed brushing her hair. "Just leave it be, Lyla. You have time. It'll work out."

"You think we can have a happily ever after?" Lyla asked quietly.

"You and Gavin deserve it."

Lyla met her eyes in the mirror. "And you too, Carmen."

She blinked hastily and focused on French braiding her hair. "I need to tell Vinny it's over."

Lyla nodded. "And we can finally spread Manny's ashes. It never felt right before. I miss him so much."

Vinny and Manny, gone too fucking soon. She breathed through the pain as she finished the braid. "I know."

Lyla reached back and grasped her hand. "We got him, Carmen."

Their eyes met in the mirror.

"I threw a dagger in his back and crushed his bones with a shield. Gavin ran him through with eight swords, and then Lucifer cut off his head."

"You crushed his bones with a shield?"

"Oh, and I kicked his severed head into the stands."

She would have taken great delight in getting her shot at Vega for all the pain he caused her family, but it seemed that Lyla and the others had taken care of it. He died in pain. That had to be enough for her. She looped her arms around Lyla's neck and pressed her cheek to her cousin's. "You're a fucking savage. I'm so proud. You're a true crime lord's wife."

The corner of Lyla's mouth twitched. "I'm the wife of a retired crime lord."

"Yes. I just met Angel."

"I'm worried," Lyla murmured.

"Why?"

"He's family. I don't want him in the line of fire."

Carmen read between the lines. "Angel isn't Vinny."

"But ..."

"Let Angel and Gavin deal with it. We're going to move on and watch Nora grow up and drive Gavin crazy. We're going to laugh, eat, and enjoy life because we fucking deserve it. We made it, Lyla. He didn't break us."

"You're different today."

She smoothed Lyla's hair. "What do you mean?" She wasn't about to blurt out that she fucked Marcus while Lyla battled for her life in Hell.

"You're excited about something."

"I can finally let him go. I want to try to find some kind of normal."

"Some kind of normal," Lyla repeated and nodded. "Sounds

about right. You know, I wouldn't have been able to do this without you."

"What's family for?"

"So you're leaving?" At Carmen's nod, she said, "Tell Aunt Isabel that Mom woke up."

"Will do. I'll be in touch, babe."

She gave Lyla another hug before she went to the guest bedroom and crammed as much of her shit as she could in a bag. She would come back for the rest later. The need to see Vinny was riding her hard. It was the last step to complete before she started over. It wouldn't be official until she told him Vega was dead.

She headed downstairs with her overnight bag slung over her shoulder. Blade and two guards stood in the foyer, conversing in low tones. Blade caught sight of her and jerked his head at the men, who immediately exited. Blade had been Gavin's shadow for as long as she could remember. His position in the household blurred since he became Lyla's bodyguard and Nora's godfather. When Lyla went rogue and stole a car, she saw a break in Blade's stoic demeanor. He went ballistic, revealing that Lyla's welfare was more than just a job to him.

"You're alive!" she chirped.

Blade didn't crack a smile. His stony face was even more imposing than normal since he sported an angry gash on his cheek. He normally dressed in a suit to conceal the fact he was always armed, but today, he wore jeans and a tee with the double shoulder holster on full display. It looked damn good on him.

Blade took the overnight bag from her. She thought this was an unusually solicitous gesture on his part until he dropped her bag on the ground.

She shoved him. "What the hell, Blade? I have expensive shit in there!"

"You can buy more," he said heartlessly. "Why'd you try to shoot Marcus?"

Damn tattletale security. "Because I thought he might be in with Vega."

Blade blinked. "Marcus?" His incredulous tone made it clear he thought the suggestion was ludicrous.

"Why couldn't he side with Vega?"

"Because he wouldn't."

Blade was naturally suspicious, yet he didn't hesitate to vouch for Marcus. "Why?"

He gave her a hard look. "Ask Gavin."

"That's your answer for everything," she grumbled. "You're so dramatic. Did you sleep at all?" Knowing Blade, he hadn't slept since they returned from Hell. She grasped the edge of his shirt and lifted to see if he had wounds like Gavin and Angel. "Did you get whipped too?"

Blade knocked her hand away, but not before she got a glimpse of his carved abs. It wasn't the first time she saw his body. She'd gotten glimpses when they worked out in the past, but this was the first time she was interested in a more thorough examination. "Come on, Blade. Don't be such a baby."

He bared his teeth. "I'm fine."

She ignored his warning and gripped his chin. "Did someone clean this? You don't want another scar." Her eyes flicked up to the thin cut on his eyebrow.

"What do I care about scars?" He grabbed her wrist and yanked it off his face. "Why are you touching me?"

"I'm checking you out."

"Why?"

"Because all of you are too stupid and macho to get your injuries checked out. Gavin and Angel have whip lashes on their bodies and who knows what else? What about you?"

"I don't have any lashes."

"How did you get that cut on your face?"

"Machete."

"A machete," she repeated and shook her head. None of the guys who'd gone into battle last night left unscathed. "I should call a doctor."

"You should see the other guys."

"Oh, yeah?"

"Yeah, they're dead."

Point made. "Fine. If you want to be scarred and prolong the healing process, go for it. I have shit to do."

"Where are you going?"

"Home."

"You're moving back with your mother?"

She clapped her hands together. "Yes! Lyla isn't under house arrest, Gavin isn't the crime lord, and the psycho who murdered my husband is dead. Gavin tells me he suffered, and that's all that matters. I can move on with my life. I want to go dancing or something, but I think I should dye my hair first. What do you think about me going red?"

He couldn't control his sneer. "I don't give a shit about your hair color."

She ignored his surly mood and handed him her car key. Blade opened the door and tossed the key to a nearby guard who jogged toward the massive garage to find her vehicle among the fleet.

"You should have an escort," Blade said.

"What for? Vega's dead."

"Vega may be gone, but there are still a lot of people who hate the Pyres, and you're included."

She shrugged. "We both know I'm not a target, not like Gavin and Lyla. Vinny was the crime lord for less than a week. No one cares about me. What do you think of Angel taking over?"

Blade didn't answer immediately. His eyes moved over the guards while they did their rounds.

"Word's out that he's taken the title. Angel's young so some might underestimate him, but he's a Roman through and through. They'll learn soon enough if they didn't already hear what he did in Hell last night."

She shouldn't ask, but curiosity got the better of her. "So, he's a good fighter?"

"He survived in the pit."

That must mean yes. "And you think it's a good thing he's taking over?"

"Isn't that what I said?"

She rolled her eyes. Men. "He's not what I expected of a Roman."

His attention snapped back to her. He searched her eyes and then shook his head. "No."

"What?"

"Fuck no."

It wasn't surprising that his reaction was nearly identical to Gavin's. They were two of a kind. She could practically hear the lecture forming in his head. Fortunately, her gold convertible rounded the drive. She shouldered her bag and gave him the peace sign as she sashayed outside. "There's my baby. Take care of Lyla for me."

"I always do," he growled. "Don't do anything stupid, Carmen."

She put the top down on the convertible before she perched on the seat. Blade was doing a good imitation of an Indian chief as he watched her from the top step, legs braced apart and arms crossed over his chest.

"What do you think of cherry?" she called.

"What?"

"Cherry for my new hair color!"

Blade scowled as several guards snickered.

"Seriously, though, red hair will be cute, right?" she yelled.

Blade walked into the house and slammed the door behind him. She laughed as she put the car in gear and stomped on the gas. The gates opened as she approached. Gavin's fortress was far enough outside the city that she didn't have to worry about the speed limit for a while, and she took full advantage of that. The car powered forward, winding smoothly on the long stretch of empty road. On days like this, she and Vinny would go on long drives, park in the middle of nowhere, and lay on the hood and talk for hours. God, she missed him. There would never be another Vincent Pyre.

Too soon, she reached civilization and slowed down a little. Her city came into view. She loved this gaudy oasis in the middle of the desert. There was a manic vibe to the city that wasn't for everyone, but she reveled in the dark beat of sexual energy, hunger, and ambition of the natives. She was one herself, after all. Las Vegas would always be her home.

She parked in the garage beside the Toyota she used to drive in high school. The door that led into the house opened before she could get out of the car. Her mother ran to her with open arms.

"Carmen Marie!" Mom leaned over the car door and hugged her tight. "I've been so worried!"

"Hi, Mom."

Mom clasped her face and blinked. "You're glowing."

Carmen slid over the top of the door instead of opening it. She reached for her purse and overnight bag and put her arm around Mom's waist.

"I know we need to catch up, but I need to talk to Vinny first."

"Of course, honey."

She gave her mother a kiss before she rushed upstairs. She walked into her modest bedroom, closed the door, and leaned back against it. A pewter urn perched on her dresser with VP engraved on the front. She dropped her bags and approached slowly.

"Hey, baby."

She stopped in front of the urn and spread her hand over the curves she knew so well. How many days had she spent wrapped around this urn, willing Vinny to make an appearance? This was all she had left of him. It didn't seem right that a man with such vitality could fit into a container. It had been almost three years, and she still couldn't believe he was gone.

"It's over. They caught him, Vin. It was Paul Vega's son, Steven. He's dead. Gavin made him suffer."

She rested her forehead on the urn and hung on tight.

"I miss you," she whispered against the cold metal. She tried to imagine it was Vinny's warm flesh against hers. "Everyone says time heals all wounds, but that's a fucking lie. Every day without you is worse than the one before."

She bit her lip as her eyes flooded with tears. It had been years since he passed, but she'd never said goodbye. She refused. How could she with his killer on the loose? Now, the time had come to say goodbye to her best friend, lover, partner, husband, and soul mate.

She took a deep breath. "I told you I was staying with Lyla because she was on lockdown. The other night, shit went down. The fortress got attacked, and we had to go to a safe house. Lyla told me to take Nora and run while she stayed behind. I hid with Nora, and when I heard a soldier coming, I had to make a decision."

Was it her imagination or did the air vibrate with tension?

"I decided to live." Facing a future without Vinny wasn't something she had ever contemplated. Even now, the realization that she was going forward alone was debilitating, but she breathed through the panic. She raised her head and saw her tear-streaked reflection in the urn. "I can't grieve you anymore."

Guilt engulfed her, but she gritted her teeth and continued, "I can't take the pain. You're not here, but I am. I *need*, Vinny." Her words hung in the air, and she mentally braced before she confessed, "I slept with Marcus Fletcher."

She closed her eyes and waited for a reaction. When none came, she lifted her chin.

"It was good." Honesty forced her to add, "Better than good." She waved her hand. "Fucking brilliant if you really want to know." She pursed her lips and then added, "He did doggy style. You know I've always had a thing for rough and doggy."

Her lips twitched, but she bit back the smile since it seemed inappropriate.

"When you died, I thought I did too. I've been living in this purgatory, but the other night, I decided to live. When I pulled the trigger, I came back to life. I can see, feel, taste ..." Her mouth watered at the memory of Marcus's kiss. She swallowed. "I can't imagine loving anyone the way I love you, but I can find small pleasures in life. At least until we meet again." She placed her hand on the urn. "I'll always love you." She tapped her chest where her heart was trapped in a never-ending cycle of restitching itself back together again. "The pain will always be there. I know that now. I just have to find some sense of satisfaction in the small things." Lyla's words tripped through her mind, and she shook her head. "I don't think I can spread your ashes. I'm not ready for that yet. I don't know if I ever will be."

She sat on the edge of the bed, chin balanced on her hand as she regarded the urn.

"Till death do us part," she whispered. "We put off that trip to Bora Bora, that couple's painting class, and you learning the tango. We thought we had a lifetime." She mustered up a smile. "You should see Nora. She's gorgeous."

She waited, but she didn't hear his voice in her mind. The silence stretched, and a tear slipped down her cheek when she realized she was truly alone. She'd broken their tie. She went up to the urn and touched the metal with her broken fingernail.

"I love you," she whispered. "I built my life around you. My heart beat for you. You loved me, even my flaws, and I loved you with every breath I had." Her face crumpled. It took a minute to regain her composure, and when she did, she forced a smile. "I'm going to live enough for the both of us. That fucker took you from me, but he didn't break me. I want to dance on his grave, you know? I have to show everyone that your widow's still smoking hot. I love you, babe. I always will."

She kissed the metal and walked away. She closed the bedroom door and leaned back against it as tears streamed down her face. She didn't want Vinny to see her cry. He'd seen enough of that already. She had to do this for the both of them; Lyla needed to know life went on even after you went through war.

Mom paced in the kitchen but stopped when she entered.

"Are you okay?" she asked and gave her another hug.

"Yeah."

Mom rubbed her back. "You've been crying."

"I..." She swallowed and tried again. "I had to tell Vinny it's over. Gavin got him."

Mom's hand stopped at the top of her spine. "He's dead?"

"Yeah."

"Thank God."

Her lips curved, and she pulled back. "Yes. It wasn't official until I told Vinny."

Mom pushed her into a chair. "Everyone's all right?"

"Yes."

Her mother murmured prayers under her breath as she turned to the stove. She came back with a steaming bowl of mac and cheese. "Eat that. You're too skinny."

Carmen didn't hesitate. She grabbed the fork and took a bite. Her taste buds moaned in delight, and she dug in with gusto. Her queasy belly instantly leveled out as cheesy goodness filled the emptiness.

"Carmen?"

She looked up to find Mom staring at her. "What?"

"You're eating."

"Yes."

Mom beamed. "I haven't seen you eat like this in years. You're getting better."

"Better than what?"

"Just... better. You smiled, laughed, and ate, but you can't fool me. I know you, Carmen. You were wasting away and now..." She clasped her hands together. "You're back."

Apparently, her acting skills needed work. "I couldn't move on with that fuck still on the loose, but now I can. I just said goodbye to Vinny."

Her mother nodded. "I understand."

"Did... did you say goodbye to Dad?"

Mom hesitated and then said, "Yes, I had to."

She eyed her mother who didn't look recently widowed. Mom looked a decade younger than when her father had passed. Mom had adapted amazingly well, unlike her. "You're good? You've been living alone for four months."

"Yes, I'm great, dear. Are you moving back in?"

"Yes. Now that it's over, everything will go back to normal."

Mom reached out and grasped her hand. "Are you really okay?"

"I will be."

Mom pulled up a seat, and she told her everything. When she finished, her mother's hands were over her mouth.

"Oh, poor Beatrice..." she whispered. "I have to go see her."

"I'm sure Lyla will go down there today even though she's exhausted. You should call her."

"Yes, I will." Mom ran her hands over Carmen as if to reassure herself that her daughter was whole. "You don't seem as upset as I thought you would be."

"That fucker's dead. I'm ready to move on." She straightened and said, "What do you think about me with red hair?"

Her mother didn't miss a beat. "What shade?"

"I can do cherry, burgundy, or an in-between shade."

"You always look great no matter what."

She pulled her phone from her pocket. "I wonder if Shonda can fit me in today at the salon."

"You're going to the salon after everything you just told me?" Mom asked.

"Yes, I have to start right now."

"Start what?"

"Living. And changing my hair is the first step. Everything will fall into place after that." She dialed and paced around the kitchen. "Hey, Shonda, it's Carmen. I know it's been forever. Can you fit me in? You're the best! Wait, hold on." She put her hand over the phone and asked Mom, "You want to come with me?"

"No, you go ahead."

"Yeah, Shonda. Just me. I'm on my way." She hung up and kissed Mom's cheek. "I love you."

"Love you too. You be safe."

"Always."

Carmen snatched her purse and rushed out to the car. She fired up the engine and dashed across town. She wasn't sure why changing her hair was so important to her, but it was. Her appearance was a reflection of how she felt, and the black hair had to go. Red was a power color, a defiant color that showed a zeal for life. On impulse, she swung into a Dunkin' Donuts drive-through, and when she walked into the salon, she balanced two boxes of donuts on one hand while she pushed her sunglasses up on her head with the other.

"Bitch!" Shonda shouted and opened her arms wide.

Carmen tossed the donuts on the counter and threw herself at Shonda who wrapped her in a bone-crushing hug before she pulled back and held Carmen at arm's length to examine her from head to toe. She suddenly gasped and slapped her chest as if she was putting out a fire.

"You took out your implants?" Shonda shouted.

The hairdressers left their clients to gather around and pat her chest as if they couldn't see with their eyes that her chest was smaller.

"I'm going au naturel," she announced proudly to the salon at large.

"Why?"

The question came not only from the salon staff but also several clients.

"Back pain," she said.

"No pain, no gain," Shonda said and got several grunts of agreement from the onlookers.

"My clothes didn't fit right, and I can get a man without water balloons on my chest," Carmen said.

Keenan, a black man who could work wonders with hair, tapped his sneakers and regarded her as if she crawled out from under a rock. He wore a striped button up shirt with a fuchsia scarf and a hat pointing sideways.

"I don't like it," he announced.

"Well, I do, and I have proof that not all men are repulsed, *so*..." Carmen put her hand in his face.

Shonda snickered. "You could cut off your tits, and you'd still have men lining up to fuck you."

"Stupid white bitch, walking in here with that face and body," Keenan muttered and snapped his scissors irritably. "Making everyone else feel like crap."

"I missed you too," Carmen said and kissed his cheek.

"And what the fuck is this?" Keenan snapped as he prodded the donut box as if it was a snake.

"It's donuts," she said and reached in to grab a frosted strawberry one with sprinkles. "Help yourself."

"And she comes with fucking donuts," Keenan muttered before he walked back to his client. "Who does she think she is?"

Carmen took a bite of doughy goodness, stopped in her tracks, and grabbed another before she skipped toward Shonda's chair. She ignored the incredulous stares from the rail thin, high-maintenance broads who visited the salon every two weeks to make sure their glossy appearance never wavered. She made a show of eating the donuts, moaning in delight, and licking her fingers because she was in the mood to fuck with people. If there had been any straight men around, she would have licked off every sprinkle and made a spectacle of herself just for shits and giggles.

"Bitch, why'd you bring these donuts?" Shonda asked as she devoured a cake donut.

"Because life's too short not to eat donuts."

Shonda finished her donut and eyed Carmen in the mirror. "Don't insult me by calling for an appointment. You know any of us would drop everything for you. You're part owner, idiot."

"Silent partner."

Shonda rolled her eyes. "Whatever. You saved our ass. You can come in whenever." She put a hand on her shoulder and squeezed. "You're okay? I know you've been having a hard time since Vinny died."

She gave Shonda a determined smile. "I'll be better once we do my hair."

Shonda nodded as if she understood completely. "What am I doing to you?"

"First, this needs to go," she said, pointing at her black hair.

"You want to go back to blond?"

"I'm thinking red." Carmen waggled her brows at Shonda in the mirror.

Shonda put a hand on her hip. "Are we talking red or red?"

"I'm feeling..." Carmen did a little shimmy under the tarp she was wearing. "You know?"

"I know just what I'm going to do to you, girl." Shonda handed her a glass of champagne. "Now, sit back, relax, and tell Shonda all about it."

Six hours later, Carmen stood in front of a mirror and examined the woman staring back at her. Shonda stripped away the black and replaced it with the color of rich wine. Long layers highlighted her features and gave her a sultry, seductive air. Her fingers and toes were the same shade of dangerous red. She had been waxed and received a facial that made her skin glow.

The woman smiling back at her held no resemblance to the exhausted creature she had been this morning. She spent the day catching up with the salon staff she'd known for years. She laughed, had food delivered, and willed the past away. The hours spent being waxed, prodded, and primped made her shiny and new again.

When she was a little girl, her favorite pastime was dress up. She loved that a shade of lipstick could make an impact and the right outfit could strike an audience speechless. She experimented as a kid and reaped the benefits as an adult. She knew which silhouettes suited her body type and what shoes made her legs go on forever. She used her looks and wiles shamelessly against Vinny who had been poleaxed and ripe for the picking. She had been fortunate that they fell in love and were perfect for one another. Many suspected she was a gold digger. She enjoyed playing the role because that meant she had the upper hand since they underestimated her. She was restless by nature and had a wild side Vinny didn't try to tame. She didn't care what people thought about her. All she cared about was how she felt about herself, and right now, she felt better than she had in years.

Keenan ambled up behind her. He'd been watching her progress throughout the day and sent many sour looks her way. They used to party ages ago. He never forgave her for hooking Vinny. It didn't matter that Vinny was straight. If Keenan coveted, he believed he should be able to have. That was just his way.

"Jealous?" she asked as she fluffed her hair so it caught the light and fell perfectly around her face. She pouted at him in the mirror and posed, exposing her midriff and slight curves, even though she knew it did nothing for him.

"You're back," he declared.

"Back?"

"To yourself. You're not moping around like a wannabe biker chick anymore. You're Carmen. You can't waste that look," he said with mock solemnity.

"What do you mean?"

"Tell me you're not going home to watch TV. We need to go out like old times."

Carmen grinned. "Just tell me when and where and I'm there."

6

Carmen pulled up to a Pyre Casino and took the hand of the valet who reached in to help her out. She unfurled from the car, grabbed her silver clutch, and headed toward the casino. Her hair bounced with every step, and the skintight dress with long sleeves and an open back hugged every curve. She wore the highest heels she owned, which made her feel invincible. She knew from experience that the diamond choker would catch the light and sparkle like a fucking disco ball. She felt like a million dollars, and the stares from the men and women confirmed it.

She absorbed the energy from the crowd as she blazed a path through the throng. She was ready to dance, drink, and drown herself in Sin City delights. A night on The Strip was a gamble, and she loved tossing the dice. She would take whatever came her way. No plans or responsibilities, just impulse and pleasure.

She ignored the losers who catcalled and the ones who tried bad pickup lines. She was an Amazonian, and Amazonians didn't bother with boys. Maybe luck would be on her side tonight, and she'd find someone who could rev her engine. Her body hummed with energy.

Shonda, Keenan, and the other stylists were standing in line to enter Ecstasy. Carmen waved them over, and they ducked under the velvet ropes.

"Girl," Shonda said and looked her over, "you look amazing!"

"Thanks to you! Come on, let's get drunk."

Carmen linked her arm through Shonda and Keenan's and led the way to the entrance. The bouncers recognized her and held up the line so she and her squad could pass. She thanked them with a big smile and ignored the slew of insults from those waiting in line.

"Oh, my fucking God," Keenan breathed.

Ecstasy was a small, intimate club. For that reason, they were extremely selective of who entered. The club was built like an amphitheater with wide stairs for people to dance on since it was standing room only. The top tier of the club had a white backlight to highlight the silhouettes of the professional dancers. The floor glowed a glassy blue that made it seem as if they were wading into a sea of exotic people. Carmen and Keenan made a beeline for the dance floor while most of the girls headed to the bar.

Keenan wore a see-through plaid button up shirt and the tightest pants she had ever seen. He wasted no time twerking and grinding his butt against her crotch. Carmen laughed as she moved with him.

"Rules!" Keenan barked. "If he's bi, then I get first dibs!"

She ran her hand down his chest and breathed, "If I want him, I'll have him."

"You're so greedy!" he protested.

"I'm starving," she said as she wrapped her arms around his waist and bucked her hips against his ass.

Keenan glanced back at her, brows raised. "If you do that in the bedroom, no man will leave you!"

"I know!" she shouted back.

Keenan shook his head. "Damn, girl. Let's do this!"

Keenan had energy to spare. They took turns grinding against one another before Keenan spotted a group of gay men dancing outrageously on the fringes of the crowd. Shonda and the girls joined her on the floor. They cheered as a Beyoncé hit blasted through the speakers. Carmen downed the drink they handed her. She couldn't decipher the complicated mix of liquor and didn't really care since it made her feel as if she had wings.

When the girls were ready to bounce, they searched for Keenan and pried him away from his new friends. Keenan's shirt was unbuttoned, proudly displaying his new hickey. They laughed and stumbled into Kaleidoscope. It wasn't a Pyre club, but they breezed in anyway because they looked so damn fine. The club had neon strobe lights and a DJ who knew what he was doing. They refueled at the bar before they made it to the dance floor, which was filled with half-naked people having a grand time. She accepted Shonda's dare and took a shot glass from a man's underwear using only her mouth. That was just the beginning.

Around two in the morning, they stumbled into Incognito. Carmen accepted a scarlet lace mask at the door and surveyed the crowd. There was a distant twinge in the region of her heart. She would never be able to enter this club and not think of Vinny. She made a beeline for the bar. Two shots later, she was feeling remarkably lightheaded and fuzzy. She headed to the main floor and danced with a bunch of strangers she would never see again.

Even though her feet felt like they were about to fall off and her calves were cramping, she kept going. The energy of the crowd was infectious. These people were living at the moment. No one was thinking about the consequences of tomorrow, so neither would she. When she found herself in the middle of a hot man sandwich, she didn't try to get away. Her dress was plastered to her body with sweat, and she didn't give a shit. The feel of two hot muscular bodies pressed against her felt fantastic.

When one man tried to lift the back of her dress, she shoved him away and boogied through the crowd. Stupid men, always ruining her fun. She was a tease, yes, but that didn't mean she was easy game for just anyone.

She moseyed aimlessly through the crowd in a euphoric state of bliss. The press of bodies, the liquor, and the drugging music made her happy to be alive. She didn't take being petted and kissed personally. She understood the need for human contact better than most.

Besides, that was why most people were here—to live out their fantasy of hooking up with a stranger. That was part of the club scene, and something she'd been doing since her teenage years. The night swirled with possibilities. Anything was possible in this desert oasis.

She cast her eye over the VIP section and felt her giddy delight dip when she spotted Regal, a sleazy pimp known for his brutal treatment of his girls. He was dressed all in white with at least ten gold necklaces resting against his wife beater. He was surrounded by women who were clearly on something. Regal was all flash and no brains. How he managed to stay in the game was beyond her. A nerdy man with a sour face sat on the edge of the booth, glaring at Regal, who looked like he was getting a hand job beneath the table.

Carmen stopped in her tracks when a beautiful brunette stepped in her path. Before she could go around her, the brunette kissed her. She closed her eyes as the woman pressed soft marshmallow lips against her own. She'd had her fair share of kisses from women, but never while in this heightened state of awareness. The woman placed a hand on her chest and squeezed one breast while she tilted her head to the side and deepened the kiss. She tasted like Pina colada and smelled like Chanel. Although Carmen was intrigued, she didn't feel any heat. As she ran a hand down the brunette's cheek, she found herself more interested in her moisturizer than feeling her up. She was distracted by a slide of tongue before the woman pulled back. She was drop-dead gorgeous with full candy apple lips, dark eyes, and long, straight hair. She also had a great smoky eye, a dress with a daring plunge, and five-thousand-dollar shoes.

"You into threesomes?" she asked.

"No," Carmen said apologetically. Apparently, a pretty face wasn't all it took to get her in the mood. The human needed to own a dick. Good to know.

"You sure? I thought you'd be up for it."

Carmen was too selfish to be involved in a threesome. "Maybe another time."

The woman pouted. "Boo. That sucks. My boyfriend won't let me invite a guy, only another woman. I've been scoping out the floor for an hour. You're the only one we both agreed on."

"I'm flattered, but I'm not into women, only men. Where'd you get your dress?"

The woman's eyes lit up. "You a local?"

"Yes."

"There's this great boutique on Westin and Lincoln called The Look."

"I'll check it out."

"You sure you're not interested?"

"Yes, but thanks for asking," Carmen said courteously.

"You taste good. Just one more."

Carmen accepted the second kiss. It wasn't an unpleasant sensation aside from the lip gloss, which was messing up her own.

"Looking for a third?"

Carmen pulled back and felt her euphoria vanish when she saw Angel. He was dressed much as he had been this morning in black jeans and shirt. He was seriously underdressed, but he stood out among the crowd. It was that face and his arrogant, bad boy vibe that made women take notice and men edge out of his way just in case he was the real deal.

"Hey, babe," he said.

Did he think she was someone else?

"I like the red," Angel said and winked. "It suits you."

The fact that he picked her out of the crowd when they had only met once, and she had a new hairdo and wore a mask was stretching coincidence too far. "Are you stalking me?"

"Does that turn you on?"

"Yes," the brunette gushed and flushed when Angel turned to her. "Hi."

"Hi," Angel said genially. "You two looking for a third?"

The brunette bit her lip. "I'm supposed to find another girl, but you're..." The brunette cast a furtive look around. "If you're around later, I think I could slip away from my boyfriend."

Angel looked back at her with a raised brow. "And you, Carmen?"

"I don't do threesomes. I'm selfish."

Angel grinned. "What a coincidence. Right now, I feel the same way."

Carmen tried to slip into the crowd but was brought to a halt by Angel, who wrapped an arm around her middle.

"Seems like neither of us can help you tonight," Angel said.

The brunette opened her mouth to negotiate, but something over Angel's shoulder caught her eye. She sighed and gave Angel a look full of yearning. "Maybe another time?"

"Sure," Angel said, and she disappeared into the crowd.

"Seriously, what are you doing here?" Carmen asked.

"I'm working."

It was a shot in the dark, but she tried. "You're here for Regal?"

She saw a flash of surprise, which he quickly hid. "You know Regal?"

"Of course."

He shook his head. "Don't worry your pretty head about it."

She scowled at the condescending tone. "He's the most skittish man on the planet. This isn't the place to approach him."

His hand stroked her bare back. The streak of fire he left in his wake made her suck in a breath. It was only then that she realized they were swaying lazily to the music. She had no problem grinding against a guy she would never see again. Angel Roman was something else.

"You're not wearing a mask," she said.

"This is my mask."

He smiled, but it didn't reach his eyes. His sharp gaze was a blatant contrast to the relaxed body moving in tune with hers. Behind that rough accent and pretty face, something twisted and ruthless lurked.

"I don't know what to make of you," Angel mused.

"What do you mean?"

"Just looking at you, I wouldn't think you knew what to do with a gun, much less have the balls to kill a man. This morning, I pegged you for a smoking hot nanny, and now you've morphed into a man-eater."

"I'm not a man-eater."

"You have trouble written all over you."

"Then you should stay far away," she said.

His finger wove a distracting design on the small of her back. "I like challenges. Are you here alone?"

"No, I'm out with friends."

He made a show of looking around. "Doesn't look like it."

"They're"—she waved vaguely—"around. Somewhere."

He raised a brow. "How smashed are you?"

"Not drunk enough to fuck you."

He threw back his head and roared with laughter as he drew her even closer. "When I fuck you, you're gonna be stone cold sober. I don't want to fuck a limp body. I need you to be able to brace yourself."

Oh, fuck. Did her pussy just spasm? Angel smiled. He definitely knew what he was doing. Men underutilized their best feature, and it wasn't their dick or muscled body. It was their mouth. Words could make a woman hotter than touch, and he fucking knew it. Damn Roman.

"You sober yet?" he murmured.

She bared her teeth. "No!"

He continued to move with her as if he had all the time in the world. Despite his words, he wasn't feeling her up or trying to kiss her, which made her wonder how he kissed... which he also knew. He was definitely a playboy, the most dangerous type. He might not dress in suits, but his image was carefully crafted all the same. She bet his jeans were fucking tailored. Gavin and Angel were definitely cut from the same cloth. They were from wealthy families but willing to get their hands dirty. She inhaled his cologne. It was a light, clean scent. Not overpowering. She labeled him forbidden sin. Apparently, she wasn't into women or the other males who approached her tonight. Instead, she was attracted to Vinny's replacements in the business and underworld: Marcus Fletcher and Angel Roman. Not good news.

"You swing both ways?" Angel asked.

"No." She liked dick too much.

"But you kissed her."

Carmen shrugged. "Why not?"

He grinned. "So, you like to experiment. You're my kind of woman."

"I don't think so."

"Why not?"

"You want a pretty face, banging body, and a woman who will leave the moment you're done with her. I'm not your gal."

Some of the easiness faded from his expression, and the hunter that made him crime lord material examined her more closely. "You think that's all I want?"

"For now," she allowed. Maybe one day he'd want to settle down like Gavin. Maybe not.

She prided herself on her ability to size up a person. Angel Roman was hot. Make that smoking hot. That was enough reason to make most women go stupid around him. Add the fact that he was rich, dangerous, and probably had the skills of an assassin, and he became irresistible. Most women would be fooled by his friendly, easygoing demeanor, but she grew up around men like him. There was something vicious and insatiable inside him. She wasn't dumb enough to think she could tame it. She liked her men civilized with a naughty streak. She wouldn't bend for an alpha male and had no wish to be in a one-sided relationship that would end in death or more heartache.

"Don't be so quick to judge me." One of his hands left her bare back to play with the ends of her hair. He held it up to the light. "Looks like fresh-spilled blood."

She made a disgusted sound. "You're such a crime lord."

"Does that turn you on?"

"Nope," she said with complete honesty.

He leaned close enough for his warm breath to breeze across her lips. "You have a wild side, Carmen. I can taste it."

Her insides squirmed. Yes, he was good at this. But then again, so was she. She cupped the side of his pretty face and ran her thumb over his bottom lip. She felt him tense ever so slightly against her.

"You can't handle me, Roman," she said.

He captured her thumb and sucked it into his mouth. She ignored the heat that speared straight to her lady bits. Holy fuck. No wonder men liked to stick their hands in women's mouths. They were thinking about being sucked off... and so was she. His wicked blue eyes told her he would make her scream, and she believed him. From her position, she could tell he was packing and ready. It wasn't fair. A man with a face like his should have a small dick.

She ripped her thumb from his mouth. "That's not fair! We can touch, but no sucking!" Sucking was too close to the actual act, and she needed to keep her wits together.

"Who said I play fair?"

"True. You are a Roman."

"Right. And we play to win."

He was clearly baiting her. It took every ounce of control she possessed not to challenge him. It would be monumentally stupid to get involved with the new crime lord and a Roman to boot. His eyes glinted in the dim light, enticing her to pit her will against his. He would be dirty, animalistic, raw... Carmen bitch-slapped her inner hussy.

"Not this time, baby," she said and patted his cheek. She eased back and was relieved when he released her.

His eyes swept her from head to toe. "Damn."

"Eat your heart out, Roman," she said before she walked away.

She perched on a stool at the bar to give her poor feet a rest. This time she ordered a water. She twisted off the cap and surveyed the club. It was impossible to find Shonda, Keenan, or any of the others in the crush. A compulsive beat hit the club, and the urge to dance was nearly irresistible, but she was half convinced she might not have feet tomorrow if she didn't have mercy on them. Instead, she was forced to shimmy from a sitting position while she turned down men left and right.

"No speak English," she said in a heavy accent to an especially pushy guy.

As the song faded and another began, she spotted Angel meander toward the VIP section. When he approached the wall of bouncers, Regal glanced over. When he spotted Angel, he leaped to his feet and pulled a black pistol from his pants.

"Oh, fuck," Carmen cursed.

Regal fired wildly and jumped off the VIP dais onto the dance floor. People fell like bowling pins. More shots were fired, and everyone scattered. Carmen climbed on top of her stool as the crowd stampeded like wild animals toward the exit, pushing and shoving at the people they had been making out with seconds before. Angel and Regal were lost in the crowd, but she caught sight of the nerdy man who had been a part of Regal's party hiding beneath the booth with his hands over his head.

She kept her eyes on Regal's assistant and moved when he did. She trailed behind him as he tried to shove himself ahead. His eyes darted in every direction like a trapped rat. She made sure to keep him within arm's length as they poured into the casino. He made his way to the next casino and went out front to grab a taxi. She used tears and a glance down her modest cleavage to snag a taxi. She made a show of seeing Regal's assistant and waved to him.

"Do you want to share a taxi?" she called and was grateful she still wore her mask. She wasn't sure if Regal's assistant would recognize her, but it was always better to be safe than sorry.

The assistant hesitated and looked around at the accumulating crowd before he ran toward her. "You don't mind?"

"No, let's get out of here. This is *scary*!"

They ducked into the cab and pulled away from the pandemonium in front of the casino. She waved her hands in front of her eyes as if she were fighting tears.

"We can drop you off first," she said in a small voice. "I'm not sure where I'm going to stay tonight. I have to call my friends. I don't want to be alone after that. I can't stand guns." She gave an exaggerated shiver.

Regal's assistant gave the cabbie his address, and they were off. She texted Blade for Angel's number and got an instant reply.

No.

She was amused rather than irritated. God, she loved Blade. He was like the disapproving uncle she never asked for. She liked pushing his buttons since he had no sense of humor.

He caused a shooting at a club. I have info he needs.

Her phone began to ring. She answered with a tearful, "Hi, Daddy."

A pause and then Blade snapped, "What the fuck are you talking about?"

"T-there was a shooting at Incognito. I wasn't doing drugs, Daddy, I swear."

Blade was silent for a moment, and then he hissed, "Where are you?"

She sniffled. "Don't be mad at me, okay? I wasn't even drinking."

"You're with someone, aren't you? Fuck, Carmen, can't you stay out of trouble for a fucking day? Goddamn," Blade growled.

"I don't need this right now. I could have died, okay? Have you ever been shot at?" She milked her performance for all it was worth and felt tears trickle down her cheeks. "You're being so mean. I can't handle you right now."

She hung up on him as the cabbie turned on the radio just loud enough to conceal the sound of her pitiful whines. Blade texted her Angel's number and an order.

Call me as soon as you can.

She replied with, *Thanks, Daddy.*

She added Angel's number to her contacts as the driver pulled up to the assistant's house, and she made a note of the address. Regal's assistant bailed out of the cab and ran to his run-down home. She gave the driver her mother's address and texted Shonda and Keenan to make sure they were okay. They replied immediately, saying they went to another club. She gave her apologies and said she'd party with them again soon.

She paid the cabbie and walked up to her house while she dialed Angel's number. He answered on the third ring.

"Who is this?"

The voice on the other end sounded menacing and definitely not like the man who danced with her half an hour ago. She paused with her keys in the front door.

"Angel?" she asked to confirm.

"Who is this?"

"It's Carmen. I got your number from Blade."

A pause and then, "He shouldn't have done that."

No charm or clever lines now. Angel was in business mode. This was the crime lord, the heartless asshole. "Didn't I tell you not to approach Regal?"

He hung up on her. She sighed. Men and their egos. She walked into the dark and quiet house and tiptoed to her room as she redialed his number.

"I'm busy," he snapped.

"So, you lost him?"

Silence.

"Why do you want Regal?"

"This is underworld business."

"Do you want Regal or not?"

"You know where he is?"

"Why do you want him?" she persisted as she kicked off her heels and sighed in relief. God, that felt amazing.

"Do you know where he is or not?"

"I might."

"This isn't a fucking game."

"I know," she said as she put him on speaker and peeled off her dress. "That's why I want to know why you want him."

A pause as he mulled that over. "He did a lot for Steven Vega; things you don't need to know about."

That's all she needed to know. "I'm going to text you his assistant's address."

"Why the fuck would I care about his assistant?"

"Because his assistant is actually his life partner. They've been together for years."

"Isn't his assistant a man?"

"Yeah. So?"

"But he fucks his whores."

"Yeah, yeah." She waved a dismissive hand. She didn't have time to dissect people's sex lives. "He swings both ways, and he uses the women as a cover since he knows people wouldn't respect him. His assistant is really his husband. Not legally, of course, but you know..."

"How do you know this?"

"This is my city, Roman. My father was an enforcer, and I married Vincent Pyre."

"How do you know the husband's address?"

"I caught a cab with him."

There was a stark silence on the other end. "Why would you do that?"

"Because I knew Regal would get away, and it must have been important if you're looking for him."

"Where are you now?"

"At home."

"Send me his address," he said and hung up.

"You're welcome, asshole," she muttered and texted the address.

She called Blade, who answered halfway through the first ring.

"How badly are you hurt?" he asked.

"I'm dandy. Angel tried to approach Regal in a club. He bolted, of course. I caught a cab with his partner and gave Angel the address. No biggie."

She gaped at her reflection. Between partying like a rock star and her crying jag, her makeup had melted into a goopy mess that made her look like a nightmare.

"You're a pain in my ass."

"I know. I'm going to shower and go to bed. Thanks, Daddy."

She hung up before he could say anything else and hopped in the shower.

7

"CARMEN?"

Someone prodded her shoulder.

"Carmen Marie, it's your mother."

She rolled over and stared blearily at Mom. She wasn't sure why her mom felt it was necessary to reiterate her title. She knew very well who she was. "Hello, *Mother*."

"I have a cha-cha class in an hour. Want to come?"

Her temples throbbed, but one look at her mom's hopeful expression, and she caved. "Sure."

"Great!"

Her mother bustled out of the room, leaving Carmen to roll out of bed and stand in the shower until she woke up. She found tangerine heels and a matching dress she hadn't worn in years with sassy fringe on the hem. She put on a chunky turquoise necklace and couldn't decide between three rings, so she decided to wear them all. She posed for Vinny and gave him a kiss and an, "I love you," before she met her mom in the kitchen.

"I love your hair," Mom said.

"Thanks!" She fluffed her hair. "I feel much better now."

"Where's your car?"

"I took a cab home. Can you drive me to the hotel after?"

"Sure. Did you have fun last night?"

"Yes. I went out with Shonda and a bunch of other people. I felt a little old dancing with twenty-somethings, but it's all good."

She snatched two bananas and a water bottle as she followed her mother out to the car. Her mother handed her the car keys, which she accepted without comment. Putting the old Toyota in gear filled her with nostalgia.

"You doing good, Mama?" Carmen asked as she ate her banana and drove.

"Of course."

Her mother's friends bullied her into participating in so many classes and clubs that her mother was barely home. She appeared to be happy, but Carmen wanted to make sure.

"Do you need money?" she asked as she pulled into a Starbucks drive-through.

Mom patted her knee. "No, thanks, honey."

"Are you sure?"

"I have what I need."

"You'd tell me if you didn't, right?"

"Yes."

"Okay, what do you want to drink?"

By the time they entered the dance class, Carmen was ready to cha-cha her ass off. She was the youngest person in the class, but that didn't bother her in the least. She hugged and kissed her mother's friends and was bathed in their heavy perfume. Everyone was friendly and welcoming. There were only a handful of men in the class. They made a big show of kissing her hand and making jokes like, "If I was forty years younger, baby, you'd have to make a run for it."

Carmen was glad to see that she hadn't overdressed. The room was a colorful mix of dresses, heels, and scarves. These women were dressed to impress. The instructors started the class with a walking step, which was torturously slow, but she passed the time by getting to know her rascal dance partner, Marv, a widower with two sons and a daughter in college. The class started to get more interesting when the instructors added side steps and rock steps. The pace picked up, and her brow became slick with sweat. Holy cow, no wonder her mom looked forty. Geez. She really needed to get back into her stripper workout classes. This cha-cha class was kicking her ass.

After the class, they went to a restaurant within walking distance. Carmen became the topic of conversation as the women offered their advice on love, loss, marriage, and tips to find an eligible man. Most of the women offered their own sons. She politely declined and said that she was happily single and independent. This started several heated discussions about whether it was better to be alone or with a man. She had to distract them with a platter of desserts and decaf coffee. In the middle of the commotion, her cell rang.

"Hey, Alice, what's up?"

"Do you want to help with an animal adoption?" Alice sounded a bit breathless.

"Sure. When is it?"

"Next week. I contacted the shelters, and they're overloaded, so I had to move up the event. We're doing the adoption at Cimarron Elementary next Saturday at eight. I'm having a meeting here at five today if you can make it. We can do dinner after."

"Okay, I'll be there." Carmen looked at the group of elderly people. Maybe some of them needed a furry companion?

"I tried to call Lyla, but she didn't pick up. Can you check with her?"

"No problem."

"Thank you so much. See you in a couple of hours!"

She snatched the bill from their pregnant server before anyone noticed and gave her credit card before she announced at large, "There's going to be an animal adoption at Cimarron Elementary next Saturday. It starts at eight. Do any of your grandkids want a pet?"

She answered their questions to the best of her ability as the server asked her to sign the receipt. She added a large tip for the server who, despite being exhausted, had been kind and patient with the inquisitive, indecisive elders. Her new friends were shocked, and a bit outraged when they discovered she paid the bill.

"You can repay me by bringing someone to the animal adoption next Saturday," Carmen said.

"You're a good girl. Isabel raised you right," a woman said and patted her on the cheek.

It took over fifteen minutes to say goodbye to her new friends. She linked her arm through her mother's and was about to duck into the car when the server hurried out of the restaurant.

"I think you made a mistake! Did you add an extra zero to the tip by accident?"

Carmen put on her sunglasses. "No, I didn't. Are you having a boy or a girl?"

"I'm having one of each. But this tip is—"

"Buy the twins something from me," Carmen said as she slipped behind the wheel.

"What's your name?"

"Carmen Pyre."

"Pyre? As in Pyre Casinos? You're related to Gavin Pyre?"

Carmen resisted the urge to grimace. "Through marriage."

"I heard the Pyres have been doing great things in the community," the server said. "It's a shame what happened at the hospital last week."

"It is." The hospital attack had slipped her mind since it had been eclipsed by later events. "If you want the twins to have a furry friend, there's going to be an animal adoption on Saturday at Cimarron Elementary. You should come. It'll be fun."

"Thank you so much. You don't know how much I needed this!"

"You're welcome. Take care of yourself," she said before she ducked into the car and started the engine.

"That was nice of you, honey," Mom said, taking her hand.

"It's the least I could do. What am I going to do with all my money?"

Her mother shuddered. "I don't even want to know how much money Vinny left you."

"He left me a bundle," Carmen said with a shrug, "and I have investments of my own."

"Are you sure you're my child?" she asked, shaking her head.

"Of course, I am! How dare you?" Carmen asked in mock outrage and couldn't resist singing, "I wanna be a billionaire so fucking baaaaad."

"Carmen Marie!"

She laughed and tried to accelerate, but the old Toyota wasn't cooperating. "Mom, we have to get you a new car."

"No, we don't. I don't need to get everywhere in a hurry like you."

"Still, this isn't safe. What if your car breaks down somewhere? You know what you'd look cute in? A Lamborghini!"

Mom laughed. She grilled her mother all the way to the casino about what car she would like and what color. Pulling answers out of her modest, conservative mother was like trying to grill a guilty person about a crime. Her mother didn't want anything and didn't believe she should have more than what she had. Carmen didn't believe in that shit. Her mother raised her, which meant she should have the best.

Carmen pulled up to the front entrance of Pyre Casino and kissed her mother on the cheek. "Thanks for inviting me to class. That was great."

"You liked my friends?"

"They're awesome."

"What did you think of Marv?"

Carmen grinned. "He's an old rascal."

Her mother looked affronted. "Don't say old, Carmen."

"Fine. He's mature and funny."

"That's better. What are you going to do today?"

"I'm gonna head to Lyla's, and then I have dinner plans with Alice here later. Don't wait up for me."

She handed the valet her ticket and looked around for a familiar face even though the chances of running into Marcus were slim to none. She would be lying to herself if she didn't admit that she had been hoping to run into him last night during their bar hopping.

While she was still curious about his background and motives, she found herself more intent on discovering if he tasted as good as she remembered or if her adrenaline high made him taste better than any man she'd sampled since Vinny. She was almost disappointed when her car pulled up.

On the way to Lyla's house, she called Shonda, who didn't mention the club shooting at all and instead regaled her with tales of their exploits and extracted a promise that they would go out again soon. She agreed and asked if Shonda would put up a flyer in the salon for the animal adoption event as she pulled up to the Pyre fortress. When Carmen stopped in front of the house, she was met by Blade who guarded the front steps, arms crossed, expression grim.

"Hey, Daddy!" she called and was delighted by the sudden silence in the front drive as all conversation ground to a halt.

A muscle clenched in his cheek. "Don't call me that."

She baited the beast by going on tiptoe and giving him a loud smack on the cheek. "You know you like it," she whispered before she moseyed inside.

Blade was too serious by half. Her father had been more bark than bite, and she suspected Blade was the same. She paused for a moment, listening for voices before she headed upstairs to Nora's nursery. She burst in and came to a dead stop. Gavin and Lyla were caught in a lip-lock that was seconds away from being rated R. Seeing Nora's parents getting it on within feet of their daughter made her feel a little better about hooking up with Marcus. Apparently, the nursery gave off some kind of sex pheromone that got people in the mood.

Gavin lifted his head and glared at her over Lyla's shoulder. "What do you want?"

Lyla shoved him away and turned. "Oh my God! I love your hair!"

"I was due for a change." She gave Gavin a steely smile. "What do you think of my hair, Gavin?"

"I don't give a shit."

Clearly, Gavin wasn't happy that she interrupted, but she didn't care. She approached the crib and looked down at Nora, who was fast asleep. She had to clasp her hands together so she wouldn't grab the baby and smother her with kisses.

"I missed her." She loved Nora before she was born, but the latest turn of events bonded her even more to the baby. Shit, between her, Lyla, and Gavin, Nora would never need a crib to lie in if she didn't want to. They would gladly hold her all she wanted.

"Where have you been?" Lyla asked.

"And why didn't you stay there?" Gavin asked rudely.

"Don't get your panties in a twist. I'm just visiting."

"You're always welcome," Lyla said and shot Gavin a warning look. "Ignore him. He's insatiable at the moment."

She held up both hands. "Oh, my God! Are you guys trying for another baby? Because if you are, I'll leave."

"No," Lyla said and glared at her husband.

"You want our kids to be close together, don't you?" Gavin asked.

Lyla's eyes flared. "We never talked about having more kids."

"We haven't had a chance. I think we should have a couple."

Lyla waved her hands as if she was clearing away smoke. "I don't want to talk about this right now." She turned her back on him. "Carmen, you're dressed fancy."

"I just came from cha-cha with Mom."

Gavin left the room with an irritated growl. The moment he left, Lyla sat in the rocking chair and moaned with her hands over her face.

"What's wrong?" Carmen asked.

"I don't know how Gavin gets over stuff so quickly," Lyla said in a muffled voice. "Once he's done with something, he's *done*. I'm still trying to process that Steven Vega is the man who haunted me all these years, and Gavin is talking about kids." She dropped her hands. "Between Gavin, my mom, and Nora, I can't even think about having more kids."

"You don't have to decide right now."

"I know he's going to bother me about it tonight. Once he latches onto something, he doesn't stop until he gets it. He's such a bull-headed ass."

Carmen had to resist the urge to do a dance. She would be ecstatic if Lyla got pregnant again. She could already imagine a little boy with his father's grumpy disposition. She would make sure to do her godmother duties and embarrass the hell out of Gavin Jr.

"How's your mom?" Carmen asked.

"I haven't been to see her yet. I've been catching up on sleep, but the hospital says she's stable. She's in and out of consciousness. Her memory is cloudy."

"Hopefully, it stays that way." It would be a blessing if Aunt Beatrice's mind erased the horrors of being gang raped and tortured.

"Yes." Lyla twisted her hands together. "She's going to be in the hospital for a while. After she gets out, I'll ask her if she wants to live with us, but I have a feeling she won't want to."

"Why not?"

"She told the nurses she doesn't want to see me."

"What?"

Yes, Aunt Beatrice went through a trauma, but cutting herself off from her daughter wasn't going to help matters. When she lost Vinny, she clung to her family for all she was worth. She couldn't understand Aunt Beatrice wanting to be alone.

"Do you want me to go down there and talk to her?" Carmen asked.

"No, I'm going back tomorrow. If she's up to seeing people, I'll let you know."

"Alice asked if I wanted to help with the animal adoption next Saturday. I said I'm down. We're having dinner at the casino tonight. She said she couldn't get in touch with you?"

"Gavin." Lyla rolled her eyes. "Now that he's out of the underworld, he doesn't want any distractions. He wants his four months back. It's like he's trying to fuse us together, but I need time to feel like a person again. My head won't accept that it's over yet."

"Guys communicate through sex. It's his way of reassuring himself that you're both alive."

"How do you know?"

"Because I think like a man," Carmen said with a shrug. "And it's what I'd do if Vinny was alive." On second thought, it was what she'd done with Marcus. It took every ounce of control she possessed not to turn her head and look at the spot where they'd done the deed. Her fingertips tingled just remembering his hand collaring her throat.

"I don't think I can help with Alice's event. I'm too..." Lyla wrung her hands.

"It's fine. You can't do everything, and there will be other events. Other than your mom, how are you doing?"

Lyla stared at her with eyes that revealed her conflicted, rocky emotional state. "I don't know."

Carmen wrapped her arms around her. "You did what you had to, Lyla. You did good."

"Carmen, I killed my dad," Lyla whispered.

"If I killed him, would you hate me?"

Lyla considered her for a long moment. "No."

"It was either Nora or him."

Although Lyla's expression hardened, she still said, "It's not that easy."

No, it wasn't. No amount of logic could erase the bonds of blood. "You'll get past it. Are you breastfeeding again?"

When they returned home after their near-death experience, Lyla had some harebrained idea that her breast milk was contaminated. Carmen was sure that a psychologist would have an explanation as to why Lyla was convinced that breastfeeding would turn Nora into a sociopath. The fact that Lyla was afraid of infecting Nora was proof that she wasn't psychotic. Carmen witnessed Lyla shut down completely, like a soldier who did what had to be done—no emotion or second-guessing, just action.

"Gavin made me breastfeed." Lyla crossed her arms over her chest. "Then he got turned on, which is why we were..." She waved to the spot in front of the crib where Carmen caught them making out. "Did you know men are turned on by breastfeeding?"

Carmen considered. "I've never thought about it, but it makes sense. I mean, they like to suck on boobs anyway. I guess if they do it when you're lactating, they get something extra. I can see how they'd—"

Lyla held up a hand. "I don't want to know."

They left the nursery and started downstairs.

"It's weird without you here," Lyla said.

"Well, your husband needs to fucked regularly, and I need to get a life."

"What do you mean, get a life?"

"I've been taking care of Mom, and then I moved in with you. I'm thinking about traveling, helping Alice, partying my ass off, going back to my stripper workouts... and I want to get a kickass hobby. What do you think it should be?"

Lyla gave her a wan smile. "I have no idea, but I know it's gonna be nuts."

As they passed Gavin's office, she saw Angel sitting across from his cousin in a slick black-on-black suit that made her stop in her tracks. Fuck. She'd hoped he didn't own a suit. She was a sucker for a well-dressed man. He looked as comfortable in his current ensemble as he'd been in jeans.

The cousins looked nothing alike. They were both tall, but while Gavin bulged with muscles, Angel was lean. If Gavin didn't tailor his suits, they would look ridiculous on him. Instead, he looked like a buff, dangerous god. No amount of prettying up could disguise Gavin's intensity. Angel lacked Gavin's aggressive energy. That could be a problem for him. The dogs in the underworld wouldn't be able to resist testing him even though he was a Roman. She should know. Vinny's relationship with Gavin didn't keep him alive.

As if they sensed her regard, Gavin and Angel turned their heads. They didn't look alike, but their hot factor was definitely off the charts. They oozed testosterone, had arrogance to spare, and were definitely all male. They rose from their seats and started toward them. Her thumb began to throb, the same one he'd sucked on last night. She tucked her thumb safely away and tried to shrug off the sexual vibes emanating from him.

"Carmen," Angel said with a smile.

The asshole she talked to on the phone was gone, and Mr. Smooth was back in place.

"Angel," she acknowledged coolly.

Lyla glanced at them, and then her eyes got big. "Oh, my God."

Gavin glared at Carmen. "No."

"You keep saying that like it's gonna make a difference," she said.

Angel chuckled and pulled his ringing phone from his pocket. He glanced at the screen and held the phone up as he answered. "Hey, Luci."

Angel turned the phone toward them, and Carmen saw an exotic woman staring back. She had a perfect oval face with an olive complexion, sea green eyes, and shiny brown hair. Jade chandelier earrings highlighted her good looks and instantly captured Carmen's attention.

"Did you kill him?" the woman asked in a no-nonsense New York accent.

"Yes," Gavin answered.

"How'd you do it?" Luci asked brusquely.

Gavin clasped his hands behind his back and reported, "Lyla stabbed him in the back and tried to dismember him using a shield. I ran him through with eight swords, and then he was beheaded."

The woman gave Gavin a Miss America smile and then bounced excitedly. "So it's done. Can I come?"

"Not yet, princess," Angel said before Gavin could answer.

Sea green eyes narrowed dangerously. "Why not? That fucker's dead, so what's the problem?"

Carmen grinned. Whoever this woman was, she wasn't intimidated by Gavin or Angel and had spunk. Luci was her new best friend; she just didn't know it yet.

"We're transitioning. It isn't safe yet," Angel said.

Luci glared. "Gavin?"

"Sorry, Luci, not yet."

Gavin's voice was noticeably gentler when he spoke to Luci, which piqued her interest even more. The only woman Gavin toned it down for was Lyla.

The woman waved her hands imperiously. "I don't want to talk to either of you. Where's your wife and baby?"

Angel angled the phone toward her and Lyla. Luci squealed, and Angel handed his phone to her.

"Oh, you two are gorgeous! Who's who?" Luci asked.

"I'm Lyla," Lyla said, looking a little bewildered.

"I'm Luci!" she exclaimed with a hand pressed against her chest. "I'm Angel's sister."

There was a Roman sister? She had no idea. No one had ever mentioned Luci.

"Oh, hi," Lyla said with an awkward wave.

"Where's the baby?" Luci asked.

"She's asleep."

Luci curled up in a fabulous white leather chair and rested her chin on her fist. "What does she like? How old is she? What does she need? I want to send a gift!"

Gavin and Angel drifted toward the office again while Lyla and Carmen settled on the couch.

"Um, Nora doesn't need anything right now. Having another aunt is great, though," Lyla said.

Luci kissed the camera and then wiped her lipstick off. "I can't wait! Ugh, I want to come so bad. Who are you, gorgeous?"

Carmen grinned. "I'm Carmen, Vinny's wife."

Luci's mouth formed on O. "I'm sorry about Vinny, honey. I know what it's like to lose someone you love. It's the worst pain in the world. You never really get over it."

Luci's sincerity radiated through the phone and made her nose sting with tears, but she forced a smile and said, "Thank you."

"I can't wait to meet you two! I need to be around women. It's been my brothers and me for so long. I can't believe Angel left me here with Raul. I mean, Raul's fine and all, but all he does is work. Angel was my lifeline. I don't know when Raul will tell Roque that Angel took over Las Vegas. Roque is gonna be pissed, but, hey"—Luci shrugged—"Angel wants to make his own way, and it's perfect since Gavin wants out. That's his right." Luci beamed at Lyla. "Gavin is so gone for you. I never thought he'd get out of the game, but family is more important. Besides, you and Gavin need to give me more cousins. We're supposed to have big families. We need the next generation to take over, you know? Besides, it sounds like the fuckers in the underworld need a new flavor of crime lord, yes? Angel loves fucking with people. He'll do well there, I'm sure."

Luci was clearly confident about Angel's ability to take over the underworld. Even as they stared at her, something cold and calculating replaced her friendly warmth.

"I heard what happened to Uncle Manny. Everyone involved will pay," she said simply. "You don't fuck with our family."

Lyla looked awed by Luci's unapologetic creed. Maybe Luci was exactly what Lyla needed to help her come to terms with her bloody deeds. Speaking to another woman who had grown up in the underworld and adopted the same cutthroat principles as her brothers was breathtaking to behold.

"You know, Luci," Carmen said. "I think we're going to be best friends."

The ruthlessness vanished, and once again, Luci's face flooded with warmth. "I know, right? I haven't seen Gavin in years, and when he showed up and told us he was married with a baby, I was like, 'we need to reconnect with our family outside of New York.'" Luci looked hopefully at them. "Sounds like I can't come there, but maybe you two can visit me here!"

"I'll come," Carmen said promptly.

"You will?" Luci was clearly thrilled. "When?"

Lyla clamped a hand on her thigh and squeezed. Apparently, Lyla wasn't ready for her to be on the other side of the continent.

"Maybe in a couple of months. I'll keep you posted," Carmen said smoothly and squeezed Lyla's hand. Of course, she wouldn't leave when her cousin needed her.

Luci looked a little disappointed, but she nodded. "Yes, keep me posted. It's probably for the best since it hasn't even been a week since Angel left, and things are a bit out of sorts here."

"Where did you get your earrings?" Carmen asked.

"Oh! You like them?" Luci did a close up of the gorgeous, glowing jade. "I made them."

"What?"

"I'm a jewelry designer. I take on clients every now and then and make custom pieces. I spend most of my time sketching."

"They're beautiful," Lyla said.

"I can make anything! What's your favorite stone? Do you want a ring, earrings or necklace—?"

An incoming call interrupted the video. Angel materialized behind the couch and snatched the phone from Carmen.

"Luci, you'll have to chat with them later," Angel said.

"Give them my number and call me tonight, asshole!" Luci snapped.

"Will do," Angel said indulgently and answered the call before he ambled away.

Carmen looked at Lyla. "Well, that was interesting."

Lyla nodded. "For sure."

"You should talk to her about"—Carmen waved her hands—"your stuff. Sounds like she's been there, done that."

"Yes." Lyla stared fixedly at the glass coffee table. "She called us family."

"Well, she is your family. She's first cousins with Gavin."

She blew out a breath. "It would be nice to have more family, especially after..."

After Lyla was forced to kill her own father and her mother was on the skids? Yes, family was important. It was time to rebuild after years of terror and death. "Yes. I'm gonna head out, okay?"

"Okay. Tell Alice and Janice I said hi and give my apologies for not being able to help with this event."

Carmen rose and kissed Lyla's temple. "It'll get better, babe. Call me if you need me."

"Okay," Lyla said softly.

Beau jumped on the sofa, interrupting Lyla's solemn contemplation. He licked her face, making her sputter and laugh. Carmen walked out of the house and saw her car parked beside a black

Lamborghini Aventador. She paused to admire the sweet ride and heard the front door slam. Angel sauntered down the front steps with his hands in pockets.

"Yours?" she asked.

"For the moment. I'm trying it on for size. Nice Ferrari. I should have known you would have a gold car."

Angel lifted the door, and she got a whiff of that new car smell that anyone who gave a shit about cars craved. She liked luxurious things and fast cars. Put those things together and she was close to orgasmic. It was surprising she hadn't married a race car driver. She attended the Formula 1 race every year since she was a kid.

"I got a place on Grove Crest Lane. You want to see it?" Angel asked.

"Grove Crest?" It was an exclusive community where the most affordable homes were in the twenty-million-dollar range. Her interest was piqued. "Sure."

Angel gestured at the Lamborghini. "Want a ride?"

She hesitated for a second before she shook her head. "No, I'm good. I'll follow you."

"Suit yourself." He climbed into the car and revved the engine.

Carmen slipped into the Ferrari and raised her brows as he roared past. "Oh, no, you don't."

She put her car in gear and chased after him. When they reached the deserted highway that led back to the city, she cruised beside him on the opposite lane before she cut in front. Angel didn't like that and tried to overtake her, but she didn't give him an opening. When a truck approached, Angel was forced to fall into place behind her, which made her laugh maniacally. She loved winning, fast cars, traveling, and so much more. How could she have forgotten how much fun it was to play?

Once they reached the city, she allowed Angel to lead the way to the exclusive community. He pulled up to a gated property and punched in the code. They drove up the drive and parked in front of a lavish house. Palm trees offered shade and privacy. The mansion was a two-story monstrosity with a cascade of water on either side of the front door.

"This place is ridiculous," she said.

Angel grinned as he unlocked the front door. "I know. It's Las Vegas at its finest."

The house had a European flair mixed with gaudy Las Vegas. The shiny marble floor was cream colored. Elaborate chandeliers hung above their heads while candelabras and mirrors reflected light. Marble columns gave the place an elegant, stately feel.

"Oh, my God," she said, voice echoing in the massive foyer.

A curved double staircase led to the second story. She walked beneath the staircases into a massive living room. The main feature was an eight-foot water wall that splashed gently into a pool and trickled into a larger outdoor one.

"How big is this place?" she asked.

"Six bedrooms, eleven baths."

"Decadent," she said as she peeked into the rooms decorated with luxurious furniture and custom chandeliers.

"It'll do," Angel said.

"Are you planning to host pool parties while handling the underworld?"

He slanted her an amused look. "I always make time to play. I never had the chance to have anything this massive in New York, so I wanted to take advantage."

"No kidding?"

"It has a movie theater, gym, elevator... you get the drift."

She nodded and then turned to face him. "Did Regal show up at his husband's house?"

"Yes."

"And?"

"And he understands that his services are no longer needed." He cocked his head to the side. "Do you always jump into situations like that?"

"I wasn't in danger."

"The assistant could have turned on you."

"I would've handled him." Angel gave her a skeptical look that made her inwardly bristle. "My dad was an enforcer. He taught me how to fight dirty and shoot a gun. Also, I've been training with Blade for months."

"It still could've gone wrong."

"But it didn't. You should be thanking me."

Angel slipped his hands into his pockets, which made him appear proper and boyish, an appealing mix she wasn't falling for.

"What did you think of my sister?" he asked.

The abrupt change in topic was odd, but she went with it. "I love her."

"I thought you might."

"I'm going to visit her."

He didn't look surprised. "She'd be over the moon to have company. I'll have to warn Raul before you visit."

The other Roman brother, the one that handled the legitimate side of the Roman empire. Vinny had mentioned him in the past. "Warn him? Why?"

"Dealing with Luci is almost more than he can handle. If he has both of you, he's going to need reinforcements. Besides, I have a feeling Luci's going to try to convince you to move to New York. She's always trying to befriend..." He paused and shrugged. "Hired help."

She mulled over that telling pause for a few seconds before she arched a brow. "Hired help? Does that include prostitutes?"

Angel grinned but otherwise ignored her question. "Raul prefers to deal with figures and paperwork. He won't know what to do with the two of you."

"I don't need a babysitter. Why doesn't she have friends? She's obviously friendly."

"It's safer for her not to have much contact with the outside world. We have too many enemies."

Now she really wanted to see Luci. God, it sounded like the poor girl had been locked up for years. "That sucks. I'll make a point to call her."

"She'd like that."

Angel Roman might be an undercover ruthless asshole, but his love for his sister was genuine. She didn't like the spear of warmth that spread through her chest. She turned away and toured the massive kitchen he would never cook in and the stately library filled with books he would never read. The house, like so many things about him, didn't add up. It was an expensive prop to intimidate, attract, and manipulate.

She and Angel were chameleons. They used their pretty exteriors to get what they wanted and took great pains to conceal dark insides that had the ravenous cravings of a junkie. She hid her intelligence while he concealed his ruthlessness by portraying an amused, controlled façade.

She turned and found Angel leaning against the wall, watching her.

"Dinner?"

He threw that out there so casually. Her inner devil jumped up and down and clapped her hands in excitement. The look in his eyes promised it would be a night to remember. The silence stretched. Her toes curled, and she resisted the urge to shift restlessly. He was doing it deliberately, using his magnetism to reel her in and make silent promises with those dreamy blue eyes. It would be easy to accept the invitation and see where the night took her, but...

"I'm meeting someone tonight." Alice needed her, and the animals at the shelter needed homes.

One eyebrow rose. "Another night on The Strip with your friends?"

"I have a meeting." She couldn't stop herself from running a hand through her hair. Dark temptation urged her to forget the animal adoption and indulge in some dark fantasies.

"A meeting."

His tone implied that she was lying. She narrowed her eyes. "There's a meeting to discuss an animal adoption event being put on by the Pyre Foundation next Saturday. I'm helping." She made a show of looking around the huge room and pointed at a spot in front of the window. "That would be a great spot for a scratching post."

Angel blinked. "A scratching post for what?"

"A cat, silly. A cat would really add to the crime lord thing too. When you invite people over, you can answer the door with it in your arms. No one would suspect how evil you are."

He coughed. "Uh, I'm not a cat person."

"A dog then."

"I'm not an animal person."

"What kind of person are you?"

"A busy one."

She sighed theatrically. "Fine."

Angel shook his head. "You're something else."

She put a hand on her hip and posed. "I know. You can't handle this."

His eyes moved over her. "Vinny was a lucky bastard."

Her husband's name was as effective as a slap in the face. One moment, she was enjoying the sexual tension and banter, and the next, guilt had her by the throat. Suddenly, the colors in the room seemed less bright, and her lightheartedness drained away.

"Oh, fuck." Angel was suddenly in front of her. "I'm sorry."

She dropped her face to hide the pain twisting her features into something ugly and uncomfortable to witness.

"I'm sorry," he said again.

Anger came to her rescue. She slammed her hands on his chest and shoved. He hissed through his teeth as he rocked back. His hand trembled as it hovered over his chest, face screwed up in pain. Only then did she remember his wounds from Hell.

"Oh my gosh! I forgot," she said and reached for him only to stop several inches shy of his body. "What do I do?"

He gave her a pained smile. "Not hit me again. I know I deserve it, but..." He took a deep breath and fisted both hands at his sides.

"Did you go to the doctor?"

"Yeah, I'll live."

"You have pain medication?"

"I can handle it."

She wrapped her arms around herself. "I'm sorry. I didn't mean to hurt you."

"Yeah, you did," he said easily. "But I deserved it."

She tried to compose herself. She couldn't break down every time someone mentioned Vinny's name.

"I'm sorry," Angel said again.

"Don't worry about it."

"Let me make it up to you. Dinner. I swear, I won't fuck you unless you beg me."

She stared at him. "What?"

"We'll do whatever gets you off. Toys? Audience? Dirty talk?" He grimaced as he glanced down at his chest. "You definitely need to be bound. Fuck. That was a damn good hit. You weren't holding back either."

"I don't pull punches for anyone."

"Good to know. So, dinner?"

"You're insane."

His mouth crooked at the corner. "It distracted you."

He was right. His talk about sex definitely distracted her from having a breakdown.

"Dinner?" he pushed.

"No."

"I won't fuck you."

"No." She headed for the door. "I have stuff to do."

He followed. "I don't get off on making women feel vulnerable. If I'd known, I wouldn't have said his name."

She tried to put a cap on her embarrassment. "I know you didn't know."

"We're good?"

She nodded. "Yeah."

He took her hand, and she jerked.

He slanted her an amused glance. "Jumpy, are you?"

She scowled. "I'm not jumpy."

He laced their fingers together and squeezed. His hand was warm and a little calloused. She was close enough to smell his cologne. It wasn't the same one he wore yesterday. It was darker, spicier. Did he change his scent to match his suit? The hand-holding was odd, something high schoolers did. Why was this simple gesture more effective than a kiss? She tried to stifle the warmth in her chest. She didn't want to like him. He was the new crime lord.

"I don't even know you," she muttered.

"You will," he said as he led her to her car. "We're not going to be able to avoid one another."

"Why would we run into each other?"

"Besides Lyla and Gavin? I get the feeling you and I have a lot in common. Vegas isn't New York. We'll be seeing a lot of one another. It's inevitable."

He opened her car door. She started to duck inside and then paused. She looked up at him. He looked refined and invincible, but she knew he was as human as Vinny had been. A memory of Vinny's lifeless body flashed through her mind, and her heart clenched.

"You need to be careful," she said.

"I know."

"No." She searched for the right words to make him understand. "Vinny thought his name was enough, that Gavin's support was enough, but it wasn't. You don't know these guys. They'll test you, try anything to kill you to make another mark against Gavin. Even though everyone knows your family, even the lowest drug dealers aren't gonna come running if you whistle. You have to start from scratch. You need as much help as you can get."

Angel searched her eyes. "I'm not an easy mark."

She knew he wasn't but… "You need a second, someone who knows the players in the underworld, someone to watch your back. Gavin had Blade. You need a beta."

He cocked his head to the side. "Are you volunteering?"

She blinked. "Me?"

"You know the players, and you say you can fight."

"Hell, no."

"Why not? You obviously get off on danger."

"Dodging bullets isn't my idea of fun." The memory of clutching

Nora to her chest as she ran for her life chilled her even though she was standing under the warm sun.

"What's your idea of fun?"

"Anything that doesn't include me running for my life. Just... get a beta, okay?"

"Worried about me?"

"Yes." They lost Vinny and Manny to the underworld. She didn't know Angel, but she didn't want him to be the next victim.

His amusement faded, and a taut silence fell between them. It took a concentrated effort to break their eye contact. It was easy to fold into the car since her legs were a little weak. She didn't look at him as she buckled herself in.

"You have my number," he said.

She nodded and turned the key in the ignition. "Right."

"Carmen."

She mentally braced before she looked up. "What?"

"If you change your mind and want to hear what my version of fun is, call me," he said and closed the car door.

She watched him saunter into his house and let out a long breath as she clutched the steering wheel. That man should be locked up. She could just imagine the havoc he would wreak on the city's female population. Having a Roman take over as crime lord was definitely an unexpected turn of events. Thankfully, she had nothing to do with that. She would keep her promise to herself and live free of the worries of the underworld and the death and heartbreak that came with it.

When she reached home, she was disappointed to find her mother was out. The house felt cold and empty. She hated it, especially when she was keyed up. Restlessness prodded her between the shoulder blades. Thank God, she had the meeting with Alice to distract her or she might have taken Angel up on his offer of dinner. Being the wife of a COO fit her personality like a glove. There was always some event to attend, a party to host or contact to schmooze. Besides that, she grew up in Las Vegas and always had a list of friends to party with, but times changed. Most of her friends had settled down and were strapped with kids while she had nothing.

She stripped off the tangerine dress and showered before she sat on the counter in her bathroom to apply makeup. She was halfway through when the need for company forced her to fetch Vinny. She set him in the corner and stood in front of the mirror, hands on her hips.

She wore a thong and nothing else. Red hair spilled over narrow shoulders and pale skin. How long had it been since she had a spray tan? She cupped her breasts and glanced at the urn.

"I know you liked them big, but I'm kinda digging these little ones. I can wear whatever I want, I don't have to wear a bra twenty-four seven, and my back isn't sore."

She perused her eyeshadows and settled on a berry color. She wasn't feeling light and playful, so her makeup and outfit would have to do the work to raise her spirits.

"I saw Lyla today. She's struggling with the whole killing her dad thing." She pawed through the makeup strewn over the counter. "I mean, I get it, but it was him or us, and I'm glad I'm still here."

Her hand shook as she applied eyeliner. She paused and closed her eyes. She understood where Lyla was coming from. It was over, but it didn't feel over. The rage and discontent were still there, along with the depression and loss she couldn't quite shake. There was nothing she could do except push through. She took a deep breath and grabbed her makeup brush and eyeshadow palette.

"Did I tell you that I've been calling Blade Daddy? He really hates it."

She talked until the grip on her lungs eased. Her determination to move on didn't mean the grieving episodes and panic attacks would magically disappear. This was life. She had to learn how to keeping moving forward while a part of her wanted to curl up on the floor and cry.

Carmen slipped into a crimson colored halter dress with two thin straps crisscrossing over her bare back and two high slits. Now that she had small tits again, she could wear dresses like this without fear of having a nipple mishap—not that that stopped her in the past. Her smoky berry eye was perfection, and she found heels in the same shade. Fiery ringlets highlighted her kickass makeup job. Seeing pops of color definitely improved her mood. She added a bracelet with rubies in the shape of hearts and put a ring on each finger. One could never go wrong with bling. The more jewels she added, the better she felt. Her massive wedding ring didn't fit with her ensemble. She stared at the diamond ring for a long minute before she slipped it off. She glanced at Vinny before she placed it in the black velvet box he proposed with. Her hands shook as she placed the box at the back of her jewelry chest.

"What do you think?" she asked, turning to show Vinny her ass. He was back on the dresser where she preferred him to be, watching over her. She backed it up the way he liked it before she went to him. She went up on tiptoes to give him a kiss, leaving a berry outline on the shiny metal.

"I love you," she said as she backed away and grabbed her clutch. "Don't let me do anything too stupid."

8

"Alice, the event is going to be fine," Carmen said as Alice scribbled in a notebook.

"I need to make sure everything is perfect." Alice's unicorn pencil glided across the page. "If it's not perfect, I have to answer to Mr. Pyre, and I don't want to answer to Mr. Pyre."

"You've been to his house and threw his wife a baby gender party and baby shower. I'm pretty sure you can call him Gavin."

"I do," Janice said as she settled in the booth. "The meeting went well. I think this animal adoption is going to be fantastic. It's just what we need after what happened at the hospital last week."

"Yes." Alice pursed her lips and ran her finger down a two-column list. "After that incident, I need to make sure my events run smoothly. What if Mr. Pyre decides to fire me?"

Carmen nudged her. "Stop, Alice. What happened at the hospital wasn't your fault, and it was phenomenal. I can't believe you were able to pull this event together so quickly. You have more than enough volunteers, and everyone's on the same page."

"I know," Alice said but still looked troubled.

They made quite a trio, Carmen thought, as several men paused to study them on their way to the bar. Janice was the epitome of a career woman with her power suit and cell phone in hand. She was a savvy shark with glittery pointy-toe Jimmy Choos. Although Alice could more than hold her own in the looks department, she stood out like a sore thumb in her deep purple velvet jeans and a button-up blouse. Carmen's fingers itched to undo the buttons around her throat. How could she breathe?

A server delivered a round of martinis. Janice and Carmen took theirs gratefully, but Alice scowled and crossed her arms over her chest.

"What?" Janice asked when Carmen snickered.

"Alice is afraid I'll get her drunk again."

"You got her drunk?"

"I had to call in for two days," Alice said irritably.

"Two days?"

"One day to recover and another to clean up my apartment."

They laughed while Alice gave them a withering glare.

"I gave you two drinks, and you did the rest," Carmen said and turned to Janice. "I had to cut her off for fear of alcohol poisoning."

"I didn't think alcohol would taste so good," Alice muttered.

"Why were you drinking anyway?" Janice asked.

Alice opened her mouth, but Carmen beat her to it.

"I was trying to get her laid."

Janice looked intrigued. "Did you hook up?"

Alice's eyes darted back and forth between them and then away. "No."

"Did you try?"

Alice played with her utensils. "Yes."

"And?" Janice pushed.

"He said no."

"How many did you ask?"

"One."

Janice sighed. "Well, you can't expect the one and only guy you ask to say yes."

"How many should I have asked?" Alice asked.

Carmen bit her lip to stop herself from laughing aloud. Any moment now, she expected Alice to start making notes.

"I think five is a good number," Janice said after a moment. "Carmen?"

She'd never had to ask even one to hook up. "Sure, five sounds good."

Alice and Janice glared at her.

"What?"

"You've never had to ask, have you? Bitch." Janice downed her drink and signaled for another. "I don't have time in my schedule to get laid. I can afford to take care of a man. All he has to do is cook for me, keep my fridge stocked, and give me an orgasm when I ask for it. That's not too much to ask for, is it?"

Alice flushed and dug through her purse. "I-I don't know."

"That's not a bad idea, Janice." Sex on tap. No emotions, just raw sex whenever she wanted it. That sounded amazing. This was Vegas. There had to be a business that catered to busy, successful women who could afford a full-time gigolo. What would be on their menu of sex services? Fifty dollars for every ten minutes of fucking? Surely, she could order—

"What about you, Carmen?"

She jerked her mind out of the gutter. "What?"

Janice bobbed her brows. "What about you and that hunk?"

"Hunk?"

"You and Kody Singer. Have you seen him since the hospital?"

"No, I haven't." He had left some voicemails, but she didn't respond. She asked him to attend the hospital event in exchange for a date. That day, a bubble of frustration caused her to shove Kody into a bathroom and have a heavy make out and petting session. Kody had been delighted. During their lunch date, she had been blind-sided when he asked her to go to Europe with him while he shot a movie. Kody wanted strings, and she didn't. She wasn't looking for a full-time man; maybe a part-time one… one that didn't talk. Maybe the gigolo service had a mute who was a god in the sack…

"He's still in-house," Janice said.

"Who?"

"Kody Singer."

"Oh," she said without much interest.

"Seriously, you're not interested in him? He's polite, prompt, and sexy as all get-out."

"He's a great guy, but I'd destroy him."

Janice pointed a finger at her. "I get you, girl. Us woman beasts got shit going on in our daily lives. It's when we come home, we want to make sure we got a man who can make us submit in the bedroom." She raised one brow. "So, Singer's out. What about Marcus?"

She tried to look casual even though her heartbeat sped up a bit. "What about him?"

"You gonna make a play for him?" Janice pushed.

"What are you talking about?"

"He's all kinds of hot, right, Alice?"

Alice smoothed her hands down her buttons and shrugged, evading eye contact. "He's attractive, I guess."

"He's sex on a stick is what he is," Janice said passionately and immediately snatched up the second martini put in front of her.

"Why don't you make a play for him?" Carmen asked curiously.

Janice was hot, blunt, intelligent, and dressed like she shopped on Fifth Avenue. What man wouldn't want her?

"I don't fuck co-workers," Janice stabbed an olive and munched vigorously. "And I don't fuck bosses."

"Is that the voice of experience talking?" Carmen asked.

Janice gave her a deadpan look and sipped without answering. So, Janice fucked a boss in the past. Interesting. Alice shifted restlessly in her seat, looking anywhere but at either of them. Poor girl had no idea what she was getting into when she started working at Pyre Casinos.

"Ladies." A server set down three cosmopolitans. "Compliments from the men at that table."

The server nodded to three men dressed conservatively in button-up shirts and sports jackets. They appeared to be in their forties, and she pegged them as businessmen on a work trip at a glance.

"Maybe my night's looking up, after all," Janice said and raised her glass to salute the men. "One's a moose, but the other two aren't bad."

"Moose?" Carmen and Alice echoed in unison.

Janice frowned at them. "Moose, a cosmetically challenged man."

Carmen slammed her hand on the table, rattling their glasses and making a commotion, but she didn't care. She threw back her head and laughed uproariously. She laughed until her belly hurt and her eyes were wet, this time with happy tears.

"Oh, man, I needed that," she wheezed when she could speak.

"Anytime," Janice said, all business now. "So, who gets the moose?"

Carmen hid her face behind Alice's back and snickered as their food was served.

"Why don't you take him, Carmen? Take one for the team?"

"Fuck, no," she said as she straightened. "I'm not fucking a moose. I don't care how much you pay me."

The male server dropped the plate a little too hard on the table. Alice let out a nervous laugh and flapped her hands at them urgently, but they ignored her.

"Usually the moose is better in bed since he has to be. He can't be ugly and bad in bed, you feel me?" Janice said.

"Why don't you take him?" Carmen argued.

"I don't need the guy to be good in bed. I'm good enough for the both of us, and I want something pretty to look at while I'm bringing it home, you know?"

"Makes sense," Carmen said.

Janice looked at the server who was frozen in place. "Can I help you?"

"Uh, no, ma'am," he said and gave them a little bow as he left.

"Carmen?" Janice prompted. "Moose?"

"Hell, no."

Janice gave Alice a megawatt smile. "It's your lucky day, honey."

"I, uh, I have things to do," Alice stammered and began to stuff her face.

It was obvious that Alice was planning to dine and dash to get away from them. Unluckily for her, the men made their way over before she finished her meal. Alice looked like a deer in the headlights. The men were tourists from Germany with great accents and not a clear reason for being in Las Vegas. Carmen added little to the conversation despite the men's interest. She wasn't tempted by polite, vanilla businessmen. Besides, watching Alice flounder was much more entertaining.

Carmen paid for the meal and hid her wince when Alice grasped her arm in a death grip. She gave the moose and his friend a polite brush-off as Janice disappeared with the best looking of the trio. Carmen silently wished her a happy fuck. She could feel the night coming to a close. She tried to bury her anxiety as she hooked her arm with Alice. She was wide-awake and ready for anything. The last thing she wanted was to go home to her empty bed and count the hours until daylight. The night was young, and she needed to do something to cure the restlessness thrumming through her body.

"Thanks for that," Alice said and leaned into her.

"I guess you're still a virgin."

Alice gave her a frosty look. "Do you have to keep bringing it up?"

"Are you planning to be a nun?"

"No."

"Then what's the deal?"

"Men don't look at me the way they look at you."

"I beg to differ. That guy would have given you a one-night stand in a heartbeat."

"The moose?" Alice tipped her nose up. "If I wanted a one-night stand, I could get one. Men don't have to like a woman to have sex with her."

"True. So, you want the white knight?"

"I want a guy who likes me for me. What's wrong with that?"

Men she dated in the past said they had a hard time keeping up with her. She was restless and manic and always into something, whether it was real estate, cooking, driving race cars, skydiving, or painting. She was a jack-of-all-trades, master of none. Most men saw her as arm candy and a body to fuck. She was much more, but no one cared what was inside her. Vinny was the only one who accepted her, flaws and all.

"Carmen?"

She cleared her throat. "There's nothing wrong with waiting for the right guy."

Alice looked surprised. "Really? I thought you said—"

"Forget what I said. I don't know anything."

"Are you okay?"

Before she could answer, two hands gripped her waist and lifted her. She aimed her heels down to impale the buffoon holding her aloft, but her irritation disappeared when she recognized him.

"Connie!" she squealed.

"Jesus, woman." Cormac, aka The Heat, didn't look pleased. "Don't be saying that pansy ass name so loud. It's Mac or The Heat." He bobbed his brows. "Or the man who's gonna make your dreams come true." He set her down and then tucked her under one arm. "I caught a glimpse of your ass and told The Punisher it was mine until I realized it was you. Gavin would have my hide, wouldn't he?"

"He would," she agreed and smiled at The Punisher, aka Walter, who she hadn't seen since Incognito's opening night. "What are you assholes doing here?"

"My buddy's having a get-together in the penthouse, and we're bringing the party."

Behind Cormac and Walter was an entourage of men who had the bodies of Chippendale dancers. Alice stared at Cormac as if he was the devil incarnate. Carmen had to admit that Cormac looked outlandish in a ridiculous white fur coat, baby blue sunglasses, thick gold chain and red Mohawk. He wore jeans and no shirt beneath the fur coat. His abs and beautiful tattoos were on full display. Cormac was brash, uncouth, flashy, and a shit talker of the highest order, which wasn't a surprise since he was the reigning UFC Lightweight Champion. She met Cormac years ago and watched him get his ass whooped more times than she cared to remember. But Cormac was a stubborn bastard and kept getting in the ring. Now, he was a millionaire and a champion determined to suck life dry. She could relate to that. A night with Cormac was just what she needed.

"And who's this?" Cormac asked, following her gaze to Alice.

"This is my friend, Alice. She works for Gavin."

Cormac raised his ridiculous sunglasses to examine Alice with dark eyes. "What do you do for Pyre, honey?"

Alice opened and closed her mouth without uttering a word.

"She's the community outreach coordinator for the Pyre Foundation. You know, Connie," Carmen said, stroking his bare chest absently, "you could really help Alice out. We always need huge celebs to up the ante for press at her events."

"No problem," Cormac said and flexed his pecs.

Alice looked like she might faint.

"Of course," Carmen drawled, "you'd have to be a gentleman and not cause a ruckus."

"I thought you wanted press," he said with a wink and focused on Alice. "You want to come with us, sweetheart?"

"Uh, no, I have—" Alice began.

"Great." Cormac yanked her under his other arm and propelled them through the casino.

"Uh, I have stuff to do," Alice stammered.

Cormac held up her bare left hand. "No ring, no claim."

"Claim?"

"No man, so you have no reason not to come with us." Cormac surveyed her and gave her a broad smile. "You have potential, sweetheart."

"Potential?" Alice echoed.

Carmen was about to intervene but decided to let it play out when she noticed that Alice no longer looked nervous but offended.

"You dress like you're forty, but you can't be older twenty-five. Why are you hiding your body under these ugly ass clothes?"

Alice dug her heels in. "I'm not going anywhere with you."

Cormac released Carmen, so he could pick up Alice who let out a piercing squeal. "Wanna bet?"

Carmen laughed and fell into step beside Walter. "Cormac hasn't changed. He's more arrogant and obnoxious than ever."

"That's part of his charm," Walter said and tossed an arm over her shoulders. "By the way, you are looking fine."

As they passed Partition, a popular Pyre nightclub, the people in line spotted Cormac, Walter, and the other fighters. Several women jumped over the gold ropes and rushed them, screaming and begging to take selfies. Cormac smiled broadly and let a woman suck his nipple while she took a picture. Alice struggled madly to get away, but Cormac held onto her despite being fawned over by admirers. In less than a minute, the crowd that headed for the elevators swelled to over fifty people. Cormac led the way with Alice clamped to his side. They jammed into three elevators while the rest had to wait for the next set.

Two men who could play for the NFL guarded the penthouse and opened doors that led into complete mayhem. Carmen was familiar with this particular penthouse. It was three stories of chrome and glass with five master suites, two pools, three bars (one for each floor), a bowling alley, billiard table, around-the-clock butler service, and more. At the moment, every square inch of the penthouse was filled with people. The energy saturating the room urged her to throw herself headlong into trouble.

"The party's arrived!" Cormac crowed, and everyone converged on him.

Carmen lost her grip on Walter in the scuffle. She looked over the railing at the first story below. The pool that took up most of the floor was filled with people dancing, laughing, and drinking. She heard the crack of balls from a billiard game while strippers danced on tables. Servers dressed in lingerie with body jewelry strutted. The heavy bass made the floor vibrate beneath her heels.

Alice appeared at her side, looking panicked. "We have to get out of here! This is out of control!" She focused on a fighter getting a lap dance and flushed. "They're heathens!"

"Let's get you a drink," Carmen suggested and started toward the bar, which she could barely make out since so many people crowded around it.

"I'm going to get fired! I'm leaving."

"You're off duty," Carmen pointed out. "And Cormac will be disappointed."

"Don't be ridiculous. He's disgusting," Alice snapped.

Carmen grinned. Seeing Alice riled was a pastime of hers that she hadn't indulged in enough lately. "He's really sweet once you get to know him."

Alice shot her a disbelieving glance. "I doubt it. Come on, let's get out of here."

"I'm going to stay."

Alice shook her head. "He's no good for you, Carmen."

She had no intention of fucking Cormac. She just wasn't ready to go home and lay in her empty bed. No, she wanted to join in the chaos and forget about tomorrow. Alice could go home to her peaceful apartment and relax. She would indulge in excess until the fire in her gut was gone.

"Carmen?" Alice tugged on her hand. "I can help you."

That warmed her. She hugged her friend and gave her a small push toward the exit. "If I need someone to post bond, I'll give you a call."

Her eyes bugged. "Post bond? Why—?"

"I'm kidding. I've only been arrested three times, and I'm not planning to get into that kind of trouble tonight."

"What kind of trouble are you planning to get into?" Alice asked, hands on her hips like a disapproving parent.

"That's not for your innocent ears. Scat, babe."

Alice sighed. "I'll keep my phone on just in case."

"You're the best."

Alice gave her a worried look before she dodged through the crowd and made her getaway. Carmen snatched two glasses of champagne from the half-naked server and downed it. She welcomed the flush of heat and grabbed a second glass, which she held above her head as she made her way through the crowd, so it wouldn't spill. She received many admiring glances and ignored the catcalls as she made her way to the pool. She was debating whether she wanted to strip off her dress and get in when a muscled arm wrapped around her waist and drew her back against a hard body.

"I thought you left," Cormac said.

"Me, miss a party? Not a chance."

"Where'd Alice go?"

"She slipped away. She has to work tomorrow, and you scared the crap out of her." She glanced back at him and smiled. "She called you a heathen."

Cormac grinned. "I like that." He cupped her face. "I heard about Vinny. Did Gavin get the fucker?"

"Yeah."

Cormac searched her eyes. "You good?"

"I'm getting there," she said and drained the rest of her glass.

He tossed his fur coat on a couch, which was occupied by people dry humping and pulled her flush against him.

"Time to live, babe," he said before he began to move.

Like everything else about him, he danced outrageously. His athleticism showed as he switched from Latin to break dancing. He kept her laughing and entertained while sipping champagne. She was having a great time until they were interrupted by a woman in a swimsuit who gripped his arm.

"I want to suck you off," the woman said loud enough for those around them to hear.

Cormac tapped Carmen's ass. "I'll be back," he said and followed the woman through the crowd.

Those around them catcalled and hooted. She felt a twinge of envy. How many times had she dragged Vinny off during a party to have sex? Vinny. Fuck.

She snatched a shot from a passing server and downed it. Patrón. Not a favorite of hers, but it made her pleasantly cloudy, and that was all that mattered. Thick arms wrapped around her. She didn't look to see who it was because it didn't matter. Men had always come easy to her. Finding one wasn't the problem. It was finding a man who didn't bore her to tears and could give her what she needed that was the problem. She leaned back against a massive chest. She felt small and feminine but not safe. After witnessing the shit she had, she knew size meant nothing. What really mattered was how accurate you were with a gun and what you were willing to do to survive. Now she knew how far she'd go. She'd kill.

A sharp blast made her jump. She was about to go apeshit until she spotted the lingerie-clad servers opening more champagne bottles. She huddled against the mountain behind her, who pulled her even closer. Her need for human contact was pathetic, but at the moment, she didn't care. Whatever she needed to do to keep her demons at bay, she would do.

The man behind her smelled of whiskey and cigars. It wasn't unpleasant. His hands smoothed over her hips and gripped. His hands were huge, which made her mind shift gears. She rotated her ass against his groin to cop a feel and felt the hard length press between her cheeks. Okay, if he was a moose, he had a big dick to compensate. Despite how eager he was, he hadn't done anything sleazy or perverted. Maybe he was the unicorn she'd been looking for —the mute gigolo with a massive penis.

Lips touched her ear. Her eyes flared when he sucked her earlobe into his mouth. Okay, that was *hawt*—

"Do you work at Subway?" he murmured.

The beginning pangs of lust dimmed. "What?"

"Because you gave me a foot long."

She whirled and glared at the man who could have been the perfect man for her and Janice. He was over six feet and had an open dress shirt that revealed a body that rivaled Cormac's. He was a gorgeous black man with a beard, perfect teeth, and hazel eyes. Gah!

She put her hands on her hips. "Really?"

He grinned and looked down at the bulge in his pants. "Well, it's true."

"Seriously?"

"Are you a mirror?"

She took a step back. He was smoking hot but off his rocker. "What?"

"Because I can see myself inside you," he said with a boyish grin. When she stared at him, he asked, "No?"

"No!"

He held up both hands. "Fine. We can play Titanic. I'll be the iceberg, and you can go down."

Her mouth dropped open. She would have if he hadn't opened his mouth. "You did not just say that!"

He grabbed his junk and bobbed his brows. "Come on, baby."

When he opened his mouth again, she clapped her hand over it and leaned in close.

"Let me tell you something that will get you more pussy in future, okay? Women don't like pickup lines, especially sleazy ones. When a woman wants to have sex, don't joke with her, just give her what she wants. I could have made your eyes roll from what I can do between the sheets." Her hand tightened on his face, pruning up his skin. "I would have let you do me rough and dirty, and you had to fucking ruin it. No more pickup lines unless you want to fuck blow up dolls. Got it?"

He stared at her for a moment before he nodded. She dropped her hand and turned away.

"Wait, that's it?" he called.

She turned back. "Were you born on a highway?"

"What?"

"Because that's where most accidents happen." She snatched another glass of champagne as she made her exit. God, men always had to open their mouths and ruin everything. If he'd just kept silent, she might have screwed his brains out, and they'd both be feeling like a million dollars right now, but nooooo. Some men were ridiculously clueless.

She passed a half-naked poker game in progress, strippers giving private shows, and people having sex in shadowed corners. She watched a couple going at it, but the fact that they were spit swapping a pill turned her off.

Dissatisfaction ate at her soul. Yesterday, she felt shiny and new, and already, she was beginning to tarnish. The high that carried her through partying with Shonda and the gang and then dance class with her mother this morning was waning fast. The same desperate craving that hit her the night Lyla was in Hell was back. She was sliding into destruct mode.

A stripper abandoned her pole when a man flashed a one-hundred-dollar bill. Carmen climbed onto the round platform and gripped the shiny silver pole. No one paid her any mind as she reached high over her head, lifted her legs, and slowly rotated around the pole. An R&B song with a heavy, sultry beat filled the room. She climbed the pole and used her momentum to do a lazy spiral to the platform where she came to a graceful landing. She closed her eyes and focused on the music as she used the pole to pull herself up and let her body take over. The middle panel and high slits of her dress weren't a hindrance. Her skirt floated dreamily around her as she spun. Her mind quieted as every fiber of her being focused on the physicality of what she was doing. She definitely had to get back to pole workouts. They kept her fit, strong, and tuned in to her sexuality. Her muscles protested as she held her position at the top of the pole, but she embraced the burn. She had taken ballet classes when she was younger, but when she heard hip-hop music pouring from another studio, she ditched the tutu and never looked back. She moved sinuously from one pose to another, allowing the beat to mold her. Her body began to tremble as her muscles begged for a break, but she kept moving.

The last song she and Vinny made love to boomed from the speakers, and she froze. She rested her forehead against the pole. Fuck. She would never be able to forget him. Bittersweet memories threatened to kill her buzz.

She raised her head and found that a crowd had gathered around her. Apparently, she hadn't lost her touch. A stripper glared at her and tapped her clear heel, clearly annoyed that she stole the show. Well, she would finish her fucking performance. She forced herself to move to the beat even though her heart wasn't in it. Her hands shook as she slid down the pole. Men crowded close, but no one dared touch. For the moment, she was still a fantasy, but when she stopped moving, she was up for grabs.

She surveyed her options as she leaned back against the pole and continued to move. Her gaze moved over the men, but no one stood out. One man made his way forward, capturing her attention. His easy, unhurried stride was unthreatening enough that the other men let him pass. Marcus stopped in front of her and held out a hand. Even though he wasn't wearing a smile and looked unusually grim, her inner hellion was intrigued. He might be wearing a light gray suit and matching tie, but she knew for a fact that he was more dominant than the men standing around him in basketball jerseys or swim trunks.

Carmen took his hand and heard the grumble of the others as they dispersed to find action elsewhere. Dirty thoughts traipsed through her mind as she met Marcus's hooded green gaze.

"Hey," she said.

"Hey, yourself. I wasn't expecting to find you dancing on a pole."

"I'm full of surprises," she purred and wrapped her arms around him. "What are you doing here?"

"I bumped into Alice."

That explained his appearance. "Lucky me."

This was her opportunity to question him about his weird connection to Gavin, but right now, she didn't give a shit. She was feeling restless and needy and Marcus offered himself as a sacrifice. She was a bit shaky from dancing, so she leaned into him. He took her weight and moved them to an empty space against the wall.

"Are you all right?"

"Uh-huh." His silk suit felt great beneath her tingling palms. She burrowed against him and felt him stiffen a moment before she discovered his bulge. She looked up and found him staring at her intently. She couldn't stop the delighted grin that broke across her face.

"How long were you watching me?" she murmured as she ran her hands over his back.

He shifted against her. "Long enough."

He was so fucking cute. She nuzzled his neck and licked. His hands bit into her hips. "Do you have a stripper fantasy, Marcus?"

A hand skated over her ass cheek. "Now I do."

"It's your lucky night, Marcus," she panted against his ear and felt him shudder. "The stripper's easy."

"How drunk are you?" he growled.

"Why don't you find out," she whispered and kissed him. She swept her tongue into his mouth and dug her nails into his back as the dark taste of him combined with a hint of lime hit her starved senses. She moaned into his mouth and drank deep—classy sin. She didn't care about the crowd. Her whole focus was on making Marcus feel a modicum of the desperation that consumed her. She wanted him as he'd been the other night—stripped of all civilization and unwilling to take no for an answer.

He pulled back. "Carmen."

She kissed his cheek. "You woke me up, Marcus, and now I *need*. How much do you want me?"

When she tried to kiss him again, he tried to avoid her mouth while his eyes moved around the room. She surveyed her prim businessman with giddy anticipation. Marcus liked control. That much was obvious. His image was very important to him, which made him the perfect challenge. Like any man, she didn't care for anything that came easy. She liked the chase, and she respected a man who didn't bend easily to her will. The other night, she got a taste of what lay beneath his smooth professionalism, and she wanted more. She wanted to bait the beast he kept under such rigid control. This was the perfect setting for her seduction.

She kissed the curve of his jaw as she loosened his tie and undid the top buttons of his shirt so she could reach his neck.

"Carmen, let's get out of here. I have a suite..." He trailed off as she sucked on his pulse. "Carmen."

"Watch the stripper, Marcus," she breathed against his pulse.

"You should give her lessons. She doesn't hold a candle to you."

She smiled and nipped his neck. He jumped and gripped her hip.

"What are you doing?" he growled.

She leaned back to survey her hickey. "I'm having fun."

"We can have fun elsewhere."

She leaned against him to keep him in place and slipped her hand into his jacket. He stiffened when she rubbed his nipple. She kissed the corner of his mouth. "Let me, Marcus." The muscle in his jaw flexed, and she laved it with her tongue.

"Let you what?" he growled.

"Let me pay you back for the other night."

"You don't owe me anything."

Her hand moved from his chest, down his rock-hard abs to his dick. He tensed, but he didn't push her away. She traced his length and enjoyed the shudder he tried to suppress. She teased him through the material and was pleased to see that he was now one hundred percent focused on what she was doing to him.

"I've always had a thing for a man who knows how to dress," she said as her hand left his dick and traveled along his zipper. Her fingers trailed up and down, up and down. A muscle twitched near his eye. "I like the way you dress, the way you smell, the way you taste..."

When she leaned toward him, he did the same, but her aim was his neck. She worked on her hickey. She would make it big as fuck. He'd be wearing her mark for a couple of days. He shifted, rubbing his erection against her. She sent her hand back to his junk and gripped harder this time. He dropped his face into her hair and let out a heartfelt groan.

She moved from his neck to his ear and nipped. "How'd you know doggy's my favorite position?" She cupped his face and brushed teasing kisses over his smooth skin. "Can you give me what I need?"

He pierced her with lusty green eyes. "What do you want, Carmen?"

She leaned close, so their lips brushed as she said, "I want you mindless."

His Adam's apple bobbed as he swallowed. "Why?"

"I want the real you."

"This is the real me."

"There's more." She was sure of it. "How much do you want me?"

His lips firmed, and he didn't answer. She was ready for him, but he still had a modicum of control. It was time to break him. She placed her hands on his chest and ran them slowly down his body as she dropped to her knees. His eyes bulged. He glanced around, but when she ran her hands along the inside of his thighs, his eyes came back to her.

Carmen kept eye contact as she nuzzled his erection through his slacks. She traced his cock with her tongue, leaving a damp trail in her wake. She found the head of his cock and kept eye contact as she gripped it between her lips, which was quite a feat since his slacks were stretched to the breaking point. His eyes went blind with need, and she knew she had him.

Even as he reached for her, she was already rising. He opened his mouth, and she slipped her pointer and middle finger into his mouth. He grabbed her wrist to hold her hand still as he sucked on her fingers, tongue swirling between both digits. Her body felt as if it was going up in flames.

Marcus pulled her hand from his mouth and clasped it in his before he pulled her through the crowd. He charged down a hallway and tried both master suites, which were occupied. The bathroom had a line, and she was beginning to feel feverish. She needed him now. Marcus seemed to be feeling the same because he opened a random door and they were greeted with the sight of an unused laundry room complete with a marble island to fold clothes and two sets of stainless steel washers and dryers.

"There's no lock on the door," Marcus snapped.

"Who cares?" She grabbed handfuls of his jacket. "Fuck me."

He glared at her. Desire warred with reason.

She cupped his face. "Marcus." Her voice was harsh with lust.

He picked her up and placed her on the marble table. The icy surface under her ass made her hiss in surprise. He tossed the middle panel of her dress to one side and paused to look at the damp lace between her thighs.

"You're a dangerous woman," he said as he slipped two fingers past her underwear. She braced her hands on the table and tossed her head back as his fingers stretched her and then curled. "You're soaked."

"I told you," she panted, "I need you."

Marcus withdrew his fingers and dropped. His head went between her legs, and she spread wide. She moaned when she felt the first swipe of his tongue. She was too hungry and needy to play coy. She mashed his face against her pussy and rocked her hips against his mouth. When his tongue slipped inside her, she dropped her head back as pleasure wiped her mind clean.

Someone in the hallway cheered. Marcus didn't pause. He was too far gone, and so was she. There was only a door between their hookup and one hundred guests, and she didn't fucking care. All that mattered was that he kept doing that with his tongue. She shuddered and grabbed a handful of his hair as ecstasy nipped at her.

Marcus raised his head, and she screamed, "No!"

"I'm not going to last," he bit out as he undid his buckle and slacks. He pulled his cock out of his boxers and yanked her to the edge of the table. He pressed the head of his cock to her entrance, and she held her breath. She wasn't prepared when he grabbed her by the throat and yanked her forward so they were nose to nose. His hot breath fanned her face.

"Have you been with anyone since me?" he growled.

She couldn't think. "What?"

His hand flexed on her throat while the other slid his dick up and down her slit. She moaned and tried to take him, but his grip on her throat kept her at his mercy.

"Have you fucked anyone since me?" he said against her mouth.

"No. Now fuck me!"

His hand disappeared and then he was sinking into her, stretching her deliciously. She grasped handfuls of his shirt as he pressed his forehead against hers and panted as he sheathed himself to the hilt. They stared at one another in the dim light as the party carried on mere feet away.

"Would you have given me a blowjob in front of everyone?" he murmured.

"You'll never know, will you?"

"You make me crazy," he said as he dropped his head on her shoulder.

"That's how I want you."

"How do you want me to fuck you?" he whispered in her ear.

"Surprise me."

He raised his head. She had a split second to see his grin before he shoved her on her back on the table. Before she knew what was happening, he climbed on with her. He knelt, spread her legs, and dragged her ass along his hard thighs until he slid inside her. His hands spanned her waist and controlled her involuntary jerk as he impaled her. She couldn't hold back a loud groan as the position caused him to rub against her G-spot. She tried to grab onto something, but there was nothing but cold marble beneath her.

"Holy shit. Marcus, I—"

He gripped her hips and began to move her on him. Hard, grinding thrusts that made her kick and jerk. She was flat on her back with her legs splayed wide on either side of him. The contrast of cold marble beneath her bare back, the soft material of his slacks under her ass, and the heel of his hand on her pussy made her crazy. She tried to lever her ass up so she could hit the right spot and bring it home, but he wasn't allowing it. He was toying with her.

"Marcus, I swear I'm going to—" she began hoarsely, but a hard thrust made her clamp her mouth shut.

He hit that spot again, and she screamed. The door opened, and she closed her eyes against the flood of bright light.

"Holy fuck!"

Marcus hauled her so she straddled his lap. "Get the fuck out and close the door."

Carmen was too far gone to care about their audience. She wrapped her arms around him and kept riding him, so lost in her high that nothing would stop her.

"I'll pay to watch," the voice tried to bargain.

"Get out."

"Fuck," the man grumbled before the door closed, and they were once again locked in semi-darkness.

"I'm going to bring it home," she said and launched herself at him so he tipped backward. She didn't pause to savor the sight of Marcus Fletcher splayed out beneath her, hair a mess, clothes in disarray. She was too hungry. She braced her hands on his chest and began to move. She tipped her head back as she rode him, seeking her pleasure.

He yanked her down so her hands were braced on either side of his head. He latched onto her breast through the thin material and bit. She cupped the back of his head, holding him to her as she fucked him. He bucked beneath her, going deeper than she believed possible. She swiveled her hips and had the pleasure of watching his eyes roll and then flutter shut.

"I-I can't," he said through clenched teeth.

He didn't have to because she was already there. She pumped her hips, impaling herself on him and moaned as she fell headlong into one of the most intense orgasms she ever experienced. His groan echoed in the small space. He gripped her ass and rocked her on him as she hissed through her teeth.

"You're going to kill me," he puffed.

She laughed weakly as she slumped on top of him. "You're a wonderful man, Marcus Fletcher."

Her body was one throbbing mess, but she didn't care. If anyone walked in, they'd have no doubt what they'd been doing, but they were both fully clothed, which made the whole encounter that much more titillating.

All worries faded into the ether. Those dark emotions clawing at her throat, threatening to drag her under, were banished for the moment. She basked in the glow. Her body ached from the pounding she took, but it was worth it.

Someone hit the door, making them both jolt, but the door didn't open. Raucous, drunken laughter reached their ears as the assholes continued down the hallway.

"We better get out of here," Marcus said.

They slipped off the table. He ran his hands through his disheveled hair and made an attempt to look presentable before he turned to her.

"All right?" he asked.

Carmen gave him a lazy smile. "Fabulous."

He grinned and began to straighten her clothes. "How did you end up at this party?"

"Cormac got me in."

"Cormac?"

"Cormac Hart."

Marcus's brows rose. "The UFC Lightweight Champion?"

"Of course."

"Of course," he echoed and cupped her chin. "You good?"

"Now I am."

He fingered her hair. "I like the red. It suits you."

The door opened, and a man with a woman under each arm entered. He scanned them while the women giggled uncontrollably.

"Dude," he drawled and bobbed his brows.

Marcus grasped her hand and tugged her out of the room. He navigated through the raging party. It wasn't until she saw the NFL security guards that she realized he intended to leave.

"What are you doing?" she asked.

"You're done for the night."

"I'm not."

"Yeah, you are." When she tried to dig in her heels, he wrapped an arm around her waist and propelled her past security. "What have you had to drink?"

"Champagne... and a shot of Patrón, but I have a high alcohol tolerance," she said with a shrug and added, "And I sweat out most of it when I dance."

"Of course, you're drunk on champagne."

"Who said I'm drunk?"

"I do," he said and pulled her into the elevator.

Her head was pleasantly fuzzy, so she leaned into him. He pulled her under his arm and kissed her temple.

"You smell amazing," he said.

"So do you." She yawned and nuzzled his neck. "Like classy sin."

"Classy sin," he repeated and shook his head. "Whatever you say, babe. I'm glad I didn't find you wrapped around some loser this time."

The champagne prompted her to admit, "I was going to bang someone, but he ruined the moment with a lame pickup line."

"How bad was it?"

"He asked if I worked at Subway because I gave him a footlong."

Marcus grinned. "Accurate, but poorly put, hmm?"

He led her through the casino. A man screaming his head off roused her from her walking slumber. At first, she thought the man was in a fight but then realized he hit the jackpot. She craned her neck to get a look at his machine, but Marcus tugged her in another direction.

"Hey!"

"Tonight's not a good night," he said and shrugged back his sleeve to look at his watch. "I'm late, and I have to change."

"Don't let me hold you up," she said and tried to get away, but Marcus didn't release her.

"You're going home where I don't have to worry about you." He marched her outside and towed her toward a waiting taxi.

"I brought my car. I'm not drunk, Marcus!"

"You can barely keep your eyes open."

"I'm tired."

He settled her in the back of the taxi. When she tried to go out the other side, he stopped her with a grip on her thigh and cupped her cheek.

"I don't have time tonight. I'm late for my meeting."

He kissed her, and she forgot to struggle. Her hand fisted in his shirt. He pulled back, searched her face, and then kissed her twice more.

"You know where to find me," he said and slammed the door in her dazed face.

He gave her home address to the cabbie and strode back into the casino. Carmen slumped against the seat and closed her eyes as exhaustion pulled her under. She wasn't sure what to think of Marcus's highhandedness, but she couldn't find it in herself to be truly angry. He sated her inner demon. He would be dynamite if she ever got him in bed.

She must have fallen asleep because the cabbie had to yell to wake her up. He told her Marcus slipped him money. When did that happen? She stumbled to the house and realized she was blitzed because she couldn't walk a straight line. She knocked on the door for Mom to open, but the house remained dark and silent. Odd. She unearthed an extra key from a flowerpot. It took every ounce of concentration she possessed to unlock the door. She trudged upstairs and fell face first into her bed and moaned. She was drifting off to sleep when it occurred to her that Marcus shouldn't know her address.

9

A RINGING PHONE INTERRUPTED HER DREAMLESS SLUMBER. SHE groaned and covered her head with a pillow to block out the noise. The phone stopped and she relaxed. She pulled the blankets snugly around her and popped one eye open when the phone began to blare again. She bared her teeth and peered over the side of the bed at her clutch. Maybe there was a crisis... She tilted her top half out of bed, fished the phone out of her clutch, and peered at the unfamiliar number.

"If this is a telemarketer, I'm going to find you and kill you," she growled.

There was a pause and then a delighted, feminine laugh. "I fucking love you, girl!"

There was something familiar about that voice, but it was too fucking early to figure it out. She heaved herself back into bed and closed her eyes, so the room would stop pitching.

"Who is this?"

"Luciana Roman. I asked Angel for your number, and he wasn't happy, but I told him it's an emergency."

She tensed. "Emergency?"

"Girl, your picture's all over the internet!"

Her eyes flew open. "What?"

"You're dating Cormac Hart and didn't tell me? Oh, my God, he's so fucking hot. I want to trace his abs with my tongue and suck on his nipples... but I won't because you're dating him! Oh, my God. Does he like to go down on you? Please tell me he does. I won't tell anyone, I swear. In the picture, he's all dripping sweat. I'm staring at this picture of you guys, and you look amazing together! Your eyes are closed, and his arms are wrapped around you from behind. So romantic. Whose party is this? It looks wild! Did you fuck at the party?"

"Yeah." A smile played around her mouth as tidbits of the night came back to her. Riding Marcus in a laundry room at a party was definitely something to remember. Her body was sore from pole dancing and their fuck, but it was worth it.

Luci screamed on the other end. "Did you guys do it in front of everyone? God, I fucking *love* Vegas!"

"After that dance, some girl sucked off Cormac. I'm sure she wasn't the only one."

Dead silence on the other end and then, "You let another girl blow your man? *My* Cormac?"

Carmen grinned. "I'm not dating him, Luci."

"But you're fucking him."

"No, I'm not."

"What? Why not? He's Cormac Hart! He's undefeated. He's—"

"I know his stats, Luci. I've known him a long time. We're friends."

"You're friends," Luci repeated.

"Yes."

"Friends who kiss?"

She tried to remember if he'd ever kissed her in the past. "I guess."

"Friends who slow dance on the floor and get lost in each other?"

"I cheered him on when he was a scrawny loser. I even helped him when he was in a tight spot financially. We're close. I call him Connie."

"You can't call Cormac Hart, Connie! You're emasculating him."

"Exactly. He can stand to be taken down a peg or two." She bit back a groan as she rolled out of bed and glanced at her makeup smeared sheets. Damn. She hobbled into the bathroom and stripped as Luci chattered.

"I'm so disappointed. I wanted to know his fucking routine."

Carmen paused with one foot in the tub. "Fucking routine?"

"Yeah. Like, does he fuck after his fights? What kind of positions can he do? The other day, I was watching porn. This woman was doing a handstand and he was fucking her upside down. I think it's called the wheelbarrow. I figured Cormac would be great at it because he has amazing core strength. The woman had a big ass, and it was jiggling while—"

Carmen smothered a laugh as she turned on the shower. She poked her head out periodically to comment as Luci rattled on about sex positions.

"What site is this?" Carmen bellowed through the curtain. "And what keywords should I use?"

She scraped all evidence of last night's adventure off her body, slipped into a robe, and went searching for her mother. The house was empty, but when she glanced at a clock, she saw it was nearly noon. No surprise that her mother had already started her day. She dressed in a blue jumper with matching heels and kept her makeup rosy and fresh. She tracker her mother's phone and found that she was at a nearby Italian restaurant. The shower went a long way to making her feel better, but she was starving. She would crash her mom's lunch with her friends and then bum a ride to The Strip to collect her car. She put Luci on hold while she called for a pickup and then resumed their conversation.

"When are you coming to New York?" Luci asked.

"I don't know." Now, she really wanted to go. Luci was a hoot and a woman after her own heart.

"You let me know as soon as possible," Luci said and then asked, "So if you didn't have sex with Cormac, who did you screw?"

"What makes you think I fucked anyone?"

"Girl," Luci drawled. "You looked like a million dollars. No man who's any man would let you leave without getting some. So, who was he?"

"He's..." She didn't know how to finish that sentence. Marcus wasn't a friend. He wasn't a boyfriend. He was a fuck buddy of sorts, but it was more complicated than that. They were Nora's godparents, and he was Vinny's replacement...

"At a loss for words?" Luci sounded delighted. "This is gonna be juicy!"

"He's... He works for Gavin."

"At the casino or in the underworld?"

"The casino."

"Oh," Luci sounded disappointed. "I'm guessing he's hot."

"Very."

"You have a picture you can send me?"

"No."

"He works for Gavin? Is he on the company website?"

Carmen held the phone away from her ear and stared at it a moment before she brought it back. "Do you work for an investigation agency on the side? Geez."

"I'm good like that. Come on, what's his name?"

"Marcus Fletcher."

"Was he good?"

She smiled and slipped into the back of the car that pulled up. "Very." An image of Marcus's eyes rolling in his head made her nipples tingle. She clamped her legs together and confirmed the restaurant address with the driver.

"Holy shit!" Luci exclaimed.

"What?"

"This guy works for Gavin? What the fuck? Are all the men in Vegas hot or something? This isn't fair! Do you know if he's done porn?"

"I don't think he has, but he should," she said.

Luci moaned. "You are killing me! So, where'd you do it?"

"In a laundry room." Stark silence on the other end. "He didn't even take my panties off, he just moved them to the side and got busy. Someone walked in during, and I kept riding him. It was amazing."

"I gotta go."

Luci abruptly hung up the phone. It didn't take a genius to figure out that she needed some alone time.

The car pulled up to the restaurant. Carmen started toward the Italian restaurant and spotted her mother through the window. She was with Marv, the rascal from dance class. Even as she watched, Marv took her mother's hands and kissed it. Carmen stopped in her tracks. She hadn't seen that her mother smile like that since her father passed. Her world tore at the seams. Her mother was in a relationship. It wasn't the classes or activities that made her mother look a decade younger; it was Marv.

As if her mother sensed someone watching, she glanced out the window and spotted her. Her mother's eyes bulged. Carmen stood there like an idiot, staring at them. Mom jerked her hands from Marv's as if she'd been burned and rushed out of the restaurant.

"Honey, what are you doing here?" Mom called as she hurried toward her.

"I needed a ride," she said past the lump in her throat. "And I tracked you through your phone."

"Oh, honey, I didn't want you to find out this way."

She was so shocked; she didn't feel anything. "How did you want me to find out?"

Her mother wrung her hands. "I was waiting for a good time. You haven't been yourself since you lost Vinny and your father, and you've been helping Lyla, and that's been stressful. I wasn't sure if you'd think it's too soon."

Carmen looked past her mother to Marv, who watched them, hands in pockets. He looked hella worried and far from the jokester she met in dance class.

"Marv is a good man."

She refocused on her mother who looked on the verge of tears. "Are you happy?"

Mom hesitated and then nodded. "I am."

"Is it serious?"

"He asked me to marry him."

Carmen jerked. "Whoa. He doesn't mess around. He's a widower, right? Has three kids?"

Her mother smiled uncertainly. "Yes. They're good kids. You'll like them."

When she came back to Las Vegas to care for her mother after being on the road, she had been hanging on by a thread. She lay in bed for weeks, listening to her mother sob herself to sleep. The woman before her was a far cry from a grieving widow. Whoever made her mom light up this way was good with her. Personal thoughts and feelings didn't enter into this.

Carmen stomped on her emotions and took a deep breath. "You're finally getting around to giving me siblings? When I'm almost thirty?"

Her eyes filled with tears. "Oh, Carmen."

She stepped forward and hugged her. "Don't cry, Mom. You'll ruin your makeup. You don't mind if I crash your date, do you?"

"I-I was so worried you…"

She kissed her cheek and wrapped an arm around her waist. "I'm fine."

Carmen led her back into the restaurant. Marv looked uncertain and wary as she approached. She didn't allow herself to think. She released her mother and hugged him.

"I knew you were trouble when I met you," she said.

Marv returned the embrace. He had a similar build to her father and Marv's hold was just tight enough to make her feel cherished.

"Thank you," he murmured into her hair.

She breathed through the emotions clamoring in her chest. She was so focused on Vinny that she hadn't been able to deal with the loss of her father and now… Memories of him bombarded her. She closed her eyes as a tear trickled down her cheek. She had just come to terms with Vinny's death. She thought she'd have time to deal with losing the second most important man in her life, but life was ten steps ahead, and she was playing catch-up.

Marv eased his grip. She gave him a mock scowl as she brushed away a tear. She put her hands on her hips.

"Aren't you going to ask me for my mother's hand?"

Marv grinned broadly and got down on one knee in the middle of the restaurant. He took her hand and stared solemnly up at her.

"Carmen Marie Pyre, will you do me the honor of allowing your mother to be my wife?"

She heard her mother choke back a sob. Carmen looked down at Marv, a man willing to lay it all on the line and smiled through the tears.

"Yes."

Marv kissed her hand and both cheeks before he moved to her mother and planted a chaste kiss on her lips. There was a smattering of clapping from the other patrons in the restaurant who were obviously confused. Carmen sat because her legs were shaking. When she tracked her mom down for a ride, this was the last thing she expected.

Her mother sat beside her and gripped her hand beneath the table. They were both trembling.

Carmen took a deep breath. "So, Marv, tell me about yourself."

"Are you okay?" Mom asked.

"Yeah."

"Are you really?"

"Yes." She moved to get out of the car as they pulled up to the casino, but Mom latched onto her arm.

"Carmen Marie."

She was worried. It was written all over her face.

"Mom, I'm fine."

"You aren't fine. You haven't been fine for years."

The past two hours had been an emotional roller coaster of learning about her future stepfather and his family. Marv's oldest son lived in Japan with his wife who was expecting. They would have the wedding a few months after the baby was born since the wife was too far along to fly right now. Not only had her mother been dating Marv, but she'd also been living with him for two months. She was shell-shocked but doing her best to keep an open mind. Marv was obviously head over heels for her mother. That was all that mattered, right?

She kissed her mother on the cheek. "I love you, and I'm happy for you."

"I don't have to live with him. I can move back into the house."

"Why would you do that if you're happy where you are? You moved in with him because you wanted to spend more time with him, right?"

"Yes."

"Then just stay with him and be happy."

"I want you to be happy too."

"I'll get there."

"Your dad would be proud of you."

She couldn't deal with that right now, so she banked it. "I'll be in touch."

She got out of the car, walked past the valet, and entered the casino. She didn't register the smoke or the people brushing up against her. She wasn't even aware of where she was going until a man stepped into her path.

"Carmen?"

Hands grasped her shoulders and she focused on Kody Singer.

"Kody?"

He frowned. "Are you okay?"

"Yeah, I'm good."

He surveyed her for a few beats. "I've been calling you."

"My life has been kinda crazy." Understatement of the century, but she wasn't going to elaborate. It felt like weeks rather than days since she went to lunch with him after the hospital event. Her life had turned on its head since then.

"I'm on my way out. Have a drink with me," he said.

"I don't—"

"Come."

He led her to the nearest bar and urged her onto the high stool.

"What'll you have?" the bartender asked.

"You still like mojitos?" Kody asked.

She didn't really, but a drink order was beyond her at the moment, so she nodded. She glanced at the other people at the bar without much interest.

"What's going on with you?"

She looked back to find Kody watching her closely.

"I—" No other words emerged. "I'm..."

"I asked you to go with me to Europe while I film my new movie," he said, cutting to the chase.

"Right. I..." Her mind was a complete blank. "I can't."

"So you said before. Why not?"

He led a glamorous life, but beneath the good looks, he was a simple man with simple wants. He was too good for her.

"Maybe getting out of Vegas would be good for you," Kody continued. "There was the shooting at the hospital, and now I heard a bunch of people are missing."

"Missing?"

"Yeah, it's all over the news. The governor, a judge, and gaming commissioner are missing. They're saying even people from the police force have disappeared. Vegas is going to the dogs. Come on, Carmen. There's nothing for you here."

Her mom and Lyla had been her support system and now... Lyla had Gavin, who wasn't going to be battling the underworld, and her mother had Marv. At one point, she was all they had, and now they had their own lives, and she had nothing. Everyone had moved on without her.

The bartender set the mojito in front of her. She snatched it and drank deep. Kody sipped his drink and watched as she gulped hers.

"What's going on, Carmen?" Kody asked. "You were all over me at the hospital, and then you disappear, don't return my calls... What's going on?"

How would he react if she confided that she killed a man? That she lost half of her soul when Vinny died? That all she wanted was her father here, so she could run into his arms one last time and have him say she would get through this?

"You aren't yourself," Kody said.

That was true. She hadn't been herself for years. Warm hands grasped hers and squeezed. She focused on Kody, who had a mix of frustration and yearning on his face.

"Come with me." She opened her mouth, but he pressed a finger against her lips to stop her. "It doesn't need to be like that. I can see you still need time. Let me take care of you. Let's start fresh." He cupped her chin and leaned forward. "I never forgot you. I want what we had, but I can wait."

She stared at him, her thoughts in turmoil.

"Remember, Carmen?"

He pressed his lips against hers. She stiffened but didn't pull away. He kissed her gently. The taste of something sweet and appealing made her deepen the kiss. He cupped the side of her face. She closed her eyes and tried to lose herself in him. This was what she should want, a sweet guy who wanted to take care of her. This was what women dreamed of—the white knight with money and a heart of gold. Life with Kody would be glamorous and smooth. He would put her first, and they would live happily ever after. This was what Mom had with Marv, what she used to have what Vinny. Maybe if she opened up a little...

His lips slanted over hers, deepening the kiss. It felt nice, but her heart rate didn't speed up, and her body felt heavy and lethargic. When she couldn't stand the disappointment any longer, she pulled back. Kody had kissed his fair share of women, and it showed. Despite his technique, she felt nothing. How could she have had such chemistry with him once upon a time, and now, it was just gone? Even as the thought drifted through her mind, she answered herself. She wasn't the same woman who fell into an affair with such reckless gusto. That woman flitted from relationship to relationship and never had her heart broken, never experienced the devastating loss of a parent, or watched a broken human being struggle to survive. Lyla's recovery had been painful to watch, especially since the worst of her injuries were internal where she couldn't help. Lyla had to piece herself back together, and she had, through her own strength of will. Now it was her turn to put herself back together, and she had no fucking clue how to do it.

"Carmen?" Kody asked, stroking her cheek.

"Kody—"

Out of the corner of her eye, she noticed a figure standing a little too close. She turned her head, dislodging Kody's hand, and met Marcus's dark gaze. His normally animated face was the picture of polite inquiry. All that wonderful arrogance and affection was banked.

Marcus turned to Kody and held out a hand. "I'm glad I caught you. I wanted to thank you for staying with us these past two weeks. I was hoping to offer you a drink before you left but see you already have one."

"You've been very accommodating with the suites for my staff and the last-minute company," Kody said.

"Of course. Anything we can do, Mr. Singer. Have a safe trip home." Marcus turned to her and inclined his head. "Mrs. Pyre."

The way he addressed her made her stomach twist. She swiped her thumb over her naked ring finger and tried to think of something to say. She looked like a complete slut for accepting a kiss when Marcus had been inside her less than fifteen hours ago. If she had caught Marcus kissing a woman today, she would have lost her shit. She opened her mouth to explain, but no words came out.

Marcus turned away. She reached out for his arm but stopped just shy of grabbing his sleeve. What would she say? How could she explain why she accepted a kiss from Kody? Would it make a difference if she told him that she'd been on her way to the executive offices to see him and been waylaid by Kody?

He strode away, and her heart sank. She wasn't sure what she and Marcus were, but he was a balm to her shattered nerves. He cared for her the night Lyla was in Hell, and he sated her demons last night. God knows what she would have gotten into if he hadn't stepped in.

Marcus was her gateway to euphoria and relief, and she felt a sharp pang of loss and panic as he disappeared into the crowd.

"Carmen?"

She looked at Kody and took a deep breath. "I'm sorry. You're a great guy. You're going to make some woman really happy."

"And she's not you," he said slowly.

"No." She held out a hand. "Friends?"

He didn't take her hand immediately and each passing second felt like an eternity. When she was about to retract her hand and what dignity she had left, he took it.

"If you ever need someone to talk to, you have my number," he said and slipped off the stool. He chucked her under the chin. "Take care of yourself."

Two good guys walked away from her in less than five minutes. That had to be some kind of record. She had a black belt in fucking up her life. Carmen tipped the bartender and headed through the casino to the valet and handed her ticket over. She watched the doors to the casino, expecting Marcus to appear, but he didn't. She slipped into her car, filched her phone out of her purse, and hit Lyla's number on speed dial. The call went to voicemail. She cursed and redialed as she tore out of the driveway of the casino but didn't get far because of traffic. She was about to redial Lyla for the third time but stopped herself. Between Gavin being an insatiable beast, a four-month-old baby, and her mother being in the hospital, it was no surprise that Lyla couldn't pick up her call.

She drummed her fingers restlessly and tried every single radio station, but nothing suited her mood. As soon as she reached the freeway, she slammed her foot on the gas. She cut through traffic like a madwoman, shifting gears, and dodging other cars like she was on the run. The rush didn't alleviate the pressure on her chest.

When she finally stopped the car, she rested her chin on the steering wheel and stared through the windshield at the gates of the property she once owned with Vinny. She caught a glimpse of the ostentatious mansion she spent years designing. It had been her dream home with her dream man, and now she had neither. Gavin had sold the property when she and Lyla went on the road. She would never admit it, but she was grateful he'd done so. She wouldn't have been able to continue living there without Vinny. Gavin put her belongings in storage where they'd been for almost three years, like her.

Seeing her mother with a new man had been an out-of-body experience, one she hadn't been prepared for. She assumed her mother would always be around while she figured out what to do with her life, only to discover that her mother had built a new life without her. She had truly been left behind.

She sat back and rested her hand on her aching chest. She'd lost the two most important men in her life so close together. Her father and Vinny had been her foundation. They loved her for who she was —the good, bad, and ugly—and she loved them back with the same fervor. Her father understood her nature and never tried to rein her in. He prepared her for life by drilling into her that she was capable of anything she put her mind to. The last time she saw her father was the day she left with Lyla to go on the road. Between Vinny and Manny's murder and the attack on Lyla, she'd been a wreck.

"I know this seems impossible right now, baby, but you're gonna pull through this. You're strong, Carmen. Take care of Lyla. Get her out of here, give yourselves both time." He buried his face in her hair. "When you're ready to come home, we'll be here."

She blinked back tears as the echo of his words slipped through her mind. That was the last time she saw him alive. Fuck. She missed him. He'd want her to support her mother. That was what family did for one another. No one should be alone, and her mother was a sweet woman who loved taking care of people. Soon, her mom would have more people to fuss over—a new husband and step kids who were going to love her. Who wouldn't? Her mother was the best.

Time passed. She didn't give a fuck. The fact that her phone remained silent reinforced that she needed to do something with her life. No one would take her by the hand. No one would fawn over her. Soon, her mother would marry, and she would be living alone in her childhood home...

Carmen picked up her phone and skimmed through her contacts before she found the right number. The phone rang once, and then a feminine voice came on the line.

"Carmen Pyre. Oh, my God."

"Hey, Charisse."

"Are you okay? I sent flowers when I heard about Vinny."

She nodded even though Charisse couldn't see. "Yes. I got them. Thank you."

"Are you in town? What's going on? How are you?"

"I'm back, and I need you."

"You're looking for a place?" Charisse's excitement leaked through the phone. "That's great! Do you have an idea of what kind of place you want?"

"No, but I'll know it when I see it. Can you help me?"

"Of course. When?"

"Tomorrow if you can manage it."

"You bet!"

Carmen made small talk with Charisse before they hung up. She might not be ready to move on, but she had no choice. She had to start creating a life for herself. Her dad didn't raise her to wallow in self-pity. He expected better from her. It was time to get her shit in order and get down to business. She made a few calls. One to the storage place to see just how many lockers she had, one to the RV park to check on her baby, and one to the bank to check on her accounts. She was fucking loaded—a millionaire many times over—sitting in a car, staring through the gates at her old life. She would see about getting a new place that suited her, and maybe it was time for a new ride as well.

Carmen tossed her phone and revved her car. Time to start living.

10

Carmen reveled in the growl of her new Aston Martin Vanquish S Volante as she put the beauty through its paces. The smell of new car and leather permeated the air as she sped through the city. She couldn't resist stroking the luxurious red leather interior and gleaming panels. Getting a new car definitely improved her mood. She loved her gold Ferrari, but when she pulled up to the lot and saw this beast, she knew she would be driving it off the lot within the hour. As the saying goes, money talked, and she didn't mind dropping buckets of it to get her way.

She pulled into the parking lot of a gentlemen's club called the Red Diamond. The parking lot was full of flashy cars and limos that provided shuttle service to and from The Strip. She found a spot in the back lot and stepped out of the Aston. She took two steps back to admire it. The exterior was so shiny; it looked like polished chrome. The Aston was sleek, powerful, and sexy.

Carmen strutted to the back entrance and rapped a distinct pattern on the door. She glanced up at the surveillance camera and blew a kiss. The door opened to reveal a behemoth with a craggy, emotionless face.

"Hey, boss," he said.

"Hey, Phil." She went up on tiptoes to kiss him on the cheek. "How's life?"

"Haven't gotten shot or stabbed in a year so I'd say life is good," he rumbled.

"Slow year?"

"You wish."

"Is Kiki here?"

"Yup. In her office."

"Great."

Carmen walked into a dressing room filled with well-lit vanities, a wall of hooker heels in every color, and props for the shows. Seeing this room filled her with memories of her stripping days, which felt like a lifetime ago. The music from the club reverberated through the walls and made her heartbeat pick up speed. The beat beckoned her to indulge. She would, but she had business to see to first.

She stopped in front of a mirror and admired her gunmetal strappy heels. After she picked up the Aston Martin, she went to The Look, the boutique the woman in Incognito recommended. She dropped fifteen thousand and became fast friends with the owner who waited on her hand and foot. Tonight's ensemble was definitely inspired by her new ride.

Slowly, she undid the sash of her short black trench coat and revealed the silver shift dress beneath. Liquid silk brushed over her skin. It was a barely there dress that hugged every curve and left little to the imagination. The shift rode high on her thighs and made her feel as if she didn't have anything on at all. She leaned toward the mirror to examine her porn star makeup job—the larger than life eyes, perfect lips, and flawless face. She shrugged off her trench coat and headed out of the dressing room.

The music intensified, and the urge to join in the fun increased. Her palms tingled as she nodded to mingling security and called the elevator. The moment the doors closed, the music disappeared. She took a breath to clear her head and examined her outfit. In the past, she went for straight-up sex, but her taste was changing like so many other things.

The elevator opened onto a quiet hallway lined with a wall of tinted glass that looked out at the Red Diamond. A gold, glittering stage took up one end of the club and flowed into a long runway lined with stripper poles that divided the club in two. Six girls twirled dreamily to the music. A hazy ruby light highlighted smaller stages around the club. She appreciated the glint of gold throughout the club which included the bar, chairs, and trays of the servers moving through the crowd. The Red Diamond was filled to capacity. She walked down the hallway to Kiki's office and nodded to the armed guard who moved aside as she approached. She gave a cursory knock before she entered.

The office looked as respectable and classy as any executive's aside from a few eccentricities. Gold framed nudes hung on black velvet walls, and the room was littered with life-size copper and silver sculptured men. At the far end of the soundproof office was an impressive walnut desk occupied by a formidable woman smoking a cigar. She looked up through a cloud of smoke. Her forbidding expression disappeared when she recognized Carmen. A genuine smile curved her hard mouth. Kiki rose and stood six-foot-three in six-inch stilettos.

"Give me a fucking hug, girlie," Kiki said.

Carmen ran to her friend and was caught in a bone-crushing hug. Kiki pulled back and examined her. "You're looking good, chickie."

"So do you."

Even at sixty-three, Kiki was a sight to behold in a red tailored jumpsuit, diamond choker, slick ponytail, and flawless makeup. Kiki went to the wet bar in the corner and poured Carmen a glass of whiskey.

"I haven't seen you since Vinny's funeral," Kiki said.

"I've been keeping my cousin company."

"The one who married Gavin Pyre?"

"Yes. They had a baby a couple of months back."

Kiki handed her the glass and perched on the edge of the desk. "How are you doing?"

"Better."

"You look it." Kiki let out a stream of smoke before she said, "What the fuck is happening in the underworld?"

Carmen held her gaze. "I'm sure you already know."

Kiki had connections, murky ones that Carmen wasn't interested in digging up.

"Angel Roman is the new head honcho?"

"Yup."

"What about New York?"

"There's more than one Roman brother."

Kiki grunted. "And Roque will be out soon. Fuck."

Carmen frowned and opened her mouth but thought better of it. She was out of underworld business. The less she knew, the better. She took a healthy swallow of whiskey and enjoyed the burn. Her foot bounced, which betrayed her eagerness to join the madness beyond the office.

"Why's Pyre stepping down?" Kiki asked.

"My cousin."

Kiki eyed her intently. "Your cousin slayed in the Pit. They're the perfect couple to rule the underworld. No one would dare fuck with them."

So, Lyla's exploits were already on the streets. Carmen resisted the urge to beam with pride. "They have a daughter, and Lyla's not interested in underworld politics."

Kiki made a disgusted smacking sound with her lips. "Fucking love."

Carmen toasted her. "Fucking love." It was the strongest force on the planet. Nothing on earth could erase your memories of a loved one who left you behind.

"Business would be easier without having to deal with a new crime lord," Kiki said.

"Angel Roman has bigger things to deal with than us."

"I hope you're right. Vega never bothered with us during his reign."

She tensed. "You knew it was him?"

Kiki frowned. "Of course, not. I would have told you if I knew. I fucking loved Vinny."

She downed the rest of her drink. "Right."

Vega's mind games really fucked her up. She almost shot Marcus and was even questioning her long-term business partner who she'd known almost a decade. She stepped on stage for the first time on her twenty-first birthday. Kiki taught her everything she knew about confidence, seduction, and men.

When Kiki hit a rough patch, Carmen used her stripper savings to bail her out and became a silent partner for the Red Diamond. The gentlemen's club flourished and became the most popular in the city. Carmen found it ironic that people labeled her a gold digger when she was a millionaire in her own right. Vinny was the only one who knew about her connection to the club. When Gavin needed dirt, Vinny gave her the nudge, and she visited Kiki to get the goods on the high-end clientele who frequented the club. It had been mutually beneficial for all of them.

"Even those who reported directly to Vega didn't know his identity. His name's everywhere since Pyre tortured him in the Pit. Apparently, Pyre's whole crew was quite spectacular," Kiki continued.

Carmen's curiosity was piqued, but she didn't rise to the bait. If she knew how close to death Lyla had been, it would bring up all the shit she was trying to leave in the past. She came out tonight to let loose and reconnect with Kiki, that's it.

"Gavin endorses Angel. That's all that matters."

Kiki inclined her head. "Right. I'm sure Pyre will tell him we provided the dirt to blackmail his competitors. That could come in handy for Roman."

"We'll worry about it if it happens." She set the empty glass on the desk. "Now, what do you have for me?"

Kiki went behind the desk and became all business. Before Carmen became a silent partner, the Red Diamond was a ghetto strip joint. Once she started dating Vinny, she developed the VIP side of the business and turned it into a high-end gentlemen's club. She and Kiki became wealthy bitches. Over the years, they nurtured their relationships with the casinos and their clientele. Kiki had the club running like a well-oiled machine, and business was booming.

"You look better than ever," Kiki said as they left the office and caught the elevator to the second floor.

"Thanks," she said and shifted restlessly as the elevator slowly traveled down.

"That dress is going to cause a riot."

Carmen beamed. "That's what I'm hoping for."

The elevator doors opened. The level of noise would have knocked a lesser person backward, but Carmen stepped forward eagerly. Two guards stepped aside to let them pass. The second floor had shadowed alcoves for semi-private shows or parties that overlooked the main floor, which catered to the masses.

"We have two bachelor parties tonight. Eight of the ten VIP rooms are occupied, and the limo drivers are bringing guys in groups of ten or more," Kiki shouted as they walked down the gold staircase.

On stage, four girls danced with fans, boas, and thongs. The Red Diamond kept up a steady stream of entertainment from old Hollywood numbers to twerking and everything in between. The later the hour, the more risqué the show became. What happened on stage satisfied the public and critics while the real shit went on behind closed doors.

The main floor had clusters of chairs surrounding solo platforms, which put the girls within touching distance. Bouncers were everywhere. Carmen and Kiki weaved between hyped men and servers wearing skirts and bikini tops. It was Carmen's type of bedlam. She inhaled cigar smoke with relish and slapped the ass of a passing stripper she hadn't seen in ages and received a boob squeeze in return. Several men reached for her as she passed. One hand skated over her belly before Kiki stepped in. Her imposing presence made the men think twice about waylaying her.

They found a seat at the bar. Carmen blew a kiss to the bartender and surveyed the club while Kiki talked. It was hard to concentrate when her surroundings called to the wildness inside her. Her need to push the limits led her to the stage. Being a dancer brought out her love of role playing, and when she danced, she felt alive and free. People thought strippers were at a man's mercy, yet in her experience, it was the other way around. She never felt more in control than when she worked the stage. Money rained down, and anything was possible.

Vinny replaced the stage, booze, and anything else she indulged in to sate her inner demons. He became her everything, and now, he was gone, and the taste for something dark and uncivilized made her insides salivate. Her body ached from yesterday's exploits, but she was hungry for more. Walking through her old hunting grounds was like parading a recovering alcoholic in front of a bar.

The music shifted from old Hollywood to hard rock, and the stage lights began to flash. Girls wearing lingerie or mesh dresses strutted down the catwalk and began to climb the poles. Carmen accepted a shot from the bartender and downed it without looking to see what it was. She couldn't take her eyes off the dancers writhing to the beat. Seeing the girls embrace the moment brought back memories of a simpler time when life was about fun and games and not death and loss.

"Hey, baby." A man with spiky hair and a sweat-stained button up eyed her as if she were a meal. "Can I get you a drink?"

"No." Mr. Hip wasn't going to do it for her. Even if he was the best fuck in the room (which she doubted), he wasn't going to quench her hunger. She leaned to the side to watch as a dancer did a ridiculous trick on the pole that had the men around her tossing twenty-dollar bills on her platform. Carmen's toes curled in her shoes as the need to throw all inhibition into the wind hit her.

"I don't think she's interested," Kiki said to the guy and turned back to her. "You fucked since Vinny?"

Carmen nodded.

Kiki patted her on the back. "I'm happy for you. Are you looking for a replacement?"

"No," she said as she fisted her hands in her lap.

"You been on a pole lately?" Kiki asked dryly.

"I have, actually."

"Can you dance with this?" Kiki asked, fingering her shift dress.

Carmen gave her a deadpan look that made her grin. "Rock You Like A Hurricane" hit the speakers, and her shaky control snapped. Kiki's delighted laughter followed her as she shoved her way through the crowd. She hopped on a table to get on the main stage. The men cheered excitedly, thinking she was a housewife gone crazy. Two strippers paused in their twirling to stare and then smile in welcome when they recognized her. She strutted down the runway as if she owned it. Technically, she did, but the men watching her didn't know that.

She got down on her hands and knees and prowled across the glittering stage, very aware that she was giving everyone a great view of the scrap of white lace masquerading as underwear. She crawled toward one of the dancers who hung upside down. Carmen rose to her knees and grasped handfuls of Mercedes's hair and leaned close. Out of the corner of her eyes, she saw men crowding around the stage to get in position to see their lips touch.

Mercedes eyes sparkled with mischief. "Hey, chica. Where you been?"

"Around."

"Those are bomb shoes."

"I know, right? I got them at The Look," she said as she stroked her hair. "How are the kids?"

"Good. Barry's gonna be happy to hear I saw you. He's been worried about you."

"Tell him I said hi," Carmen said before she kissed her.

Mercedes accepted the kiss eagerly and slid her tongue into Carmen's mouth. She was happy to discover that Mercedes penchant for sweets hadn't changed. She found a hard caramel candy and took it for herself and felt dollar bills brush over her thighs. Their mouths parted, and the men went wild when they saw tongue.

"Have a great night," Carmen said.

Mercedes's eyes flicked to the money littered over the stage and grinned. "I already am."

Carmen winked and tossed her hair as she slid over the money to an empty pole. Her mini dress slithered over her sensitive skin. She blocked out the roar of the crowd and soared with the amazing guitar solo. She arched her back and saw a captivated audience watching her. She smiled and imagined that the money that rained over her were flower petals. She rose slowly, using the pole as leverage with her ass out. She paraded around the pole and licked it, which made the men go crazy. One show of tongue and men forgot their names. She felt alive, desirable, and invincible.

"Man in the Box" by Alice In Chains saturated the club in sex and fantasy. Carmen moved slowly, sensuously. Men weren't here to be impressed by tricks but liked to imagine they were the pole. She made her movements jerky and sluggish to match the song. She absorbed the energy of the crowd and let it fill the emptiness inside her. She lost herself in the music, lights, and pulse of lust. It coated her as surely as the sweat that slid over her skin. She swiveled her hips, played with her hair, and stared boldly at the men lining the stage to be near her. The power she felt being on stage made her feel as if there was a sunburst in her chest. Here, she ruled. Here, she knew who she was. Here, everything was simple. She was a woman in charge of her sexuality, and these men were her slaves, here to worship their fantasy in the flesh.

Songs transitioned, and she let her body take over. She forgot about the audience unless a man tried to take the stage and was immediately restrained by the security working overtime tonight. She partied her ass off and enjoyed teasing the onlookers with slow kisses and caresses by the other dancers. She had her back against a pole and had Taryn kissing a path up her leg when she saw a familiar face in the crowd. She stiffened, and Taryn paused on her upper thighs and patted her butt.

"Okay?" Taryn asked in a muffled voice.

Even as she hoped her mind was playing tricks on her, the crowd parted again, and she saw him. Angel leaned back against the bar, watching her. He wore a white shirt tucked into well-fitted slacks. His belt buckle caught the light as he shifted when they made eye contact. A smile curved his mouth, and he shook his head chidingly. His presence intruded on her adrenaline high.

Taryn rose and kissed her cheek. "What's wrong?"

"Nothing," she said.

Taryn prowled to the edge of the stage and humped the stage to the absolute delight of the crowd. Carmen didn't move her eyes from Angel. What the fuck was he doing here? This was her haven, her business... not that he knew that. This was the second time in a matter of days that she ran into him. Shouldn't he be doing gun battles in the ghetto, not watching strippers dance in a gentlemen's club?

Angel raised his hand and beckoned with one finger. He did not just... He did it again. He crooked his pointer finger at her as if she were a naughty child or a dog. Who the fuck did he think he was? She didn't have a keeper. She was a free agent. She called the shots, not some Roman, even if he was the new crime lord.

Carmen grasped the edge of her shift and lifted it over her head. The outbreak of cheers, hollering, and shouting overpowered the music. She dropped the silk shift on the stage and faced Angel in her white lace lingerie set, which she had been waiting to reveal at the perfect moment. The moment she picked it out today, she knew her night would end here. The tulle cups embroidered with a silky floral pattern were utterly feminine and more suited to a bride's wedding night than a stripper stage. Her demure outfit stood out among the neon, animal print, or solid red or black the other strippers wore. If the men looked hard enough, they'd see her nipples through the sheer fabric. She put her hands on her hips and raised a brow at Angel. He couldn't touch her. This was her territory, her power spot. He was just passing through.

Angel dropped his hand. She was too far away to decipher his expression, but she didn't fucking care. She could do whatever she wanted. His opinion didn't enter into the equation. She climbed the pole and let muscle memory take over. She hugged the pole with her legs and twirled slowly. Time passed, and her muscles protested, but she blocked it out. She hadn't felt this empowered in years.

She was twirling upside down with only one leg holding her weight when she caught sight of Angel again. This time, he sat in front of the stage, hands steepled as he watched her with laser focus. She straightened and revolved slowly until she reached the stage, which was littered with money. She landed on her knees and rotated her hips as she faced Angel. Men jockeyed for position on either side of him.

Angel rose and took two steps to reach the stage. He held out a hand. When a guard tried to push him back, Angel said something that made the man back off. What the hell? She considered ignoring him, but she had a feeling he was seconds away from leaping on stage to fetch her. She slipped on her dress before she prepared to scoot over the edge, but Angel grabbed her arm and yanked her off, along with a handful of bills. Instead of setting her on the ground, he carried her to the bar with her clamped to his side. He set her on a stool and faced the crowd of men.

"Get lost," Angel said.

Some of the men dispersed, but a respectably large group remained. She could practically hear them panting for a chance to taste or touch. She had been the best dancer for a reason. Most girls didn't want to be on the main stage since they didn't make many tips, but it was the only place Carmen could dance where the bouncers could control the crowd. The largest tips were in the VIP lounge or from lap dances, but Carmen excelled on stage, the ultimate fantasy come to life. Despite the precarious situation, she was fucking giddy. Her arms and legs felt like jelly, but she was so fucking jazzed. She still had it.

Two men sidled up beside Angel. She recognized them from Gavin's security team. The trio knocked some sense into the last of the lust-dazed men. The thwarted men backed off and shouted for lap dances.

She grabbed a twenty-dollar bill clinging to her leg and slapped it on the bar. "Drinks?"

She took the chilled water bottle the bartender slipped her and took long gulps. When she lowered it, she found all three men staring at her.

Angel grabbed her wrist and yanked her off the stool. "I need to talk to you in private."

"About what?"

He didn't answer and dragged her toward the gold staircase. Three men tried to waylay them. They didn't even seem to register Angel's presence. Angel punched a guy in his path and nearly dislocated another man's knee when he lashed out with his shiny shoes. The third man stepped aside.

"What the fuck?" she snapped.

Angel faced off with the bouncers monitoring access to the second level and flashed a card with the Red Diamond logo on it.

"You paid for VIP access?" she asked.

He shot her a hooded glance. "I want the whole experience."

"What does that mean?"

Angel pulled her into a VIP room. She hoped it was occupied and was disappointed to find it empty. He pulled her inside and slammed the door behind them. When he released her, she put her hands on hips.

"What the hell is your problem?"

"I don't believe in coincidence," Angel said.

She blinked. "What?"

"If you'd been the nanny, this would have been easier. Now you're the nanny, the informer, and the stripper?" He shook his head in mock regret. "You can't expect me not to make a play."

A mixture of alarm and excitement coursed through her veins. "Angel."

He approached slowly. She resisted the urge to run since that would only spur him on. Angel wasn't playing the indulgent, laid back host he had at his home. His body was rigid with tension—a tension he thought he would work out right here, right now. Her inner slut screamed at her to go for it. The same euphoric feeling she got while dancing, she could get from Angel... and then some.

"Does Gavin know about this?" he asked as he stopped in front of her, so close she could feel his body heat.

She tapped her chin thoughtfully. "You know, I've never felt the need to tell Gavin what my plans are every night... and I doubt he would care."

"He'd care."

There wasn't a shred of doubt in his voice.

"Gavin knows I can handle myself," she said.

"You were about to cause a riot."

"I wasn't the only one dancing."

"No, but you were the only one doing it right."

"Excuse me?"

"You were born for the stage." He ran a hand through her tangled hair as if he had every right to. "You dance because you love it while the others are there for the money. Men can tell the difference."

Their eyes locked, and her breath seized. His thumb stroked over her fluttering pulse and her nipples tightened.

"You abandon yourself on stage. All any man can think about is how you'll be in bed."

His voice was low with the promise of sex. When he leaned forward and licked her sweaty collarbone, she shuddered. His hands slid down her sides and stopped on her hips.

"You were created to give yourself to a man so he can lavish you with pleasure." He sucked on her neck, and she bit back a moan. "You know you're the ideal woman for me, don't you?"

"I'm not," she whispered and fought the urge to let her eyes shut.

"I recognize another wild soul when I see one. I wouldn't try to tame you. I would unleash you, Carmen. It would be glorious."

He kissed her. She was swamped with his taste—dark, elusive, barbaric. He picked her up and pinned her on the couch beneath him. He licked her neck as he ground himself against her. His bulge was right there... Her hips bucked, and he swore.

"This fucking dress," he growled as he grasped a handful of silk. His hot hand slipped beneath the fabric and splayed over her quivering belly. "You knew what you were doing up there. You were hoping it would end like this, right? That's not the only place you can get a high, baby."

Her demons were shrieking at her to take what he offered. She was lost in the intoxicating weight pinning her, his words, and the hand stroking her. It wasn't until she heard the hiss of his zipper that she came back to herself.

She had sex with Marcus yesterday. Even though they weren't in a relationship, she'd never slept with two different men a day apart. Angel would be a great fuck (phenomenal, probably), but she would regret it. She knew it as surely as she knew the sun would rise in a couple of hours. Angel tried to hide behind a cool demeanor, but she saw fleeting glimpses of his true nature—lust, greed, possessiveness. Nope. Men like Angel and Gavin wouldn't be able to handle her. She needed to be free to be herself, and they wouldn't allow it. Vinny didn't force her to stop dancing. She quit on her own when she realized the high came from him, not strangers. Dominant men like Angel would enjoy her wild side for a while and then try to snuff it out when they couldn't control her.

She covered his hand with hers and felt his cock through the thin material of his underwear. She swallowed hard.

"No," she said hoarsely.

His eyes were narrow slits of lust. "What?"

She pressed both hands on his chest, but he didn't budge. She was on her back, legs splayed on either side of him, and he was in a position to penetrate. Belatedly, she remembered the cameras and hoped Kiki wasn't watching.

"We're not going to have sex," she said.

When she tried to sit up, his hand clamped on her thigh to keep her in place.

"Why?"

She glared at him. "Because I said so."

She wasn't prepared for his hand to probe between her legs. She shrieked and clamped her thighs together, but it was too late.

He licked his lips. "You're wet."

"It's sweat."

"Don't lie to me."

His fingers stroked, and she jerked.

"Angel, stop!"

His head dipped, and she heard him inhale. She went rigid when she realized he was trying to smell her arousal. She smacked his head. For a second, he looked stunned and then he roared with laughter. He dropped his face to her chest and nuzzled.

"I can't remember the last time a woman hit me."

"You deserve it. You're so sure of yourself." She hissed when he searched for her nipple. She grabbed a handful of hair and jerked his head up. "No."

"Come on, Carmen. We both want it."

His fingers curled again, and she bit back a curse. She grabbed his thick wrist and forcibly yanked his fingers out from between her legs. His head dropped to her groin. She had to use both hands to keep him away from her pussy, which was begging to be licked. She was amused and turned on and didn't know what to do with him.

"No," she said as her inner slut begged to be fucked.

"What the hell? You want this. It's not like you're with someone."

"You don't know that."

Angel cocked his head. "You're with someone?"

"I didn't say that."

"Then what's the problem?"

"I don't need a fuck."

He jerked his head at her vagina. "Apparently you do. She's hungry for dick, baby."

Carmen shoved, and this time he rocked back. She gained her feet and yanked her dress down. When she turned to confront Angel, she saw that he had his fingers in his mouth. Words dried up in her throat. He withdrew his fingers and cursed.

"Fuck. I didn't go deep enough. I can't taste you."

Her legs wobbled. She wagged her finger at him. "We're family."

"By marriage."

"Same thing."

"No, it isn't."

"You're inappropriate."

"You're the one dancing at a strip club."

"Gentlemen's club."

"Same thing."

That pricked her professional pride. "No, it isn't."

He got to his feet and zipped his pants. His erection was painfully obvious. She wanted nothing more than to kneel and blow him, but that wasn't happening. She waved a hand in front of her face in a vain attempt to disperse the sexual tension.

"This isn't happening," she said.

"Then I need someone to take care of what you started."

"I can arrange that," she said.

She had her hand on the doorknob when he called her name. She hesitated before she looked back. Her control quaked as she took him in. He was virile, attractive, and dangerous. His eye contact made her feel as if she was the only woman in the world, but she knew his type. Angel would fuck her mindless and then turn to the next woman without hesitation. No, this was better for both of them.

"I don't want you dancing without backup," he said.

It took her a moment to register what he said. "There's security everywhere."

"It would only take a moment for them to hurt you."

"I can handle myself."

"I don't care. How'd you end up on stage anyway?"

She gave him a one-shoulder shrug. "They played Guns N' Roses."

His smirked. "Is that the song that makes you drop your panties? I'll remember that for next time."

She gave him the middle finger as she opened the door and slammed it behind her. Gavin's guards were waiting in the hallway and tried to hide their smirks. She glared at them before she turned on her heel. She caught the elevator to the first floor, nodded to Phil and walked out the back door. When she collapsed in her car, she called Kiki.

"You forget to tell me something about you and the new crime lord?" Kiki asked.

"It's nothing. Send him someone who will take care of him."

"No problem."

"I'll see you later." Carmen hung up and dropped her head on the steering wheel. Her harsh breaths filled the silent interior of the Aston. Her legs were shaking, and her underwear was soaked. "Fucking Angel."

11

Tires screeched as Carmen pulled up to the Pyre fortress. She stepped out of the Aston and tossed the keys to the nearest guard before she ran up the steps and slammed the front door.

It had been three days of house hunting, one of her favorite pastimes, and she hadn't liked any of the properties they visited. She was a fucking millionaire, so money wasn't an issue. All she had to do was pick a place and it was hers. The massive estates were ridiculous since she had no one to share it with, not even a goldfish. She didn't want an apartment because it was too small, and she didn't want to share walls with anyone. She sounded like fucking Goldilocks—too big, too small, not enough light, not enough space, too much space... Charisse was beyond frustrated, and so was she. It wasn't supposed to be this hard! Years ago, she knew exactly what she wanted. Now, she had no idea, and it was driving her crazy. She decided they needed a break from house hunting. Charisse couldn't hide her relief. Carmen went on a short shopping spree, which made her feel marginally better. She was in love with her new black and white snakeskin stilettos, which paired well with her black leather wrap skirt and thin black sweater.

"Lyla!" she yelled.

Gavin would have to take one for the team if they were fucking. She was restless and manic and needed girl time.

Blade appeared at the top of the stairs. "What's going on?"

"I need Lyla. Where is she?"

"Backyard."

She marched in that direction and saw Lyla sitting in the sunken cabana in the middle of the pool with Nora on her lap. She relaxed a little as she watched Lyla bounce Nora on the cushions with Beau nearby.

"What's your problem?" Blade asked.

She turned to the fridge. "What do we have to eat?"

She was hungry as fuck. She stopped at two fast food joints and a Greek place she used to love, but nothing was hitting the spot. She fumbled through Lyla's fridge and sniffed some of the meals. Rosemary chicken, enchiladas, and ravioli. She scooped a little of each on a plate and tossed it in the microwave before she located her stash of marshmallows in the cupboard. She popped a few into her mouth, grimaced, and spotted a jar of peanut butter. She scooped out a spoonful, swallowed, and then grabbed chocolate syrup and squeezed a dollop on. She grabbed honey and put an amber drop on the peanut butter. Better, but still not what she was looking for. The microwave dinged, and she grabbed the plate, took a forkful of ravioli, and blew on it before she put it in her mouth. She burned her mouth, but that didn't stop her from trying the chicken and enchiladas as well. After one bite, she knew it wasn't going to do it for her. She just couldn't think of a food that would satisfy her craving.

"What drugs are you on?"

She turned and found Blade watching her suspiciously. She held the steaming plate out to him. "You want this? I just took a bite."

"I saw what you did. What are you on?"

"I'm not on anything. I'm just hungry." She tossed the spoon in the sink and poured herself a glass of root beer.

His lip curled in disgust. "You have to be on something to mix those foods together."

She waved her hands dismissively. Her taste buds clamored for flavor. Was she acting a bit crazy? Maybe. So what if she ordered thirty dollars' worth of food at Burger King and took a bite of everything before she realized she was over it? At least she gave it to some homeless teenagers on the side of the road and gave them a ride to the nearest shelter. She could be psycho and helpful at the same time. She was having a manic episode. No big deal. She had never been diagnosed with bipolar disorder; it was just what Mom always called it when she got like this. She hadn't had an episode while she had imitated the walking dead, but now she was awake and with that came her impulses and restless cravings. Her thoughts raced a million miles a minute, and she obsessed over strange, inconsequential things like painting her tiny bedroom in her parents' house gold or redecorating the RV with a leopard theme. Neither of those things were relevant or helpful at all, but she couldn't stop thinking about them. Sleep had been nearly impossible the past couple of days, and her frustration increased with every property fail. Her mind couldn't articulate why the homes weren't right, but she knew they wouldn't do. Once she found the right place, she could settle... She just had to figure out what she wanted.

She poured herself a glass of grapefruit juice and swished the bitter drink in her mouth and rolled her eyes when she saw Blade hadn't moved. She decided to give him a show and arched her back to elongate her body and licked her lips after she swallowed. His gaze didn't waver. He was too much of a pro to be distracted by sex, which intrigued her.

"When's the last time you had sex?"

He didn't react to her question.

She pursed her lips. "Like, you're always here. Do you ever take a day off?"

"No."

"So you haven't had sex in months." She cast her eyes over his rockin' body. "Years? Is that why you work out so much?"

"I like to be in control."

"Tell me something I don't know."

"I heard you were dancing at the Red Diamond the other night. You want to explain that to me?"

She gave a one-shoulder shrug. "Just visiting my roots."

"You're asking for trouble."

"Worried about me, Blade?"

"Lyla needs you. She can't take another loss."

She gave him an over bright smile to cover the yawning feeling in the pit of her stomach. She wouldn't survive another loss either. "Nothing's going to happen to me."

She turned her back on him and headed outside. Beau barked in welcome, and Lyla smiled as she rushed toward the cabana. She gave Lyla a tight hug and a kiss on her temple before she took Nora who beamed at her.

"Oh, I missed you so much. Yes, I did," she said as she bobbed the baby from side to side.

"I'm glad you came over. We've been playing phone tag for a couple of days now," Lyla said.

"Yes." She cast an eye over her cousin who was looking much more like her old self. "How've you been?"

"Sleeping a lot. Gavin's working in the office, so I came out here. I went to see Mom yesterday."

"How is she?"

Lyla grimaced. "She didn't say a word."

"Give her time."

Lyla nodded and took in her outfit. "You look fab. What have you been up to?"

"I've been trying to look for a new place."

"Why?"

"Mom's engaged, and I don't want to live in that house by myself."

Lyla straightened. "Aunt Isabel's engaged? How? When?"

"They've known each other for years, but they started dating six months ago. She didn't know how I'd feel about it, so she kept it on the down low."

Silver blue eyes locked on her face. "How are you taking it?"

"I want Mom to be happy."

"Who is this guy? Did you check him out?"

"Of course. He's clean as a whistle. Marvin Armstrong's never even had a speeding ticket. I talked to several of his former employees. He used to run a mechanic shop, which he passed onto his son, but he goes in on Mondays, Wednesdays, and Fridays. He owns his house, goes on hunting trips once a year, and can't golf even though he loves to watch it. His wife passed away from breast cancer eight years ago."

"Is that all?" Lyla asked dryly.

"And he loves anything lemon flavored. I don't want to stay in the house by myself. It was bad enough without Dad there." She pressed her cheek against Nora's and willed her restlessness away.

"Do you want to move back here?" Lyla asked.

"No. I need my own place."

"Have you found something you like?"

"No. I haven't found anything. Charisse thinks I've gone off the deep end."

"Give yourself time. There's no rush."

"There is a rush. I need to settle somewhere and not toss five thousand dollars shoes in a pile on the floor. I need a place to decorate and sleep and be. Vinny deserves a better place than my dresser." She made happy faces at Nora even as her insides shriveled into a ball. "I need, but I don't know what."

Lyla leaned into her. "It's gonna be okay. You're gonna find exactly what you need."

"I woke up at two this morning and went to the RV park," she said. "I went to visit Sally."

"You did? How is she?"

"She's good, but I'm thinking about redecorating her in leopard print."

Lyla laughed. "I'm sure Sally would appreciate that."

"I think so too." She stared at Beau, who rested his head on Lyla's feet. "Maybe I should get a dog."

Loyalty, love, contentment. Nothing else existed for animals. Beau was with his pack, and no matter what drama came with it, he didn't want to be anywhere else. She had no pack anymore. It was no wonder she was acting a little nuts.

"Maybe you should." Lyla leaned down and kissed Beau. "I love him. He's great."

"Are you coming to the animal adoption this weekend?"

"No, I don't think I'm ready to go to anything with a crowd yet." Lyla made a motion with her hands as if she was smoothing a tablecloth. "I just need more time."

Carmen noted her trembling hands. "Nightmares?"

Lyla closed her eyes. "Every fucking night."

A nightmare had woken her in the wee hours of the morning. It had been a replay of the night in the canyon, but in the dream, Nora was slaughtered in front of her. She woke with a gut-wrenching scream. She hadn't been able to go back to sleep, which was how she ended up at the RV park.

"I've been talking to Luci. She's great," Lyla said.

"Me too. I talked to her on the way here."

"She really wants to visit, but I agree with Gavin. It's going to take time to see how the underworld adjusts to Angel."

Kiki's words about Lyla's exploits in Hell tickled the back of her mind. Did Lyla know she was now as notorious as her husband? She probably wouldn't appreciate that little fact, so she kept it to herself. "Luci saw a picture of Cormac and I on the internet. She thought we were together."

"Cormac Hart? Oh, my God. I haven't seen him in years. How is he?"

"Same. I ended up at a party with him. Someone snapped some photos of us. Luci was over the moon for me. She's a fan of Cormac's, and she thought I would divulge his fucking routine."

"What's a fucking routine?"

"Like, does he always fuck in the morning? Does he like blowjobs on Wednesdays? Hand jobs under the table at certain restaurants?"

Lyla raised a brow. "And what did you say?"

"I never fucked Cormac; you know that."

"Just checking. What about Kody?"

"Just heavy petting at the hospital, nothing more."

Lyla's eyes tracked over her outfit. "Besides looking for a place, your mom, and this party you went to with Cormac, what else have you been up to?"

She hesitated, and Lyla's eyes narrowed. It was almost as if she knew about Marcus... He had been on her mind this morning. If it wasn't for the Kody incident, she would have visited him on the off chance that he was available for a fuck. She opened her mouth, but Beau interrupted whatever she would have said when he barked to announce Blade and Gavin's arrival.

Nora got a little hysterical when she saw her father. Before she could attempt to calm the baby, Gavin took her. Nora tucked her head under her father's chin. Gavin wore a gun holster on his hip even though he was home, which was an unpleasant reminder that Vega might be gone, but the danger the underworld posed would never disappear. Lyla went to talk to Blade who was down on a knee petting Beau.

"I heard you were at the RV park this morning," Gavin said.

She jerked. "How do you know that?"

He ignored her question. "What are you planning, Carmen?"

"I just went to visit Sally."

"Sally?"

"My RV."

"Are you planning to go on the road again?"

"I don't know."

Gavin glanced at Lyla, who laughed at something Blade said. "I think it's best if you stay put for now."

She had been planning to anyway, but she didn't like him ordering her to do so. "We'll see."

His attention snapped back to her. "Don't make me freeze your accounts again."

"What do you care what I do?" she demanded and then it hit her. "You think she'll still want to come with me? You're high."

A muscle clenched in his cheek. "I didn't say that."

"But that's what you're thinking."

"Stay put, and we won't have problems," he said through clenched teeth.

"You have someone following me?"

He hesitated and then said, "I keep tabs."

"Why?"

"You and your fucking wild hairs. You could decide to convince Lyla to go skydiving or travel to Bermuda on a moment's notice. After you took her from me twice, you think I wouldn't have you watched as closely as I do her?"

"So you have someone following me?" she pushed.

"I don't employ someone to follow you, but I will if you force me to."

"What I do is none of your concern."

"It does when it concerns Lyla." The light bouncing off the pool made his eyes appear gold instead of hazel. "She's been through a lot. She needs you, and until things settle down, I'm telling you to stay put."

"And if I don't?"

"You'll get your own security detail who will keep you grounded in Las Vegas by any means."

She lifted her chin defiantly. "If I want to leave, I will."

He crowded her, but she refused to back away.

"You talk a big game," he said quietly, "but you love her and wouldn't add to her burden."

She went on tiptoes to hiss, "Then why threaten me at all?"

"Just in case you decide to be selfish and go on the run."

"Why would I do that?"

"Because you have to deal with your life, and you don't like it, and when you don't like something, you do stupid, impulsive, and sometimes dangerous shit."

That hit far too close to home. "You know what, Gavin? You can suck it."

She stepped around him and stalked to the house. With Gavin's words ringing in her ears, the last person she wanted to see was Angel. He walked through the front door looking like something out of GQ magazine. Today, he wore a slate gray suit. The top two buttons of his shirt were undone and mirrored aviator sunglasses shielded his eyes, but she didn't need to see them since his smile spoke volumes.

"Carmen."

His voice was smooth and intimate and pissed her off even as it turned her on. The memories dancing through her mind were proof positive that she was as wild and reckless as Gavin said she was. It didn't help that the memory of Angel leaning down to smell her made her nipples tingle. Some women would have been mortified, but it turned her on. A man who liked the way a woman's pussy smelled was a man who sought to taste and therefore savor. Angel would kill between the sheets. She regretted not taking him up on his offer of no-strings sex. It would have been dirty, raunchy, and glorious. So what if she did two different guys a day apart? She wasn't going to run for office or apply to be a nun so what did she care? She blamed Vinny for training her to be monogamous.

She went to the Red Diamond to reclaim her womanhood and feel a modicum of power after having her life manipulated and torn apart by Vega. She went on stage to work out her demons and let it all hang out. Angel ruined that. He ruined it by tempting her, by making her wonder if hooking up with a crime lord wasn't the worst thing in the world. He made her question her sanity by turning him down. Over the past couple of days, she speculated more than she cared to admit about what might have happened if she gave Angel the green light, and now here he was, in her face, taunting her by looking like a million dollars.

"Hey," she said dismissively and tried to go around him.

He blocked her way. "What's the rush?"

She gritted her teeth. "I have somewhere to be."

He took off his sunglasses to show gleaming blue eyes. "Great. Tell me where and I'll make sure to be there."

She narrowed her eyes. "I'm sure you have more important things to do than stalk me through the city."

He grinned. "I can work and stalk at the same time. I'm talented like that."

"Is that what you were doing at the Red Diamond? Working? You weren't there to ogle strippers?"

"They're dancers, not strippers. I would've thought you of all people would use the correct terminology."

She made a big show of looking at her diamond encrusted watch. "Time is money, Angel."

"Right. And you know all about that."

She frowned. "What does that mean?"

Angel swung his sunglasses idly between two fingers. "You've made some lucrative investments in this town."

She froze. "Excuse me?"

"Local businesses, real estate, but most interesting to me is Red Diamond, the most successful gentlemen's club in Las Vegas." He paused for a beat and then finished, "And also a hot spot for underworld information and blackmail."

He knew. "What did you do to Kiki?" She wouldn't have given that information willingly...

"She's fine."

"What did you do to her?"

Angel kept swinging his glasses casually, as if their discussion was as mundane as the weather. "I drugged her."

She couldn't believe her ears. "You what?"

"I drugged her."

"Why?"

"I needed to know who her partner was."

"How dare you! You have no right—"

"It's my business to know who's behind a business that blackmails influential people. It's also my business to know who has financed so many projects in the valley and desperately wants to remain silent." He cocked his head to the side. "Why so secretive, Carmen?"

"None of your business," she hissed.

"Hiding your intelligence so everyone underestimates you?"

He saw too fucking much, which pissed her off. She was none of his business. "I don't know what you're talking about."

"You know the dirty secrets of every politician, cop, banker or businessman who has the money to enter your establishment. You think I wouldn't turn Red Diamond upside down and find out who runs it? You don't know me at all."

"Gavin didn't do that!"

"He trusted the establishment because Vinny vouched for it. Things change. I'm starting from the ground up. No one's safe, no one's trustworthy, no one gets a pass. You should be happy Kiki dropped your name, or I would have pushed her a little further to make sure she wasn't lying to me."

"Happy? You fucking drugged her!"

"It could have been much worse. That's how Vinny knew so much, right? You were feeding him information."

For the first time in a long time, she was speechless. She knew not to take anyone at face value, but she had grossly miscalculated Angel Roman, and it might cost her everything. His calm delivery as he dissected her world made her see red. The fact that Angel visited the Red Diamond within a week of becoming the crime lord, armed with drugs and God knew what else was alarming in the extreme. He would turn the city upside down.

"If you touch my businesses," she began, but stopped when she heard the rumble of voices as Gavin, Blade, and Lyla entered the house. "Did you tell him?"

Angel's eyes gleamed. "Not yet."

She stuck her finger under his nose. "My investments are none of his business, and if I find out that you hurt Kiki, I'll kill you!"

Angel stared at her lips. "Have dinner with me."

"What?"

"Come to dinner with me, and I won't tell Gavin you're the silent partner for a whorehouse masquerading as a gentlemen's club."

"Suck my dick," she hissed and backed away as Gavin's voice carried toward them.

Angel chuckled. "Don't tempt me."

Gavin strolled into the living room while Lyla and Blade stayed in the kitchen. Gavin stopped and glanced from one to the other suspiciously before he focused on Angel. "All set?"

Angel nodded without taking his eyes from Carmen. "Yeah."

"Everything going smoothly?"

"For the most part. There have been some bumps in the road." Angel raised a brow at Carmen. "Some very lovely bumps, but I've got it under control. You weren't kidding when you said the natives are wild."

Her hands fisted at her sides. He was baiting her. She wanted to stomp his foot with her stilettos, knock those sunglasses out of his hand, and knee him in the balls, but then he would definitely tell Gavin her secrets. Gavin might be out of the underworld, but he still had the status and power to crush whoever he wished. If he knew she was part owner of the Red Diamond, he would find out that she was CM Enterprises, which owned several properties he operated out of. Fucking Angel. He would ruin everything. Gavin would use her businesses as leverage to make her dance to his tune.

"Where you been?" Gavin asked.

"I've been making my way down your list. Chasing some of these guys down has taken me to some clubs, offices, homes..." His eyes glittered, and his smile widened. "The most interesting place by far was the Red Diamond."

Gavin grunted. "Used to be a dive before new management spruced it up. It brings in boatloads of money. Their New Year's Eve parties are more popular than some of mine. You find out anything interesting?"

Angel gave her an expectant look. "I ran into Carmen when I was there."

Her heart sank as Gavin rounded on her.

"Carmen."

His voice was disapproving and didn't bode well for her. Normally, she would smile and flip her hair at him, but she couldn't. Her investments were owned by friends and acquaintances who didn't need Gavin Pyre showing up on their doorstep. Fucking Angel. What the hell did he want from her?

"Carmen," Gavin said through clenched teeth.

"Huh?" She gave him a deliberately unconcerned look.

"What business did you have at Red Diamond?"

Angel snorted. "Business? I think it was more—"

"Weren't you on your way out, Angel?" she interrupted.

He shrugged as he continued to swing his sunglasses. "I have time."

"Not if I'm going with you," she said and slid her arm through his and pulled him toward the exit. "See ya, Gavin."

"You two are leaving together?"

Gavin sounded alarmed. Angel laughed, and she dug her nails into his bicep in warning.

"We're having dinner," she said with a wave.

"I don't think—" Gavin began.

She hauled the door open and shoved Angel out. "I'm sure you have much more pressing things to do like run your company, get Lyla pregnant again, or kill people so don't worry about us."

Gavin took a step after them. "I don't—"

She swung around. "Do you want me to move back in?"

Gavin stopped in his tracks and scowled. "No."

"Then butt out," she said and gave him a sugary sweet smile as she slammed the door.

"You two have an odd relationship," Angel observed.

She growled in his face before she stalked to her Aston Martin. No man had ever turned the tables on her, and she didn't like it worth a damn. Fuck Angel. When she reached for the driver's door, she found herself being pushed aside.

"Nice ride. I'm driving."

"I'm not going to dinner with you!" she bellowed.

Angel turned back to the house. She jumped on his back and put him in a chokehold.

"I have a gun in my purse, and I know how to use it," she hissed.

"Good. It'll come in handy." He walked to the passenger side of the Aston and untangled himself with an ease that infuriated her. He settled her in the passenger seat before he got into the driver's side. He paused a moment to survey the car. "You have excellent taste."

Of course, she did. "You can't force me to go to dinner with you."

He started the car. "Of course, I can. Besides, I already have a reservation."

"You think blackmailing me to go to dinner with you is going to make me put out? You're out of your damn mind."

"Who said anything about sex?"

She turned toward him in the seat, ready to shout, but whatever she would have said was drowned out by the roar of the Aston.

"Buckle up," he said.

He drove as recklessly as she did, so she saw the wisdom in doing as he suggested. It took less than two minutes for them to be on the open road. The Aston ate up the pavement as the last rays of light left the sky. She glared at Angel who switched gears efficiently, smoothly. This was her car, so why the fuck was he driving? This couldn't be happening to her. She called the shots in her life, not anyone else, especially a slick crime lord from New York!

"You're going to regret this," she promised.

"I can't wait." He clucked his tongue. "This really is a beautiful car."

"What do you want, Angel?"

"Why don't you want Gavin to know you're a silent partner for the Red Diamond? I'm surprised you care what he thinks. Is it because it's a strip club?"

"It's not a strip club, it's a gentlemen's club, and Gavin knew me when I was a stripper. I don't care what he thinks. I just don't want him interfering."

"Whatever you're doing, you're doing it right. Every one of your investments yielded a double return. Why would he interfere?"

She stared straight ahead with her hands clasped between her legs so she wouldn't hit him and wreck her new car.

"He's the one you want to underestimate you. Why?"

He was using an off the charts intuition that was stripping her bare, and she didn't like the sensation. In one week, Angel Roman uncovered more about her than anyone ever had, even her parents. Her relationship with Gavin was complicated, unpleasant, and filled with old hurts that would never go away. They rarely saw eye to eye, and he was manipulative and ruthless enough to use anything to make her come to heel. "That's none of your business."

"I know enough for now," Angel said. "And I have no interest in your businesses as long as they cooperate."

"We always have," she gritted.

"I'm just making the rounds, introducing myself."

"And drugging them."

He shrugged. "Sometimes I pull out my gun; sometimes I shake hands. I usually let them lead. Kiki showed me her gun, so I showed her mine." He took his eyes off the road and shot her a veiled look. "Mine was bigger. If she'd been a man, she would have met a different fate. Instead, she visited La-La Land for a couple of hours."

Hearing that Kiki tried to defend herself mollified her a little. She pulled her cell phone and gun out of her purse. Angel hummed under his breath and tapped the wheel along to the beat playing in his head. Obviously, he was off his rocker. She dialed Kiki's number and waited for her to answer. On the last ring, she heard a weary, "Hey, babe."

"Tell me you're okay," she demanded, fingers tightening on her gun.

"I'm okay. Are you?"

"Me? Of course. I didn't get fucking drugged! Did he do anything else to you?"

"No, but Carmen, I told him everything." Kiki sounded uncharacteristically shaken. "I don't know what he gave me. I'm so sorry. I can't even remember everything I said—"

"It's okay. Did you go to the doctor? Do you need some time off? I can—"

"No, I'm fine. The next day, I felt like I had a hangover. He told me not to contact you, that he'd handle you himself. I've been so worried."

She glared at Angel who continued to use her steering wheel as a drum. Crazy fuck. "I'm fine. I'll kill him."

"Carmen," Kiki said sharply, "don't. No harm, no foul."

"He drugged you!" she shouted.

Angel didn't flinch, but he rolled down his window to drown out her voice.

"I'm fine. I would have done the same if I was in his position."

Kiki was justifying his actions? She closed her eyes as her temples throbbed. She tapped her forehead with the gun, and it was snatched out of her hand.

"Be careful," Angel admonished.

"I'm fine," Kiki reiterated in her ear.

"Let me know if he fucks with you again," she ordered before she hung up. She leaned back against the door and turned in his direction with her arms crossed. "How did you know Kiki had a silent partner?"

"Bank records," Angel said as he rolled up the window.

She stiffened. "I'm not on the bank records."

"I know, but the quarterly payments she did to an off-shore account got my attention."

Her nails dug into her skin. He knew everything. "What do you want?"

He glanced at her. "I want a lot of things, but right now, I'm focused on information."

"Information about what?"

"Everything. I want to know everything there is about everyone in this city."

"That's impossible."

He shrugged. "Well, not everyone, just the ones who have ties to the underworld. I didn't hurt your friend more than necessary. Why do you think I drugged her? Less effort, more forthcoming answers. Easy."

"You can't do this!"

He slanted her a glance devoid of amusement. "I can do whatever I want. That's a crime lord's right. He doesn't ask; he takes. You know this. You were married to one."

"For a week," she said through clenched teeth.

"No matter. You've been on the outskirts of the underworld your whole life. Once you know me better, you'll understand how I work."

"I don't want to get to know you."

"You do," he said with such confidence that her hands balled into fists.

"I don't."

"If I touched you right now, you wouldn't be wet?"

Her mouth dropped. "You conceited jackass! Pull over so I can beat your ass."

He laughed. "As much as I'd like to see you try, we have reservations and can't be late."

He was unbelievable.

They left the barren desert behind and entered the city, which was lit up and buzzing. He coasted down The Strip. Her car garnered a lot of attention. She glared at Angel who waved at a bunch of teenagers drooling over the Aston. She was trying to strategize an escape plan, but that went out the window when he turned off the bustling Strip. He cruised down a deserted street she wouldn't be caught dead on. The difference one street made off The Strip was unbelievable. Most of the stores had bars on the windows and looked abandoned.

Angel pulled into the deserted parking lot of a nude bar. The sign out front said, "The Pussycat," but only "The Pussy" was lit.

"This is a joke, right?" she asked as Angel slid out of the car.

He crouched down to look at her. "What do you mean?"

"This is where you have reservations?"

"Yeah."

"Nude bars don't have reservations!"

"This one does, and I don't want to be late." He shrugged back his sleeve to look at his watch. "I heard the wings are amazing."

She looked around the empty parking lot and street. Anyone with an ounce of common sense wouldn't drive down this lane for fear of being shot or assaulted. Her skin prickled just sitting in the car. She felt as if they were being watched. She reached for her gun on the dashboard and put it in her purse.

"I'm not going in there," she said.

Angel closed the door and rounded the car. Belatedly, she tried to lock the doors, but she wasn't fast enough. He opened her door and pulled her out. She stared at the dirty building, which made her skin itch.

"I can smell the STDs from here," she said.

"You're probably right. Don't fuck anyone but me then."

While she was trying to think of something scathing to say, he opened her purse and peered inside.

"What are you doing?" she asked as she snatched it from him.

"Phone, condoms, and a gun. My kind of girl."

"I'm not leaving my brand-new car out here! It's going to get stolen or vandalized."

He slid his arm over her shoulders. "Don't worry about it."

She shoved at him and got nowhere. "Don't tell me not to worry. I paid three hundred thousand for it!"

"It'll be fine."

"You're insane. Fine. Tell Gavin my secrets. I don't give a shit. I'm not going in there. I just bought these shoes, which will be covered in piss and jizz and God knows what else if I walk in there!" She pawed through her purse for her phone. "Here, call him. See if I care. You can suck my—"

Angel grabbed her phone, tossed it on the seat, and slammed the door.

"What's your deal?" she shouted and stomped her foot. "You want to get off at a nude bar? Be my guest. Me? I got better things to do like watch my hair grow! I danced at the Red Diamond, but this isn't my fucking scene. And if you think I'm the type of woman who will let you—"

Angel leaned down and hauled her over one shoulder. She screeched and slammed her purse against his ass.

"I'm going to kill you!"

He set her down in front of the door and pinned her against it. She raised furious eyes to his and froze. The easygoing façade was gone. His body was tense and revved up against hers. Her heart leaped into her throat. He wouldn't—

"Why did you dance at the Red Diamond?" he asked.

She blinked. "What?"

"Why'd you do it?"

"I don't understand—"

"Just answer."

"Because I wanted to!" she snapped. She was scared, excited, and confused as shit.

"You like the stage, the attention, the power. That's why you did it, right? You like the adrenaline rush."

She stared at him. "Are you gonna sell me or something? I'm not a whore."

His mouth quirked. "No, you're not. This would be easier if you were."

"What the hell are you talking about?"

His eyes hardened. "I'm gonna give you the high you're looking for."

Her heart skipped. "What? I don't—"

He leaned in so close their lips brushed as he said, "Keep close."

"I don't understand."

"You will."

12

Angel clasped her hand and pulled her inside. She blinked hastily as her eyes adjusted to the darkness. The only light came from the stage where two nude women danced not to music but a monotonous, relentless bass. The club was cluttered with empty tables and chairs. She glanced at the unmanned bar and then grimaced at the booth Angel stopped in front of.

"Get in," Angel said.

"I don't—"

Angel pushed her in and followed. She glared as he made himself comfortable. This place was a fucking dump. She didn't dare touch the table, which looked as if it had a month's worth of grime on it. She could just imagine what she was sitting on. She kept her back ramrod straight so her new sweater wouldn't touch the booth, which was no doubt filthy. At first, she thought they were the only ones in the bar, but she was mistaken. She could just make out other slouched figures in the far booths.

"What are we doing here?" she hissed.

"The chicken wings are amazing."

"You can't eat what they serve you! This place can't pass a health code inspection!"

A man rounded the stage with a large tray. He came straight to their table and placed two plates of chicken wings with a linen napkin on the table before he walked away without a word.

"See, we were almost late," Angel said as he shook out the napkin and placed it on his lap.

It was hard to see the wings, but they smelled delicious. Her mouth watered, but she wouldn't have eaten those wings unless she'd gone a week without food... and maybe not even then.

"What the hell is going on, Angel?"

He dug into his meal without answering her. No one moved except the girls on stage. Her skin prickled in warning. Something dangerous was going on here, but she couldn't figure out what. No one made eye contact; they all stared at the stage as if these women were the best dancers in the world, which they were *not*. No one was drinking or eating except Angel. What. The. Fuck.

The front door opened. She squinted as a man strode through the bar and took a seat at a booth three down from theirs. There was just enough light to make out Eli Stark's sharp, handsome features. The polished image he maintained while he was a cop was gone. Now, he had a five o'clock shadow that she had to admit looked good on him. His broodiness was off the charts. She knew Eli from her stripping days. Back then, he was called out to the Red Diamond on a weekly basis. She'd witnessed him in action. He was a heartless bastard.

"Eli Stark's here," she muttered.

"What do you know about him?" Angel asked as he stared down at his plate instead of taking in their surroundings.

"He's cold and ruthless."

"Loyal?"

"He has his own code of what's right or wrong."

Angel nodded. "Sounds like my kind of man."

Several bikers came out from behind the stage and claimed stools at the empty bar. They, too, stared at the dancers as if riveted by the show. Their guns were on full display.

She gripped Angel's arm. "We should go."

"Why?"

She leaned in close to whisper, "Black Vipers."

"The what?"

"The bikers at the bar. They're the most violent gang on the West Coast. They don't have loyalties to anyone."

Angel licked his finger. "They'll behave."

"What the fuck is going on?"

"I'm eating wings."

"Fuck the wings, Angel. What—" She broke off as the front door opened again.

Another group of men filed in, but this time, they were well-dressed and definitely shouldn't be in a place like this. Their leader, George Wotherton, handled most of the Pyre fortune and was an old crony of Uncle Manny's. George knew all the loopholes to keep the Pyre's money hidden and untraceable. Despite the fact that George was essentially on their side, she never liked him. He arranged all five of his daughter's marriages and frequented The Strip with his sons-in-law, who worked for him and were currently occupying two tables in front of the stage.

She gripped Angel's thigh beneath the table. "That's George Wotherton."

He tensed but didn't stop eating. "Who?"

"He's Gavin's banker."

"You trust him?" Angel asked without looking away from his chicken wings.

"No."

"Why?" She hesitated, and he finally looked up from his plate. "Tell me why, Carmen."

"He's a pervert. He has a fetish for unconscious women. His sons-in-law are no different. They all work at his bank."

Angel considered her words and nodded before he pushed away one plate and went for the other. One of the dancers stumbled, which got her attention. She focused on the two women who couldn't dance for shit and examined them more closely. They were thin. Too thin. Their movements were jerky, awkward, and obviously untrained.

When one of the women dared to look into the silent crowd, Carmen jolted.

"She can't be older than eighteen!"

"She is," Angel said.

"How do you know?"

"Because I asked the last time I was here."

She stared at him. "You've come here more than once?" She was appalled and totally turned off. Some guys had darker tastes when it came to sex, and it appeared that Angel was one of them. He made it clear he was attracted to her, so she thought he would want a strong woman, but if he liked watching what looked like young teenagers with no curves and that scared, submissive expression, maybe he was—

"I didn't come here for the girls," Angel said. "But I asked about them because I thought they were underage. They turned eighteen this week."

"And they're on stage?" It happened but going totally nude a week into your eighteenth birthday was hardcore, and the girls on stage looked far from the defiant, rebellious teens one would expect.

"Apparently, that's what they go for here. As young as legally possible, untrained, and amateur."

The girls on stage were getting worse by the minute. She couldn't blame them. She doubted that this place was ever full, and within a half hour, nearly every table and booth was now occupied by a silent spectator. Two new dancers stumbled on stage, and the other two scurried off. These two were a little better than the first. They had a little more meat on their bones and fake boobs. They sent winning smiles into the crowd as they attempted to climb the poles and promptly slid back to earth.

Carmen fisted her hands in her lap. She wanted to drag the girls backstage and lecture them on clubs where they could make more money if they just had some training. She glared at Angel, who ate his wings as if he was at a five-star restaurant instead of a dumpy bar. She should make a scene and get out of here, but her damn curiosity kept her in place. Something big was about to go down; she just didn't know what.

More people filed into the bar. She eyed each of them in turn. The ones she recognized sent a wave of dread through her. She couldn't resist leaning into Angel to warn him about the notorious characters. Nothing made an impression on him.

The crowd in The Pussy was one of the most eclectic and confusing she had ever seen. Wealthy bankers and politicians sat next to gang leaders and criminals while police officers and other government officials rubbed shoulders with bikers and CEOs. She assumed they were here for Angel, but he seemed more concerned with finishing his wings than addressing anyone, and no one paid them any mind. She knew the upper echelon guys, the ones she and Vinny rubbed shoulders with at fundraisers and obligatory parties. She recognized the gangs and bikers from their tattoos, patches, or colors. Her dad would shit a brick if he knew she was within a quarter mile of any of these guys, much less in a room full of them.

She was trying to place a vaguely familiar face in the crowd when she spotted George Wotherton disappear down a hallway beside the stage. She tensed. There was probably a bathroom back there, but... she elbowed Angel.

"Move," she hissed.

"What?"

"Move. I have to check on something."

He held up stained hands. "I'm almost done. I'll go with you to the bathroom."

"It may be too late—move!"

Angel stood with his hands in front of him. She grabbed her purse and walked down the middle of the room to avoid the Black Vipers. She wasn't sure if the current leader, Maddog, knew that her father killed his over fifteen years ago, but she wasn't taking the chance. As she rounded the stage, she reached into her purse and felt the reassuring weight of her gun. She flipped the safety off and paused in a hallway that was just as filthy and damaged as the rest of the place. The lights flickered. A minute later, a door at the end of the hall opened, and George Wotherton appeared, dragging one of the nude dancers under one arm. He raised his head and noticed her standing there.

"Carmen Pyre," he said with a jovial smile and continued toward her.

She pulled out her gun. "Put her down, George."

"Why?"

"What'd you do to her?"

"Just a little roofie. She agreed. I gave her one hundred dollars."

Carmen blocked the entrance to the bathroom. "Give her to me."

George frowned. "She's willing."

"No."

George Wotherton wore gold spectacles, a signet ring on his finger, and an oatmeal-colored suit. One would mistake him for a civilized gentleman if it wasn't for the unconscious naked woman he had tucked under his arm like an old jacket.

George focused on her breasts. "You took out your implants? That's a shame."

Just being near him made her skin crawl. Between wife two and three, George approached her at a party and asked if she would be interested in a mistress or wife position for ten million. She had been too stunned to respond appropriately. His utter gall left her speechless then and now. "Fuck you, George."

"I wish. You know I've always wanted you. Have you fallen on hard times?" he asked hopefully.

"No!"

"Damn shame." George scanned her with a leer. "Still a knockout, I see."

"Give her to me."

"I paid for her."

He sounded like a spoiled child. He was talking about fucking a person as casually as if he wanted the last cookie on a plate. A chill ran up her spine. "Give."

George glared at her. "What are you gonna do about it?"

"George."

Angel's voice carried over the relentless beat of music that matched her heartbeat. Angel's voice was harder and deeper than it had been when he spoke to her a minute ago. George tensed as Angel looked from him to the unconscious woman in his arms.

"Put her back, George," Angel said.

George's rat eyes darted from Carmen to Angel and then to the woman in his arms.

"George." George ducked his head as if Angel yelled. "Now."

George nodded and turned to take the woman back to the room at the end of the hall. He muttered under his breath as he went. Carmen stared at the girl's feet which flopped from side to side as George dragged her. She put her gun in her purse as Angel went into the bathroom to wash his hands. She counted under her breath. Just as she started down the hall, George appeared in the hallway, wiping his face. It took her only a moment to figure out what he'd done.

"You dirty old fuck!"

George scowled at her. "I left her the hundred."

"But you licked her."

He shrugged. "She would've let me do much worse."

"You—"

Angel grasped her hand. "Fuck on your time, not mine, George. We clear?"

George's hands wove through the air. "You were eating and..."

"And it's still my time. You think I would have delayed the festivities until you finished fucking?"

"You're right, Roman. Quite right. I apologize."

George scurried ahead of them as they walked down the hallway.

"Angel," she began.

"Not now," he said quietly.

They walked into the bar, and this time, she felt every single eye on them. As Angel made his way through the crowd, the music stopped. She tensed, but Angel gave her hand a reassuring squeeze before he stepped aside so she could slide into the booth. The dancers gave dazzling smiles before they teetered off stage. Angel's plates were gone, and now that the music stopped, a foreboding, buzzing silence filled the room. Her skin prickled. The strobe lights shut off, and normal lights came on around the bar, flickering and fucking with her eyes. All heads turned in their direction, and as she eyed the men, she realized that this hole in the wall bar was filled with the most dangerous and influential men in the city. Anyone with ties to the underworld was here. Enemies, former allies, and the many, many questionable ones who flip-flopped sides on a whim. Whatever happened in Hell had brought even the Black Vipers out of the woodworks. Lecherous, greedy, soulless eyes focused on her. She resisted the urge to pull out her gun.

Angel leaned back against the table and looked around the room. "I'm Angel Roman, but you all know that. The war between Gavin and Vega is finished, but you know that as well, which is why you're here." Angel grinned. "Some of you came to plead your allegiance, others are here to assess whether they can take me, and the rest of you…" He scanned the room slowly, taking his time, letting the tension increase with each passing second. "The rest of you are here to see what I'm going to offer for allegiance."

A soundless murmur went through the crowd, but she couldn't make out any words or where it was coming from. Angel clapped his hands together. If she wasn't holding herself so still, she might have flinched. Two lawyers and one of George's sons-in-law jolted. The Black Vipers gave them disdainful sneers.

Angel spread his hands wide. "I'm not offering you shit for your loyalty."

Maddog, the leader of the Black Vipers, stirred. He had a bald head with a thick goatee. "You expect loyalty for nothing in return?"

"Yes."

The bikers weren't the only ones who muttered under their breath. There were infinitesimal shifts as the occupants glanced at one another. Angel pushed off from the table and began to walk around the room. She wanted to grab the back of his jacket to keep him by her side, but she stayed where she was. Any show of weakness would tip the scales. She slipped her hand into her purse and gripped her tiny gun and maintained an "I don't give a shit" expression that she hoped passed muster. Her senses were dangerously elevated due to the danger saturating the room. She was sure the guy at the next booth could hear her heart racing.

"Why would any of us agree to that?" Maddog asked.

"Because you don't have a choice," Angel said without looking directly at him. He clapped a man on the back who sported two black eyes and a split lip. "Tommy, I'm glad you made it."

Angel weaved through the tables, almost as if he was counting heads.

"What happened to Pyre?" a lawyer asked.

"He's out."

"Why?"

"Family."

"Pussy whipped," someone muttered.

Angel stopped in his tracks and turned to face a table of three. He slid his hands into his pockets as he surveyed each of them in turn. The way the men sat at the table spoke volumes. They weren't in uniform, but she recognized them as a unit. She recognized one as a cop, but she was sure the other two were military men from Nellis Air Force Base.

Angel put one hand on the table and leaned toward the largest man who looked like he had a steel rod strapped to his spine, his posture was so straight. "General Leeward, is it?"

If it was possible, he sat up even straighter. "Yes."

"Funny you mention pussy whipped." Angel tapped his fingers on the table. "Don't you have a sixteen-year-old mistress?"

A loaded silence filled the room. She silently willed Angel to ease back, but he didn't. He stood less than a foot from a man who looked like he could have been a professional wrestler. She didn't have to be as close as Angel to know the guy was furious.

"You're waiting for her to graduate, isn't that right?" Angel winked at General Leeward. "Talk about pussy whipped. Gavin found a woman worthy of the family name. Lyla has kills under her belt unlike your… What do you call her? Girlfriend, daughter?" Angel waved his hand. "Well, that's neither here nor there. Lyla didn't make

Gavin weak; she made him stronger, and if you think I'm wrong..." Angel pulled his phone out of his pocket and slid it across the table to the general who didn't move a muscle. "Call him and tell him yourself."

Holy fuck. Angel was insane. A bead of sweat trickled down her back as she waited for all hell to break loose. She waited... and waited.

"That's what I thought." Angel grabbed his phone and pocketed it. "You wouldn't be where you are today without Emmanuel's help, and you know you wouldn't win against Gavin financially, politically, or physically, so take my advice, General, and shut the fuck up unless I tell you to speak. Got it?"

Carmen held her breath. Oh, fuck. Oh, fuck. This was it. He'd gone too far...

The proud, wizened general gave him a minute nod of agreement. Angel turned his back on him. She waited for the general to reach into his jacket and pull out a gun or toss a knife, but he sat there, seething. Angel was making enemies of some of the most powerful men in the city. Holy shit.

"This is what I'm talking about," Angel said as he continued to meander through the tables of motionless men. "I think there's been a lot of miscommunication about this position. None of you has ever gotten close to being kingpin, so let me tell you how it goes. I take; I don't ask. I speak, and you do what I say. Rebel and your life is forfeit. There are rules, my rules, and no other. Are we clear?"

"No."

Heads turned toward Maddog, the leader of the Black Vipers, but she kept her eyes on the crowd. The tension in the room made the hairs on the nape of her neck stand up. A man at a table to the left of the general reached into his jacket and pulled out a knife. She rose and withdrew her gun, but Eli got there first. He grabbed the knife from the man before he could toss it and slit his throat with an efficiency that said he'd done this before. The man's table companions shot to their feet as blood splattered everywhere.

Eli's eyes met hers for a split second before he wiped his hands on the man's coat and retreated to the edge of the room where he leaned against the wall, cool as you please. Carmen turned her head and found Angel watching her with a calculating expression as she lowered her gun. She was breathing hard as if she ran a marathon.

"You think you can walk in here with no more backup than an ex-cop and Vinny's slut?" Maddog sneered.

She focused on Maddog as he bared silver teeth.

"You and Pyre think your money and name is enough to protect you. It isn't." Maddog tucked his thumbs into his jeans. "You're in my territory, my city. I'm not about to let some East Coast fuck take over my town." He looked around the room, proud and silently looking for votes before he refocused on Angel. "Vega showed us one thing. Gavin can be defeated, which means you can too. You bleed just as easy as the rest of us."

No one breathed.

"I think it's time for new blood, Roman."

His eyes flicked to her. Dark eyes glittered with hatred. He knew exactly who she was. Her skin prickled, and her hand tightened on the gun.

"Did Pyre tell you what happened to his other cousin who tried to take his throne? That little bitch didn't even last a week." He smiled at her. "It was a joke for Vinny to take Gavin's place. It was only a matter of time before someone gunned him down. I heard that fucker squealed and tried to run for his life. Gavin signed his cousin's death warrant—"

Carmen raised her gun. Maddog laughed and elbowed the men on either side of him who had their hands on their weapons. Maddog spread his arms wide.

"What are you gonna do with that, princess? I'll give you one free shot. I dare you—"

The first bullet went through his bicep. He grabbed his arm and cursed, but he didn't have time to reach for his gun. The second bullet got him in the chest before Angel did a head shot that sprayed the bar and everyone around him with blood. For a moment, there was absolute silence, and then the bar erupted.

The man in the booth beside her got to his feet and shoved her to the ground. He stood over her as the members of the Black Viper gang withdrew guns as everyone turned on one another. The sound of gunfire was deafening. From her prone position, she saw Angel put down three bikers with head shots. Blood splashed over the filthy floor. Rapid gunshots sounded behind her. She peered through the legs of her protector and saw Eli and several other men take down those who tried to fight back or make a run for it. The general sat in the midst of the bloodbath, splattered with blood, eyes trained on Angel.

When silence fell once more, she slowly got to her feet. The metallic scent of blood assaulted her nostrils as Angel surveyed the room.

"Never underestimate how many allies a man has in the room." He focused on her, and her stomach clenched. "And never taunt a woman who's lost someone she loves."

Carmen lowered her gun but didn't put it away.

"Let the rest of the Black Vipers know I'm coming for them. I don't believe in survivors," Angel said.

He walked to her and held out a hand. She didn't want skin contact at the moment, but she knew everyone was watching. This wasn't about her; it was about his image as the new boss. She wasn't allowed to disrespect him in front of the underworld. She grabbed her purse before she took his hand and clenched her teeth as he laced their hands together. He pulled her through the ranks of silent men. She felt a presence behind them. When she glanced back, she saw Eli on their heels with a gun in each hand.

Angel pushed the door open into the chilly night. She sucked in a breath of fresh air and jerked her hand away. He didn't push the issue. He opened the passenger door of the Aston. She got in without making eye contact, dropped her purse between her feet, and stared straight ahead.

There was the low murmur of male voices as Eli and Angel walked several feet away to talk.

In the week she'd been awakened, she'd been a slave to her

impulses—food, cars, sex. Tonight, the taste for blood ignited, and she reacted. *It was only a matter of time before someone gunned him down.* The incandescent rage that compelled her to shoot still coursed through her veins. There was a roar caught in her throat. Something dark and lethal fought to erupt out of her skin. It took every ounce of control she possessed not to give in to the need to let her demons free.

Angel slid into the driver's seat. "You okay?"

"Take me home," she said quietly.

Angel pulled away from The Pussy. He drove down the unlit lane before he turned onto The Strip. The return to civilization didn't make her feel better. Neither did the crowds or energy, which never failed to lift her spirits. All she could see was that fucker's face as he talked about Vinny—the disdain and satisfaction that they put him down. Like he was a dog or deer—something weak and vulnerable and fair game. Her senses were hyper elevated. A tangled mess of emotions rumbled inside her, demanding to be set free to wreak havoc on her surroundings.

"You had my back in there," Angel said.

She had given her allegiance without thought. Even though he blackmailed her into going and drugged Kiki, she'd been willing to defend him. The ties of family loyalty were engraved in her bones.

"Why did you take me tonight?" she whispered.

"You were looking for a rush."

"I wasn't."

"You were," he countered easily. "I recognize another restless soul when I see one."

"You don't know anything about me," she growled as she wrapped her arms around herself to conceal the fine shaking slowly creeping through her arms.

Angel coasted on the freeway, which quickly took them away from The Strip. "Baby, I know you better than you think."

"You don't know shit."

"I don't? Okay, how about this? You changed after Vinny died.

One of two things happen when people like us lose someone to violence."

"Like us?" she echoed. "I'm nothing like you."

"You're not? You wouldn't do whatever it takes to protect your loved ones?" He slanted her a look. "Even kill to protect their memory?"

She stared straight ahead.

"When you lose someone to a violent crime, it changes you," Angel said as he sped up, changed lanes, and navigated with ease. "Either you shut down and try to forget, or you embrace the dark and fight back." He grinned as he shifted gears. "You know which I chose."

"You shouldn't have taken me. I was in a room full of the most notorious cons, murderers, and rapists in the city!"

"You were covered."

"Covered?" she echoed, voice rife with disbelief. "You were practically begging them to kill you."

He shrugged. "They need to know who's boss."

"You're a fucking crazy man. Take this exit."

He followed her directions. She was too fucked up to enjoy the new car smell, the roar of the engine, or the ease with which he drove. His words sloshed around in her head.

She couldn't stop herself from asking, "Who did you lose?"

"My parents." His voice held no inflection.

She opened her mouth to ask more questions but then shut it. She didn't want anyone asking questions about Vinny, so she would let it be.

"If you're born into a crime family, there's no escape. Even if you try to fight it, sooner or later, you lose someone to the underworld, and you have to choose. You either let them get away with it and turn your back on your family, or you get even and destroy everyone associated with them."

She stared at the way the light revealed and then concealed his features as they sped past buildings lining the freeway.

"Raul handles it better than the rest of us. If it wasn't for their murders, he would probably be the fucking mayor of New York. Instead, he does what he needs to for the family. Loyalty. That's all we know. You fuck with one of us, you fuck with all of us, and you bear our wrath. I wear my parent's tainted memory on my skin for everyone to see, and I send motherfuckers like their murderers to hell with a smile. That's what pushes all of us, including you."

"No," she said faintly.

"Let me guess. What used to satisfy you won't do it for you anymore. That's why you're out every night, why you were dancing on stage at the strip club. Your cheap thrills won't work anymore."

"Gentlemen's club," she muttered.

"I know what works for my cravings." He glanced at her. "You need to find out what yours is."

Her restless, insatiable hunger jumped from food to bloodlust at the speed of light. No one could have stopped her. It was probably only sheer disbelief that she would do something so stupid in front of witnesses that kept anyone from reacting faster. The wrath Maddog ignited still burned in her gut. Tonight, she killed a man in cold blood without an iota of remorse. Even now, she felt nothing. If she could kill him again, she would. *Gavin signed his death warrant.* The words knocked around in her head. She bowed her head and curled her toes in her shoes in a vain attempt to keep memories of Vinny from intruding.

"I'll take care of the Black Vipers," Angel said.

"What?" she whispered.

"They won't touch you. That's why I took the head shot. Hopefully, I can get eyes off you by claiming the kill."

She froze. For the first time, she stopped thinking about why she killed and focused on the other part—*who*. She killed the leader of the Black Vipers, the most notorious and violent biker gang on the West Coast. Fuck. "My mom—"

"I'll get some guys to watch your place."

She dropped her face in her hand. Just when the danger should have disappeared, she reignited it by doing something monumentally stupid. "Shit."

"I'll take care of it. I was planning to kill him myself, but if it made you feel better, so be it."

He didn't give two shits that she killed a man in cold blood. Even as it soothed her bloodlust, a voice in the back of her head said something was very wrong about the fact that Angel thought killing people was appropriate if it made you feel better. And on that note...

"What the hell was that?"

"My introduction as crime lord." He gave a one-shoulder shrug. "Everything went according to plan, including killing Maddog. I just didn't expect you to be the one to do it."

"You planned to kill him all along and took me with you? Are you crazy?"

"Your father was an enforcer, and you were married to Vinny. I doubt much shocks you. Besides, you've killed before."

"That was self-defense!" she shouted and then realized where they were. "Turn left." Angel obeyed, and she continued her rant. "I don't kill people when I'm bored."

"No, only when provoked. It was your right to kill him, Carmen."

She leaned toward him, sure any moment now she would breathe fire. "You shouldn't have forced me to go with you! I fucking killed a man, and you made enemies with all the big players in the city! You need allies, not more enemies. Fuck. You have a death wish."

"I know what I'm doing."

"They are going to kill you," she enunciated, clapping her hands for emphasis with each word. "And me too. Turn here."

"They can try," Angel said absently as he looked around. "This neighborhood is..."

"Not what you're used to?" she quipped. "Yeah, I know, rich boy."

"Doesn't look like someplace you'd be either, sweetheart, when you have the fortune you do. Your shoes cost more than the mortgage for these houses."

"I grew up here."

"And live with your mom?"

"Actually, I'm looking for a new place, and the sooner, the better it seems."

"There's a property near mine. Actually, maybe it's better if—"

"No," she clipped. "Turn left on Craig Road."

"Maybe you should move back with Gavin and Lyla."

"I'm fine." She was so far from fine, it was ridiculous, but she wasn't about to tell him that.

Angel followed her terse directions and pulled up to her family house. He put the car in park in her driveway. "I was hoping to give your demons what they needed tonight."

It was almost nice in a fucked-up way. He was trying to help her. He understood her cravings and tried to feed them. She let out a long breath. "We're alive. That's all that matters."

"There was never going to be another outcome."

Arrogant. "How are you going home?"

He pushed open his door and climbed out. "Eli's tracking me. He shouldn't be far behind."

"So, he's your second?"

"If you want to call him that." A car slowed down at the end of the driveway. "I think this is him."

She heard a sharp ping that she didn't understand until his body jerked. Two more muffled shots made him reel back as he took the bullets to the chest. No. Rage blotted out common sense and fear. She grabbed her gun and tossed herself over the console and peeked her head out the driver's side. Three men approached with their guns drawn to finish him off. It was a reenactment of Vinny's murder. This couldn't be happening to her again.

Her first shot went wide, but her second got one of them in the shin, and another in the man's throat. A bullet lodged in the Aston less than six inches from her face, but she didn't flinch. She was trying to get her bearings to make the last shot count when Angel shot two of them from his prone position. Sharp, earsplitting cracks split the air as Eli jogged up the driveway with a gun in each hand and took out the last hit man.

Carmen bent over Angel, hands going to his chest, ready to apply pressure to keep him from bleeding out. She touched him, expecting to feel the sticky wetness of fresh blood, but there was nothing.

"Angel?"

"I'm wearing a vest," he wheezed.

It took her a few seconds to process. When it did, she fell back on her ass. Angel sat up with a wince and gingerly touched his ruined shirt, marred by three holes on his chest.

"Fuck, that hurt," Angel hissed.

Eli cursed under his breath and turned to confront her curious neighbors, who'd gathered in the street. Adrenaline drained from her as fast as it came. The horror of watching Vinny's murder play out right in front of her with another man who claimed the crime lord position after Gavin stepped down was too much.

"Carmen?" Angel crouched beside her and touched her clammy skin. "Are you all right?"

She looked up at his handsome, arrogant face. She wasn't sure whether she wanted to throw herself in his arms or murder him. "No, I'm not."

"What's wrong?"

She shook her head. "I can't."

"Can't what?"

She forced herself up on shaky legs and faced Angel, who thought he was invincible. Vinny's death destroyed her so badly she wasn't sure she would ever be okay again. She saw Vinny one last time before he was cremated. The memory of his blood-stained dress shirt and his open, horror-glazed eyes was ingrained in her mind for eternity. Angel's fearlessness scared the hell out of her. Was he really that good or setting himself up for a bloody ending? He thought he could conquer the world and bring these men to heel. He thought his name and smarts were enough, but she knew the truth. Nothing would ever be enough.

"I can't," she said again.

"Can't what?"

"Watch another man die. I've lost too much. I don't have much left."

Angel searched her face. He opened his mouth to say something, but Eli called his name and distracted him. She took the key out of the Aston Martin and put her gun in the purse before she walked toward the house. It was Angel's job to lie and do whatever he had to, to make the three dead bodies disappear. She was so fucking done.

It took several attempts to unlock her door since her hand was shaking so badly. When she finally got in, she leaned back against the door and closed her eyes.

"It's done," she whispered. "It's over."

Even as she said the words, she shook her head. Her mind kept replaying the way Angel jerked when he got shot, and the awful sound he made as the wind got knocked out of him. How many times had her mind reenacted Vinny's murder?

She walked upstairs, pushed open her door, and stared at Vinny's urn. Her heart cracked, and so did the wall of denial. She dropped her purse and keys in the doorway and advanced as first one tear fell and then another. She sank to her knees in front of the dresser, buried her face in the carpet, and gave into the need to scream. The carpet muffled her tortured howl, so she did it again and again. She beat her hands against the rug until her fists were throbbing. If she had the strength, she would have destroyed her room, so it matched her insides.

Tonight, her deepest, darkest secret had been shoved in her face. It was a truth she had been avoiding since his murder. She'd never spoken the words out loud, never allowed herself to think about it because it would destroy her. The leader of the Black Viper gang was right. Someone had signed Vinny's death warrant, but it wasn't Gavin. It was her.

"I'm sorry, Vinny," she whispered. "It's my fault."

13

THREE YEARS AGO

Carmen bounced on her toes as she watched Gavin and Lyla share a deep kiss. It took less than two weeks for Lyla and Gavin to pull their heads out of their asses. No one watching them would suspect they'd been apart for three years. The connection between them was electric. A couple of days ago, Lyla had been putting up the good fight and doing everything possible to hold him off and now… now, everything was back the way it should be. Her heart felt as if it could burst with happiness.

"You taste good," Gavin said.

"It's meatloaf," Lyla replied.

"Damn, that sounds good."

Gavin turned to Carmen and kissed her cheek. "Thanks for keeping Lyla company."

She and Gavin had some rocky encounters during Lyla's absence, but all of that was done now. The man looking back at her was a Gavin she hadn't seen in years.

"No problem, and thanks for keeping her here permanently," she said with a wink before she dashed to the car and slipped into the passenger seat. "Don't they look happy?" she demanded as Vinny pulled away from the Pyre estate.

"They do," he said. "How's Lyla really doing?"

Her euphoria dimmed. "As good as she can be after being kidnapped and possibly raped." Guilt lay heavy on her shoulders.

During a trip to the mall, Lyla had been kidnapped. No one had ever done something so stupid. Gavin recovered Lyla within a couple of hours, but the damage was done. She visited Lyla today for the first time since she had been recovered from an abandoned warehouse. Lyla was clearly shaken, and there was a raw fragility to her cousin that made her lightheaded with rage.

Vinny clasped her hand and squeezed. "It's not your fault."

"It is."

"No, it isn't."

"I shouldn't have let her go off on her own."

"Gavin will take care of it and send a message to whoever's fucking with us."

She turned toward him and pressed his hand against her breasts. "She's staying," she stage-whispered and then threw her arms wide. "She's staying!"

He shot her an amused glance. "I heard."

"Fucking Gavin." She sighed and rolled down the window and sat sideways with her feet in Vinny's lap. "I knew he could do it."

Vinny stroked her leg. "Was there any doubt?"

"Well, he fucked it up when he roughed her up and scared the bejesus out of her. He's such an idiot."

It had been a long week. First, Vinny told her Lyla was back; then she saw Lyla's bruised and terrified state. It was no wonder Uncle Manny lost his shit and gave Lyla sanctuary. Boy fucking lost his mind. Despite his immense stupidity, she saw the way Gavin watched Lyla. He was a hard son of a bitch, but she'd known him long enough to see past the tough exterior. He loved Lyla, always had. Why he cheated on her, she would never know, but this was the most animated she had seen him in years.

"She left him," Vinny said.

"He cheated on her!"

Vinny pat her leg. "That's done. She's staying."

She held up her hands and took a breath. "Right. Let's focus on the positives. My girl is fucking back! I missed her so much."

"I know."

"It's fucked up that it took this to get them back together." She bit her lip. "Is it bad that I'm happy about it if it brought them together?"

Vinny shrugged. "Don't think about it. Just focus on the now."

She knelt on her seat, wrapped her arms around his neck, and kissed the side of his face. "That's why I love you. You're so practical and cute." She nibbled on his ear and undid the top buttons of his shirt. "You're getting lucky tonight."

"I love my life."

She chuckled as she ran her hand through his thick chest hair. "And I love mine. I found a man who worships me."

"That you do," he said as her hand dropped to his lap. "And I have a woman obsessed with me. What's not to love?"

She stroked him through his slacks. "You think it'll ever fade?"

"No."

There wasn't a shred of uncertainty in his voice.

"How do you know?"

"Because it keeps getting worse," he said as he arched into her hand.

"Worse?" she repeated with a frown.

He unzipped his slacks and forced her hand around his dick. She obliged, and he let out a hum of delight.

"On our anniversary, I think about how I felt when we first started dating and comparing it to now..." He sighed as she stroked him. "No fucking comparison."

She smiled as she leaned down to take him in her mouth. His hand sifted through her hair.

"You don't play games anymore."

She raised her head. "What?"

"Carmen." His dick poked her cheek as he raised his hips. She pushed his hand away, which tried to keep her head down.

"What do you mean, games?"

He groaned. "You can't stop now."

"Yes, I can. What are you talking about?"

"Come on, Carmen. You were always up to something. Flirting with other guys, throwing a fit over something. You put me through the wringer to see if I would fight for you."

She smacked his chest. "You didn't want to commit!"

He grinned. "Can you blame me?"

"Yes!" She sat in her seat with her arms crossed. "You played games too."

"I did," he said agreeably and fisted his dick. "But this isn't a joke. Come on, babe."

She tipped her nose in the air. "You dated that slut, Felicia."

"Oh, hell. Don't bring her up now—"

"You dated her for two weeks!"

"You were with Kody Singer."

"So? She actually tried to talk to me. What a bitch... What are you doing?"

Vinny pulled off the highway in the middle of nowhere and turned off the car.

"What the hell are you—?"

Vinny dragged her over the console, cupped her face, and kissed her. She tried to shove him away, but he held tight and kept it up until she relaxed. He pulled her thong to the side and worked himself in her.

"We both played games," he breathed. "We both dated other people, but we always came back to each other. You know why?"

She glared at him even as she swiveled her hips to take him deep. "Why?"

"Because we love each other. There was never going to be anyone else for either of us. It's like Gavin and Lyla. We wouldn't be who we are without the other." He stared into her eyes as she moved on him. "You fought to get away from me and then you fought to get me back."

She hadn't wanted to be tied down when she was younger, but she'd never been able to let Vinny walk off with some other woman. She'd been wild and rebellious and sabotaged his relationships if he looked like he was getting serious with anyone. "You're mine."

He smiled. "Yes. Always. Now, show me."

She took her time. She didn't care that cars passed while she tortured him. The car was more likely to get someone's attention, but they had a gun if someone thought they were stranded and would be easy game. She used her years of experience to drive him crazy. She laughed when he reclined the seat, rolled her beneath him, and fucked her. A warm breeze brushed over their sweaty bodies as they came down from the high.

"I love you," Vinny whispered.

"I know," she said as she ran her hand through his sweaty hair.

He raised his head. "Gavin's stepping down."

"I know. I can't believe it."

Gavin had been born to rule, and he did so with a ruthlessness that kept everyone in check. Gavin deciding to give up his position was like giving up a chunk of his identity. It proved beyond a doubt that he loved Lyla more than anything else.

Vinny positioned them on their sides, so they faced one another. "He needs a replacement."

"I know. Does he have someone in mind?"

He tensed. "I offered."

"Wait, what?"

"You don't think I can?"

"Uh, yeah, I'm sure you could but..."

"But what?"

Her husband presented a polished and suave exterior, but he battled crippling anxiety. He had always been a worrier and was constantly making lists because he was terrified of making a mistake. Vinny concealed his disorder well, but it was still there. It stemmed from his need to fit in with the Pyres after his parents died.

"What did Gavin say when you offered?"

"He said no." Vinny sat up, and she scooted onto the console as he straightened his clothes. "He doesn't think I'm tough enough."

"Why do you want to do it?"

"Everyone looks up to Gavin. Everyone knows his name. I want that respect. I want to make Uncle Manny and Gavin proud." He gestured with his hands as he spoke, which betrayed his anxiety. "There's something about men like your dad, Gavin, and Blade... There's a camaraderie between them that I don't have. I've always been second to Gavin, as it should be, but this may be my only chance to see if I've got what it takes, you know?"

His face was creased with uncertainty. He gripped her thigh and squeezed gently.

"You think I can do it, right, babe?"

"Of course, I do. You know how to shoot a gun." She held up one finger. "You're a Pyre." Another finger. "You know all of Gavin's contacts, and your father-in-law is a legendary enforcer. No one would dare fuck with you."

"That's true." His face clouded. "Gavin doesn't think I have what it takes."

How many times had she heard that line over the years? It was always, "Gavin said" or "Gavin thinks that..." Vinny idolized his cousin and cared more about Gavin's opinion than hers. Gavin could do no wrong in his eyes. They had argued way too much about him over the years, especially after Lyla disappeared. Vinny always defended and deferred to Gavin, and it drove her up the wall. It was like having a third person in their relationship.

"Screw Gavin. Lots of times he told you that you weren't ready, and you always proved him wrong. This is no different."

"But he said—"

"Tomorrow, you talk to him again, and this time, you don't take no for an answer. You've gone to underworld meetings with Gavin. He can pass his anointing to you. This is your opportunity to prove him wrong once and for all."

"You really think I can do this?"

"Of course, I do."

He cupped her nape and drew her down for a sweet kiss. "You make me believe I can do anything."

"That's what a good wife does." She nuzzled close. "If it doesn't work out, Gavin can always find someone else, right?"

"Right."

"He just needs to stop being such a control freak." She slid into the passenger seat and clapped her hands together. "Now we have two things to celebrate!"

"We do?"

"Yes, Lyla staying and your new promotion!"

He smiled as he started up the car. "What do you think about me being crime lord?"

"I think it's fucking hot. You were born for this."

"What do you think your dad will say?" Vinny asked as he started the car and pulled onto the highway.

"He'll probably give you a lot of pointers and be really proud of you."

"That's what I think."

"He was always happy I didn't end up with Gavin, but I think it's just because it's Gavin. I don't think it had anything to do with him being crime lord. Besides, Dad worked for Uncle Manny and... Well, you know the rest. I think this is going to work out perfect. Gavin can focus more on Lyla, and we'll be good."

"We will," he said and squeezed her hand. "That's why I love you. You take everything in stride. You're the perfect crime lord's wife."

She straightened. "I need a new wardrobe."

He laughed.

"You be careful, Vincent."

"I will. I'm a Pyre, baby. We're indestructible."

"You better be."

Vinny spent the rest of the journey going over his speech for Gavin. When they reached home, she told him to start a bubble bath while she fetched champagne. When he went upstairs, she filched her phone from her purse and tapped speed dial three. She was climbing on her counter to reach the flutes from their wedding when Gavin answered.

"Carmen."

"Vinny's gonna give you a pitch about why he's the best candidate to be the new crime lord. You're going to accept his offer," she said crisply as she jumped down.

"You want him to do this?" Gavin asked.

"Yes."

"Why?"

"He wants to do it, so I support him."

"It's dangerous."

"I know that," she snapped as she retrieved a chilled bottle of pink champagne from the fridge. She always had chilled bubbly. One never knew when there would be cause to celebrate. She tended to find at least one thing every week. "My dad was an enforcer. I know the danger, and so does Vinny. If he says he can do it, then he can."

"No."

"You know what's your problem?" she asked as she pulled off the wrapper and got to work on the cork. "You're a control freak. You need to learn how to delegate. Lyla needs you, and she wants you to give this up. Vinny's the best man for the job. You trust him, he knows all your connections, and who the hell is going to mess with him? He's a fucking Pyre! Come on."

Silence on the other end.

"If he doesn't work out, fine, but let him try. You know what it cost him to get up the courage to approach you, and you just shut him down."

"I was busy," Gavin growled. "And he isn't ready."

"When is he gonna be ready? Geez. How many years has he been shadowing you? How long has he been imitating you? Copying the way you talk and walk? You and Uncle Manny have been telling him he's not ready all his life! You're the reason he has problems with his nerves. If he does this, it may give him the confidence he's always lacked—"

"Fine."

She nodded, immensely satisfied. "All right, then."

"How did she do today?"

She took the change of subject in stride. "A little shaken, but she's strong. She's gonna pull through."

"Yes, she is. You'll stay with her tomorrow?"

"Yes."

"Okay." She popped the cork on the champagne and heard a sharp, "What was that?" in her ear.

"Just a bottle of champagne."

"You're celebrating?"

"Yup. Lyla staying and Vinny's new position." She watched champagne fizz in the glass and said quietly, "Gavin?"

"Yeah?"

"You're going to keep him safe, right?"

"Of course."

"You promise?"

"Yes. He's my brother."

She closed her eyes and let out a breath. "Of course. Okay. Thank you."

He cut the connection. She hummed to herself as she grabbed the glasses of champagne and headed upstairs.

14

Carmen woke to the sound of a ringing phone. She opened swollen, itchy eyes and surveyed her bedroom from the floor. Sunlight filtered through the blinds and warmed her body, which was curled in the fetal position.

The ringing stopped. Her body ached as if she had the flu. Her eyes moved up to the urn, a constant reminder of what she had lost. She curled her toes, and even that small gesture sent a streak of pain to her temples. She swam in a sea of regret and self-loathing. If she hadn't fought for Vinny to become crime lord, he never would have been killed. Maybe Steven Vega wouldn't have pegged Vinny as an easy mark and Gavin wouldn't have gone on a bloody revenge spree, he and Lyla wouldn't have put off their wedding, and maybe Steven wouldn't have gone for Uncle Manny...

She curled into a tighter ball to combat the agony searing her insides. She buried the truth because she couldn't handle the fact that she had orchestrated her husband's demise. Vinny wouldn't have become crime lord without her interference. Gavin wouldn't have allowed it if she hadn't made that call. Why had she done it? *That's what a good wife does.* She moaned and covered her head with her arms as if that would protect her from the memories ripping her soul to shreds. She encouraged him to be crime lord to help him be more confident and prove Gavin wrong. It was she who was wrong. She ruined her life and everyone else's, and for what?

Guilt and more pain than she could bear flooded through her. She took refuge in a zombie-like state for years, but she couldn't avoid the truth any longer. *Gavin signed his cousin's death warrant.* Maddog's words lashed at her. No, it wasn't Gavin who signed Vinny's death warrant, it was her. She writhed on the ground as the pain turned her inside out. She couldn't stay still, couldn't put a stopper on it. She instinctively clawed her chest to get beneath her skin to the source of her agony. If she could have, she would have carved out her own heart. Memories of Vinny taunted her. She could feel his hands on her skin, remember the smell of their lovemaking, the touch of his hands cupping her face. She could see his face so clearly.

What did I do to deserve a wife like you?

She screamed to block out the echo of his voice. She got to her knees and gripped her head as she rocked uncontrollably. She couldn't take much more. She had to make it stop.

The sound of the phone ringing pierced through her hysteria. She spotted her purse and crawled across the carpet and turned it upside down. Phone, tampons, condoms, keys, gun. She touched cold metal and was about to wrap her hands around it when she heard, "Carmen?"

She jerked her hand away from the gun as her mother's voice broke the spell as effectively as a crowd of people stampeding into the room. She scrubbed a hand over her face and tried to get herself together, but she didn't have enough time. Footsteps sounded in the hallway, and seconds later, her mother appeared. She bowed her head in an attempt to conceal her puffy, distraught face.

"Carmen?" Her mother was out of breath. "We've been calling—"

She dropped to her knees and grasped Carmen's hand as she tried to sweep everything back into her purse.

"Carmen?"

"I'm sorry. I just woke up," she said hoarsely.

"Carmen."

Mom cupped her chin and raised it. She attempted a smile even as tears slid down her face.

"I'm fine," she whispered.

Mom's eyes filled with tears.

"I'm fine," she said again.

"You're not," Mom said gently.

"I am," she said even as her face crumpled.

She desperately tried to hold it all in.

"It's going to be okay, Carmen."

Mom drew her close. She buried her face in her mother's shoulder and fisted a handful of her starched shirt. No, it would never be okay. As if Mom could hear her thoughts, she hugged her even tighter.

"You've been so strong," Mom murmured. "We're so proud of you."

No, she couldn't hear this now. She shook her head and tried to pull away, but Mom held her tight.

"You're everything we could have hoped for and more. We raised you to be confident, passionate, caring. You give so much of yourself away and leave nothing for yourself. We were so happy you found Vinny. He understood you just like us."

"Mom, stop," she begged.

"It hurts me to see you in pain," Mom whispered.

She desperately tried to get a handle on her emotions. "I know. I'm trying."

"But it hurts me even more to see you ignore it."

Carmen gave in. She went limp in her mother's arms as sorrow swallowed her whole. She wasn't sure how much time passed, but the tight embrace never slackened. Warm, familiar hands comforted her while her body was wracked with sobs so powerful, she couldn't catch her breath. Her mother murmured soft, loving words in her ear while she rocked her. When the storm passed, she lay exhausted and empty in her arms.

They sat in silence. She noticed that the light in the room had changed, confirmation that they had been here a while.

Mom kissed her temple. "Come, I'll make you a bath."

Mom assisted her into the bathroom and filled the tub while Carmen sat, staring into space. Mom undressed her and urged her in. The sweet smell of jasmine drew her out of the darkness. The warm water soothed her aching, quivering muscles. Mom washed her hair as if she was five years old. She wasn't capable of doing anything more strenuous than sitting upright.

"Lyla called me this morning," Mom said.

It took a minute for that to make sense. "Why?"

"Something to do with the Black Viper gang." Mom didn't ask questions; she just massaged her scalp, as placid as could be. "Gavin was in some kind of uproar, and Lyla tried to call you, but you didn't answer, so she called me."

She tried to think of something to say that wouldn't alarm her mother and came up with nothing. Her mother knew all about the Black Vipers.

"Carmen Marie."

She suddenly found her chin caught in a firm grip. Her mother stared straight into her eyes, gaze strong and unflinching.

"I don't know what you're doing to work through your grief, but I won't lose you to the underworld, you understand me? I won't tell you what not to do because you'll do it, but I'm warning you, you're running toward dark stuff. Once you go down that road, there's no coming back." Her expression eased a little as she stroked her cheek and then splayed her hand over the angry red scratches on her chest. "This isn't you, baby."

Her chest quaked as she tried to keep the well of emotions in check.

"I lost your father. I can't lose you too. I'm here. I can help you through this. I need you here with me, baby. Stay with me."

Carmen gave a tiny nod that satisfied her mother. The hand wiped away her tears and resumed giving her a bath.

"Gavin's involved," Mom continued.

Oh, shit.

"Lyla doesn't know all the details. Something about you, his cousin, a shooting, the Black Vipers, and he left shortly after. Whatever happened yesterday is done. Gavin will handle it."

She rinsed Carmen's hair as she continued to talk.

"I prayed for a daughter because I knew your father would forbid you from becoming an enforcer."

Yes, she had heard that more than once over the years.

"Your father never worried about you because he believed you could handle anything, and he was right. And what you couldn't handle, Manny and Gavin would."

"Mom—"

"Hush."

Mom wrapped her in a robe and combed her hair before she led her downstairs. Mom pushed her onto a chair at the table and put a glass of water in front of her along with two aspirin. The cold water soothed her raw throat. She heard the sizzle of butter hit a hot pan as Mom bustled around the kitchen. It seemed that it took less than a minute for Mom to place a grilled cheese sandwich in front of her.

"Eat."

She obeyed because she didn't have any fight left. Mom sat across from her with her own sandwich. They ate in silence. When she finished, she felt better, but the heavy weight on her chest was still there. Mom watched her with quiet expectation. She opened her mouth and then closed it. Her hands fisted in her lap, and she swallowed hard.

"You're going to get through this, Carmen."

"I used to be strong," she whispered as a tear slipped down her cheek.

"No one is strong all the time. You've been taking care of people for a long time. You took Lyla under your wing when you were kids, you took care of Vinny, and then you took on Lyla after the attack. Then you came home and took care of me." Her voice shook, and she reached for Carmen's hand and squeezed. "I know it wasn't easy. You have a good heart, Carmen. You take on so many things without thinking twice. You don't have a mean bone in your body."

"I killed the leader of the Black Viper gang."

Mom paled. "What? Why?"

"H-he said Vinny becoming crime lord was a joke, that Gavin signed his death warrant, but he was wrong..." She shook her head as memories cascaded through her. "He was wrong."

"Carmen?"

"It's my fault," she whispered.

"What's your fault?"

"I killed Vinny." Her mother shook her head and opened her mouth, but she spoke over her. "I did. I told Vinny to do it. I encouraged him. I called Gavin and told him to make Vinny crime lord."

Silence filled the kitchen.

"I knew what to say to make Gavin give in. I'm the one who made it happen. It's my fault." She stared straight ahead as she said, "Hearing him mock Vinny's life, hearing him blame Gavin..." She hung her head, too ashamed to meet her mother's eyes. "If Vega hadn't killed Vinny, Gavin wouldn't have gone crazy. Uncle Manny would still be alive, and Lyla wouldn't have s-scars."

"It's done, Carmen."

She shook her head. "No, it's not."

"Carmen, let it go."

"I can't."

Mom gripped both of her hands hard enough to get her attention. "Do you know why I married your father?"

"You loved him."

"Yes, but I didn't marry him until I got pregnant, and I knew there was no going back."

This was new information, but a little out of the blue. "What does that have to do with—?"

"I don't know why I fell in love with a bad man, but I did. I knew what your father did for a living. I didn't want to worry about him every time he went to work. I didn't want to live like that, wondering if he would come home to me, but I got pregnant, and I committed." Mom leaned forward. "Sometimes, innocents get hurt. Sometimes, he made mistakes. I saw the news, and I could put two and two together. I should have turned him in."

She stared transfixed at her mother. She had never seen this side of her. Her mother had never voiced anything like this in her life. She had always seemed totally accepting of the ways of the underworld.

"Your father did what he did best. He was the best father to you and an amazing husband to me. I never turned him in."

"Why?"

"Because I loved a good man who did bad things for a living. Even though some of the battles in the underworld are fought for money and territory, I told myself what he did was for the better good." Mom stroked her face. "Your father had a code. It's not one that everyone would understand, but he had one, and he was a good man."

"He was the best," she agreed.

"I supported your father even when I shouldn't, even knowing people would lose their lives. Do you understand?"

"But—"

"Even if Vinny hadn't become crime lord, there was always a possibility he could be targeted because he's a Pyre."

"Yes."

"You supported your husband because you wanted what he wanted. That's what millions of women have done for men who risk their lives for country or code. Loyalty, that's what we bred in you. You're your father's daughter. He gave you grit, but he also gave you heart. You took action last night to defend your husband. I'm just glad you're breathing today."

"Mom—"

She grasped her face between both hands. "You loved him, Carmen, more than life. You love me, which is why you gave your blessing when you found out about Marv."

"Yes, but—"

"You love, and there's no shame in that. You care. You deserve to be happy. Vinny wouldn't blame you, would he?"

"I don't know," she whispered.

"No, he wouldn't. What's done is done. You did what you thought was right at the moment, and there's no going back. You have so much life to live, Carmen."

She sniffled. "I do?"

"You give so much you don't even notice. My friends are fighting over whose son you get to meet first. You listen to them, spend time with them, take care of them. You tip the pregnant waitress without hesitation. You spread good wherever you go. You help with your friend's businesses, volunteer, and don't hesitate to drop everything if someone needs help. You're a good person, and you won't convince anyone otherwise." She eyed her sternly. "Let it go, Carmen."

"It's not that easy," she whispered.

"You'll get there."

"How?"

"Be around people who love and appreciate you." She stood and hugged Carmen from behind. "We'll love you back to life. It's the most powerful force on the planet. It can do wonders."

She let out a long breath and let her mother's love soothe her raw wounds. "Okay."

"I love you."

"I love you too."

"We're gonna get through this. One day at a time."

"How do I do this?"

"You find something that makes you happy. You do that, and it'll give you a break from the pain. Then you find something else that makes you happy, and you do more of that. Eventually, the good beats out the bad." Mom stroked her hair. "How many shots?"

It took her a moment to figure out what she was asking. "Two. I missed on the first, but the second got him in the chest."

Mom kissed her temple. "Your father would be proud."

Carmen's lips curved. "I know."

The faint ring of a phone echoed through the house.

"It's probably Lyla," Mom said and rushed out of the kitchen.

Carmen folded her arms on the table and rested her aching head on top. She took a deep breath and then another. Mom's ministrations definitely worked. The bath to wash away the memories, the food to fill the emptiness, and the love to hold her in the present.

"Carmen." She grunted as Mom walked in the kitchen. "It's Gavin."

She tensed. He was the last person she wanted to talk to when she was feeling this way. She played possum and didn't raise her head.

Mom sighed and said, "She can hear you."

Gavin's angry voice filled the kitchen. "What the hell were you thinking, Carmen?"

She raised her head and glared at Mom who shrugged.

"Neither of you can stay there. It isn't safe. Pack a bag and stay with us," he said.

Carmen felt the blood drain from her body. Oh, shit. It was starting all over again. Her impulsive stupidity put Mom's life in danger.

"I just moved in with Marv," Mom said,

"Who's Marv?" Gavin asked brusquely.

"My fiancé." When Gavin didn't comment, she added, "I'll invite you to the wedding, of course."

"Of course," Gavin echoed.

"Carmen will stay with us."

"I guess that should be okay since I didn't even know you were engaged," Gavin said after a pause. "Congratulations."

"Thanks, Gavin," Mom chirped gaily. "You're going to love him. He's so sweet."

"I'll take your word for it. There are two guards outside, Mickey and Frederick. They stay on Carmen at all times. Keeping you out of sight is just a precaution, Isabel."

"I understand," Mom said.

"I want you gone in the next fifteen minutes."

"Will do. Thank you, Gavin." Mom waited a good twenty seconds before she lowered the phone. "I guess he hung up. Let's go, Carmen."

Someone pounded on the door, which made them both jump. Her survival instinct kicked in. She shot up from the table, climbed on the counter, and pulled the shotgun from the top of the cabinets. Mom pulled a tiny pistol from its hiding place behind the bread maker. She tiptoed to the door and waited.

"It's Mickey and Frederick. Pyre says you need to be gone in fourteen minutes," said a male voice.

She relaxed slightly. Fucking Gavin. She opened the door with the shotgun still in hand. Two men stood on her doorstep. They looked FBI rejects with the blinding white shirts, black ties, and black suits. The Mexican built like a tank had sprawling tattoos on the back of his hands that twined around each finger. Probably covering up a gang tattoo. The second guy couldn't be older than twenty-five. He looked bright-eyed and excited before he noticed the gun. He took a step back while the other guard's lip curled.

"I hope you know how to use that," Mexican Hulk said.

She lifted the barrel. "Want me to show you?"

Mom bumped her to the side. "Carmen was taught to shoot when she eight years old, and I'm not such a bad shot myself." She waved to Lamar, a teenager who lived three doors down and who was currently parked at the end of their driveway on his bike, watching avidly. "Hey, Lamar!"

"They straight?" he called.

"Yes, they work for Gavin."

Lamar threw the peace sign and pedaled down the road. Mom turned back to the guards and waved them inside. "Carmen needs help with her things."

It finally penetrated that she would be moving again, and this time to her future stepfather's house, a man she'd met twice in her life. "Maybe I should get a hotel."

"No." Mom pushed her toward the stairs. "You have ten minutes. Don't dawdle. Just take what you need. I'm sure you can always send someone to get more if you need it."

"Marv doesn't want—"

"You don't know what he wants, Carmen Marie. Now, hush and hurry."

It wasn't until she felt an uncomfortable breeze that she realized her robe had loosened, giving a glimpse of her modest cleavage and stomach.

"You're hurt?" the smaller guard asked as he stared at the angry scratches on her chest.

"No," she said shortly as she cinched the robe and headed upstairs with the shotgun under her arm. She surveyed her room and heard the two guards stop behind her.

"I want those piles," she said, pointing at four mounds of shoes, clothes, and shopping bags.

"All of those?" Wannabe Blade grunted.

"Yes."

She could feel his irritation, but he didn't argue. He opened her closet, found a duffel she used in high school for cheerleading and got to work. She kicked through a pile of clothes and found a purple velvet tracksuit. She went into the bathroom to change as the guys got to work. She looked in the mirror at her bloodshot, puffy eyes and took a deep breath. There was no time to think. No, once again life was propelling her forward. She found a bedazzled Ed Hardy hat, which she pulled low over her face, oversized sunglasses, and slipped into a pair of black platform sandals decorated with studs.

She packed her makeup and jewelry and handed it off to the younger guard before she hefted Vinny. She waved them off as she carried the urn to the Aston Martin. Her things had been loaded into an SUV.

"Will one of you drive her?" Mom called from the beat-up Toyota. "She's under the weather."

"Mom!"

"Don't argue, Carmen. I gave them the address. They know where we're going. I'll see you there!"

Mom waved as she backed out of the drive. She probably needed a head start to explain to Marv why she was showing up with her twenty-nine-year-old daughter in tow.

"Ma'am?" the young guard asked tentatively.

She tossed him the keys, got into the passenger seat, and settled Vinny on the floorboard between her feet. She sat back and closed her eyes as the car began to move.

"I'm Mickey."

"Carmen," she said with her eyes closed.

"Of course, we know all about you, Mrs. Pyre."

She ground her teeth. "Just call me Carmen."

"Okay."

She felt congested and lightheaded from her crying fit. All she wanted to do was lay in a dark room and sleep, preferably for a week or two. Her phone rang. She hesitated before she fished it out of her purse.

"Hey," she said.

"Hey. I just wanted to remind you about Saturday," Alice said.

"Saturday?"

"The animal adoption. You're coming right?"

The meeting she attended with Alice about the arrangements felt like a month ago. "Oh, right. Yes. What's today?"

"Thursday. Are you all right?"

No, she wasn't, but she was a world-class actress. "I'm good. I went out last night and am only getting my day started now."

"Oh, okay. Saturday, Cimarron Elementary."

"Right. I'll be there. Do you need anything?"

"A crowd to get these animals adopted."

"Right. I'll see you then."

"Bye."

After she hung up, Mickey said, "I doubt Pyre's going to allow that."

She held up a finger. "Don't."

He glanced at her. "Don't what?"

"Tell me what I can or can't do." It was Maddog's dare that put her over the edge last night. Mom was right; if someone told her not to do something, she would be compelled to do just that.

She sat back and stared out the window. She felt dead inside. It took a week for her new outlook on life to plummet to its death in a hail of blood, violence, and a reminder of past sins. Angel thought she needed to risk her life to keep her restlessness at bay. Mom didn't want her going down that road, and neither did she. The last thing she wanted was to rub shoulders with people like Maddog and

George Wotherton. Mom was right. She would find little things that made her happy and hold on for dear life.

She spotted a familiar building. "Turn here."

"What?"

"Turn!" she snapped.

The tires screeched as Mickey made a sharp turn.

"The drive-through is around the corner," she said.

"What the hell are we doing?"

"I want a donut," she said.

"What?"

"Do-nut," she enunciated. "Strawberry, chocolate... whatever they have, I want it. I had one a week ago, and it made me happy, so we're gonna get a dozen and hope it perks me up. Comprende?"

Mickey gave her a glance that suggested she'd lost her mind. His phone rang as he pulled up to the microphone. Carmen leaned across him and hollered out her order as Mickey talked on the phone.

"She wants a donut. I know. We'll be out of here in a sec." He hung up. "Frederick's covering us."

"Of course, he is." She handed him her credit card. "I didn't ask if you wanted anything."

He grinned. "I'm sure I'll like something from the three dozen you ordered."

"I want Mom and Marv to have some too."

Mickey handed her three hot boxes, which she placed on her lap. She waved at the Dunkin' Donut's worker who drooled over her car. She closed her eyes and sank her teeth into the pink frosting of a strawberry donut and let everything else cease to exist. It was pathetic to seek solace from a donut, but she would take what she could get. Anything had to be better than wallowing in a pit of self-loathing.

"Is that as good as it looks?" Mickey asked, ruining her moment.

She opened her eyes to find him watching her instead of where he was going. "Eyes on the road."

"Yes, ma'am."

She bit into two other donuts, but none gave her a rush like the strawberry one. She sucked her finger and then smacked the door.

"Turn here."

"Frederick's not going to—"

She reached for the steering wheel. He cursed and brushed her hands away. "Okay, okay. Where are we going?"

She gave him directions and then handed him the donut boxes as she got out of the car. Frederick parked beside her and jumped out with his hand in his jacket.

"What's going on?"

"I need stuff," she said and started toward Petco.

"What the hell?"

"There's an animal adoption event in two days."

"What the hell does that have to do with...?" Frederick began but broke off when he saw she wasn't going to wait around to talk.

She walked into Petco with Frederick and Mickey flanking her. She found two workers to assist her on her shopping spree. She bought beds, leashes, food and water dishes, collars, toys, treats, etc. She situated a delivery time with the manager and also managed to get him to advertise the event with the local stores as well. After handing over her credit card to pay over ten grand, she caught the look her guards exchanged.

"How'd you two get stuck with me?" she asked. "Is Angel or Gavin punishing you?"

"Neither. We volunteered," Mickey said.

Carmen frowned. "Why would you volunteer?"

"You're with Roman, right?"

She stiffened. "Excuse me?"

"You were with him last night. He basically claimed you in front of everyone. We figured you were bound for action since you're his." He finally registered her outraged expression. "You're not?"

"No! You were duped into playing babysitter for someone who is going to make you take her on fast food runs and animal adoptions."

"So why were you with Roman last night?" Mickey persisted.

Why, indeed? Fucking Angel. She thanked the cashier and crumpled the epic receipt into a sizable ball as she marched out of the store. She pulled her phone out of her purse and pointed at both men to stay put as she paced and dialed Angel. He answered on the fifth ring.

"I'm busy."

"So am I," she quipped. "Why did you really take me with you last night?"

"I told you."

"For the rush?" she asked as she paced with a hand on her hip. "Is that all?"

"What else is there?"

"How about the fact that everyone thinks I'm yours now?"

"It's for protection."

"What?"

"The next time you do some wild shit, they know they'll have to deal with me as well. I put you under my wing."

"You put me on the map, jack off!"

"You wouldn't be on the map if you hadn't decided to shoot Maddog. I took the killing shot, but everyone who was there knows you would have kept shooting until he keeled over. Did you work through whatever shit was going on with you last night? It has to do with Vinny, right?"

She stomped her foot. "Stop trying to play my fucked-up therapist! You don't know me!"

He chuckled. "I do know you. It's like looking in a mirror. You, Luci, and I are cut from the same cloth. I don't need to analyze you because I already get it."

"You don't get shit."

"Right. Where are you?" he asked suddenly.

"In a Petco parking lot. Why?"

"You're alone?" His voice was suddenly sharp.

"No, I have my guards."

"Stop fucking around and get to your safe place. Once Gavin got involved, the Black Vipers went to ground. Stay low and if you have to go out, don't leave without them. Got it?"

"If you hadn't taken me, I wouldn't need guards," she sassed back.

The line went dead. She cursed and turned to see Frederick and

Mickey standing closer than they had been a minute ago. She glared as she pushed between them and got in the car. Mickey said nothing as he drove. Her foot tapped against the floorboard in irritation. If Angel hadn't taken her last night, she would still be encased in her impenetrable wall of denial, a much-needed buffer that kept the guilt at bay so she could function. Now, it was in her lungs. With every breath she took, pain swirled around in her chest like fine shards of glass, leaving razor thin cuts on her insides.

Mickey pulled up to a house painted in baby blue and white with big bay windows and rose bushes in front. She stepped out of the car as the front door opened, and Mom and Marv appeared. She waited with her hand on the door, bracing herself for a lecture or disapproving look from Marv.

"I thought something happened to you," he said as he gave her a hug.

The smell of Old Spice and the burly feel of him went to her head like whiskey. *Oh, Dad, I miss you so much*, she thought and willed back the tears. Dad wasn't here, but Marv was doing a damn good job of stepping up. He roused good memories that made her want to burrow against him and hang on tight.

"I brought donuts," she said as he pulled away. She made a big show of reaching into the car to grab them.

Marv's eyes widened. "You'd be a hit at the mechanic shop."

"Really? I can deliver—"

He laughed and swung an arm over her shoulders. "No, that's okay. Come inside."

"Wait, let me get Vinny."

He released her and watched as she hefted the urn. He didn't comment as he led the way into the house. The Armstrong home had high beam ceilings, wood floors, and a big fireplace. Everything was open, airy, and filled with personal touches that said it had been well lived in. She got a glimpse of a well-kept backyard with thriving plants.

"This is it," Marv said. "It's simple but—"

"It's perfect," she said quietly as she clutched Vinny to her chest.

"I think so," Marv said with his hands in pockets.

A young, exotic looking woman walked out of the hallway wearing jeans and a shirt two sizes too big for her. She had the perfect mix of both parents—creamy white skin from her father and slanted hazel eyes and pin straight black hair from her Asian mother.

"This is my daughter, Maddie. She's a freshman in college. Maddie, this is Carmen, Isabel's daughter," Marv said.

"Hi," Maddie said faintly.

"Hi," Carmen said and hefted Vinny awkwardly on her hip.

"What's that?" Maddie asked.

"My husband."

Maddie's eyes widened and then softened. "Oh."

"Maddie's going to school for hotel management and business," Marv said.

"Really? I might be able to help you with that," Carmen said.

Maddie's brows rose. "You can?"

"I own shares in Pyre Casino, and I have an in with the CEO."

Maddie's mouth formed the word, "Wow," but no sound came out of her.

"Where are we putting her stuff?" Frederick asked from behind her.

"This way," Marv said and started down the hallway.

"You know, Marv, it's not a big deal for me to go to a hotel," Carmen began.

"Don't be silly. You're family," he said.

He led her to a beautiful guest room with doilies on the dresser and everything done in white. It was simple, rustic, and soothing. It wasn't the type of room you cried your heart out in. She settled Vinny on the bedside table and winced when it creaked under the weight. Frederick and Mickey began to bring in her stuff, and she attempted not to trash the place by making semi-organized piles. When she finished, she padded back into the living area. Through the front windows, she saw Mickey and Frederick parked across the street in the SUV.

"Are you in trouble?" Maddie asked.

Carmen plopped onto the opposite end of the lush couch and faced her future stepsister.

"Yeah," she said.

"What kind?" Maddie asked.

She hesitated. This house belonged in Better Homes and Garden. If Maddie grew up in a house like this, underworld shit wasn't for her innocent ears. She might not even know it existed.

"The bad kind, but it'll be over soon."

"I like your shoes."

Carmen smiled and held up her foot so they could admire the kickass shoe together. "Thanks. What's your shoe size?"

"Eight."

She winked. "Your shoe collection just imploded. You and I are the same size. Whatever you want, feel free to take."

Maddie's mouth dropped. "What?"

She waved a hand. "I mostly use my shoes once anyway. Actually, Lyla's the same size too, so you can steal her shit too."

"Lyla?"

"My cousin. She's married to Gavin."

"You mean, the CEO of Pyre Casinos?" Maddie asked in a strangled voice.

"That's him," she said dryly.

She jerked her head toward the kitchen where their parents were eating donuts, drinking decaf coffee, and giggling like teenagers.

"How long have you known about them?"

"From their first date." Maddie gave her a small smile. "Mom's great."

Hearing Maddie call her mom gave her all the feels. She cleared her throat. "She sure is."

"My mom died when I was eleven. Breast cancer," Maddie said quietly. "Dad's been alone for a long time. I'm happy for him."

"So am I."

"I know about your husband," Maddie said quietly. "It was in the papers."

She let out a long breath. "Yes."

"I'm sorry."

She nodded because there was nothing to say.

"We spread Mom's ashes in the backyard. We'd never sell this house because of that."

Carmen looked around at what felt like a sprawling ranch house. "I can see why. It's beautiful."

"I'm boarding at college to give them privacy." Maddie tilted her head toward their parents. "But I like to come home when I don't have classes. Levi is going to freak out."

"Levi?"

"My brother." Maddie crossed her arms and grinned. "I don't know what he's going to notice first. You or that Aston Martin Vanquish S Volante."

Carmen grinned. "You know your cars."

"It's a requirement when you live with mechanics."

Carmen hugged an oversized pillow to her chest. "This is nice."

This house seemed untouched by anything twisted or evil. Mom looked comfortable and settled here. The pictures on the mantle and walls showed a happy family who had lived a full life. Despite the years since Marv's wife passed, the house still maintained the essence of her. Marv didn't become resentful or abusive. He took care of his family and worked hard, and the result was here in front of her. Maddie had grown up without a mother, but she seemed secure and grounded. She wasn't resentful of their presence.

"You're taking this well," she said.

Maddie's brows rose. "I am?"

"We're moving in on your turf."

Maddie laughed, and the beautiful sound was music to her ears. "I freaked out when I first found out, but I met Mom and..." She shrugged. "Some things are meant to be, you know?" She glanced into the kitchen before she leaned forward. "Dad told me how you reacted." She gave her two thumbs up. "What's good for them is good for us, right?"

That painful clenching sensation in her chest eased ever so slightly. Maddie's innocence made the night at The Pussy seem like a bad dream rather than something she participated in. Carmen rose and gave her new sister a long hug before she settled beside her on the couch.

"Yes, what's good for them is good for us," she agreed.

Maddie's wise eyes tracked her face. "You need a nap."

Carmen let out a choked laugh. "I do." She needed a lot of things, but a nap sounded like the best at the moment. Maddie smelled of vanilla and honey. She settled against her sister who didn't seem the least bit uncomfortable. Marv's house seemed like a good place to lick her raw wounds and recover.

"You want to watch Psych?" Maddie asked.

"What's Psych?"

"It's a show about a guy who's super observant and solves crimes from clues police post on the news. When he tries to collect his reward money for solving a crime, they think he's a suspect, so he has to act like a psychic instead. It's really funny."

She settled against Maddie. "That sounds perfect. I'm in."

15

CARMEN PULLED UP TO CIMARRON ELEMENTARY AND STEPPED OUT OF the car. She put her hands on hips and glared at Frederick and Mickey as they strolled up to her.

"Pyre and Roman approved the outing," Frederick said.

"I would have attended without their approval," she retorted and turned as Maddie climbed out of the passenger seat of the Aston. She wore Carmen's thigh-high boots with jeans and a white tee. Carmen grinned as she glanced down at the scuffed Converse sneakers she had borrowed. Maddie had been horrified when Carmen found them in the back of her closet, but she was in love with them. It brought her back to a simpler time. She was loving Maddie's olive-green bomber jacket paired with her black knit body con dress. Little things. That was how she was getting through.

She'd spent the past two days at Marv's house, doing nothing more strenuous than sleeping, eating, and watching Netflix. She had a few breakdowns, but they didn't last long. How could it when she was surrounded by such nice, caring people? She told Charisse that something came up and that they would have to resume their house hunting next week. After two days at Marv's house, she had a better idea of what she wanted for her next home, and it wasn't as grand as what she'd had in the past. It would be smaller, homey, safe. Despite the love bursting at the seams in Marv's house, she couldn't stay there. She was sharing a bathroom with Maddie, and the closet was the size of a linen closet. Nope.

"You made it!"

Alice rushed toward them wearing a ball cap, fluorescent jacket, and gold shoelaces. She was also accompanied by a dachshund wearing a red bandanna. Alice's eyes were shining and she looked adorable. If men saw this version of her, she'd have to beat them off with a stick.

"Hey," Alice gushed and smiled at Maddie. "I'm Alice."

"This is my sister, Maddie," Carmen said.

Alice blinked as she shook Maddie's hand. "Oh, wow. That's awesome."

"Maddie's in school for hotel management and business and interested in helping out with your events. I'm going to see if I can get her into the intern program at Pyre Casinos."

Alice beamed. "That's fantastic." She looked past Maddie as Frederick and Mickey helped a large truck back up. "What's going on?"

Carmen clapped her hands together. "I bought some goodies."

"Goodies?" Alice echoed as two delivery guys opened the back of the truck.

"I got things a new pet owner would need. Scratching posts, puppy pads, leashes, food. I thought it would help. What we don't use, we can donate to the shelters."

"Did Gavin authorize this?" Alice was clearly ill at ease.

"No, this is my contribution."

"Carmen, we can't accept this."

"Why not? I'm a Pyre, aren't I? I can do good Samaritan shit." She had enough money to feed a country. Maybe she should do that—

Alice gave her an enthusiastic one-armed hug. "You're amazing; you know that?"

"I've heard that once or twice," she said.

Alice hollered to some volunteers to help before she grabbed Maddie's hand. "Come, let me show you everything!"

Alice led them toward a cluster of tents and volunteers wearing gold Pyre Foundation T-shirts. There were pens full of puppies, kittens, and older dogs wearing bandannas or cute sweaters. Kids ran with the dogs on their heels, and manly men with tattoos allowed their faces to be pawed by tiny kittens. The elderly bonded with the mature dogs who needed a pair of feet to snooze beside for the handful of years they had left.

She was pleased to see her mother's friends from cha-cha with their grandkids. Alice flitted from here to there with Maddie in tow. There was happy madness everywhere she looked. She ran into Shonda and Keenan from the salon and chatted with them for a minute. Keenan adopted a black cat with mesmerizing blue eyes. She pointed them toward the free stuff and was happy to see that the pregnant waitress and her boyfriend had adopted an old, gray-faced Chihuahua who sat docile in her arms.

Mom and Marv arrived holdings hands. Her mother was glowing.

"Carmen!" Marv boomed as if he hadn't seen her in days when it had been less than two hours.

He hugged her tight. If she'd had any doubts about her mom's relationship, they were put to rest after spending time with the Armstrong's. Marv and Maddie were amazing. She felt as if she had known them all her life. She'd been so absorbed by brutal tragedies that she couldn't see past that to anything clean or normal until now. It took Marv almost a decade to recover from losing his wife, so he didn't think her inability to move on after two years was odd in the slightest.

"Levi's here," Marv said.

Before she could ask who that was, a brawny arm slid over her shoulders. She looked up at a handsome guy with Maddie's hazel eyes and dark hair. "So, you're my new smoking hot sister?"

Marv sputtered. "Levi, don't talk like that to your stepsister!"

"When's the wedding?" Levi asked without looking away from her.

"We're not sure yet. Why?" Marv asked suspiciously.

"I want to take her out before she becomes my sister."

Carmen grinned as Marv made a choking sound.

"Show some respect, son," Marv admonished.

"I had to try. Is that Aston yours?" Levi asked.

Carmen pulled the keys from her pocket. "Knock yourself out."

Levi dropped the flirtatious act. "Are you kidding?"

"Nope."

"You're smoking hot *and* have good taste in cars? Where have you been all my life?"

Marv shoved his son good-naturedly. Levi and Maddie raced toward the car as she headed toward a group of pit bulls that most people were giving a wide berth. They wagged their tails as she approached. She went on her knees and was immediately rushed by eager to please dogs. She considered the situation for a minute before she grabbed a handful of toys. When the dogs began to gnaw on squeaky toys, it drew the attention of a small crowd. Alice gave her a thumbs up.

One dog, a beautiful rust-colored one with bright green eyes, was flat on her belly. As she approached, the dog turned her face away. She was shaking and clearly in distress.

"What happened to her?" she asked a volunteer.

"Don't know. She was found on the streets. Looks like she's been in a few scrapes." The volunteer pointed at some scarring around her neck and rump. "She's terrified. She won't even eat."

Carmen lay on the ground a good two feet away. The dog wouldn't meet her eyes, though her ears twitched in her direction. Her tail was curled under her body.

"She has to get adopted, or she'll be put down," the volunteer said quietly.

Carmen got to her feet. "If no one adopts her, let me know."

She gave the volunteer her number and looked around the gathering. Everyone was having a good time. Her heart swelled when she saw families walking away with new pets. A familiar figure caught her eye. Marcus was dressed in a light gray suit and white button-up shirt, no tie. He looked suave and cultured, but she knew what lay beneath the clean-cut image. She'd always had a soft spot for a good guy who had a dark streak and fucked like a bad boy.

He spotted her and stopped in his tracks. Memories of their hookups made her palms tingle. She took a step toward him but had to stop when a group of kids ran in front of her. He made no move toward her. After the week she had, the Kody Singer thing seemed inconsequential in comparison. Marcus couldn't still be mad about that, could he? As the little crowd passed and Marcus continued to watch her, she realized he was definitely still mad. Before she could figure out how she wanted to handle this, an arm slid over her shoulders.

"That was amazing," Levi said as he handed back her car keys. "I think you're my new favorite sister."

"I'm standing right here," Maddie said.

"You smell that new car smell on me?" Levi asked.

He was drunk on the Aston. "You smell like grease," she said, but it wasn't unpleasant.

He shrugged. "Inevitable when you work at a garage."

"How many of your clients are women?" she asked.

He winked at her and was about to say something flirtatious when he was interrupted.

"Carmen."

She turned her head and locked eyes with Marcus who was standing two feet away. He gave her a long look through cool green eyes before he extended his hand to Levi who still had an arm around her.

"I don't believe we've met. I'm Marcus."

Levi took the outstretched hand. "Levi."

"You're the COO of Pyre Casinos," Maddie piped up.

"He is," Carmen said. Maybe he wasn't mad after all. "Marcus, this is Maddie. She's a freshman in college and taking courses in hotel management."

"I took the same courses," Marcus said, making direct eye contact with Maddie who blushed furiously. "If you're interested in an internship at Pyre Casinos, let me know."

"T-thank you," Maddie said.

Marcus switched his attention back to her. He eyed her expectantly, obviously waiting for her to say something. She clapped her hands and gestured to Maddie and Levi. "Our parents are getting married."

Marcus blinked. "Excuse me?"

"My mom's marrying their dad, Marv, so we're getting to know one another."

Marcus focused on Levi. "Looks like it's going well."

Something about his tone made Levi drop his arm. Carmen gave her future step siblings a sunny smile as she went to Marcus and linked her arm through his.

"We'll catch up later. I need to talk to Marcus about something," she said before she pulled him into the crowd.

"Your mom's getting married?" Marcus asked.

"Yes."

"You're happy about it?"

"Of course. I don't want her to be alone." *Like me*, she thought.

"You seem comfortable with your stepbrother."

They stopped on the path leading up to the school, a good distance from the happy ruckus taking place. "I let him drive my new Aston, and he's a car nut, so he's dubbed me his new favorite sister."

With the sun highlighting his features, he looked chic and unattainable. His cool demeanor made her want to provoke him, but that would have to wait.

"My stepdad asked for my mom's hand in marriage an hour before you saw me in the casino with Kody," she said bluntly.

His expression revealed nothing. "I see."

"I was on my way to your office when Kody stopped me."

That caught him off guard. Out of the corner of her eye, she saw Mickey and Frederick milling around. They were keeping their distance but observing every move she made. She looked around and focused on the open door of the school. Without a word, she started walking toward the building after shooting her guards a warning look.

"Where are you going?" Marcus asked as he followed.

She didn't answer as she walked down a hallway lined with pegs and cubbies. The walls were covered in crayon artwork, and the smell of Play-Doh and tiny, sweaty humans filled her nostrils. She walked into a classroom filled with tiny desks. A guinea pig burrowed into shredded newspaper while the burble of the aquarium filled the room. A map of the world covered one wall and a dry erase board littered with math problems hung on the other.

She strolled around the classroom while Marcus watched from the doorway. He didn't step into the classroom, of course, because he liked rules. Even as a child, she didn't acknowledge rules. That was partly her father's training, but she continued the practice in her adult years since it got her what she wanted in life.

She sat in the tiny plastic chair, which felt as if it had been made for a doll rather than a human. She propped her chin on her hand and clamped her knees together in the classic schoolgirl pose. Maddie's shoes really got her into character. She pouted as Marcus watched her suspiciously. He was a wise man. She was definitely going to fuck with him.

"Did you ever have a student/teacher fantasy?" she asked.

"Excuse me?"

"Did you ever fantasize about a teacher?"

"Not that I can remember."

"That's a shame." Carmen rose and sauntered to the teacher's desk. She perched on the edge and crossed her legs. "Did you ever want someone who worked for you?"

Marcus leaned against the wall just inside the classroom. His pose was casual, but his eyes were alert and held a tinge of heat. Warmth pooled low. He wasn't walking away. He was willing to play her game.

"Several employees have dropped hints, but I'm not interested in someone who wants to use me to get ahead."

"In all fairness, she could really want you." That was probably more likely. Anyone who worked for Marcus knew he was a slave driver, so he wouldn't promote anyone who didn't deserve it.
"You're hot."

"You think so?"

She took her time examining him. She imagined what was beneath the tailored clothes and saw his pockets bulge as he fisted his hands. She hid a smile.

"Did you ever do anything about your teacher fantasy?" Marcus asked, breaking the taut silence.

"Yes."

His brows drew together. "A teacher took advantage of you?"

"I took advantage of the college TA."

He shook his head in mock regret. "He probably didn't know what hit him."

She leaned back on her hands. It was a provocative pose, and Marcus responded beautifully. He took a step forward before he caught himself.

"Did you ever seduce an employer?" he asked.

"No, I only had one boss, and she was a friend of mine."

"What did you do for your friend?"

"I stripped."

Marcus took another step forward. "I'm sorry?"

"My friend owned a club. I did it right out of high school."

"You were a professional stripper? That explains a lot."

She swung her foot idly as he approached. "What does that mean?"

"It means you know how to exploit every weakness a man has." He stopped so close that she could smell his cologne. "So, you were on your way to me, but got sidetracked by Kody and ended up kissing him. How did that happen?"

"I was sad."

"So, you kissed him?"

"I was in shock. I had just found out about Mom and Marv."

He placed a hand on her bare thigh. She couldn't help the goose bumps that erupted over her skin and hoped he didn't notice. Despite the sexual tension, Marcus was waiting for an answer. She hadn't explained herself to any man for years. It was uncomfortable, but the knowledge that she would be getting fucked soon was a great incentive.

"Kody said things I should want to hear..." She shrugged. "I wanted to have feelings for him. It would have made things simpler."

"You let him kiss you."

"Yes."

He planted his hands on either side of her and leaned in. "If you need kisses, you can come to me."

She smiled. "I'll remember that."

"What do you want, Carmen?" he murmured as he dragged her to the edge of the desk, forcing her to open her legs so he could fit between.

He stared at her with an intensity that made heat blossom in her belly and spread. She straightened so their faces were a hairsbreadth apart. Classy sin teased her nostrils.

"I want to play."

He searched her eyes. "Play?"

She had a thing for role playing. Not all men were game for this kind of thing, but it definitely got her going. She waited to see what Marcus Fletcher would do. "I'll be the student; you be the teacher."

His hands flexed on her, but he didn't move. She could almost hear the wheels turning in his head. She kissed his chin.

"Mr. Fletcher, don't you want me?" she asked in a high-pitched voice.

She ran her hand down his chest.

"I know I haven't been doing well in class, but"—she looked up at him and made her eyes as wide and guileless as possible right before she cupped his hardening cock—"I'm sure I can make up my grade by doing something special for you."

Marcus was rigid as a board. She wasn't even sure he was breathing.

"I really need to pass your class," she continued.

"You pick the damnedest places."

Disappointment coated her throat. She dropped her hand. Maybe he wasn't—

"On your knees."

"What?"

Marcus sat in the teacher's seat and pulled her backward off the desk before settling her on her knees in front of him. Her heart pounded as she spread her legs, so her dress rode up her thighs. Excitement drowned out all other thoughts. He was really going to let her do this. Either he wanted her fucking bad, or he had secret kink. She hoped it was both.

Marcus raised a brow. "If you want an A, you have to work for it."

"Yes, Mr. Fletcher," she said in a meek voice and reached for his belt.

He watched her with an unwavering focus that made her fumble with his slacks for real. She pulled down his zipper and bit back a moan when she saw his Calvin Klein's. He could be a serious contender for an underwear model. Jesus. She took a deep, audible breath and made a big show of touching his dick through the thin material and then pulling him out of his boxer briefs. She made an O with her mouth and looked up at him.

"It's so *big*!"

He gripped the peeling arms of the desk chair. "It'll fit in your mouth… and other places, I promise you."

"Is it painful?"

"Yes," he growled.

"Maybe a kiss will make you feel better?" She kissed the head and made an ooh sound when it jerked. "Did that work?"

Marcus glared at her. "If you want an A, you need to suck me."

"I've never done this before."

"Christ," he bit out. "Carmen, I'm gonna come on your face if you keep talking like that."

She gave a little shrug. "That's fine with me."

He shuddered and ran his hands down his face. "You're killing me."

She gave a theatrical gasp and grabbed his thigh. He jolted. "I don't want you to *die*!"

"Then suck me."

The order, said through gritted teeth, satisfied her immensely. "I heard I'm supposed to lick it like an ice-cream cone." She lapped at it and watched a muscle in his cheek flex. She licked the base of his cock and then kissed her way to the tip. "Am I doing okay?"

"It'll be better if you put it in your mouth and suck it."

"I really want an A. My dad will kill me if I get a B so..."

She closed her mouth around him. His feet moved restlessly, knocking into her legs before dropping to the floor with a soft clap. Kneeling in front of him suggested that she was the submissive, but she had him by the balls, literally, and could turn the tide whichever way she wished. She always liked giving blowjobs and now had the opportunity to push Marcus Fletcher over the edge. She kept up the innocent schoolgirl role, peeking up at him shyly.

She pulled him out of her mouth with a pop. "How's that, Mr. Fletcher?"

"Do you want an A plus?"

"Yes."

Marcus yanked her to her feet and placed her on the edge of the desk. She gasped as he forced her legs apart and stepped between.

"How badly do you want that A?" he asked, face less than six inches away.

He was completely still, like a predator waiting for the right moment to pounce. Her heart pounded double time in her chest. She resisted the urge to lick her lips in anticipation and tried to stay in character.

"I really need an A," she breathed.

"How far are you willing to go?"

He placed his hand high on her thigh. It was her turn to jolt. Her body was revved up and begging to be used. She was breathless with anticipation to see what he would do next.

"A-as far as I need to go." Her shaky voice wasn't an act. Her throat was dry and dusty.

His hand slid beneath her dress and between her legs. His fingers touched her, and she had the pleasure of seeing his eyes dilate with desire. "You'll let me fuck you?"

"Yes," she said hoarsely. If this hadn't been her idea, she would have ordered him to get on with it. Instead, she had to play the game even if it killed her.

"You let any other guy touch you?" he murmured against her cheek as he slid one finger in.

"No," she moaned as she squirmed.

"I saw you kiss that boy in the hallway, the most popular boy in school," Marcus hissed as his thumb rubbed her clit.

She broke character. "Huh?"

"You kissed him. I saw you."

He was weaving Kody into the storyline? Hell. "He said he really liked me," she said plaintively as her legs began to tremble.

"Boys will say anything to get this," he said as he dragged his fingers out and then slid deep. "You're not going to give it to him, are you?"

"No."

"Why not?"

"Because he can't give me an A?"

He yanked her off the desk, whirled her around, and bent her over. Her breath whooshed out as he kicked her legs apart, fit himself against her, and slammed home. She gasped at the unexpected intrusion and then bit back a delighted laugh as he stretched her.

"You don't give him anything because he can't give you what you need," he whispered in her ear.

Her eyes nearly rolled back in her head as he began to move. *Hell, yeah.*

"Carmen?"

"Yeah?" she huffed.

"Hang on."

He straightened, gripped her hips, and began to thrust. She splayed over the teacher's desk, vaguely aware of the fact that she was on a chart which listed the student's name and tasks with smiley face stickers. She gripped the other side of the desk for leverage and moaned as she stared at the classroom of empty desks. She imagined that she really was fucking a teacher and got even wetter.

"Fuck me, Mr. Fletcher!" she moaned.

He ground against her. "Carmen."

"Yes, fuck me!"

He sped up, and she held on for dear life. The taboo environment sent her over the edge. His thrusts became erratic and frenzied as she rode her orgasm. Her teeth clamped together to hold back a scream as he gripped her hard enough to bruise. He slammed deep and came in one gush.

"You're so bad for me," he muttered into her hair as he rested on top of her.

She laughed weakly as she stared out the windows at the crowd in the distance. The door of the classroom was wide open, and anyone could find them like this, but she wasn't concerned. Even if Frederick and Mickey weren't guarding the hall, she would have seduced Marcus to see how far he would go. She loved pushing boundaries, and she was pleasantly surprised to find that he kept matching her.

"That shouldn't have worked on me," he grumbled as he pulled out and collapsed in the teacher's chair.

She slid off the desk and found some paper towels to clean herself. He didn't move. He sat in the chair with his eyes closed, utterly drained. She smiled as she sat sideways on his lap and wrapped one arm around his neck. Straitlaced Marcus was bending his rules for her.

"You played the teacher part perfectly," she praised.

He opened one eye. "You have these urges often?"

"Urges?"

"Fantasies."

"All the time."

His eyes closed. "I figured."

She wanted to pet and stroke, but she rested against him instead and floated in the aftermath of great sex. Marcus seemed willing to bust it loose anytime, anywhere. He was a man after her own heart. Too soon, he shifted and tapped her butt.

"We better go," he said.

She reluctantly slipped off his lap and did the schoolgirl pose while twirling her hair around one finger. "Do I get an A, Mr. Fletcher?"

He paused in the middle of straightening his clothes. "I'll give you an A, but I have to reevaluate for next quarter."

She giggled as they cleaned up the teacher's desk and walked out of the school. The adoption event was winding down. From this distance, she couldn't see how many animals were left, but she knew they had saved a lot of lives today. That fact combined with her orgasm made her feel as if she was emanating sunshine.

"We had a great turnout today," she said.

"Alice said you had a big hand in that."

She shrugged. "I just told a few of my friends."

"Is one of your friends the manager of Petco?"

She grinned. "He was a sweetheart."

"I heard you donated over ten thousand dollars' worth of items for the new owners as well."

"It's not a big deal."

Marcus stopped and turned to her. "It is a big deal. Alice says you're a big reason these events have become such a success."

"All I do is talk and donate where I see fit. Alice is the one that spends weeks preparing and making sure they turn out amazing. They're for good causes, and I love Alice."

His gaze shifted over her shoulder. "Can I help you?"

She turned and saw Mickey and Frederick standing nearby. "They're with me."

"What do you mean?"

"They're watching over me."

Marcus tensed. "Why?"

Reality was coming back with alarming speed. She wrinkled her nose as she tried to think of a delicate way to put this so she wouldn't scare him off. "I kind of …"

His brows rose, and she realized there was no nice way to put it. Actually, if threatening to shoot him didn't make him run for the hills, he could handle anything.

"I killed someone." No change in his expression. "Gavin and

Angel are taking care of it, but I'm laying low at my soon-to-be stepdad's house. When I go out, I have my guards."

"Who did you kill?"

No inflection in his voice. He had the best poker face she'd ever seen. Control personified… unless she provoked him with sex.

"The leader of the Black Viper gang."

He cupped the back of her neck and drew her against him. "You killed Blaine?"

"Blaine?" She was confused by the question and the smell of her cotton candy perfume mixing with classy sin on his suit.

"He was Blaine Carter before he became Maddog."

Hearing Marcus say Maddog sounded wrong on so many levels. "How do you know that?

"We went to the same school. He dropped out in seventh grade." His hand tightened on the back of her neck. "You need a place to stay where no one will find you?"

"No one knows my mom is engaged."

"The Black Vipers could track you after a public outing like this one."

She rocked her hand from side to side. Possible, but unlikely. The Black Vipers were bound to be more worried about Gavin and Angel than her.

"Why don't you move back in with Gavin?"

"Gavin and I don't see eye to eye. Besides, I need my own space. I'm going house hunting next week."

"If you need a place to stay, I have one."

"What?"

"I have a house I don't use since I stay in a suite at the hotel. I didn't even unpack, and it's in a gated community."

"You're offering to let me stay at your house?" she asked, just to clarify.

"Why not?"

"Wouldn't that be weird?"

"No. Come, you can see it now." He grabbed her hand and towed her toward a silver Audi.

"Um, okay." She turned and hollered, "You have my keys?" to Mickey who gave her a nod as she ducked into the passenger seat of Marcus's car. This was an interesting turn of events.

"Why are you involved with the Black Viper gang?" Marcus wasted no time asking as they left Cimarron Elementary.

She hesitated and then said, "Wrong place, wrong time." She didn't want to bring up the fact that Angel took her there. She was sure Gavin and Marcus would both be pissed about it. They wouldn't understand that in his own fucked up way, Angel had been trying to help.

"Why'd you kill him?" Marcus asked.

She tried to hang onto the bliss of climax and not the slap of rage that threatened to blow her high. "He said something about Vinny, and I snapped." She felt his quick glance and stared straight ahead.

"Blaine never respected women. Not surprising that he underestimated the wrong one," he said mildly.

She didn't like hearing that his name was Blaine. It made him sound more human and less like the leader of a violent, notorious biker gang. "My dad killed his. We have history."

"Your dad's the one who shot Cannon?"

She stared at him. "How do you know all this shit?"

"I grew up in Conklin."

She straightened. "The housing projects? Are you serious?"

He flicked her an amused glance. "You didn't think I was born into this, did you?"

"I did, actually." He wore power like a second skin and had the manners of a fine gentleman. She couldn't imagine him in a rough neighborhood. Not even cops wanted to answer calls in that area. It was gang infested and poverty-stricken. "How is that possible?"

"Long story," he said and reached for his phone when it began to ring.

She sat back as Marcus drove. Unlike her and Angel, he was cautious and controlled, which amused her. She closed her eyes and listened to the rumble of his voice as she basked in the afterglow of her orgasm.

Twenty minutes later, they entered a private community with its own shopping center. The homes were built around a massive golf course and lake. Marcus drove up a picturesque street lined with trees and generous properties before he pulled up to a house with a stone front. He parked in an empty three-car garage. She got out of the car as Frederick and Mickey parked in the driveway. Marcus unlocked the front door and waved her through as he continued his conversation on the phone.

She wasn't sure what to expect. She paused in the foyer and surveyed the space. Directly before her was a living room filled with light. A short staircase led to an upper level where the kitchen and dining room were. From where she stood, she could see everything, including a short hallway on the second floor that must lead to the bedrooms. There was no furniture or decorations. The only room that had anything in it was an office. Marcus kicked aside some boxes to get to the computer as he talked.

She walked up to the second level and looked out at a surprisingly well-maintained backyard with a bench, trees, and shrubs. The house had three bedrooms, two bathrooms. The master had a bed, nightstand, and not much else. The closet held a handful of suits, workout clothes, and shoes. The second bedroom was filled with boxes, and the third was empty.

The house had been designed with beautiful stone accent walls, built-in shelves, and a corner bathtub in the master that invited her to take a load off and soak. This place had a sense of peace and tranquility about it. It wasn't something she would have considered in the past, but at this point in her life, it was perfect. Charisse expected her to choose a super luxe home comparable to what she had with Vinny. This... this felt just right. Both she and Marcus could afford something much grander, but maybe he had been drawn to the same sense of well-being embedded into the walls.

She walked back to the dining area and leaned on the metal railing and surveyed the first floor. She was already mentally decorating when Marcus walked out of the office and pocketed his phone.

"I'll buy it from you," she said immediately.

"Buy?"

"You said you're never here."

"My stuff is," he said as he climbed the steps.

"I can put it in storage and help you find another place."

"You like it," Marcus surmised.

"Yes, it's perfect for me."

"You don't have to buy it from me. I told you, you can stay here."

"I know, but I want it, and I have to settle somewhere. I looked at twenty-six houses in three days, and I hated all of them. Besides, who knows how long it'll take Gavin to kill all the Black Vipers?" She cocked her head. "And if you think I can live here without decorating, you're crazy. Let me buy it from you. I'll pay you double what you bought it for."

"You want it that bad?"

"Yes!"

Marcus went to the fridge and pulled out two bottled waters. He handed one to her and drank from the other. "I'm not selling."

"Why not?"

"Because I like it." When she opened her mouth to argue, he held up a hand. "If you still want it after you've been here a while, maybe we'll negotiate."

"But you're a businessman! You'll make a profit!"

He leaned against the railing. "I don't need the money."

"Hard ass," she muttered.

His mouth crooked at the corner as he sipped his water. He studied her silently as if he was waiting for her to say something.

"What?" she asked and looked down at her dress to make sure she didn't have cum stains or something.

"You got your head sorted out?"

Her head snapped up. "Excuse me?"

"You've been on a wild bender. I want to know if you're done or still going."

"I haven't been on a bender."

"Carmen, you fucked my brains out three times, twice in public, once in front of our goddaughter." When she opened her mouth to argue, he added, "I caught you pole dancing in the penthouse suite, kissing Kody Singer, and now I hear you killed the leader of the Black Vipers, all in two weeks." He crossed his arms. "And I'm sure I'm missing a whole lot of other stuff."

She tossed her hair. "What's your point?"

"My point is, I want to know if you're done trying to cheat death."

"I'm not suicidal," she said even as her mind supplied a flashback of her reaching for the gun in her bedroom.

"The night Gavin went to Hell, you told me you wanted to live. You told me to wake you up." He placed his hands on the railing on either side of her, caging her in. He leaned down and tilted his head to the side, so their lips were mere inches apart. "You're awake, you're alive, and I want to keep you that way."

Her heart thudded in her ears as warmth spread to every part of her body. "I'm fine."

"You're far from it, but you'll get there. Are you done with your bender?"

"I haven't been—"

He kissed her, and she sank so fast, everything around her ceased to exist. One hand gripped her hair while the other cupped her face to hold her to him. Classy sin. His taste tempted, teased, and calmed her all at the same time.

Marcus lifted her. She wrapped her arms and legs around him and kept his mouth busy. She didn't care where they were going or why. He settled her on her back on something as soft as a cloud. She broke the kiss to press a hand against the mattress.

"This bed is amazing. I'll buy this from you too."

"We'll share it," he said as he grabbed her face and turned it back to him so he could continue ravishing her.

She grinned as he shrugged off his suit jacket and lay on top of her. They made out like teenagers while they explored through their clothes. When she couldn't take the teasing any longer, she thumped his shoulder.

"I want your dick!"

Marcus buried his face in her hair and laughed. She hit his

shoulder again and tried to roll him on his back, but he was too heavy.

"I'm serious!"

Marcus slid off her and began to undress. She came up on her elbows to watch the show. Despite the fact that they had hooked up several times, she hadn't seen him completely nude. She waited with bated breath as Marcus bared his body for her delectation. Marcus Fletcher was *fine*. He had a sculpted body with hair on his chest that led straight to his moneymaker. He had broad shoulders and muscles in all the right places—arms, abdomen, thighs. His hip bones were prominent and made her mouth water with the need to trace them with her tongue. She sat up and stripped off her jacket.

"No, let me," he said.

He pulled her to the edge of the bed and pulled off the bomber jacket. She worked the dress over her hips and held her hands in the air so he could pull it off. He stilled when he saw her matching black lace lingerie set. She grinned, enjoying his bemused reaction. When thirty seconds passed without a word, she decided to speed things up by widening her legs.

"Mr. Fletcher, I've been soooo naughty," she said in her high-pitched schoolgirl voice.

Marcus visibly stiffened. She was about to muster up a girly giggle, but that wasn't necessary. He launched himself at her. Her back hit the mattress even as he ripped her flimsy string bikini off and sank into her.

"I told you about that voice," he growled.

"You like it," she whispered as she ran her nails down his back.

He cupped her breast and thumbed her nipple. "I finally have you in a bed. I wanted to take my time—" He broke off as she rocked beneath him. "Carmen."

She ran her hand through his damp hair. "You can take your time next round."

He took her at her word and got to work. He did her missionary style. Rough, hard, and deep. She urged him on with her schoolgirl voice until she was too lost in the moment. He came first, but she didn't mind. She rolled him onto his back and rode him until she found her own orgasm. She flopped on top of him, cheek pressed against his heaving chest.

"Twice today without a condom," he said, "You been with anyone besides me?"

"No," she murmured sleepily.

A hand cupped her cheek. She opened one eye to see him smiling and looking extremely smug. "That's good news, babe."

"I've had a slow week," she joked.

He chuckled as he tipped her to the side and curled himself around her. One arm wrapped her close as he buried his face in her hair and took a deep breath.

"You have anywhere to be?" he asked.

"No."

"Then sleep," he said and twined his leg with hers.

He rested heavily against her. She closed her eyes and absorbed the feel of a man holding her close. She could feel the differences between Marcus and Vinny's bodies and immediately stopped trying to compare and just let it be. It hadn't just been a long week; it had been years of stress and heartache, but right now, she was at peace, and she wanted to savor it.

"You're safe here," Marcus murmured into her hair.

"I know." She closed her eyes, took a deep breath, and let it all go.

16

Carmen cracked open one eye and surveyed her bare surroundings for a full minute before she remembered where she was. She was with Marcus in her future house. She stretched beneath the sheets and found that she was alone in bed. She padded into the amazing bathroom and gave the bathtub a longing glance before she stepped into a shower big enough for four people.

Her mind was cloudy from sex and sleep, but she felt better than she had in days. Sex had always been her drug of choice. She liked sex with food, sex with alcohol, sex with costumes... She wasn't picky. Sex made her feel alive, wanted, powerful, sensual. Marcus was doing a damn good job of keeping her topped up.

She stepped out of the shower and felt no qualms about going through Marcus's closet to find something to wear. She settled on a thin white tee with a small V neck. It was soft and rode high on her thighs. Her stomach rumbled as she made her way to the kitchen. She turned on the lights and fell in love all over again. The house wasn't too big or too small; it was just right. Everything was strategically placed and tailor-made for her. This was her house; she just needed to convince Marcus of that.

She heard the rumble of his voice coming from the office. She went into the garage to fetch her phone from his car. She had three missed phone calls from her mom, one from Lyla, and one from an unknown number. She dialed her mom as she walked into the house.

"Carmen, are you all right?" Mom asked quickly.

"Yes. Sorry, I forgot to call. Mickey and Frederick are with me," she said as she peeked through the curtains. They sat in their SUV, staring straight ahead. When and where did they pee?

"Where are you?"

She hesitated only a second before she said, "I'm at Marcus's house."

"Marcus Fletcher?"

That managed to surprise her mother.

"Yes. He heard about my trouble and offered to let me stay at his place."

"You're going to live with Marcus?" Mom sounded stunned.

"He doesn't live here. He lives in the casino, and I'm going to buy it from him."

"I didn't know you two were so close. This is great news."

"It is?"

"You sound happy, and that makes me happy. Are you coming home tonight?"

Mom sounded supremely unconcerned now.

"I don't know. I'll keep you posted."

"Okay. Tell Marcus I said hi."

"I will," she said.

"Carmen?"

"Yeah?"

"I always liked him," Mom said.

"I know you have."

"Okay, baby. Have fun."

Carmen hung up, shaking her head. She had seen Mom and Marcus talking at several get-togethers. He was a natural charmer, and her mother wasn't immune to him. She listened to her voicemail as she headed toward the kitchen. It was the volunteer from the event. The terrified pit bull hadn't been adopted.

She paced around the living room. Gavin put her things in storage before selling the house she shared with Vinny. She had no idea what was in the storage unit since she never had the balls to go through it, but now that she had a house to decorate, she was eager to comb through her old belongings. She could imagine several pieces that would be perfect here.

"Hey."

Marcus gave her a sweet kiss while one hand slipped under her shirt and cupped her ass.

"You had a good nap?" he asked.

"Yes." She took in his workout shorts and white tee, which was identical to the one she wore. "This must be the longest you've ever been away from work."

He chuckled and gave her ass a squeeze before he let her go. "I come here maybe once every two weeks."

"How long have you had this house?"

"Almost two years."

"And you don't have a dining table or something to sit on?"

"All I need is a desk and bed. Everything else is unnecessary."

"Spoken like a true workaholic."

"And proud of it. I can make us sandwiches or call for takeout."

"A sandwich is fine." It sounded amazing, actually. She was starving.

She leaned against the counter and watched Marcus pull out the fixings for sandwiches. He poured pretzels into a bowl and slid them across the counter to her. Amused, she took one and munched.

"Since you're my new landlord, I guess I should run this by you," she hedged.

He glanced at her as he arranged bread on a cutting board. "You're not going to pay me rent, so you can't call me your landlord."

"What am I supposed to call you?"

"A friend."

Friend. She silently tested the word and liked it. "Okay, friend, I want to get a dog."

Marcus carefully smeared mayo on bread. "A dog?"

"There was this dog at the event today. No one will adopt her. She's a wreck. She needs a second chance, and I want to give it to her."

Marcus carefully placed thin slices of turkey on top of the bread. "What breed?"

She crossed her arms. "What kind of dog do you think I'd pick?"

"A Pomeranian?"

She smacked his arm. "Seriously?"

"It's not?"

"No, she's a pit bull."

He shook his head. "If the dog has been abused—"

"Beau was abused, but he's one of the best things that happened to Lyla. Even Gavin loves him. Besides, you can't judge from the outside, and everyone deserves a second chance." *Like me*, she thought.

"I should've known you'd choose a breed no one would imagine you with. Always doing the unexpected."

He spent an inordinate amount of time choosing the right pickles. She had to admit, the sandwich he was building looked delicious.

"Is that a yes?"

"You can do whatever you want," Marcus said as he slapped a slice of provolone on top of a stack of turkey.

"You'll let me take over your house? What if I end up staying here longer than a month or two?"

Marcus slid her sandwich over and took a bite of his own. "Fine with me."

"What about when you want to get away from the hotels and need somewhere to go?"

"Then I'll come here."

"What if our sex turns to shit before Gavin and Angel kill all the Black Vipers?"

"We'll still be friends, and you can still live here."

"What if I annoy the hell out of you?"

He grinned. "I'm sure I can handle it.

"You're right. It's more likely you'll annoy me."

He frowned. "Why would I annoy you?"

She examined his sandwich, which was commercial worthy. "You're too perfect."

"I'm far from perfect."

"I have yet to see your bad. It's fucking annoying."

He laughed. "Trust me, I have a lot of bad traits."

"Well, let's hear it."

"I'm competitive."

She frowned. "You think that's a bad trait?"

"It is when you're as obsessive about it as I am. I want to be the best in every aspect, especially business."

"You need to be competitive to be successful. That doesn't count."

"I'm hyper focused."

"Not impressed."

"I'm selfish."

"There's no proof of that. You go out of your way for everyone, and you're offering to let me stay at your house."

"I don't want anything to distract me from work, which is why I'm not in a relationship," he said.

"Okay..." she drawled. "That's a little selfish but not surprising. You've been carrying the load for a long time, so I'm not surprised you haven't had time for a relationship. Come on, what else?"

"Gavin says I'm never satisfied. I'm obsessed with improving everything."

She fake yawned. "Seriously, you have no idea what a bad trait is."

"Okay, what are your bad traits?"

She blew out a breath. "Where do I start? I'm impulsive, manic, have a hair trigger temper, I love things that glitter and shine, I love presents, and I have a hard time letting go." She sped past that last one. "I'm also high-maintenance, vain, selfish, arrogant, bitchy, bratty, lusty, and according to you, occasionally go on benders. And that's just off the top of my head."

"Is that all?"

She grinned at his dry tone. "I believe in embracing one's flaws. It's what makes me irresistible."

"I'll remember that when you start being bratty. What does that mean, by the way?"

"That I may throw tantrums and want to be babied when I feel like it."

"Thanks for the heads-up," he said as he finished off his sandwich.

Unruffled, as usual. "You aren't concerned what people will think about me being here?"

"No. Are you?"

"No, but you have a squeaky-clean image."

"I'll survive."

She munched on pretzels between bites of her sandwich. "What if I refuse to move if you don't sell it to me?"

He grinned. "I'm sure we'll work it out. Besides, we have to make it work since we'll be co-parenting."

She froze with her sandwich an inch from her lips. "Excuse me?"

"We're Nora's godparents," he said and laughed. "You should see your face."

She scowled. "Gavin's right. You're annoying."

"You like the house, and I work a lot so I'm not going to demand sex every night."

"And if that's what I want?" she challenged.

His voice lowered. "You have my number."

He went to a wet bar in the dining area and made himself a gin and tonic with an efficiency that made her stare.

"You want a drink?" he asked.

"Sure. Were you a bartender in a past life?"

"Bartender, valet, bell boy, cashier... you name it, I did it."

"What? You were a cashier? Where?"

"Target."

She lowered her voice to a purr. "You still have the red vest and khakis?"

He stiffened and stared at her with wary eyes. She slapped the counter and waved her sandwich at him.

"You should see the look on your face," she said gaily.

"You should warn a man before you use that voice on him."

She fluffed her hair. "It's my specialty."

"Driving men crazy? Yes, it is. Every time I see you, some guy's trying to get your attention."

"It was worse when I had big boobs."

He walked back with their drinks and paused to lean down and kiss each breast through his shirt. "I think they're perfect."

She tried to ignore the flash of heat he evoked as he sipped his drink and leaned against the counter. This should have felt strange—standing in Marcus's kitchen eating sandwiches, but it felt easy, casual, as if they'd been doing this for years. How strange.

"Tell me about when you and Lyla went on the road," he said.

"What about it?"

"Where did you go?"

"Everywhere. I'm sure we hit almost every state."

He shook his head. "I can't imagine you and Lyla on the road by yourselves. It must have been dangerous."

"It can be, but we had guns, and we didn't stay at ghetto RV parks, only the best. When we wanted to settle down, we'd rent a place for a week or two before going back on the road. It was a good break."

"From what?"

"Life." She sipped her drink and thought of how reckless she had been. "I used to be a fighter."

"You still look like one to me."

"You don't know me," she said quietly.

"Of course, I do."

She frowned. "You don't. If you really knew me, you'd run."

Marcus raised a brow. "Try me."

She clamped her mouth shut. She wanted to stay at the house, wanted the sex, and she liked his view of her even if it wasn't accurate.

"You are one of the most complex women I've met," Marcus said thoughtfully. "You and Lyla are thick as thieves, yet you two couldn't be more different from one another. You're the mastermind behind a lot of Vinny's projects and can network even better than me, and that's saying something. You're gorgeous, reckless, and the best I ever had. Is there something I'm missing?"

She liked his description of her more than she should. Damn, he was good with that mouth. "I'm a killer."

"Yes. You killed to protect yourself and Nora, and then you killed the leader of the Black Vipers because he said something about Vinny."

It wasn't a question, so she didn't answer.

"Blaine went over to the dark side a long time ago. If you hadn't pulled the trigger, someone else would have." He cocked his head to the side. "I doubt an evil person would have donated ten thousand dollars' worth of items to an animal adoption or want to rescue an abused pit bull."

"I'm a wreck," she said, determined to make him see the real her.

"You've been through the wringer. You have reason to be."

"You're making excuses for me."

"Someone has to. You're human. You have feelings; you make mistakes."

"You're trying to make me feel better." His dismissive attitude was working wonders on her, which relieved her of the perpetual weight on her shoulders. That same sense of good she felt while being with Maddie and Marv now had a new and unexpected source.

"You're hurting. It makes people do crazy things," he said.

She looked down to hide her reaction. She grabbed a handful of pretzels and focused on the tiny bits of salt instead of his words, but his voice was penetrating when she didn't want it to.

"Carmen?"

"Yeah?"

"Look at me."

She braced herself before she met his gaze.

"I don't know what you're searching for, and I'm not going to help you find it, but I'll keep you company until you do."

She blinked hastily and nodded. "Thanks."

"No problem."

She mentally scrambled for another topic, but he provided one when he said, "I can't imagine living on the road. I've never been out of Nevada."

She gaped. "What? How is that possible?"

"I was born and raised in Las Vegas. I started working at fifteen. I have everything I need here. Traveling was never an option."

"You need to take a vacation ASAP," she said and then gasped. "You've never seen the ocean?"

"No."

"How can you live without seeing the ocean? It's only a three-hour drive to the beach!"

"I'll go one day."

"You should go right now!"

He laughed. "One day, I will. I don't think now's a good time."

"Is Gavin back at work full-time?"

"Not yet. I've got it handled, though."

"Of course, you do."

"Is that sarcasm?"

"No. I know you can handle it. You graduated at the top of your class and have a business degree."

"Checking up on me?"

"Yes," she admitted without shame. "I wanted to make sure."

"Wanted to make sure I was qualified to stand in for Vinny?"

That sounded ludicrous since Marcus had done more to advance the company than Gavin or Vinny had in the past five years.

"It's not about Vinny. I wanted to know why Gavin picked you." She paused deliberately. "And I still want to know."

"He picked me because of my background."

"Because you grew up in the housing projects?"

He nodded. "I knew Emmanuel Pyre as a crime lord before I ever knew he owned casinos. I know the players in the underworld since I grew up among them." Marcus shrugged. "I knew the only way out was an education. I got a scholarship at UNLV and was picked for an internship. I worked in low level management for a couple of years before Gavin approached me for this position. He saw my background as an asset rather than a liability. He gave me an opportunity no one would have trusted me with. I would never betray him. I owe him for everything I have."

"It may have taken longer, but you would have made it without his help," she said.

His eyes gleamed. "You think so?" He picked her up and placed her on the counter. He nuzzled her chest. "I can see your nipples through my shirt."

"Want me to change into something else?"

"No," he said lazily as he licked her nipple. "This is great." He ran his hands up her thighs. "I can't believe you would have given yourself to that boy in the club. You choose the most mediocre men who could never give you what you need."

She gripped his hair to pull his mouth off her nipple. "It was just sex. It didn't matter."

"It matters. You can't find anyone compatible if they're not on your level to begin with, and we both know one-night stands are shit."

"What?"

"Hookups take care of the itch, but it doesn't tide you over very long, so you keep having shitty sex with people you don't give a fuck about, and it becomes an endless cycle of crap."

"And you have experience with this?"

"I don't have time for relationships, which only leaves one-night stands or friends with benefits."

"Which do you prefer?"

He looked up. "Friends with benefits."

She considered him for a long minute. "I'm open to that."

"Good, because that's what I can give you."

"I'm not looking for a relationship." That was the last thing she needed while she was trying to put herself back together.

"Then maybe we can help each other out." He spread her legs and stared down at her bare pussy. "You've been playing hell with my concentration at work."

He leaned down and licked her. She groaned and reached up to grip the cabinets as his tongue slid through her folds. He went deep, and her head kicked back. She thought she was having a visit from God, but it was just the blinding track lights.

"Marcus," she moaned.

He straightened. "You want me to get a condom?"

"No."

He captured her lips as he slid inside her. He watched her, green eyes burning and bright.

"I've been craving you," he husked.

"Crave away," she panted.

His tongue slid into her mouth, and she clutched him as he overloaded her senses. When he pounded into her, she couldn't concentrate on the kiss. She wrapped her arms around his neck and held on tight. His head tipped back as he came. He slumped against her, and she took his weight.

"I'm loving this friend thing," she said.

He let out a breathless laugh and kissed her neck. "Me too, but I have to go to work."

They cleaned up the kitchen, and he showed her how to use the security system. She went into the bedroom with him and cleaned up while he morphed into the slick COO of Pyre Casinos. She slid beneath the covers and eyed him appreciatively.

"I'll tell Frederick or Mickey to get you clothes for tomorrow," Marcus said.

"You're the best friend I've ever had," she yawned.

He kissed her forehead. "You'll stay here?"

"Yes."

"Good. I want to know you're safe." His hand slipped beneath the cover and smoothed over her naked skin. "You need anything, you call me."

"I will."

He kissed her and left. The smell of classy sin hung in the air. She turned on her side and hugged his pillow to her chest. Everything would be okay. It would all work out. For the first time in years, she caught a glimpse of her future, and it looked promising.

17

"WHAT THE HELL, CARMEN?" LYLA DEMANDED.

"Hey, girl, what's up?"

"What's up?" Lyla repeated in a dangerous tone. "What's up is you haven't been answering my calls for three days. What's up is Gavin told me you took out the leader of a biker gang, and Angel got shot. What's up is you're now a target. What the hell?"

"Yeah, I'm over it," Carmen said as she navigated the freeway and stroked the quivering pit bull on her passenger seat. "I wouldn't say I'm a target, technically. Angel did the head shot, and besides, I have two guards. Don't worry about me."

"Carmen." Lyla sounded as if she were trying to stay calm. "I need you to be safe."

"I am!" she insisted as she blared her horn and flipped the bird at an old woman who shouldn't be on the freeway. "I found a place!"

"You did?"

"Yes. My shit that was in storage is being delivered today, and I got a dog."

"You got a dog," Lyla repeated flatly.

"Yeah, she's shaking like a leaf, though. They were gonna put her down, but it isn't her fault that she's had a shit life. I'm going to make her a princess."

"Okay... where's your new place?"

"The Gillian Estates."

"Never heard of it."

"Yes, it's pretty new, and it's on the other side of town from you, but you gotta see this house. It's perfect for me."

"Well, I'm happy for you." Lyla sounded much more relaxed. "You're getting settled in. That's good."

"Yes. How are you?"

"Worried sick about you, bitch."

Carmen laughed. "I'm fine."

She woke up with a ton of energy. No tears this morning. No hard, cold weight in her gut. Three orgasms worked wonders on her state of mind. Despite the fact it was Sunday, she started making calls. At times like these, she liked being rich because it produced results. She called the dog shelter to tell them she would be picking up the pit, a call to a moving company to go to the storage facility to pack up her shit, a call to a couple of personal assistants who were in her employ years ago who would help, and her relator to find out if there was another house available in this area.

Marcus was true to his word. This morning, a duffel of her clothes was on the front step. She blew a kiss to Mickey as she hauled it in and got ready for the day. Her first stop was the dog shelter. It seemed the poor pit was worse today than she was yesterday. When they tried to move the dog, she peed herself. Carmen volunteered to bathe the dog and murmured sweet nothings to her as she ran her hands over the terrified dog, but nothing soothed her. When Frederick picked up the dog to put her on the passenger seat of the Aston, the dog let out a heart-wrenching cry that ripped at her heart. She tried to reassure the pit that she was safe now. Whatever happened in the past was done, and there was only good in her future, but of course, the pit ignored her. She decided to call her Honey because her life would be sweet from now on. She and Mickey did a quick run to Petco for doggy supplies while Frederick kept an eye on Honey, and now they were on their way back to the house. Hopefully, they'd beat the movers there so she could direct everyone.

"When Gavin heard Angel got shot, he was furious," Lyla said quietly.

"I bet." Another cousin of his trying to claim his crown, getting gunned down within a matter of days.

"You were there? You saw it happen?"

The ball of sunshine in her chest began to dim. "Yes."

"Three times in the chest," Lyla said and paused. "You okay?"

Thanks to Marv, Mom, Maddie, and Marcus... "Yes."

"I'm glad. Gavin's been going to work, which is good. I need some breathing room."

"You're doing okay?" she asked belatedly.

"I have my moments, but Nora yanks me out of it pretty quick. She's getting more active every day, and Blade's training me again, so I've been keeping busy."

"Good. What about your mom?"

"Same. Still doesn't want to see me, slow recovering. I decided to wait until she's ready to be released instead of hanging around the hospital, making Gavin crazy."

"Good idea. I'll come over soon, or you can visit me once I get settled."

"Okay, good. I love you."

"I love you too."

"Stay out of trouble for fuck's sake," Lyla snapped before she hung up.

Carmen pulled into Marcus's driveway and saw that the movers were already there, as were her assistants. Frederick carried Honey to the backyard so she wouldn't bolt as they got busy. There were five twenty-six-foot moving trucks with items from her past life. She wouldn't be able to keep everything, but she was due for a purge.

The men opened the back of the trucks. She climbed in, surveyed the clutter, and took a moment to get her bearings before she got to work. She locked her emotions up tight, examining the items objectively while blocking out the memories that came with them. She started pointing at what she wanted and in which rooms. Her assistants made sure the movers put the items in the right place. By the time everyone cleared out, she lay exhausted but extremely satisfied on her red velvet couch. Marcus's house had been transformed in the span of a few hours. They still had a lot of work to do, but the large pieces of furniture had been put in place, and the house was much more livable and welcoming. She added paintings, statues, and accents to give the house personality. Everyone would return tomorrow to continue the transformation.

Her phone rang. It was within reaching distance, so she answered. "Hello?"

"Angel likes you!" Luci sang.

Carmen's eyes popped open. "What?"

"I've never heard him talk about a woman like this ever. OMG." Luci sounded like she was jumping around. "Where ya been, chick? I've been calling you for days."

She sat up. "I've been busy. What are you talking about?"

"Angel told me you killed the leader of some motorcycle gang. That was badass. I wish I could've seen it. He also told me you tried to protect him when he got shot." She sucked her teeth. "Gavin wasn't kidding when he said these motherfuckers are out of line. Angel's going to make Sin City his bitch. I'm glad Gavin called him in. They're gonna find out real quick what makes us crime lords of New York."

She got to her feet and checked on Honey who was in the same spot she'd been in for the past three hours. She lay on the ground beside her doggy bed in a ball, her food and water untouched. As Carmen approached, she tensed. Carmen sat on the floor just inside the kitchen, giving Honey space but also letting her grow accustomed to her presence.

"So?" Luci prompted.

"So what?"

"Angel likes you."

"Because I killed someone?"

"Because you're the ride or die chick. Girls have always come easy to Angel. You can see why. He's pretty and has the carefree, bad boy vibe that we both know is a sham. Angel's a dark one, but that's part of his appeal, right?"

"Angel's suicidal."

Luci giggled. "I know, right?"

Carmen couldn't hold back a smile. Luci was obviously damn proud of her brother. If she had a brother, she would be the same. The more badass he was, the better.

"It's hard to come across a woman who has balls and heart, you know?" Luci asked.

"Wait, what are we talking about?"

"You. Brass balls, guns, badass motherfucker, my brother and you…?"

"There is no Angel and me."

"Why not? You think he's hot, right?"

"Yes, but—"

"And he's badass!"

She bit her lip to hold back her laughter. Honey's eyes flicked to her, but when she saw her watching, Honey immediately looked away. "He's definitely a badass with a chip on his shoulder."

"Don't we all? Only someone who got everything they want in life wouldn't have a chip on their shoulder."

The chip on the Romans' shoulders was their parents' death. Angel hadn't explained it, and it wasn't something you brought up so she agreed. "True."

"Angel needs a woman."

"Excuse me?"

"Well, he needs a good woman, you know?"

"And you think that's me," she said dubiously.

"He likes you."

"That's nice, but I'm not about to get mixed up with another crime lord."

"Why not?"

She sighed and tipped her head back against the wall. "Angel got shot three times in the chest."

"So?"

"That's exactly how my husband died. Three to the chest."

A pause and then a very quiet, "Oh."

"It was my nightmare come to life right in front of me." She could still hear the sound Angel made as he got hit, and the image of the men coming to finish him off, just as they'd done to Vinny. The surge of helpless rage threatened to sweep away her satisfaction over her productive day. "I can't do it twice."

"But Angel's a beast."

"I can't take the chance."

"This fucking sucks," Luci whined. "I already designed a Roman tattoo for you."

"What?"

"We all have eagle tattoos. It's tradition. I was getting one ready for you."

Holy shit. "Uh, thanks, but I'm good."

Luci blew a raspberry. "Fine. No new sister-in-law. You know, I've been waiting for one of my brothers to get with someone, but they're taking their sweet time."

"I'm sure it'll happen soon," she said consolingly as she inched toward Honey. She grabbed a handful of food out of the bowl and put it near her. Honey turned her face away. If she didn't eat by tomorrow, she'd have to take her to the vet. Fuck.

"You don't understand! I'm like Rapunzel stuck in this brimstone. It's not fair! When are you gonna come visit?"

"I actually just moved into a place."

Luci moaned. "No! I was going to tell you there's another brimstone for sale three down from mine. It would have been perfect!"

Carmen chuckled as she padded down the hallway to the master bedroom and ran the water in the luxurious tub. Thanks to her amazing assistants, all her toiletries were unpacked, and a basket of salts and oils sat on the ledge of the tub. She put in a generous amount of eucalyptus oil while Luci tried to sell her on living in New York.

"I'll just have to convince you when you visit. Angel told me you and I would get along swell, not that I needed his input. I already knew we're sisters from other misters. Other than killing that guy and buying a house, what else have you been up to? Banged anyone new lately?"

"I adopted a dog. I just brought her home, and she's scared stiff. It'll take time for her to unwind, and as for banging, I'm still doing Gavin's COO, Marcus."

"Oh, the hottie with the nice eyes? Yeah, I'd hit that. You guys are dating?"

"Friends with benefits." She put the phone on the ledge and stepped into the tub. She moaned as she submerged her aching body.

"That good, huh? Damn, Angel needs to step up his game."

"No Angel," she snapped.

"But you're not super committed to Mr. COO. You haven't even tried Angel yet, so there's still hope."

"There's no hope."

"Yes, there is."

She rolled her eyes. "Whatever you say, Luci."

"Ah, I like hearing that. My brothers never say that to me, those assholes. Anyway, I'll check in later. Keep me posted on your shenanigans. I need to live vicariously through you."

"Sounds good. Bye, chick."

She took a deep breath and sank chin deep in the warm, scented water that turned her bones to mush and made her skin tingle. Bubble baths were the unspoken cure for many things. Some woman had to make a living off cure-all bubble baths for overworked, overstressed women. She'd have to look into that and buy stock in bath bombs or oils or whatever.

Her phone rang again. She scrunched up her nose and peered at the screen before she reached for it. "Hey."

"Hey, baby," Marcus said.

Her toes curled. "I'm taking a bubble bath."

"Send me a picture."

"Why don't you visit and see me in person?"

"I would, but there are some issues in the casino tonight. I'm taking a break."

"What happened?"

"Someone tried to rob the cage cashier, and now, I'm all tied up in paperwork and cops."

"Did they get away?"

"No. He was shot in the leg by a guard. He didn't reach the doors."

"Nice."

He chuckled. "I'm glad you're impressed."

She held the phone up and made sure to shoo away the bubbles to expose her body as she took a selfie. "Poor baby."

"What about you? You moved in yet?"

She glanced around the bathroom, which bore no resemblance to what she walked into yesterday. An iron mermaid stood near the tub with seafoam-colored towels draped over one arm. Her assistants organized all her shit across the length of the vanity. Her jewels winked at her and begged to be shown off. Marcus's meager belongings took up one corner while she dominated.

"You wouldn't recognize the place," she said.

"Really?"

She could tell from his voice he didn't believe her. She took a variety of selfies before she settled on one and sent. "I brought home Honey."

"Honey? Who the hell is that?"

She blinked. "My new dog. Her name's Honey."

"Oh, the pit bull."

"Who'd you think I was talking about?"

"Knowing you, it could be anyone."

She raised her brows. "I'm not going to bring any guys here."

"Good."

She grinned. "Jealous, Marcus?"

"I've got my shot, and I'm gonna hold onto it for as long as I can." A pause and then he said hoarsely, "You shouldn't have done that."

"Done what?"

"Seriously? You can't send me pictures like that."

"You told me to."

"God, I can see everything. Fuck. I'll come home when I can."

She did a long, fake yawn. "Promises, promises."

"I gotta go. I'll talk to you soon."

She grinned as she tossed the phone on the ledge and sank back into the water. "You gotta keep up, Fletcher."

She soaked until the water turned cold and then reluctantly hauled herself out. She wrapped herself in a silk robe and checked on Honey. The food on the floor and in the bowl was gone, and there was a pool of water under her mouth to show she drank water. Carmen clapped her hands together excitedly and instantly regretted it when Honey went rigid.

"Fuck, Honey, I'm sorry. Mommy's just so happy. You're such a good girl." She slowly approached, but Honey's wide, terrified eyes stopped her in her tracks. She pressed her hands against her aching chest. "It's going to get better. I promise. You're safe here."

She cracked open the sliding door, so Honey could go outside and padded toward the velvet sofa and mound of pillows. She flopped on the couch and turned on the TV. She put on Psych, which Maddie had gotten her addicted to and settled down with a contented sigh.

An earsplitting howl jerked her out of sound sleep. She lurched upright as a light flipped on to reveal Marcus coming through the door that led into the garage. She looked around wildly for the source of the noise and saw Honey on her feet, emitting that awful sound.

"It's okay, Honey," she said as she rushed toward her. "He's a friend."

Honey stopped immediately and backed into a corner. Carmen stopped a few feet away with her hands out, unsure what to do.

"You were protecting Mommy. You're such a good girl. Thank you," she said.

Honey curled into a ball and tucked her face away. She turned to find Marcus surveying the living room in silence. He touched the head of a gold and white elephant near the front door before he examined an oil painting of a woman covered in flower petals of every color.

"You weren't kidding when you said you decorated," he said.

She rubbed her eyes. "I told you. What time is it?"

"Just after three."

She dropped her hand. "In the morning? Oh my gosh. What are you doing here?"

He came up the steps and glanced at the marble top dining table, which had a cheery arrangement on it before he focused on her. She realized her robe had come undone. She was too tired to care about her nudity. He took a step toward her, then stopped when Honey let out a warning growl. When he looked at the dog, she immediately averted her face.

"She okay?"

"Yes. She's just on edge." That was an understatement, but she wasn't going to lose hope.

Marcus went to the fridge and pulled out a slice of turkey and went on his haunches near the dog. Honey sniffed the air but didn't turn her head in his direction.

"You're fine," he said and dropped the turkey near her nose. "I'm one of the good guys."

Carmen's heart warmed. She smiled as he rose and came toward her. He picked her up, and she wrapped her arms and legs around him and dropped her head on his shoulder.

"You are a good guy."

He tucked his face into her neck. "You smell good."

"Eucalyptus," she mumbled sleepily.

He settled her on the bed. She closed her eyes and floated. She heard him flip on the bathroom light. She turned her head and watched as he disappeared inside. He wouldn't mind the seashell chandelier she put up, would he? Maybe the mermaid was a bit much, but a tub like that deserved an ocean theme. Marcus reappeared and then went into the closet. She came up on her elbows and waited for the explosion. He had a tiny section of the closet since he didn't have much clothes here. Her assistants unpacked her new wardrobe, and she was thinking of having a carpenter come in to see if he could do something to create more room.

"What are you looking for?" she called.

Marcus came out of the closet. "You did all of this in one day?" he asked as he began to strip.

"I had help. I told you I would move in," she grouched and turned on her side. "If you don't like it, you can sell the house to me. By the end of this week, you won't even recognize this place. I can't believe you've had this house for two years and never—"

Marcus flipped her on her back and crouched over her. He cupped one side of her face before he kissed her deep. He rested his body over hers and tilted his head to the side as he made love to her mouth with his tongue stroking hers. She ran her hand through his hair. His muffled groan made her nipples tighten. His hand caressed her cheek, slid over her neck, and then rested on her breast. He massaged gently, which made her nails dig into his shoulders. He detached his mouth from hers and kissed the curve of her jaw and then her neck.

"Never," he muttered.

"Never what?" she asked distractedly as he sucked on her pulse.

"Never settled anywhere in my life."

She shifted restlessly beneath him. "What are you talking about?"

"Never unpacked." He licked her pulse and then kissed it before he moved lower. "Never bought furniture. Never decorated anywhere I lived."

She clutched his hair as he sucked on her breast. "Why?"

"Never stayed anywhere long enough."

"What about when you when you lived with your parents?"

"I never had parents."

Her eyes opened. "What do you mean you didn't have parents?"

"Went into the system at six. Never stayed anywhere long."

"You were a foster kid?"

"Yes."

She shook her head. "That's not possible."

"Why isn't it possible?" he asked as he pressed gentle kisses over her face.

She was having a hard time concentrating when he was drowning her in affection he claimed to never have experienced, judging from his background. "Because you're Marcus Fletcher." He knew how to dress, how to talk. He was intelligent and business savvy and didn't have a mean bone in his body. What the fuck? The man she knew had no correlation to the story of his childhood he was painting.

"Someone gave me that name. I didn't have one before that." He raised his head and looked down at her. "The house looks great."

"Marcus," she began and didn't know what else to say.

"Bought this house to start my new life, to make it my first home, but I didn't know how." He kissed her still lips. "You did more in one day than I've done in years. Thank you."

She swallowed hard. "You can have it all."

"What?"

"Don't sell it to me. Keep it... and all the stuff."

"Even the elephant and mermaid statue?" he teased.

"Everything."

He ran his hand down her body. "Why would you do that? The painting in the living room must be worth thousands."

"Fifteen thousand."

"Why give it to me?"

"Because everyone deserves a home."

He stared down at her for a long moment before he pressed his forehead to hers. "There she is."

"Who?"

"The woman Vinny raved about." She stiffened, and he cupped her face. "I wanted you before I met you."

She stared into his eyes and had the sensation of falling.

"I wanted to meet the woman behind his projects, the woman in the photos all over his office. And now you're here." He stroked a hand down her body. "I never had access to beautiful things until recently." He licked her skin. "And it tastes amazing."

He slid down her body and paused at her belly button to lave it with his tongue. He looked up the length of her body, eyes glittering shards in the dim light.

"You never gave me an opening." He stroked her belly. "You weren't ready. Now that you're awake, now that you see me, I'm gonna take advantage." He spread her thighs and surveyed her body. "A lot."

He went down on her. She hissed through her teeth as his tongue went deep. She lifted her legs and planted her feet on the bed so she could lift her hips up to his mouth. He was damn good. She was moaning and thrashing within minutes. He didn't let up until she erupted beneath him, her limbs going rigid as pleasure rocketed through her. Marcus slid into her as she orgasmed and rode her rough. The sound of slapping skin filled the room. She raked her nails down his back.

"Fuck, Carmen," he panted.

"Harder."

He obeyed, doing her so hard she knew she would be feeling the effects tomorrow. His face was carved in animal ecstasy as he fucked her. No teasing or laughing this time. He gripped her hair and yanked her head back as he pounded into her. She took what he offered and reveled in his possession as he planted himself deep and came. He panted in her ear as he collapsed on top of her. His hand loosened in her hair and then began to stroke.

"Too rough?"

"Just right," she husked.

"I don't know what you're bringing out in me."

She nuzzled his face. "I like it. Whatever you need, Marcus."

He didn't respond, and she sensed he wasn't happy about what happened. She stroked his face.

"We all need an outlet. Let me be yours. You won't break me."

"I've never been like this with a woman," he said finally.

"You've been with pussies, that's why."

He laughed and rolled, putting her on top. "So, what are you?"

"A badass motherfucker."

He grinned. "Yes, you are."

She settled over him. "I'm going to ruin you for all other women."

"I can't wait."

"Corrupt you," she said around a yawn.

"Already done."

"I'm gonna make you get hard every time I say Daddy." She paused and then shook her head. "Wait, I can't call you Daddy. That's Blade's name."

Marcus stiffened beneath her. "What?"

She raised her head, which felt as if it weighed fifty pounds to investigate his incredulous expression. "It's a nickname."

"Why?"

"Because he doesn't want to be one." Marcus relaxed, and she tucked her face under his chin. "You're getting possessive."

"We're nowhere near done."

"And when we are?"

He wrapped his arms around her. "Then we'll still be friends."

"How can you be sure?"

"Because we understand one another. Neither of us is looking for a relationship and both of us need this."

She couldn't argue that point.

"We'll cross that bridge when we come to it, and we'll make it through."

"Promise?"

"Yes. Now, go to sleep."

She didn't need telling twice.

18

"Come on, Honey. You're safe here. You wanna go for a walk? Toss a ball? Cuddle on the couch?"

Carmen lay on the floor two feet away from Honey, who was still curled into the fetal position. Her ears flicked back and forth, but otherwise, she didn't move. It had been five days with no improvement. She felt so fucking helpless. She tried to tempt Honey with food, toys, and a soft voice, but nothing worked. She even slept on the sofa a couple of nights to see if proximity would work. It did nothing.

She sighed and got to her feet. She opened the front door and waved at Mickey and Frederick. Mickey got out of the car and came toward her.

"What's up?" he asked.

"Can you carry Honey? I want to go to Lyla's house."

Mickey winced. "I'll ask Frederick to do it."

She was due for a visit, and she was hoping Lyla had some doggy advice for her. Honey let out a howl and began to whimper when Frederick picked her up. Carmen tried to comfort her as Frederick deposited the trembling dog into the passenger seat of the Aston. She turned off the radio and backed out of the driveway with Frederick and Mickey following in their SUV.

Aside from Honey's lack of progress, it had been a satisfying week. With help from her assistants, the movers, and a professional decorator, she had been able to transform Marcus's house into a real home. Everything was in its place, and she couldn't be happier. Her belongings that didn't fit in the house would be auctioned off with all proceeds donated to the Pyre Foundation. Alice had been ecstatic and then alarmed when she found out how much some of the paintings were worth. She reluctantly accepted them when Carmen said they would be locked up in a container somewhere.

Marcus hadn't visited her since their late-night encounter, but he called almost every day. Their conversations were quick and casual. There was no awkwardness between them. She began to believe this could work although she caught the skeptical look her assistants exchanged when she explained their arrangement.

She pulled through the gates of the Pyre estate. She put the car in park and was about to open her door when Beau dashed around the corner of the mansion, barking madly. She hastily got out of the car and put her hands up to shush him. She glanced at Honey to see how she was handling this and was stunned to see her standing on the seat with her ears perked up. Beau jumped onto the driver's seat, sniffed Honey, and gave an excited bark before he jumped out again. Honey didn't move, so Beau jumped back in. He lunged playfully at her before he dashed out again, and this time, Honey followed. She stood in the middle of the drive as Beau ran circles around her and then took off around the house. Honey hesitated only a few seconds before she followed. Carmen stared after them, mouth open. What the hell?

She walked into the house with Frederick and Mickey on her heels. She peeked in the kitchen and saw that the door that led into the backyard was open. Beau and Honey ran across the yard, barking and leaping on each other. Blade had his gun out and was standing protectively in front of Lyla who was carrying Nora.

"It's okay, she's with me," Carmen said as she walked outside to join them.

Lyla turned. "Look how happy he is! I've never seen him like this."

Nora smiled and drooled as she approached. She took her goddaughter from Lyla and covered her face in loud, smacking kisses. Her guards drifted toward Blade and talked in low mumbles.

"What's her name?" Lyla asked as she went on her haunches to pet Beau who sat at her feet.

Honey stopped a few feet away and examined them all warily.

"Her name's Honey. I brought her here because she hasn't moved in five days," Carmen said dryly.

Lyla gave her a puzzled look. "What are you talking about?"

"Frederick had to carry this dog to the car because she won't walk on her own. She doesn't eat unless I leave the room, and she just sits in the corner facing the wall all day. I brought her here to get some pointers from you, but when she saw Beau, she lit up."

"Come on, Honey," Lyla coaxed.

"I've tried that—" She broke off as Honey inched forward and hit Lyla's palm. "I can't believe this."

"Maybe she needs another dog to teach her how to trust people," Lyla mused as she stroked Honey's head.

Carmen sat and bounced Nora on her knees. Blade stood nearby, watching the dogs play with his gun still out.

"You've settled into your new place?" Lyla asked.

"Yup and it's *gorg*."

"I'm sure it is." Lyla let out a long breath as she stroked the dogs. "I had a panic attack today."

Nora chortled and pulled on her top. Carmen kissed the baby's cheek and watched her mother closely.

"It was a bad one," Lyla continued. "I swear, I thought I saw a man in the nursery. I grabbed my gun and was ready to shoot, but no one was there." She shook her head. "I'm going crazy. Blade heard me scream and came with his gun. When he told Gavin, he almost left work, but I made him stay." She shook her head. "I'm a fucking mess."

"Have you been sleeping?"

"Probably not as much as I should." Lyla plopped on the bench beside her and leaned against her. "I'm glad you came over and brought your new baby. Liven things up around here. I definitely need a distraction. Tell me something interesting."

"I'm going to have three step siblings. Levi is a mechanic and too hot for his own good, the second son lives in Japan, so they're holding off the wedding until his wife gives birth, and Maddie is a freshman in college and has the same shoe size as us so she may steal some of yours."

Lyla scrunched up her nose. "That's all you got?"

Carmen hesitated only a moment before she dropped her bomb. "I'm banging Marcus."

Lyla didn't react. "Marcus who?"

"Marcus Marcus."

"His name is Marcus Marcus?"

"No, Marcus Fletcher."

Lyla's head turned so fast, Carmen was surprised she didn't get whiplash.

"What?"

"We're friends with benefits."

Lyla shot up from the bench and held up both hands like a traffic cop. "What? How? When?"

"The first time was the night you were in Hell. He came over to keep me company."

She put her hands on her hips. "When I was in Hell, you were getting busy?"

"Pretty much. Sex is a great stress reliever."

"You two hooked up that night, and now you're friends with benefits?"

"Well, we hooked up a couple of times before we agreed to be friends with benefits."

Lyla threw up her hands. "And only now you're telling me?"

"We've both been busy."

"Bitch, this is the kind of shit I want to know as soon as it happens."

"Well, now you do."

"What does this mean?" Lyla asked.

"It means I have sex on tap."

"But what changed?"

"I decided to live, and he's helping me with that. We finalized a few things at the event at Cimarron Elementary. By the way, the animal adoption was great. Over one hundred pets found homes."

"Aw, I'm so glad," Lyla said and then narrowed her eyes. "Stop trying to change the subject."

"I'm not. I'm segueing."

"No segueing. You're just banging him, and that's it?"

"Yes."

"You know I love Marcus." Lyla smiled suddenly and leaned forward. "How is he?"

"Girl."

"Really? Well, if friends with benefits works for you, and you're happy, then I'm happy too."

"Thank you."

"Speaking of segues." Lyla shoved her shoulder. "What the hell's up with you killing the leader of a biker gang?"

"He said shit about Vinny."

"And you shot him in a room full of people?"

"Pretty much," Carmen said as she made faces at Nora.

Lyla shook her head. "We're really messed up."

"We're badass motherfuckers."

Lyla scowled. "Don't swear in front of Nora."

"We're bad mothers," she said gravely.

Nora grinned and tried to stick her hand in her mouth.

"You look good," Lyla said, taking in her knee-high gladiator sandals, white shorts, and skintight top.

"I feel better now that I've settled somewhere. If Marcus hadn't offered me his place, I don't know what I would have done."

"Hold up. Marcus offered his place? The place you're staying is his house?"

"Yes."

"You're living with Marcus?" Lyla looked stunned.

"No, he lives at the casino. He offered me his place since it was a risk to stay with Mom and Marv, and I loved the house."

"But technically you're living together."

"He's been there once this whole week."

"But you two have slept under the same roof?"

"For one night."

Lyla stared at her for a full minute before she smiled so huge, it must hurt her cheeks. She clapped her hands together and did a little jig. "My day just perked up."

"Because I'm banging Marcus and staying in his place?"

"I'm happy because you're happy to be banging Marcus and living with him. I never would've thought… and now you are! I love Marcus. I love that you two are together… I mean, are friends with benefits. I don't have to worry about you because he'll take care of you."

"I don't need to be taken care of."

"We all need someone to watch out for us," Lyla said and took Nora from her. She put the baby on her hip. Mother and daughter stared at her with identical silver blue eyes. If Gavin had more daughters who looked like Lyla, he would definitely become more psychotic.

A happy yip made her look at the dogs who were running to their heart's content. "I'll take them both."

Lyla stiffened. "Excuse me?"

"I'll take Beau and Honey."

"You can't take Beau. He's mine."

"But Honey needs him."

"Then *I'll* take both of them."

"But I just got her."

"And she wasn't happy. You can adopt another dog."

"You're gonna take my dog?" she asked, outraged.

Lyla glared at her. "You bring something into my house, they're fair game. Isn't that the Pyre way? Claim what I want?"

"Gavin's not a crime lord anymore."

"So?"

"Fine. You can have Honey. It's just... I was hoping I would be the one to help her."

"You did. You found her the right family. I was thinking about finding Beau a friend anyway, so this is perfect."

Carmen drove across town as the sun began to set. Honey picked a new home, and it wasn't with her. Her fantasies of going on the road with Honey in the passenger seat disappeared in a puff of smoke. Lyla was right. It was best for Beau and Honey to be together, but she had been looking forward to having a companion. This was just another thing that didn't pan out. She parked in the garage, walked in the house, and paused to take it all in.

Her style had always been over the top, bold, and a mishmash of different elements. Nothing had changed. Pops of color meshed with metallic gold and white. Each room made a statement and was filled with knickknacks from her travels, one-of-a-kind art, and love. Marcus didn't know it, but his house held a quarter of a million dollars' worth of art. She wasn't about to tell him since he would probably freak out. Art wasn't supposed to be admired but experienced. She was having a painter come by next week to paint an ocean wall mural in his office. Maybe if Marcus saw it enough, he'd feel the urge to see it in person.

Nothing had been left untouched. The empty rooms had been filled with furniture, and all of Marcus's boxes had been emptied and tidily put away. His office had been made into the ultimate man cave. She couldn't wait to see his reaction. She was a little disappointed that he hadn't visited, but even during their short conversations, people were always interrupting. He was hella busy. It hadn't been that way with Vinny. Back then, everything had been on automatic, and Gavin was in control. Now, Marcus handled most of the load and with all his new business endeavors and expansions, Pyre Casinos was busier than ever.

She walked down the hallway, now lined with dreamy oil paintings of land and cityscapes. The master bedroom had a gold, black, and red theme. It was a sultry haven she was proud of. She sat on a chaise lounge to unzip her sandals and strip. While the tub filled with water, she walked to the kitchen and poured herself a glass of chilled white wine. She drank while 90s R&B bounced off the walls and she soaked. She was building brand-new memories here, and therefore, everything felt warm, comfy, and new—exactly what she needed.

When she finished, she pulled on her silk robe from the life-size geisha standing guard in front of her closet. She refilled her glass and climbed into bed. She played Psych on the brand-new massive flat screen mounted on the wall and opened her laptop. She laughed at Shawn's shenanigans as she clicked through her bank statements and checked her stocks and other business investments. She checked in with Kiki and several other local business partners that included local pizza parlors and helicopter rides along The Strip. When she had enough of business for the day, she set the laptop aside and called Maddie.

"I'm watching Shawn and Gus," she said.

Maddie laughed. "I'm re-watching season four."

"You want to come over?"

"I can't. I have a test tomorrow morning."

"On a Saturday?"

"Yes, it's my only class. I'll be free after that, though."

"Okay, I'll think of something."

"What happened with you and the COO?"

"You mean Marcus?"

"Yes." A pause and then, "He seems really nice."

"He is."

Marcus was definitely a puzzle she wanted to explore, but was trying not to. They were friends with benefits, which nixed deep, meaningful conversations and emotions. But what he revealed the other night had been on her mind all week. It didn't make sense for Marcus to come from such a background because he emerged from the ghetto unscathed. There was no sign of it on the surface, which meant there was something internal that she couldn't see. She hoped he had major flaws because he was almost too perfect to be real. She was missing something about him, and it was bothering the hell out of her.

"He seemed upset," Maddie hedged.

"Just a little."

"Levi said you two were probably low-key dating."

Carmen snickered. "I like that. Low-key dating. No, we're not dating, just banging."

Silence on the other end. "You're sleeping with him?"

"We're friends."

"Oh."

"He's really nice. If you're interested in an internship, he'll hook you up. He's good at what he does."

"Okay, I'll do that."

"Okay, Smarty, I'll let you study."

"Okay, bye."

"Bye." She shook her head as she called Mom. "Hey."

"Hey, baby. The house looks fantastic."

Carmen looked around the room. "It does."

"How you been? How's your new baby?"

"She wasn't doing good with me, but she came alive when she met Beau, so Lyla took her."

"Oh, no. Are you gonna adopt another?"

"I don't know. I felt like I couldn't really go anywhere since I didn't want Honey home alone. Maybe I'll wait a while and see."

"That sounds good."

"I just talked to Maddie. I'm hoping we can do something together tomorrow. You know, sister time."

"Carmen." Mom took an audible breath on the other end. "That makes me so happy."

"I know. She's a good kid. I like her." She tipped her foot from side to side. "What are we gonna do about the house? Neither of us is there now."

"It's up to you. Marv and I have cleared out almost everything."

"You want me to take care of it? Sell it?" It would be official—letting go of the past.

"Are you okay with that?"

"I have this place, and even if I have to move later, I can always find something."

"Okay, well, if you need me to help, just let me know."

"I will."

"I'm so happy, Carmen."

Her heart lightened. "I know you are. I'm happy for you too."

"I didn't think I could feel this way again after your dad died. You can too, Carmen. I think you're on your way there."

She cleared her throat. "Yes, I feel better now that I'm settled, and I have Marcus on tap."

"He's good in bed?"

"Better than good."

"He's compatible with you?"

"Very."

"I always liked that boy."

Carmen laughed. "I know you have. I just wanted to check in."

"Yes, thanks for calling, baby. Marv says hi. We're going out dancing with friends."

"That sounds great. I think I'm going to turn in early tonight."

"You do that. You've been working hard all week. I'm proud of you, Carmen."

"Thanks, Mom. Have fun tonight. I'll talk to you later. Love you."

"I love you more. Sweet dreams."

19

THREE YEARS AGO

He should have been home hours ago. Carmen paced around the living room with her phone in hand, willing it to ring. She called Vinny twenty-three times. His phone stopped ringing and now went straight to voicemail. Maybe he forgot to charge it. He called her six hours ago and said he had one meeting and then would come home. She dressed in new lingerie and waited... and waited. She was tempted to call Gavin, but she couldn't show him how worried she was. She insisted Vinny get the position, and now she had to live with it.

There was a tight ball of dread in her stomach. This was so unlike him. He wasn't the type not to call to let her know he'd be out longer, and he wasn't the type to forget to charge his phone. He was compulsive about things like that. Is this what her life would be like now? Long nights waiting up for him? How did Mom do this?

A knock on the door stopped her in her tracks. Maybe Vinny got in touch with one of the guards, and he wasn't sure if she was awake. She rushed to the front door and opened it. Gavin and Lyla stood on her front step. She was vaguely aware of SUVs parked in her driveway and the unusual amount of security milling around. It took her a split second to take this in before she focused on Gavin. She knew him well enough to know something was very wrong. The light cast his face into stark relief. His hazel eyes were fixed on her, unwavering, trying to communicate something… There was only one reason he would be on her doorstep at this hour, only one reason he would be staring at her with a mixture of pity and rage.

Her heart stopped. Color bled out of her world. She stepped back, shaking her head.

Gavin reached for her. "I'm sorry, Carmen."

"No!" His hollow apology echoed in her head. This couldn't be happening. It wasn't possible. "No! Don't say it."

"I'll find who did this and—"

His placid calm ripped at her. She launched herself at him and beat her fists against his chest. "You promised me, Gavin!"

Someone pulled her back, but she wasn't finished with him. She lashed out and was nowhere near satisfied when her open palm cracked against his cheek. She ripped herself away from whoever was tugging on her. She didn't want to be touched. She reached for the closest object and hurled it at the wall. The sound of smashing glass was satisfying so she grabbed something else and then another. She embraced fury and denial because she couldn't handle the guilt ripping her soul to shreds. This was her fault. If she hadn't convinced Gavin to… She picked up another object. She didn't care what it was because it could be destroyed and that was all that mattered. She maimed, slashed, stomped, and demolished everything she could get her hands on. Art she worked so hard to acquire and preserve wasn't safe from her. Her life, her perfect, beautiful live was shattered and so was she.

She saw an iron poker and swung it at a statue. The statue weighed a ton and didn't move when she attacked. She felt the impact reverberate up her arms, but she didn't stop. Her hands were numb, and she was out of breath, but she didn't stop waging war.

A sharp, stabbing pain broke through her rage. She whirled to kill her assailant. The poker was wrenched from her hands with such force that she landed on her hands and knees. She panted as her limbs began to feel heavy and unresponsive. As if from a long way off, she heard the burble of voices but couldn't make out the words. She stared down at her hands, at the diamond ring on her left finger. No Vinny. No husband. No future. Nothing.

"He can't be gone," she whispered. "I can't live without him."

Gentle hands stroked her face. "I'm so sorry," Lyla said.

Her eyes slid shut against her will. She felt herself being lifted. She tried to fight, but her body didn't obey. She forced her eyes open and saw Blade's ugly mug instead of Gavin's and let her eyes slide shut again. He set her on a soft bed. Her limbs flopped uselessly around her. She lay on her side, staring straight ahead as tears leaked out of her eyes. Vinny was dead. She would never see him again. How did he die? No, she couldn't handle that. Did she kiss him before he went to work this morning? She couldn't remember. She and Lyla went shopping for a wedding dress today and now… now, Vinny was gone.

A warm, wet washcloth wiped her sweaty, tear-streaked face. Fresh tears replaced the ones Lyla wiped away. As the full ramifications hit her, she began to shake. Lyla climbed into bed and hugged her tight. She grabbed fistfuls of her clothes because she needed something to hold onto and began to sob. Lyla's voice was soothing, but it couldn't penetrate the pain that engulfed her.

Vinny was gone. She killed him.

20

CARMEN WOKE, FACE WET WITH TEARS, AND HER HEART THREATENING to explode. She lashed out and heard something crash to the floor. She threw her head back and screamed before she dropped her face on her knees and sobbed as hard as she had the night she lost him. She rocked as she tried to contain her emotions. The sound of her pathetic whimpering filled the room.

Vinny was her everything. Aside from her parents and Lyla, no one had ever accepted her as she was. Vinny understood her moods and impulses better than she did. He handled her far better than her parents ever had and didn't try to curb her wild ways. He allowed her to run free, knowing she would come back to him. He was her anchor, her everything, and he was gone along with her father, the only other man who loved her unreservedly.

She reached for her phone to call... who? A glance at the clock revealed she'd only been asleep two hours. Mom was out dancing, Lyla was with Nora and Gavin, Maddie would have no idea what to do with her, and Alice would probably give her a pint of ice cream and suggest they watch HGTV. She wanted to rage, to scream, to curl into a ball and die. She wanted to jump out of a plane, race headlong at another car to see who would swerve out of the way, or strip on stage to cast out her demons and give them to someone else. She needed something to draw her out of the darkness or it would forever consume her.

It took her several tries to find Marcus's number since her hands were trembling and she couldn't see through the tears. When the phone began to ring, she rolled out of bed and paced, one hand flapping to keep herself from completely losing her shit.

"Hey, babe," Marcus said.

Just the sound of his calm, soothing voice made the pain lessen. She clutched the phone with both hands. "I need a purge."

"What?"

"I-I need..." What did she need? She needed to lose herself in something, anything to take her mind off the memories stabbing at her. Sex was the best antidote. Touch, adrenaline, oblivion. Yes, sex. She needed it so bad, she was shaking. She wanted it rough and dirty. "I need a fuck."

There was a short pause. She stopped in the middle of the room and closed her eyes, tears streaming down her face, silently pleading for him to say what she needed to hear. She couldn't be alone right now. He couldn't leave her like this, but if she told him how fucked up she was, he would definitely avoid her at all costs.

"Can you come to me?"

Relief so heady that she became lightheaded made her bend over at the waist. She attempted to sound normal as she said, "Yes, I can."

"There are several events going on tonight, and I'm not sure how long I'll be. You can attend with me, and then we'll leave when we can."

Knowing ecstasy and oblivion were in her near future allowed her to think past the pain. "Yes, I can do that."

"You okay?"

No. "Yes."

"Come to me."

"I will. I'll get ready now."

"See you soon."

She hung up and flipped on the bedroom light. A lamp with a

gold base lay shattered beside the bed. She ignored it and went into the bathroom. She splashed cold water on her face and sprayed a cooling mist over her swollen eyes and fanned her face. Her desolate reflection was familiar. Too familiar. She hated herself. The empty wineglass was filled with ice and Crown Royal this time. She sat at her vanity and placed the chilled glass against her eye.

No! Don't say it.

She flinched as the memory of her heartbroken voice echoed in her ears. She shot to her feet and tore through the bedroom until she found her earphones. Noise cancelling earphones blocked out everything but the sound of her racing heartbeat. She blasted the most "don't give a fuck" music she had. Cardi B was up first. She clung to the dark beat with the desperation of a drowning woman. She said the lyrics with an intensity Cardi B would have been proud of. She ignored the agony and forced herself to move to encapsulate the mood.

She planted her hands on the vanity and examined the woman in the mirror. The chilled whiskey helped with the swelling and redness. Her mouth was set, eyes glistening, but she refused to let another tear fall. She suffered every day for almost three years. It had to stop. She tipped her head up when she felt tears crawling up her throat.

"Don't cry, don't cry," she chanted but couldn't hear herself over the music.

She blew out a breath and let Eminem's attitude seep into her. When she had herself under control, she sat on the vanity bench made up of two snarling lions she had rescued from storage. Through the power of makeup, she could become whoever she wanted. She painted herself into a character who showed no sign that she possessed a hemorrhaging heart with a busted a stitch that was bleeding out with every beat. With every layer of makeup, she became less herself and more the character she wanted to emulate.

Forty minutes later, the sultry badass bitch in the mirror bore no resemblance to the out of control one who wanted to curl up in a ball and die. She wore a crimson velvet sleeveless dress with a high neck.

It was skintight, rode high on her upper thighs, and showed off her slight curves. She was decked out in diamonds from her glittering stilettos to the bracelet and rings decorating every finger. It was extra as fuck, but that's who she was. Her smoky wing tipped eye and matte, wine-colored lip was perfection. She was so deep in character that she didn't feel anything. It was a relief, but she knew the reprieve wouldn't last. Hopefully, Marcus worked his magic before the stroke of midnight and she became herself again and fragmented into a million pieces. A black velvet clutch completed the look. She filled it with necessities—cell phone, lipstick, gun.

She walked out the front door and turned to lock it. It took less than thirty seconds for Frederick and Mickey to breathe down her neck.

"What's going on?" Frederick asked.

"You're taking me to The Strip," she said and turned to face them.

Mickey and Frederick surveyed her in silence before they exchanged a look.

"I don't think that's smart," Frederick said.

"I didn't ask for your opinion," she said and started toward the SUV.

"I'm calling it in," Mickey said.

She ground her teeth as she slid into the back of the SUV. "I'm meeting Marcus."

"Fletcher? Oh, that changes things," Mickey said as he climbed into the passenger seat. "Although I still don't think The Strip is the best place for you. Too much exposure."

"Angel and Gavin haven't killed all the Black Vipers yet? It's been almost two weeks."

"They've killed a bunch, but the Black Vipers contacts have come to play as well."

If she wasn't buzzed from whiskey and high on rap, she might have worried about that. Instead, she clung to the beat playing in her head that kept her focused on her role. She balanced on a knife's edge. One push and she would topple into the endless depths of self-loathing, guilt, and depression. She hoped Marcus was able to fuck her out of the past and into the present. It was the only course of action she could think of. If that didn't work, she had no idea what she would do.

It took too long to reach The Strip, and the lights and manic energy didn't penetrate her armor. She texted Marcus as they waited in Friday night traffic. He was at Lux, which was hosting a wealthy businessman's thirtieth birthday. Apparently, the businessman had the dough to fly in the hottest celebrities to help him celebrate. Due to the high-profile event, the wait to reach the valet station was taking forever.

Her patience snapped, and she stepped out of the car. Mickey immediately followed and grasped her arm as she slipped through the crowd. This time, the press of bodies didn't make her feel better. The excited tourists flocking the sidewalks irritated her. She was tempted to shove and elbow her way through. As if he sensed her volatile mood, Mickey stepped in front of her and cleared a path while she pressed against his back. It was marginally better once they entered the casino. She took the lead while Mickey scanned his surroundings. He didn't look so young and bright-eyed now. He was tense and alert. She welcomed an attack right now. She was armed and good to go.

The crowd in front of Lux was ridiculous. She hadn't seen such a crush in a while. Once again, Mickey cleared a path. When they reached the front, she stepped up to security. The club manager spotted her and waved her forward.

"Mrs. Pyre, Mr. Fletcher told me you would be attending," he said and glanced at Mickey.

His address caused a hairline fracture in her shield. Her body locked, and she sank deeper into character and turned up the rap in her head. "This is my security guard, and I have another, Frederick. He's ripped and looks like he works for FBI," she shouted over the sound of the crowd.

The manager nodded and waved her through. "I'll make sure he gets in."

Lux was built like an amphitheater with five levels. It was a grand club that hosted the largest events on The Strip. The DJ booth on stage was wreathed in gold lights, as were the dancers being spotlighted on high platforms around the club. The club was bursting at the seams. A quick look at the amount of security in the VIP sections told her it was a star-studded night. No wonder Marcus couldn't get away. He had a ridiculous amount of high-maintenance celebrities and their entourages to accommodate.

The last time she visited this club, she'd been with Vinny, Gavin, and Lyla. Lyla tried to set Gavin up with another woman that night. That felt like a lifetime ago. The hyped crowd should have improved her mood, but it did nothing for her. Every beat of her heart flooded her with such agony, she was surprised she could walk. It felt as if there were nine-inch nails in her body. The urge to do something reckless made her temples pound. She was locked down so tight that she didn't feel the bodies brush against her, didn't hear the music, and didn't register the smell of alcohol, lust, or excitement in the air. She needed something cataclysmic and powerful to cancel out the feeling of impending doom. She hoped sex would wash away her raw fragility and replace it with something else. She hoped Angel was wrong—that it wouldn't take blood to cure her. If that was so, her mother would lose her because she would do anything to stop the pain.

Using her phone to get in touch with Marcus would be impossible. No one would hear their phone above the deafening music, and with the floor jolting beneath her, he wouldn't feel his phone vibrate either. She had no choice but to circulate. A server wearing pink bunny ears offered a glass of pink champagne, which she declined. She headed to the VIP section where she figured Marcus would be. Despite it being three years since Vinny died, the staff acknowledged her. Staff came and went but her face was intrinsically linked to Pyre Casinos as surely as Gavin's was.

Celebrities greeted her. She allowed hugs and pecks on the cheek. She had no idea what they were saying or how she responded, but they left with smiles and waves. She was so used to her role as hostess that she could have a discussion without needing to think. She felt Frederick press in on her other side as he joined them.

The fourth and highest VIP tier had alcoves set far back from the railings for privacy. One U-shaped alcove could sit up to thirty people, so VIPs could have their entire entourage around them while watching the action on stage or the crowd of thousands rock out below. Carmen passed a popular talk show host and an elderly politician doing body shots off a server in a bikini, a bunch of rappers popping Dom Perignon as if it was Coke, and a boy band who wasn't old enough to be in the club being fawned over by a hoard of women. She scanned the security in each section, trying to figure out who was the highest profile by the amount of guards.

Eli Stark stood near the last alcove closest to the stage. He turned as she approached and didn't look pleased to see her. He wore jeans with a navy button up that looked good on him. She suspected he only wore the jacket because he was packing.

"You shouldn't be in public," Eli said.

She ignored him and waded through the milling security guards into the alcove. Frederick blocked a guard who tried to grab her while Mickey stuck to her like glue. What she found in the VIP area stopped her in her tracks. Angel sat with retired football star (and douchebag) Carter Raymond and Phillip Marquee, Nevada Attorney General. Angel was getting a lap dance from a Hispanic woman wearing a barely there dress that couldn't contain her boobs, which were hanging out. The woman on Angel's lap had her arms around his neck and was riding him as if she were on a galloping horse. Having a big ass drop on his crotch like could be dangerous if he had an erection. The woman whispered something in his ear, which made him smile. The woman did a reverse cowgirl and then braced her hands on the floor, planted her knees on the seat and began to twerk, exposing her ass and black G string. Angel put one hand on each cheek and squeezed.

A hand wrapped around her arm. "Let's go find Mr. Fletcher," Mickey said.

Angel looked up and spotted her. His hand paused in its caress over smooth tanned skin. His gaze skimmed her and lingered on her breasts, thighs, shoes, and then fixed on her lips. The girl on his lap air humped as if her life depended on it. Angel's mouth curved as his hand slipped under the woman's ass. Carmen saw the woman's body jolt as Angel inserted his finger in one of her holes.

"Carmen," Mickey said and tried to drag her back, but she stayed where she was.

Angel's arm moved as he fingered her. When the woman tipped her hips up, Angel smacked her ass hard enough to make her yelp.

"Don't move," Angel ordered, voice barely audible over the music.

The woman hung her head and nodded as she held her position, legs splayed on either side of him, giving him access to everything. She was at his mercy.

Carmen kept her eyes fixed on his. He stared at her with an amused, faintly cruel expression that put her on edge. Was he trying to shock her? She couldn't deny that something inside her stirred at the lewd act. She'd seen him in many moods. This one was melded to the darkness in him. He was unaffected by the woman whose movements became increasingly frenzied. He was getting off on controlling her, on exploiting her. He cared nothing for the woman begging him for release.

The attorney general and Carter Raymond were staring at him, transfixed by his ability to make the woman his bitch. The woman moaned and clawed the carpet. Her hooker heels bounced as she fought her pleasure. Angel licked his lip and winked at her as the woman jerked and screamed.

"You want some of that, Carmen?" Carter Raymond asked, reaching for her.

Even as Mickey stepped forward, Angel said, "Don't touch her."

Carter's head whipped around. "What?"

"Don't touch her."

"Carmen and I go way back," Carter said.

Angel shook his head. "Not Carmen."

He was just like Gavin. He thought because she was part of the family that he could call the shots in her life. He, on the other hand, could do whatever he wanted, whenever he wanted. The woman on his lap did push-ups to shove herself against his hand. He laughed, well pleased with her out-of-control state. He did something with his hand that made the woman shriek and collapse on the ground, shuddering as if she was having a seizure. The attorney general laughed and beckoned to her. The woman crawled to him. He unzipped his pants, and she took him in her mouth.

Angel raised a mocking brow, eyes gleaming dangerously. "You need a release, Carmen?" He beckoned with a glistening hand and patted his lap. "I'm free."

The guards behind her were shuffling like a bunch of teenage boys. She could smell their lust. She needed something to get her off, but she wasn't so far gone that she'd allow herself to be used in front of a crowd for his amusement. His eyes dared her to come to him, silently promising her that he could banish the darkness he knew festered within her. He saw too much and would use his knowledge to destroy her. Luci's voice drifted through her mind. *Angel likes you.* The man waiting for her capitulation wasn't the brother Luci knew and loved. This was the crime lord, the one who didn't give a shit about anyone or anything. High on power, pitiless, and shameless.

She'd never been able to walk away from a dare.

Carmen handed her clutch to Mickey. Angel's eyes gleamed and his mouth began to curve in victory, but he stiffened when she walked toward Carter. She perched sideways on the footballer's lap and looped one arm around his neck. Carter was looking at Angel, but she cupped his face and turned it to her. Carter was good looking. Unfortunately, he was one of the most self-centered, arrogant men she knew. He thought he was God's gift to women and had been hitting on her for years. It was time to make him her slave.

She placed a soft kiss on the corner of his mouth. He leaned toward her, reflexively seeking more. She obliged while she stroked his cheek with a feather light touch that was worlds away from what he was used to getting from prostitutes. She ran kisses across his cheek, down his neck, and sucked delicately, laving his skin with her tongue. His pulse flickered beneath her tongue as his erection prodded her hip. She straightened and straddled his lap. He looked up at her, eyes cloudy with desire. He was in her thrall. Her dress was short enough that she didn't have to pull it up as she planted her knees on either side of him and rode him nice and slow.

"You're fucking beautiful. Always have been," Carter said through gritted teeth.

She didn't respond. She swiveled her hips. His head dropped back and he panted as if he was in pain. Seeing his insolent masquerade fade urged her onward. She did a reverse cowgirl on him. His arms wrapped around her waist, and he buried his face in her hair with a groan. She continued to move achingly slow. No less than fifteen men watched her with rapt attention. She placed her hands on Carter's knees and rocked forward. She panted as if she was getting off on this. In reality, the lap dance was doing nothing for her. It was the dark lust emanating from the crowd of men who fed her inner demon. She made her eyes heavy lidded and let tendrils of hair drop over her face so she looked like she was in the throes of ecstasy. She opened her mouth obscenely wide as she rocked on her victim. Her eyes locked with Angel's. She couldn't read his expression, but that didn't matter. All she cared about was that he was watching her. He wasn't smiling anymore. He liked to play with his food in front of an audience? Two could play at that game.

She leaned back against Carter's chest and allowed his hands to move over her, tugging at her clothes and pawing at her breasts. She reached up and looped her arms around his neck as she ground on him. He groaned and shifted restlessly beneath her. One guard took a step forward before he caught himself, drawing Angel's attention. The guard cleared his throat and looked away.

The music in the club built to a crescendo while she undulated her body, using every feminine wile she had picked up in her years. The Hispanic woman who sucked off the attorney general was curled up in a ball on the couch, forgotten. She allowed the men to use and wring her dry. Amateur move.

She spread Carter's legs wide so she could brace her feet on the ground and swiveled her hips against his dick. Angel shifted. It was a small movement, but she knew what it meant. Mission accomplished. He was aroused. She kept up the charade until Carter had an arm banded around her waist and was basically trying to fuck her through his clothes.

"How much do you want?" he growled in her ear.

"What?"

"How much do I have to pay to fuck you?"

"You can't afford me," she whispered before she tapped his arm to be released.

"What do you want?"

"I'm sure you can find someone to finish you." She looked up and gave him an arched eyebrow. "Let me go."

His eyes narrowed, but something over the top of her head caught his attention and he released her instantly. She smoothed her dress down and calmly walked toward Mickey who had beads of sweat on his forehead. She grabbed her clutch and raised a brow, completely ignoring the wall of guards staring at her.

"Let's go," she said.

For a moment, no one moved but then Mickey made a path through the motionless men. They gave way reluctantly. She felt hands brush against her as she passed. Mickey led her away from Angel's alcove. The other VIPs weren't nearly as risqué as Angel. He made the rappers look like old women knitting.

"What was that?" Frederick growled.

"I don't know what you're talking about," she said.

"You're fucking with him." Frederick sounded pissed.

She glanced at him. "So?"

"You don't fuck with men like him, especially in front of his men."

"Angel didn't do anything."

"He will. Later."

"Don't be dramatic."

Angel taunted her by bending that woman to his will in front of her. It was his way of showing her what he could do to her if she submitted to him. She slammed his suggestion back in his face by showing him he wasn't the only player in the room. She wasn't a toy to be played with. She was a woman, one who would spit in his face if he tried shit like that on her. Being objectified like that in front of other men to be used and discarded wasn't something she would sink low enough to participate in.

"There's Fletcher," Mickey said, sounding relieved.

She followed his gaze and spotted Marcus talking to Bridgette Mackee, who was now married to an A list actor. She had definitely come up in the world since her days of seeking out publicity. Bridgette noticed her and waved. Marcus turned and scanned her appreciatively. She did air kisses with Bridgette and shook her husband's hand before she stood beside Marcus.

"Glad you found me in this crush," Marcus said and nodded to the couple. "Have a great night."

Marcus took her hand and led her from the fourth tier and paused on the third. He pulled her against him and leaned in close.

"I have two people to talk to and then we can go," he said.

Classy sin teased her senses. His presence made that tight, destructive ball in her chest ease. He had a numbing effect on her pain. It didn't cure her, but it was something. She followed him into the fray. He talked to a bunch of politicians and lawyers and introduced her while he kept their hands clasped. She spoke when she needed to and even managed a smile although she couldn't hold it long since her head was messed up and her insides were mangled and heavy.

That lascivious scene with Angel fed her dark cravings. She couldn't deny that it gave her a degree of satisfaction to arouse Carter, Angel, and the other men, but... now what? Depraved, erotic needs swamped her. Involuntarily, she squeezed Marcus's hand. He squeezed back and shot her a reassuring smile. She focused on his smooth, polished voice. He was good at what he did—making everyone feel welcome and important, extracting information, offering future services, and solidifying their relationship with personal tidbits. Marcus was a natural. Vinny worked hard to maintain that level of poise. Vinny... She forced her mind away from that dangerous path and took in Marcus's thick eyelashes she would have stolen if she could. He was freshly shaved and well-groomed, as usual. Being on the arm of another COO, it should have felt like Deja vu, but it didn't. Marcus was definitely his own person, and she wasn't the carefree, vivacious woman who once graced Vinny's arm. She felt like a shadow of the woman she used to be, a stitched together version that could fall apart at any moment.

Marcus wrapped his arm around her waist. "Let's get out of here."

Frederick made a way through the main floor with Mickey following behind. Marcus paused to talk to the nightclub manager before they reached the casino.

"You look amazing," Marcus said as he led her to the elevator.

She raised a brow. "You like my badass bitch look?"

"Bitch?" he echoed as he swiped a key card and pressed the highest floor. "You may be a badass, but you're not a bitch."

She glanced at Frederick and Mickey who gave them a modicum of privacy by standing in front of them. What she'd done to Carter was a bitch move—arouse, taunt, desert.

"I am a bitch."

"You won't convince me of that," Marcus said.

He leaned against the wall of the elevator in a charcoal gray suit with a navy-blue handkerchief in the pocket. He was effortlessly stylish and handsome and a sight for sore eyes. He was relaxed and amused and worlds away from what she experienced with Angel ten minutes ago. He was smiling and happy while she felt wanton and vicious. Angel guessed what was going on with her at a glance because he was experiencing it himself. He could control and exploit a woman to get off, but what the hell was she going to do? She was on the verge of another bender as Marcus called it. Three steps forward, six back. She was good for a couple of days before something dragged her back to square one. She instinctively called Marcus. She hoped he could help her because she had no plan B.

She crossed her arms as she faced him across the lift. "I have bitch moments. Do you have a thing for dangerous women?"

He cocked his head to the side as he examined her. "Dangerous?"

"I'm armed," she said.

He shrugged. "So am I."

He was dismissing her claims, as usual. She wasn't sure if that irritated or charmed her. He refused to see how fucked up and crazy she was. A part of her hated that she wanted to be the woman he thought she was. Well, she couldn't say she hadn't warned him.

The elevator opened to reveal a short hallway that led to two imposing doors. Marcus turned to Frederick and Mickey.

"No one can reach this floor without a key card. I'll take care of her. Take a break."

Frederick and Mickey looked at her for confirmation, and she nodded.

"You're staying in the penthouse?" she asked.

"No, but since you were coming, I thought we could enjoy the view."

Marcus swiped his key in the door. The sound of running water tickled her ears as she entered. There was a five-foot-tall lion fountain to the left of the door. Its mane was perpetually slick from the water cascading down his back and tapping pleasantly in the pool he stood in. A wall of unbroken glass showed The Strip in all its glory. The bright colors bounced off the gleaming black floor. There was a full-size kitchen to the left and a massive living area that could easily sit up to fifteen people. On the long black dining table was a bucket of ice with two bottles of wine and several covered trays.

"What's this?" she asked.

"Thought you might be hungry."

"It's midnight."

"So? Are you hungry?"

She was a lot of things, but she wasn't sure if hungry was one of them. She watched him uncover the trays to reveal rows of tiny, elegant appetizers.

"I told you I was coming an hour ago. How did you put this together so quickly?"

He raised a brow. "This is Pyre Casinos, babe. We're ready for anything."

He opened a white wine with a French label as she walked toward the wall of glass. The huge balcony along two sides of the penthouse was everything. There was a full-size Jacuzzi, lounge chairs, and a covered cabana along with an untended bar. The penthouse was definitely made for entertaining.

"Here."

She accepted the glass of wine. "Thanks."

She let the chilled wine wash away the bitter taste on her tongue. Marcus watched her intently, gauging her mood. How much did he see?

"I'm glad you came tonight." He swirled the wine in his glass. "You're wearing your armor tonight."

Her heart skipped a beat. "What are you talking about?"

"You look hard, untouchable. You use clothes the same way I do —to make a statement." He grasped her free hand and carried it to his mouth. He kissed the inside of her wrist. "You may think you're a badass bitch, but I know your secret."

She tensed. "Secret?"

"You're soft." He unfurled her hand and kissed her fingertips. "Delicate. You champion those who need it. Lyla, Honey, Alice... What war are you fighting tonight, Carmen?"

An internal one she was losing. Angel enhanced her carnal hunger into debauched desires that chased through her mind. Marcus's gentleness made her feel like a depraved pervert.

He cupped her chin. "Tell me what you need."

The hand holding her wine glass trembled as she tried to gather her skittering thoughts. If Angel hadn't publicly humiliated that woman, he would have been the perfect candidate to help her out tonight. Angel was right. Vinny's death changed her. She'd always had a high sex drive, but now there was a dark edge to it—a craving she wasn't comfortable with because it was new and unexplored. She was in the mood to be used, pushed to her limits, and wrung dry. She needed a man who wouldn't use her dark needs against her. Was Marcus up to the challenge or was she about to destroy their tentative friendship by asking for too much?

21

"Carmen, tell me what you want."

She drained the glass of wine before she took the plunge. "Do you have fantasies?"

"What?"

She tugged on his tie to reel him in. He came willingly and towered over her. His lips were close, but she knew it wouldn't be enough. She cupped the back of his neck and ignored her heart which sped up as anxiety and lust mixed with alcohol and heated her blood.

"Fantasies, Marcus. Do you have any?"

Witnessing what Angel was capable of and what he dared made her hungry to be dominated. She was a strong, capable woman, but right now, she wanted someone else to call the shots and rule her life so she could take a break. Marcus watched her closely, probably trying to figure out where this was headed.

"You," he said.

"What?"

"You're my fantasy."

"Me doing what?"

"Anything." He shrugged. "Everything. You're doing a good job of giving me variety."

She looped her arms around his neck and went on tiptoes so their lips brushed as she said, "I want you to use me."

"What?"

She stared into his eyes as she said, "Whatever fantasy you have, make me do it." One hand slipped into his hair. "Make me submit. Wring me dry."

There was a lot of activity in his eyes, but he didn't speak. She wasn't even sure he was breathing.

"I'm going to fight you," she whispered, and his body locked against hers. "I need to battle tonight, and I want you to win."

She stroked the side of his face. Her stomach jittered as she waited for him to respond. Only the sound of the gently dripping water filled the room. He hadn't shoved her away and called her crazy yet. Words tumbled out of her mouth, desires she didn't know she possessed.

"I need you to make me believe I'm yours. Completely, irrevocably. I need to believe things will go right in my life because it's yours, and you won't let anything happen to your fuck toy."

The night of Vinny's murder marked the beginning of her perfect life being torn to shreds. She lost Vinny and her future, her father, and Uncle Manny. Fast forward three years and she was still floating through life with no anchor or true North. She wanted to imagine she belonged to someone, even if it was only for an hour. She had been alone for so long. The need to feel bonded to someone, to be connected on a visceral level burned in her gut. Before, she arrogantly believed she could control her life, Vinny's life, Lyla's life. Vinny was gunned down, Gavin cheated... She couldn't control people, she couldn't control *anything*, so she would give someone else the reins temporarily, if he accepted. She didn't know who she was anymore. She wanted someone to mold her into someone worth keeping.

She stroked the side of his face with a trembling hand. "Use me, Marcus."

He searched her eyes. "I don't know how to do this."

Oh. My. God. He was willing. Her eyes stung with tears of relief and that awful wrenching feeling in her chest subsided. Her heart swelled with emotion. Holy shit. Marcus Fletcher would let his caveman free. Anticipation and excitement made her breathing heavy. This was dangerous, but she trusted him. Marcus matched her time and again, and he was willing to step off the cliff with her again. She role played with Vinny but never like this. She'd never had these urges before, but they were here now and not going away. It was time to purge. She hoped Marcus was up for it.

"Let yourself go," she whispered as she kissed the side of his mouth. "You're a man. Let your animal instincts take over. Forget about morals and proper behavior. Do what feels good. You're in control here." She pressed a close-mouthed kiss on his lips before she looked up at him. "That's the last one you get unless you make me."

She shoved him hard. He stumbled back and dropped his cup. Glass shattered, and expensive wine leaked across the floor. Neither of them acknowledged it. They stared at one another as the colored lights from The Strip played over their faces. She couldn't read his expression. His rigid body, narrowed eyes, and silence was so unlike him. It made her heart flutter with excitement. She'd caught glimpses of his dominant side, but he'd never given it free rein. He was always cool, effortless control. He was comfortable playing the nice guy, but there was more to him. She knew it. Now, how to incite his beast?

She hurled her glass at him. He sidestepped and turned to watch the cup shatter before he turned back to her with a scowl. Her badass bitch rose to the surface and raised a brow.

"What are you gonna do about it?" she asked with a hand on her hip.

Marcus stared at her.

"Nothing?" She sighed dramatically and examined her nails. "Figures. I know I should have fucked—"

One moment, he was standing three feet away, and the next, he was in front of her. He clamped a hand over her mouth and propelled her backward until she collided with the glass wall. Her nails dug into his wrist, but he didn't loosen his hold. She looked up and her heart stuttered. Holy fuck. The polite, amused businessman was gone. His whole demeanor had changed. His eyes were calculating, cold, and hungry while the lines of his face seemed sharper as he morphed into a character who would match hers.

He leaned down so their faces were inches apart. "Behave."

She brought her leg up, but he jerked back in time and gripped her by the throat. He squeezed hard enough to make her aware of his strength. No man had ever manhandled her before. No man dared and now... now she could let loose as she never had before.

She went for his eyes with her nails. He blocked her hand at the same time that he kicked one of her legs out from under her. She screamed as she fell backwards. Marcus followed her down and stopped the back of her head from hitting the floor with the grip on her throat. He crouched over her, a beast in his six-thousand-dollar Brioni suit.

"I told you to behave," he said.

His placid tone sent a chill down her spine. His actions were nothing like the Marcus she knew. What had she unleashed... and how could she get more? She made her eyes as wide and vulnerable as possible and let her lips quiver.

"M-Marcus?"

He blinked twice and the hand on her throat fell away. "Carmen?" When she didn't answer, he cupped her face. "Did I hurt—"

She grasped a handful of his hair and yanked savagely. As he toppled to the side, she leaped to her feet and ran as fast as she could in her stilettos. She was feet from the stairs when Marcus tackled her from behind. She lost her breath as she took his weight.

"You're going to pay for that," he said.

He stood and yanked her up with him. She sucked in a breath as he twisted her arm behind her back. She walked quickly to avoid him breaking it. He shoved her on her knees in front of the couch and sat in front of her. He spread his legs and dragged her forward so she was between his thighs. The angle he kept her arm twisted at made her bend forward so her nose was pressed to his crotch.

"Undo my pants," he ordered.

"I need both hands."

"You can do without one."

She fumbled with the belt buckle, undid his button, and tugged the zipper down. Her hand brushed against his dick, which was already hard. She looked up at him as she pulled his cock out of his underwear.

"Suck me."

She bared her teeth at him. "Make me."

His hand clamped on her cheeks, making her mouth fall open. He pushed her head down, and the next thing she knew, his dick was in her mouth, and he was balls deep. She gagged and tapped his hard thigh. When that didn't work, her hand dug into his chest, but it made no difference since he was still clothed. He had a grip on her hair and her arm still bent behind her back, effectively pinning her. Holy shit.

"Suck me."

She wriggled her tongue, and his grip on her hair eased. She bobbed tentatively and was rewarded even more. The piercing pain in her arm eased. Rewards for good behavior. He held her too close for her to see his face. He could have been anyone except that his scent reassured her she was safe. She tried to relax as she worked him, but she couldn't. She had never done anything like this before. She expected this of Angel, but Marcus? She wasn't sure if she was exhilarated or terrified.

"Use your hand."

She hesitated, and he forced her head down. She immediately wrapped her hand around his dick to stop herself from deep throating him again. Her diamond rings sparkled as she fisted him hard.

"Good girl."

That made her pause, but the grip in her hair forced her to keep moving.

"I learned to hold back from a very young age. I've never done what I wanted, I always did what was required, and I was fine with that." His voice roughened as she swirled her tongue over the tip of his cock. He stroked her hair. "You come to me, asking me to forget years of conditioning."

He yanked her head back and stared at her, eyes devoid of anything civilized and gentle.

"It's dangerous to tell someone to let go when you don't know what's inside them."

She licked her lips as her heart galloped in her chest. "What's inside you?"

"I'll show you."

He yanked her up with that brutal grip on her arm and threw her on the couch. He ripped off her thong and pinned her thighs against his chest with his forearms before he rose. Her top half hung upside down, back arched and hands planted on the couch cushions for balance. She wasn't prepared for him to enter her. She let out a choked scream. Before her body could fully adjust to the intrusion, he was moving—hard, brutal thrusts that took her breath away. He was hitting spots that made her eyes roll. She was as helpless as the girl Angel finger fucked.

"Marcus." She wasn't sure whether she was pleading for mercy or for more.

She would come. It had to be the fastest climax on record. That couldn't happen. It wasn't enough—not yet. Her body might be sated, but her demons were still bloodthirsty for more. It would be over too soon. She began to fight—twisting, screaming, thrashing.

"What the fuck?"

Marcus dropped her, and she landed on the couch. She rolled off and stumbled toward the stairs on unsteady legs, but once again, she didn't make it. Marcus grabbed a handful of her dress and yanked. The sound of ripping fabric made her scalp tingle as she fell forward. She ignored the sting in her hands and tried to get away, stilettos trying to find purchase on the slick floor. They ripped her dress as they fought, and she felt a draft on her back before the dress fell away.

He pinned her on her stomach and placed his thighs on either side of hers as he entered her again. He rode her hard. She cried out and clawed the floor as she tried to get away from him. He was so deep, he was stabbing her cervix. The pain and pleasure of it silenced her clamoring demons. Color returned to her world and her senses came back to life, throbbing and pulsing. She could smell a faint lemon scent wafting off the cold, unforgiving ground beneath her as she panted. She could feel the tiny hairs on Marcus's arm brushing against her cheek with each thrust. He was fucking her back to life.

"Do you know what it does to me to see you like this? At my mercy?" Marcus growled.

She thrashed beneath him. Her pussy was burning; she was high on lust and craved more. She wanted her head to explode. As if he sensed this, he pulled out. His weight disappeared, and she lay shaking on the floor until he grabbed her by the hair. She followed on her knees to the glass wall. He leaned against it and forced his dick in her mouth with both hands clenched in her hair. The taste of them made her moan. She gripped the leg of his pants as he fucked her mouth.

"Your lipstick is all over my dick. I love that. What did you say before? That you were thinking of fucking someone else?"

She hummed, and he yanked her away from his cock. She needed it so badly that she wrapped her hand around it and continued to stroke it. His face was carved with savage lust. He was out of control and so was she. She was cock drunk and loving it.

He gripped her face. "Who owns you?"

"You do."

He leaned down and kissed her, biting, licking, sucking as she panted with her eyes closed.

"You give yourself to me?"

"Yes. Take me. Everything."

"I'm glad you said that."

He yanked her up with a hold on her throat. She staggered on legs that felt like water. He bent her over. Her hands came out instinctively and hit the glass. She moaned as his fingers slid into her raw pussy. She was dripping, even down her legs. His slick fingers circled her asshole and then slid in. The new burn made her clench her teeth.

"Did he fuck your ass?" Marcus murmured.

"I-it wasn't his thing."

His chuckle made the hairs on the nape of her neck stand. She opened her eyes and saw his reflection in the glass as his fingers played with her ass. He looked as if she was putting him through excruciating pain. It made her lightheaded with anticipation.

"It's my thing," Marcus said as he stretched her.

She pranced on her stilettos. "No."

His fingers paused. He yanked out without warning and slapped her hard enough to make her shriek and ram into the glass to get away from him. Holy shit. He crowded her and gripped her throat. She reached back and grabbed his wrist in panic as his hand slid back into her ass.

"You take what I give you," he hissed in her ear as he fucked her brutally with his fingers.

She trembled and nodded.

"Tell me again."

"Tell you what?" she panted.

"Who owns you?"

She took too long to answer and screamed when he jammed three fingers into her. She bounced up on her tiptoes.

"You," she cried. "You. Only you."

"That's what I want to hear."

She stilled when she felt the head of his penis touch her puckered ass. It felt as big as a fist. Good thing she had slobbered all over his dick. She blew out a breath, which caught in her throat as he eased in. He grabbed her shoulders and pulled her backward until he was embedded inside her. She shrieked and bowed her head, her nails threatening to snap off as she pressed them against the wall.

"Take it," he said.

She hung her head and did as he said. Her body was lax as all the fight left her. She trembled uncontrollably as he eased in and out of her until he was balls deep.

"Now who owns all of you?" he whispered.

"You," she whispered back.

"That's right."

He bent her over and began to move. His movements were rough and uncontrolled, betraying how far gone he was. He sounded more animal than man while she felt more like a throbbing ball of need than a human being. He shoved her forward, pinning her face, breasts, and half her abdomen against the wall. Pain and pleasure made her buck against him, inciting him to go faster and make him more aggressive.

"Marcus!"

Starbursts went off behind her eyelids as ecstasy crashed into her. She screamed as she came—the contrast of the freezing glass and the hot male behind her blowing her into oblivion. Marcus rode her through it and continued to fuck her, grunting and grabbing handfuls of her skin as his control shredded.

"Down."

She heard the command a second before he spun her around and kicked her legs out from her under. Her knees hit the floor, and she looked up as Marcus stroked himself.

"Open your mouth," he said.

Before she could comply, he gripped her cheeks again and her mouth dropped open to accept his cum. Jets of milky white covered her face and spurted into her mouth. She closed her eyes as he climaxed and licked the cum from her lips.

"Carmen," he panted.

She opened her eyes and saw him staring down at her, dazed and shell-shocked. She took his cock into her mouth and sucked gently. He shuddered, tipped his head back, and stroked her hair. When he released her, she began to sink to the floor, but he pulled her up. There was a marked difference now in his grip and the way he picked her up and held her to his chest. She was limp as a noodle.

"Okay?" he asked gruffly.

His voice echoed strangely. She opened one eye and saw that they were in a lavish bathroom. He leaned into a shower and turned on the water.

"Can you stand?" he asked.

"Mm." She couldn't talk.

He set her on her feet, and she threw out a hand for balance.

"Lean against the wall," he ordered as he unbuckled her shoes and stripped off his suit.

He carried her into the shower. She leaned her head back and enjoyed the warm water cascading over her aching body. Marcus washed her while she leaned against him for support. When he finished, he picked her up again. She dropped her face on his shoulder and allowed him to take her wherever. She roused when icy wind touched her wet, nude body. She shifted and burrowed against him.

"Marcus."

"Hold on."

He walked into the Jacuzzi with her in his arms. She relaxed once she was shoulders deep in hot water. He set her on her feet, and she floated.

"I'll be right back. Don't drown."

She giggled weakly as he left her. She tipped her head back and spread her arms wide. She felt empty in the best way possible. No needs, compulsions, guilt. It had all been burned away. She had been cleansed. The purge had been successful, better than she could have imagined. The sound of a shutting door made her eyes open. Marcus came toward her with a tray of appetizers in one hand and two bottled waters in the other. He was buck naked. She watched his muscles shift beautifully as he moved. He set the tray and bottled waters near the edge before he jumped in. He waded toward her and took her in his arms. She wrapped her arms around his neck and closed her eyes.

"You're all right?" he asked.

"Mm." She couldn't think of anything else to say.

He sat on the underwater bench and maneuvered her to sit sideways on his lap. He snagged a water and held it to her lips. She didn't realize she was thirsty until the first cool drops hit her tongue. She drank half of it before she pulled back.

"Thanks," she rasped.

"Here."

He pressed something against her lips. She didn't hesitate. She opened, and he placed something crunchy in her mouth. She hummed as the flavor burst on her tongue.

"Yum. What is it?"

"Lobster wonton."

Something else touched her lips, and she opened. She chewed and swallowed.

"Amazing," she said.

"Grilled artichoke with roasted garlic aioli dipping sauce," Marcus said.

He fed her while she floated, utterly content and at peace with her world.

"Borsin breaded mushrooms."

Marcus went on and on until she tucked her head under his chin in surrender. "I'm full. Thank you."

She could hear the faint traces of a musical score playing for the Bellagio water fountain show. Between the warm water bubbling around her and Marcus's body, she felt as if she was near a roaring fire. She was lax, lethargic, and for the first time in a long time, knew everything would be okay. She would get past the pain, the relapses, the guilt. The battle with Marcus challenged her physically, mentally, emotionally. She had never felt better.

"You scare me."

For a moment, she thought she was hearing things. She raised her head to see his face.

"What?" she slurred, so exhausted she was having a hard time thinking straight.

"You scare me," he repeated as his eyes tracked over her face.

"Why?"

"You have no fear. I could have... If I had been a different man..."

He shook his head and tightened his hold on her. "You bring out things in me. I don't like the man I am with you."

She chuckled. "I love him. He's perfect for me."

His eyes narrowed. "You like the man who mouth fucked you? Pulled your hair? Almost broke your arm?"

Just the memory of it made her pussy tingle. "I loved that it was you doing it. I would have killed any other man who tried. I knew I was safe. I trust you."

His silence was fraught with tension. She shifted to straddle him. She wrapped her arms around his neck and pressed gentle kisses over his face.

"Thank you."

"For what?"

His grumpy, disgruntled tone made her smile. She sat back and looked straight into dissecting green eyes.

"For always being there when I need you." She stroked his cheek. "I cried during our first hookup, and you still came back for more." She kissed him, soft and sweet. "I pulled a gun on you, turned you into a teacher, fucked you in a laundry room, and just now you gave me something you've never given anyone else."

He stared at her for a long minute. "What's that?"

She rested her forehead against his. "The real you." He tensed, and she wrapped herself around him. "The one you don't show people, the one you're ashamed of." She looked deep into his eyes. "I love that guy."

He closed his eyes and shook his head. "You've got me all fucked up."

She laughed and nuzzled him. "You're fine; you're just freaked because you lost control."

He fixed her with a bad-tempered look. "I did. That can't happen again."

"It will," she predicted and gave him another kiss. "I'll make sure it does."

She dropped her cheek on his shoulder and sighed. He slipped off the bench while she clung to him. He bounced around the Jacuzzi as he held her.

"What happened tonight?" he asked.

She hesitated only a second before she said, "I had a dream."

"About Vinny."

It wasn't a question, but she answered anyway. "Yes."

She was so sated that she didn't feel even a flicker of pain. She girded herself to collect her thoughts and show her cards. After going to war with her, he deserved to know why. "I made a lot of mistakes. I have a lot of guilt." Her chest tightened fractionally, but she soldiered on. "I don't know how to handle the pain, so I obsess about other things. Food, shopping, volunteering, taking care of others, sex. Nothing satisfies me for long before I'm on my next bender."

Marcus said nothing, and for that, she was grateful. Her sheltered position allowed her to confess without seeing his expression while she spilled her guts. In her current state, there was no embarrassment, guilt, or sorrow—only still waters.

"I needed something more tonight. Seeing Angel finger fuck that chick in Lux didn't help. He goes through the same manic episodes that I do, but we handle them differently. He thought I would submit to him, to let him do whatever he wanted to me to get my fix, but I gave Carter a lap dance instead."

Marcus tensed, but that could have been her imagination.

"I needed something more tonight. I needed a fight, and I didn't know how I would get one." She tightened her arms around him and kissed his shoulder. "You gave me exactly what I needed. Thank you."

"I didn't scare you?"

"You did, but in the best way." She smiled against his skin. "A good guy with major kink. I love it. You make me happy, Marcus Fletcher."

He pulled away slightly, forcing her to raise her head and look up.

"Is there something going on between you and Angel?" he asked.

"We've had... encounters," she admitted, "but we haven't slept together."

He cocked his head to the side. "But you were close to it?"

"Yes."

He collared her throat. "I don't want anyone else touching you."

She beamed and wrapped her arms around him. "Really? That's sweet!"

"I mean it. We're exclusive," he said in a rough voice that said his beast was still near the surface.

She liked the hand on her throat and the possessiveness in his voice. It made her feel wanted and cherished instead of lost and alone. "I'm good with that."

"It means no lap dances for other men too." She smiled as his thumb feathered over her pulse. "Is there anything else I should know?"

She nodded, and he tensed.

"What?" he bit out.

"You were bloody magnificent tonight."

The hard glitter faded from his eyes and was replaced by something much softer and the slightest bit arrogant. "Really?"

She nodded emphatically. "Best hate fuck ever."

He frowned. "I don't like that term."

"Fine. Best purge fuck ever."

"I still don't like it, but it's better."

She kissed him. "How about you're the best purge a girl could ask for?"

"Better," he murmured. "I'm glad you came to me."

"Me too."

She wasn't sure how long they stayed wrapped in each other, but when he carried her out of the water, she moaned in protest.

"You're falling asleep on me."

She shivered as he moved through the penthouse. Once again, he stepped into the shower with her and washed away the chlorine and all traces of the purge. He shampooed her hair while she floated in the throes of her high. He wrapped her in a warm, comfy robe and placed her in bed. He slid in beside her and pulled the heavy duvet over them. He buried his face in her hair as he wrapped her close from behind.

"I ripped your dress," he said.

"I think we both did," she mumbled.

"You need clothes," he said.

She wasn't worried about it. She was warm, calm, safe. Nothing else mattered.

22

Carmen opened her eyes and found herself alone in bed. She sat up and bit back a moan. She felt battered, but deliciously so. The room was empty, curtains drawn. She slipped out of bed and sucked in a breath. Her ass and pussy throbbed (no surprise), and her back and legs felt as if she had been beaten with a cane. She hobbled into the bathroom and turned on the light. Despite the pain, she was smiling. Apparently, her purge carried her through to the next day. It was a fucking miracle. She turned her back to the mirror, but there were no bruises, not even one blemish despite their rough play last night. She washed her face and brushed her teeth before she noticed the clothes waiting for her. Jeans and a familiar sleeveless turtleneck and even her bra from Marcus's house. She slipped into the clothes and slicked her hair into a bun. She was still decked out in diamonds. It never occurred to her what she must have looked like, fisting him with diamond rings on every finger. It must have been fucking hot. Despite the fact she wore no makeup, she thought she looked damn presentable.

She slipped into her diamond stilettos and winced as the new position tilted her hips, making her calves ache. Holy fuck, next time she would make sure he fucked her on a carpet at least. She walked out of the bedroom and down a short hallway that led into the main part of the penthouse suite, which was now filled with sunlight.

Marcus stood with his back to her, looking out at The Strip as he talked on the phone. He was dressed in a different suit than the one he wore last night. Today's ensemble was a pale blue number tailored to perfection. She paused to admire the long lines of his body as he set up a meeting for this afternoon and hung up. He turned, showing that he wore a white and blue pinstriped shirt opened at the collar, no tie. He looked amazing.

"You're awake," he said as he strode toward her.

"How did you get my clothes?"

"I went home and got them for you."

"I thought you sent Mickey or Frederick."

Marcus frowned. "I wouldn't want another man pawing through your underwear drawer."

He cupped the side of her face as he kissed her. He tasted sweet and tropical. She slid her tongue into his mouth, seeking more. He gripped her hip and pulled away.

"What did you eat?" she asked.

"Papaya."

She licked her bottom lip and watched his eyes fixate on her mouth. "Yummy."

His eyes were mossy green and mesmerizing in the blazing sun.

"How do you feel?"

"I'm a little sore." Understatement, but he was a worry wort and she didn't want him to hold back next time. "But I feel marvelous." She paused and then added, "I'm hungry."

He searched her eyes. "You're fine?"

"Yes."

"I didn't know if you'd feel differently this morning."

"I feel fantastic."

"I'm glad."

She cupped his cheek. "You didn't do anything wrong. If anything, you did everything right. You helped a lot."

"Always happy to lend a helping hand."

She tipped her head back and laughed. "And to think I was thinking about hiring a mute gigolo for sex services."

"Mute?"

His disgruntled expression made her snicker. "Most guys are sexier with their mouths closed."

"And what about me?"

She pressed her finger against his lips. "You weave magic with that fucking mouth."

His eyes dilated and he stepped back. "You're sore, and you're hungry. Let's feed you."

"Okay." She reached for the button of her jeans and laughed when he cursed and backed away as if she was contagious. "Kidding."

The dining table had a fruit tray, toast, oatmeal, and bacon. She winced as she sat and reached for a strip of bacon. Marcus poured her a glass of orange juice and placed an assortment of fruit on a tiny plate. He was careful and deliberate in everything he did whether it was making sandwiches or choosing fruit. She was charmed and smitten and liking him more and more. Marcus was capable of beating his chest with the best of them, but he chose to adopt the opposite of Gavin's demeanor, which made him more interesting to her.

"You're a control freak," she said.

Marcus paused in the act of shaking two pain pills from a bottle. "Excuse me?"

"Last night, you said you learned control at a young age." She speared a piece of cantaloupe on her fork and raised a brow. "So, spill."

Marcus placed the pills beside her plate. "I didn't have control over my life when I was younger. The only thing I could control was myself, so that's what I did."

She reached for another piece of bacon between pieces of fruit and ignored his grimace. "You mean, when you grew up in foster homes?"

"Yes."

His tone was perfect—even and smooth. His expression was

composed and unruffled. Even his body language was fluid as he spooned oatmeal into a bowl, sprinkled raspberries and blueberries artfully over it, and placed in front of her. Nothing on the surface suggested he was uncomfortable in the least, but she sensed it. She didn't want to be the girl who thought because he slept with her that he had to spill everything, but she couldn't help being curious.

"What happened to your parents?"

"I don't know."

"You don't know?" She downed the pain pills and accepted the spoon he offered, clearly indicating he wanted her to eat the oatmeal.

"Never met my father, don't know what happened to my mother. I was taken from her and put in state custody." He sat at the head of the table and angled himself in her direction. "I was put in an institute before doing a round of foster homes." He shrugged. "It's inevitable that I would get mixed up with kids like Maddog and others connected to the underworld. It's what happens to most strays."

Her spoon clattered to the table. "Stray?" she choked out in outrage. "You're not a stray!"

He grinned. "I'm not?"

She smacked her hand on the table. "What are you smiling about? This isn't funny!"

"Carmen, that was a long time ago."

"You're not a stray," she muttered as she grabbed another piece of bacon. Just the thought of Marcus labeling himself like that pissed her off.

"Strays don't have family."

"Strays don't have people, but you do! You have me and Gavin and Lyla..." Her voice trailed off. She sat back as it hit her. "That's why you're so loyal to Gavin. He's your first family."

He stared at her for a long moment before he inclined his head. "Yes. Gavin's stuck with me whether he likes it or not. I would never betray him."

Her eyes stung with tears. She looked down to hide them. "Right. Well, that means you aren't a stray anymore. You have somewhere to go during the holidays." She silently vowed that even when this thing between them ended, their relationship would remain civil. Everyone needed family.

"Carmen?"

She cleared her throat as she brushed invisible lint off her thigh. "Yeah?"

He cupped her chin and lifted it so she couldn't avoid his gaze. He examined her shimmery eyes and wiped away a tear that leaked out of the corner.

"I'm fine," he said.

She nodded. "Yes, you are. I just... didn't know."

He retracted his hand. "It's not something I blab about."

Of course, he wouldn't. She waved a hand. "I'm sorry. It's none of my business." She grabbed her spoon and dug into her oatmeal. "Subject change. Do I snore?"

He blinked. "What?"

"Did I snore last night?"

"No," he said slowly.

"Good to know. I do that when I'm really exhausted."

Her cell rang. When she looked around for it, Marcus rose and fetched it from her clutch. He glanced at the screen and his brows came together before he handed it to her. She answered on the last ring.

"Connie?"

"What kind of rock do you want?" Cormac Hart asked.

"What?"

"I was doing an interview, and you came up. Apparently, a picture of us is circulating the internet. I figure we'll be engaged next, so what kind of rock do you want?"

She didn't even have to think about it. "I want a six-carat pink diamond ring."

She winked at Marcus who towered over her.

"How much is that going to set me back?" Cormac asked.

"Just one million," she said airily.

"Fuck that. I'm never getting married. Hey, if Gavin isn't cock-blocking, I have a friend who's bugging the hell out of me about you.

You want to meet the asshole?"

Marcus did not look happy. She beamed at him. He was so dang cute.

"I'm with someone, but thanks," she said.

"Not surprised. Only a matter of time before someone picked you up. You coming to my next fight?"

"Sure. Just let me know when and where."

"Will do. Gotta go, babe."

"Bye, Con." She hung up and scrolled through her messages.

She had missed calls from Lyla, Mom, Maddie, Kiki, and Luci. Maddie was done with her test and wanted to do something. She sent her a quick text, saying she wanted to do nails and hair before she texted Shonda.

"Cormac Hart asked what kind of jewelry you want?" Marcus asked.

"Some reporter asked him about us. There's a picture of us on the internet from that party where you and I fucked in the laundry room. He was messing around, asking what kind of engagement ring I want."

"He calls you often?"

"No, but we party from time to time. Con and I go way back."

Marcus sat. "How far back?"

"I sponsored him when no one else would."

His brows shot up. "You sponsored a fighter?"

"I believed in him. He had heart." She shrugged. "I met him in my stripper days. He came in, and we clicked. He's a good guy although he acts like a douche. I have a thing for underdogs."

"A stripper who invests in fighters, dates one of the wealthiest men in the state, is behind the most successful clubs and restaurants on The Strip, knows how to handle a gun, and looks like a supermodel..." Marcus shook his head. "Like I said, you scare me."

"You should be afraid," she said loftily as she popped grapes in her mouth. "I'm a kamikaze with a cause."

He grinned. "That you are."

"My parents let me be who I wanted." She ignored the dull ache in her chest. "My dad was an enforcer, so I know the good, bad, and ugly of Las Vegas. He kept me from it as best as he could. He told me I was a princess." She smiled sadly as she stared out at The Strip, which lacked the punch and magic that it had at night. "He was a great dad. The best. If you think I'm a brat, blame him."

"I think he did a damn good job."

She rose from her seat and leaned down so they were face to face. "You're sweet." She kissed his lips but pulled away before he could open his mouth. "You're sexy." Another kiss, this time on the corner of his lips. "And you fuck like a porn star." One last kiss before she looked into his eyes. "And you'll always have a friend in me."

His hand curled around her nape. "Promise?"

She nodded. "Promise."

Marcus was just as much a part of the family as she was. No matter what, they would find a way to remain friends. No man had been able to put up with her for long. What he thought was sexy and exciting now would fade. He needed order and routine and control—those words weren't part of her vocabulary. She would ride the wave for now and try to find herself before it ended.

"I guess I'll let you use my body then. That's what good friends do, right?" he murmured.

She ran a hand down his chest. "Yep. Whatever's required. It's in the best friend contract."

"What about the family contract?"

"That means you put up with my craziness. You're doing a damn good job so far." Her phone beeped, and she straightened. "I have to pick up Maddie."

"Your future stepsister?"

She shrugged. "She's my sister now even though we're waiting for them to get married." She tucked her clutch under her arm and headed toward the exit. She paused beside the large lion fountain and bobbed her brows at Marcus. "We could have done crazy shit on this lion."

His eyes gleamed. "Next time."

"I'm counting on it," she said as they left the penthouse.

"Everything's all right at the house?" he asked.

"Everything's great. Now that I've settled in, I can focus on other things. I want to start my pole classes again, see my friends, spend time with Lyla, get her out and about..."

"You're supposed to stay out of sight," he reminded her mildly as they boarded the elevator.

"I'll let Mickey and Frederick worry about that." Because he looked concerned, she added, "I won't take unnecessary risks."

"Good."

The elevator doors opened, and Frederick and Mickey stepped in.

"Hey, boys," she said.

Frederick didn't respond, but Mickey winked at her as they traveled down to the ground floor. They strolled through the casino with Frederick and Mickey flanking them. They were passing the bar when someone called out to Marcus. He paused as a handsome, exotic-looking man held out a hand.

"Best birthday bash ever," he said as he shook Marcus's hand.

"You're welcome. Khalid, this is Carmen Pyre. Carmen, this is our guest of honor. He's visiting from Dubai and interested in some Pyre Casinos projects," Marcus said.

She shook Khalid's hand. "Happy Birthday. Your bash had quite the guest list."

"Pyre?" Khalid echoed.

"I was married to the former COO," she said.

Khalid nodded. "I see. Very nice to meet you. Where are you off to?"

"I have an appointment," she said.

He gestured to the bar, which was packed with men. "Have a drink with us. I'm sure your appointment can wait."

She retracted her hand and gave him a plastic smile. "Sorry, I'm busy. I'm sure Marcus can find you some companions for the day."

Khalid handed her a black business card with gold script. "When you're finished with your appointment, call me. I'll be in town for the rest of the week." He cocked his head. "Have you ever been to Dubai?"

He was forward as fuck, not surprising since he was a billionaire. He thought she would fall at his feet or rearrange her life for a day with him. If he hadn't dropped so much money for his birthday she would have told him to shove it. Instead, she took the card and slipped it into her back pocket.

"I haven't been to Dubai yet. It's on my list." She elbowed Marcus. "We should go someday."

"Maybe we will," Marcus said.

Khalid looked between them before he inclined his head. "I'll let you get to your appointment."

"And we'll let you get back to celebrating," she said and took Marcus's arm. She waved at Khalid's entourage who were watching avidly and continued along the heavily carpeted path. "We really should go to Dubai. You need to travel, and I can add another destination to my list."

"Does that happen a lot?"

"What?"

"Hitting on you?"

She glanced at him. "Of course."

"Must get annoying."

She sighed dramatically. "A cross I have to bear."

"Gavin's here."

She looked ahead and saw Gavin cutting a path through the crowd with Alice at his side. She was half running to keep up with his long strides. Gavin clearly wasn't going to slow down for her, the jerk. Alice had a clipboard in hand and wore a long, hideous jean skirt with black leggings and a sweater vest. When Gavin spotted them, he stopped in his tracks, and his eyes narrowed to slits. Alice stopped and looked to see what had captured Gavin's attention. She spotted them and her mouth dropped open.

Carmen gave him a broad smile. "Hey, psycho!"

Marcus snickered while Gavin bared his teeth. "What the fuck is this?"

"What's what?" she asked, playing stupid and enjoying every moment.

Gavin's finger drifted between them. "This." His voice dripped with venom.

"We're friends," she said, sounding bewildered.

"You're touching him," Gavin said through clenched teeth. "You used to avoid him, and now you're touching him, and it's morning. What are you doing here so early?"

"Didn't Lyla tell you we're living together?" she asked.

Gavin looked like he chewed rocks for breakfast. "What the fuck, Marcus?"

"Don't worry about it," Marcus said.

"Don't worry?" Gavin stepped up to Marcus and hissed, "You don't know her like I do. She'll ruin your life."

His words splintered her sunny demeanor. Did he mean if it hadn't been for her, Vinny would still be here? She raised her clutch to bash him across the face, but Marcus pulled her back.

"I'll take care of this," Marcus promised. "I have business to discuss with him, and you have an appointment."

She glared at Gavin over Marcus's shoulder. "You're going to pay for that," she promised before she wrapped her arms around Marcus and gave him a long, deep kiss. "Thanks for last night, baby."

She turned and found Alice staring at her with bulging eyes. She hooked her arm through Alice's and announced, "She'll be gone the rest of the day."

"What? No, I—" Alice squeaked.

"You need to talk to me about the auction, don't you?" She turned to Marcus and Gavin and said, "All the proceeds for my donations will go to the Pyre Foundation. Alice and I haven't discussed the details, which we'll do at the salon. Toodles."

She dragged Alice toward the exit with Mickey leading the way.

"Good news, you have some time off," she said brightly to Alice. "I cleared it with your bosses. Don't worry."

"Carmen, I couldn't possibly—"

"You can and will. We do need to talk about my donation, don't we?"

"Well, yes. I was just talking to Mr. Pyre about it before he noticed you and... Wait, you and Marcus?"

Alice's incredulous excitement raised her flagging spirits. She grinned. "Yup. He's the best fuck. I'll tell you about it while we get our nails done."

She ignored Alice's scandalized gasp as they walked out of the casino and waited for their car to be brought around.

"We're swinging by the university to pick up my sister and then we're going to the salon. You guys can get whatever you want done," Carmen said to Frederick and Mickey before she called Lyla. "Heya, I'm doing a girls' day. You should come. You need to meet Maddie."

"Gavin's calling me, and it hasn't even been an hour since he left," Lyla grumbled.

"It's about me. I just told him I'm fucking Marcus, and he said I would ruin his life."

"He what?" Lyla snapped. "Who you bang is none of his damn business!"

"No worries. Marcus is tougher than you think. So, hair? Nails? Gossip? Salon?"

"I'll be there," Lyla said before she hung up.

"Excellent." She texted her mom and Janice. "You know what Janice's schedule is?"

Alice shook her head as their SUV pulled up. Mickey opened the back door, and they climbed in. She let Maddie know they were on their way and turned to Alice, who was biting her nails.

"What?" she asked.

"You can't just tell Marcus and Mr. Pyre that I'm going to get my nails done!" Alice burst out.

"Why not?"

"Because they're my bosses."

"Technically, I'm also your boss," she said casually. "I inherited Vinny's shares, which means I own a piece of Pyre Casinos. I let them do what they want, but I can make their lives hell if I want to." She shrugged. "But they know what they're doing, so I don't intervene."

"Y-you own a part of Pyre Casinos?" Alice asked faintly.

"Yup."

"You and Gavin don't seem to be on the best terms. I mean, if you wanted to, you could do major damage to..." Alice stopped, looking horrified. "I mean, not that you *would*—"

"Hmm." Carmen tapped her lips. "You know, that's a great idea."

"Oh, my gosh! I didn't mean it like that!"

"You're right. I should make his life a living hell. How dare he say I'm going to ruin Marcus's life? I have a good thing going, and he's trying to take away my sex on tap. What an ass, right?" She pulled out her phone, which Alice snatched and hid behind her back.

"Alice, give."

"Obviously, you know how to handle Mr. Pyre. You two have history. You're family! Don't take my advice."

"Fine. Noted. Now, give me my phone."

"What are you going to do?"

"Sell my shares or blackmail Gavin into saying sorry."

Alice's eyes bulged with panic. "You can't! Oh my God!"

Carmen burst out laughing. "Alice, I'm kidding."

"No, you're not."

"I am. If I really wanted to hit him where it hurts, I'd just take Lyla on vacation without telling him and set up cameras to watch him combust." She held out a hand. "Gavin's an ass, but I would never mess with Pyre Casinos. Business is business, and we both know that. Now, give."

"You promise?" Alice asked.

"Yes." When Alice extended the phone, she snatched it and saw that Janice and her mom were gonna meet her at the salon. "Girls' day! Woohoo! I am feeling *good*, baby!" She leaned between the front seats. "What about you two? Feeling good?"

"Fletcher put us up in a room. Nicest bed I ever slept on," Mickey said.

"What about you, Freddy?" she asked, poking him in the arm.

"Fine," he grunted.

"You guys gonna get pedis?"

"No," Frederick snapped. "We're trained guards, not pansies."

"Suit yourself."

She sat back and rolled down her window as they pulled up to the university. Maddie sat on the stairs with ripped jeans, a baseball cap, and her nose buried in a book.

"Maddie!" she hollered, making a bunch of college kids look around. She winked at a cutie who could be a double for Justin Bieber before she moved over so Maddie could get in.

"Hey, baby," she said as she tossed an arm over her shoulders. "What's shakin'?"

Maddie eyed her. "You're happy."

Alice leaned forward so she could inform Maddie, "She's dating Marcus."

"Banging, not dating," Carmen corrected as she took off Maddie's cap and ran her hands through her hair. "You're a virgin, aren't you?"

Maddie jerked. "What?"

Alice elbowed her in the ribs. "Leave her be, Carmen. I am too, Maddie. There's nothing to be ashamed of."

"I meant her hair is virgin," Carmen said and elbowed Alice back. "You want to do something to your hair?"

"Do something?"

Carmen fluffed her own blazing red hair, which needed a touch-up. "You want to be a mermaid, a unicorn, a Playboy bunny? What are kids doing these days?"

"I wouldn't know," Maddie said.

"What do you mean? You're in college. You're boarding, surrounded by your peers. What are your classmates doing?"

Maddie shrugged. "I don't really pay attention. I just study."

"You don't have friends?" Carmen asked and got another elbow in the ribs, which really fucking hurt. "Will you cut that out? I'm already sore."

"Oh, I'm sorry," Alice said, instantly contrite. "What happened?"

"Marcus is a beast. That's what happened." She turned back to Maddie. "So, what's the deal?"

"Marcus hit you?" Maddie looked outraged. "Dad will kill him."

She wanted to throw her hands up in exasperation. Mickey

turned in his seat to watch the drama. The grin on his face said he knew exactly why she was bruised and couldn't wait to hear the juicy details.

"He didn't hit me. We just went at it like a bunch of animals. It was fabulous," she said airily.

Alice made a faint wheezing sound. Maddie looked relieved.

"So? What kind of hair or nails do you want?" Carmen persisted.

"I don't know." Maddie picked up Carmen's hand and examined her nails, which were grown out. "What are you going to do?"

"I still love the red, but I may add highlights or something. We'll see what Shonda says. She's the hair queen."

"I guess I'll get a trim," Alice said.

"Whoa, calm down," Carmen said dryly. "You don't want high-lights? What about layers?"

Alice shifted uncomfortably. "No, I think a trim will be just fine."

Carmen badgered her all the way to the salon because she enjoyed seeing Alice riled, and sooner or later, Alice would give in to a makeover. When she entered the salon, she found it empty. Shonda had cleared her schedule for them. She did air kisses with Shonda and Keenan and had a glass of champagne in her hand within five minutes. Mom and Janice arrived at the same time, followed shortly by Lyla, Blade, Nora, and an entourage of no less than ten guards.

"Marcus told me I had to attend a meeting with you two," Janice said, eyes sparkling. "What's the deal?"

"I wanted a girls' day, my treat," Carmen said.

"But what we really need to discuss is the art items she donated to be auctioned off," Alice said primly.

"Those pieces are amazing. I can't believe you're giving them up," Janice said.

"It's for a good cause." She hugged her mom and snatched Nora who wore adorable overalls with a white long-sleeve with tiaras and diamonds on it. "Oh, my baby! Why are you so cute?!" She gnawed on Nora's neck, which made her shriek in delight.

"Hey, girls." Lyla hugged Alice and Janice before turning to Maddie. "Nice to meet you, Maddie."

Maddie looked a little dazed as she shook her hand. "Nice to meet you too. You're married to Gavin Pyre."

Lyla's mouth curved. "That's me."

Maddie's eyes flicked to all the guards. "Is that why you have so much security? Because you're rich?"

Lyla's mouth twitched. "Gavin's over the top." She slipped an arm over Maddie's shoulders and gave her a squeeze. "You'll meet him later, when he's not on edge and psycho."

"Psycho?" Maddie echoed warily and glanced at Carmen with big eyes.

"He's a lot, but you'll get used to him. Carmen tells me you're going to school for hotel management and business."

"Yes."

"I'll tell Gavin to give you a spot if you're interested. I used to work for his father, Manny. He was amazing."

They were directed to two chairs side by side. Alice, Janice, and her mother were deep in conversation, which left Carmen with Nora. She hugged her goddaughter close.

"Pretty girl," she cooed and nibbled on her fingers.

"I thought we would get action with this job, but nothing's happened," Frederick grumbled.

She turned and saw Blade standing near the door with Frederick and Mickey while the other guards milled around outside.

"This job may be over soon," Blade said in his neutral tone. "Roman's been rounding them up quicker than expected."

"I heard it's not just the Black Vipers he's been working on, but several gangs," Mickey said eagerly.

"He hasn't wasted time declaring war on the city," Blade said. "He also had a group of men arrive from New York, and they're proved to be very effective."

"And we're missing out," Frederick grumbled.

"I'm fine," Mickey said.

"Don't get complacent. Carmen's a handful. If it wasn't this thing with the Black Vipers, it would be something else," Blade said. "She's a magnet for trouble."

"Blade, you know you love me!" she called.

Blade walked over to her and crossed his arms. "I heard it took you two shots to put Maddog down. You need to train more."

She glared. "Do I get to use you as a target?"

"If it would improve your aim. Two shots is pathetic. Your father would be embarrassed."

"Don't talk about my father!"

"Then don't give me something to talk about. You need to come to the house for more training."

"I got the guy in the desert with one shot!"

"At point blank range. A blind man could have taken him out."

She bared her teeth at him. "I'm busy."

"Fucking around with Marcus?" He shook his head. "It'll never work out."

"Since you and Gavin share the same brain, I'm not surprised you think so. But both of you fail to realize that we're not in a relationship. We're just friends."

"Friends," Blade repeated in a flat tone of voice that said he didn't believe her.

"Yes, friends with benefits. You should look into it. I think you're going numb below the waist." She dipped her eyes down to his crotch and then back up again. "That would be a shame. Women could write sonnets about that cock. You're packing."

His eyes narrowed. "It works fine."

"How would you know? When's the last time you got laid?"

"I find the time."

Carmen leaned in close and stage-whispered, "Is it the cook?"

A muscle clenched in his cheek. "She's fifty."

"Desperate times call for desperate measures."

"Carmen, you ready?" Shonda called.

"Yeah!" She handed Nora to Blade and patted his chest. "Take care of the baby, Daddy."

She skipped over to her seat and jumped when Janice came running across the salon wearing a cape with her hair dripping wet.

"You and Marcus?" Janice shrieked.

"Yep."

Janice jumped up and down and nearly fell because stilettos weren't built for exercise. "Holy shit! I'm so happy for you."

"Friends with benefits, Janice."

"Is he good?"

"Good? You think I'd bother with just good? I'm insulted."

Janice clapped her hands together. "I knew it! He's a god, isn't he? Tell me he's raw and sexy and tells you to call him daddy."

She grinned. "Yes, yes, and we'll work on the last."

Keenan stomped over. "Missy, you're dripping everywhere."

"Sorry, I had to get the scoop." Janice winked at her. "I want details later."

"New man?" Shonda asked with a broad grin.

"Yes, ma'am."

"Tell Shonda all about it."

Carmen moaned as she climbed into the steaming bathtub. Spending the day at the salon with friends and family was just what the doctor ordered. It didn't take long for Maddie to relax. Her dad and brothers had neglected Maddie's female education, so she and Mom were happy to help her catch up. They chatted, ordered in food, and gossiped. Because Alice felt so guilty for taking the day off, a portion of their time was dedicated to discussing the upcoming auction. Carmen noted the date and would send out some emails to people she knew who coveted those pieces. She wondered if Alice realized that they could easily raise half a million dollars with what she'd given. Janice would handle the press, and it would be good all around. She wasn't sure if she wanted to attend the event. The memories connected to each piece were still there, and she was trying to move on.

Her body still ached, but the champagne had gone a long way to making her forget about it. Janice grilled her mercilessly about Marcus's performance. She didn't give a blow-by-blow, but she told her Marcus was more than up to the challenge of keeping up with her. Marcus was extremely private, and she didn't want to betray his trust. He might be one of the most complicated men she had ever met, which made him so intriguing. She liked layers and the different facets of a person's personality. It was what made everyone unique. In her experience, men were simple creatures, but Marcus wasn't. Unlike most men, he didn't try to assert his dominance, and he wasn't interested in being acknowledged for his accomplishments. He kept everything close to his chest, and she liked that. It meant he could be trusted.

Carmen soaked in the tub until she was in danger of falling asleep. She fluffed her hair and examined it in the mirror. Shonda had outdone herself. Her hair was now a swirl of ruby and rose that was dreamy and romantic. She was obsessed with it. Her nails were a matching dusty rose that suited her mellow mood.

Her phone rang as she slapped on moisturizer. She answered with her elbow. "Hey, Luci."

"Please tell me you're coming to visit."

"Not yet."

"Ugh. New York's so dull without Angel, and now he's so busy I barely hear from him. It's not fair that he's having so much fun. Distract me. Tell me something exciting."

"Hmm. Today, Cormac asked me what kind of ring I want."

Silence.

"Luci?"

"Excuse me?" Luci wheezed. "I didn't hear you right."

"You did."

"But I thought you were banging the COO."

"I am."

"You're doing both of them? You can't have two! That's not allowed!"

"Says who?"

"Me! You can't do my Cormac like that."

"He's a whore."

"Don't talk about my man like that! He's *my* whore."

She laughed. "A reporter asked about us, and he was joking around."

Luci let out an audible breath. "What'd you ask for?"

"A six-carat pink diamond."

Luci whistled. "If they're gonna ask what you want, you should definitely ask for the best."

"Amen, sister."

She chatted with Luci as she finished her nighttime routine and climbed into bed in a pair of lacy hipsters. She bit back a moan as she slid between the luxurious sheets.

"I'll visit, I promise," she said before she hung up. She tossed her phone on the nightstand, hugged a pillow to her chest, and yawned.

She awakened a couple of hours later when a body wrapped around her.

"It's me," Marcus rumbled.

She relaxed instantly and allowed herself to be drawn against his bare chest. "What time is it?"

"Two."

She groaned and tossed her leg over his and got comfortable. He ran his hand over her body and kissed her neck.

"You're okay?" he murmured.

She grunted in reply, and he chuckled.

23

THREE MONTHS LATER

"How's it going with you and Marcus?" Lyla asked as they strolled through the mall.

"It's going great," Carmen said.

"God, I love him. I'm so happy you guys are together."

"We're not—"

"Yeah, yeah. You're friends with benefits. How many times are you gonna say that?"

"As many times as it takes for you to get it."

"You and Marcus aren't friends with benefits."

"We are!"

"You're in a relationship. Why are you two dancing around it?"

"We're just having fun."

"Oh, my God, you're killing me," Lyla groaned. "You care about him. You talk about him all the time, and you freaking play house."

"I should be looking for a new place, actually. The Black Vipers are probably all dead. Nothing's happened for months!"

"Gavin said we should still be cautious." Lyla cast a pointed look behind them at the guards following in their wake, a crowd of assassins itching for action. They didn't look happy to be holding shopping bags.

"He's such a drama queen. What did he say when you told him we're throwing a dinner party at your house tonight?" Carmen asked.

"He grumbled, but I told him he would get lucky later, so he gave in."

"Of course, he did." She patted Lyla's stomach. "Is there a new niece in there yet?"

Lyla slapped her hand away. "Cut it out! You're just as bad as he is."

She clapped as she jumped up and down. "Are you trying?"

"No!" Lyla growled.

"Why not?"

"Nora's not even one!"

"So?"

"I'm fine with just one. She's a handful."

"She is."

Lyla bit her lip. "How do you think your mom's doing with her?"

"She's fine. Besides, she has Marv and Maddie there too."

"Right." Lyla blew out a breath. "It's still hard to leave her. It's been almost four months, and I still wake up, thinking that fuck is still out there."

"Me too," she admitted.

"What do you do about it?"

"Fuck Marcus's brains out."

Thank God for Marcus. She didn't know how she would have survived the past three months without him. Some days were harder than others, but he had been there for each bump in the road. On the nights when she couldn't bear to be alone, she went to him on The Strip and worked her demons out in his suite. Since the night of her purge, he had become more dominant and demanding in bed, which suited her just fine.

"I do that to Gavin, but he's not home in the mornings, that ass," Lyla said.

"What do you do?"

"I've started running on the treadmill."

"It shows. You look great."

Lyla smiled and ran her hand though her shiny blond locks. "Gavin thinks we're ridiculous for throwing a dinner party just because we feel like it."

"We're celebrating that fucker's four-month death anniversary." It was a struggle for all of them. No one could survive years of death and uncertainty and shrug it off so easily. It was important to regroup and celebrate the small victories. "Although I'm not surprised Gavin made a fuss. He doesn't have a social bone in his body." She steered Lyla into a jewelry shop. "I haven't bought bling in a while."

They peered in the glass cases and acknowledged the eager saleswoman with polite smiles.

"You should ask Gavin for something," she said.

"We're going to Bora Bora in two days," Lyla said.

"So? He's a billionaire. He has cash to burn."

Lyla laughed. "If I start asking him for jewelry, he might get me something daily."

She bumped her cousin with her hip. "And what's wrong with that? You need to train him."

"Train him," Lyla repeated dubiously. "Do you not know my husband?"

Carmen grinned. "I'm just saying. He'd do anything for you."

"He's nervous about leaving Angel," Lyla confessed, "but we need a break. Mom's out of the hospital and wants to be in a home by herself with just her nurses."

"Your mom is..." She bit back her harsh words.

"I took Nora to see her, but she still turned us away." Lyla sighed. "I need a break. He does too; he just doesn't know it. It'll be great, our first family trip. I hope we can relax and recharge."

"Bora Bora is just what you guys need, and Mom and Marv will take care of the dogs." She brought the dogs to Marcus's house, but it had been a disaster. Beau and Honey were like two giddy elephants. They knocked over tables, vases, and they freaked out about the small yard. Mom and Marv offered to take the dogs, and it had been a much better fit. "They're going to have fun at Marv's cabin in Utah. They're leaving for their mini trip right after you."

"I'm actually looking forward to this," Lyla said.

"You should. I'd go with you if..."

"If Marcus could come too?" Lyla asked. "Sounds like you're a couple."

"Shut up. You know he's never left Nevada?"

"So you keep telling me."

"After Gavin comes back, I'm taking Marcus to see the ocean whether he wants to or not."

"Sounds like something a couple would do."

She shoved Lyla, who laughed delightedly. She hid her smile. Lyla teased her mercilessly about Marcus, and she denied the allegations just to be contrary. Everything with Marcus was going great. Better than great, actually. He had become her rock. It had been a challenging but rewarding three months. She cleaned up and sold her family home. Saying goodbye to her childhood and her father who was embedded into every room of that house was emotionally taxing. Mom was relieved it was taken care of and had officially moved in with Marv. She had dinner at Marv's house every other Sunday. Maddie and Levi came as well, and it was something she had come to look forward to. Marcus even made it to one of the dinners. Marv approved of him, no surprise there. There was nothing objectionable about Marcus. Mom was over the moon about her and Marcus even though she cautioned her that they were casually seeing each other. Of course, Mom didn't listen.

Marcus was a busy man, but he always seemed genuinely happy to see her. He never made her feel as if she was interrupting or being too clingy. They led separate lives that intersected here and there. They were amazingly compatible in and out of bed. Three months into their affair, and he was as sweet and affable as ever. He was so fucking cute. She kept doing things to rile him—provoking him sexually usually backfired because he wasn't submissive in the bedroom, and she loved it.

Besides selling her family home, she reconnected with old friends, went back to pole dancing workouts, coaxed Lyla out of the house, trained with Blade, checked on her business ventures, and fucked Marcus's brains out. With no action from the Black Vipers, she was down to one guard a day. Mickey didn't mind and had become an enjoyable companion. Frederick was a grump and ignored her as much as possible. She forced him to do fast food runs just to irritate him.

Carmen paused in front of a glass case that held a necklace fit for a royal. The necklace glittered like a fallen star and silently begged to be worn. Diamond encrusted leaves gave way to a pear-shaped drop diamond that was extra as fuck. She stared at it long enough to get the sales woman's attention.

"You have excellent taste, ma'am," she said eagerly.

"I know," Carmen said with a wink. "May I see it?"

"Of course."

The saleswoman set the necklace on the counter. It sparkled like a living, breathing thing on black velvet.

"This is a three-carat diamond." The sales clerk gestured to the massive pendant.

Carmen lifted the heavy necklace and put it on. She posed in a massive mirror. Her off the shoulder rock band top and ripped jeans clashed with the elegant piece, but she didn't care. She took a breath, which made the necklace sparkle. Her updo showed off the necklace to perfection.

"It's amazing," she said reverently.

"It sure is. Are you attending something special?"

"Always." Diamonds made every day special. Just the other night, she decked herself out in almost every piece of jewelry she had while she soaked in the tub. This necklace would be her crowning glory. It had been years since she'd added a new piece to her collection.

She pulled out her phone and took a selfie. She sent the picture to Marcus and bounced on her tiptoes as she waited for a response.

"Of course, you had to pick the most expensive thing in the shop," Lyla said as she joined her. She shook her head ruefully. "You look amazing."

"Of course, I do. Diamonds love me, and I love them." She fiddled with her phone. "Do you know if Marcus and Gavin are in a meeting?"

"I have no idea. Why?"

"I just sent Marcus a picture."

Lyla frowned. "Okay...?"

"I want to see if he likes it."

Her face lit up. "You send him pictures of what you want, and he buys it for you like Vinny?"

Carmen froze. In her excitement, she reverted to an old game she used to play with her husband. She would go shopping and send him pictures of things she wanted. He would send his assistant to buy the items and present them to her gift wrapped. She would gush about his excellent taste and thank him for being so thoughtful. It was a habit, one she fell back on without even realizing it.

"Carmen?" Lyla touched her arm. "What is it?"

"Help me take it off," she whispered.

"Okay." Lyla unclasped it and held both ends of the beautiful necklace. "Are you going to get it?"

"Thank you for letting me try it on," Carmen said to the confused and disappointed clerk.

Lyla surrendered it and took her hand as they walked out of the shop.

"What was that about?" Lyla asked.

"Old habits die hard." She tried to play off her blunder. Her phone chimed, which made her clench her teeth.

"Are you gonna check if that's him?"

"No."

"Does he buy you gifts?"

"No. Why would he? We're just friends... and I have my own money."

"Of course, you do, but that's not the point, right?"

"I need something sweet," she said and steered Lyla into an ice-cream parlor.

Mickey and another guard accepted her offer to buy them ice cream while the others turned her down with poorly concealed impatience. She ignored them and licked an ice-cream cone overflowing with chocolate, sprinkles, and bits of brownie.

They parted ways shortly after. It wasn't until Mickey was driving her home to get ready for the party that she glanced at her messages. Marcus responded, *You look beautiful.* She tossed the phone in her purse and stared out the window. Marcus wasn't Vinny. She knew that, though, there were definitely similarities between the two men. They were both reserved, easygoing, affectionate. On the surface, Vinny appeared confident, but that was a carefully preserved image he worked hard to maintain. With Marcus, she couldn't discern any weaknesses. He showed no signs of fatigue, frustration, anger. She was drawn to his strength and steadfast calm. No matter her mood, he never missed a beat. If she wanted to be in control, he was happy to give up the reins. If she wanted to be dominated, he was happy to oblige. He countered everything she did with an ease that stunned her. No man had ever been able to keep up with her. Vinny didn't even try. He just allowed her to be herself; he never tried to match her like Marcus. Some nights, he came home only long enough to sleep for a few hours before he was off to work again. He was up for whatever she offered and never turned her down. He was an enigma.

It didn't take long to get ready for the impromptu dinner. She slipped on a slinky sapphire gown with a high slit and silver slingback heels. Chandelier earrings completed her look along with a cat eye and a soft rose lip. Mickey eyed her appreciatively as she climbed in the back seat.

When she arrived at the Pyre fortress, it was business as usual with milling guards everywhere. When Mickey helped her out of the car, she felt the eyes of every man on her. She sashayed into the house and heard a, "Damn," in her wake, which gave her an extra spring in her step.

The smell of cooking meat and tangy sauces assailed her nose as she walked through the house. There was a long table set with candles and bouquets of peach-colored roses beside the pool. Mom, Lyla, and Maddie chatted off to the side while Marv, Gavin, Blade, and Angel conversed. Honey and Beau sat near the waterfall, playing contentedly with a mountain of doggy toys.

Marcus wasn't there. She ignored her disappointment. She'd invited him earlier, but he didn't confirm that he would make it. He must be really busy. As she approached the women, she felt Angel's eyes on her. She hadn't seen him since he finger fucked that woman in Lux. She hadn't expected him to be here, but it shouldn't surprise her that Gavin invited him.

"Hi!" She hugged Mom and Maddie, who were both dressed up. "The food smells amazing!"

"Yes, they'll start serving any minute now," Lyla said.

"You met Gavin?" she asked Maddie as she slid an arm around her waist.

She felt as if she'd known Maddie all her life. Maddie was smart, practical, and ecstatic to have her and mom in the family. She might have lost Dad and Vinny, but she now had the Armstrong's. Seeing them here tonight with the Pyres felt right. Marv didn't have the hard edge that her father had, but he had the same heart.

"I met Gavin," Maddie said quietly.

"Did you tell him you want to intern there?"

Maddie paled. "No!"

"Let me—" When she would have walked away, Maddie grasped her arm.

"I already talked to Marcus about it. You don't have to ask him," Maddie hissed.

Apparently, Maddie wasn't comfortable with Gavin. No surprise. "Okay, Marcus will take care of it."

"Dinner's ready!" the chef called.

The men sat on one end of the table and the women on the other. The mood was lighthearted, the food was amazing, and the conversation was varied and interesting. Nora was passed from person to person. When Carmen got her turn, she balanced her goddaughter on her lap as Nora jumped and tried to grab everything, including her earrings. She held Nora at arm's length. Nora Pyre would be a terror. She was a fearless hellion who was putting Lyla through the wringer. Nora hated having bows in her hair, so her black locks flowed wild and free around her face. Her silver blue eyes were piercing and filled with zeal. Carmen snuck a kiss and jerked back before Nora could grab a handful of hair. She laughed when Nora glared at her. Vinny would have doted on her. Vinny loved kids, and for a few months, he bothered her daily about having their own, but eventually bowed to her wishes to wait. If they had a child together, she would still have a piece of him… She shook herself and passed Nora to Blade, her favorite person. Blade took the baby and gave Nora a blank stare. This didn't deter the baby in the least. Nora grinned at him and smacked his broad chest.

Long after they finished eating, everyone stayed seated under the blanket of stars. Carmen sipped wine and rested her cheek on her mom's shoulder and hugged her tight. After all she'd lost, moments like this had so much more impact. She silently willed everyone to stay put to prolong the moment. She kept looking at the door, expecting Marcus to arrive, but he didn't. Mom, Marv, and Maddie were the first to call it a night. She hid her disappointment even though it was late and they had a great time. She hugged and kissed them goodbye.

"Where's Marcus?" she asked Gavin as he took a sleeping Nora from her.

"Working," he said shortly.

"I know, but on what?"

He gave her a long look. "You two are still fucking around?"

She grit her teeth. "We're friends."

"Who are fucking." He glared at her. "He's not Vinny."

"You think I don't know that?"

"He doesn't have time for your games."

"Shut up, Gavin. We're happy. Go to Bora Bora, visit the spa, and ask them to pull the stick out of your ass." She took a few steps away and then turned back. "And when you come back, Marcus is taking a vacation, got it?"

"Marcus can do what he wants."

"Then he's taking a vacation."

Gavin shrugged. "I want to hear it from him, not you."

"Fine."

Knowing her departure would be imminent, she moseyed over to Honey and Beau who lounged near the pool. As she approached, Beau met her halfway. She scratched him behind the ears and watched Honey debate whether she wanted to be touched. In the end, her competitive nature won out. Honey nudged Beau aside and took his place. It was amazing what a few weeks in a loving, safe environment could do.

"You're such a good girl," she praised. "I told you, only good from now on, baby."

"Ready for dessert?"

She turned and saw Angel standing behind her with two slices of cake. She stared from the cake to him and back.

"Where'd you get that?" she asked.

"It's the last two pieces of a cake Blade wants out of the house."

Angel was back to his relaxed vibe—jeans and a black tee, but neither his appearance nor the cake fooled her. But if he wanted to play nice and bring her cake, why not enjoy?

"Thanks," she said and took the plate. "I think you can take Mickey and Frederick off babysitting duty."

"Not yet."

"You haven't killed all the Black Vipers yet?"

"Getting there, although they reconnected with the Spade gang from California. They've been quite entertaining." He shrugged. "It's only a matter of time before they flee."

Beau and Honey ran toward the house as Gavin and Lyla went inside. Honey had really bonded with her new family. She was a whole new dog. Gavin seemed taken with her in particular. According to Lyla, the dog's favorite place was his office.

The staff cleared the table, leaving them alone on the patio. The tranquil sound of the waterfall and the dim light made this strangely intimate. She ignored all of that and took a bite of cake.

Her eyes fluttered shut. "Oh my God. What is this and how do I get more of it?"

"You're with Fletcher."

Her eyes popped open. "What?"

"You live together."

It wasn't a question.

"We're friends, and I'm staying at his place. He's mostly at the hotel."

He tilted his head to the side. "And that's working for you?"

His incredulous tone made her tense. "It's working perfectly. Why?"

He ignored his fork and picked up the cake with his hands. "I didn't think vanilla would do it for you."

"Who said he's vanilla?"

"Come on. We both know he isn't like us."

"There is no us."

"Of course there is. You're just playing hard to get."

"Excuse me?"

"You want me."

He finished his cake and licked frosting off his thumb while he stared at her. She ignored the tummy clench.

"I don't want you." Her voice didn't come out as nonchalant as she wanted.

"You do," he said with an arrogance that made her want to slap him.

"You know what I really want?"

He tensed. "What?"

"More of this cake." She held his gaze as she forked up a piece and opened her mouth wider than necessary to accept the spongy piece of heaven. Angel watched silently as she chewed and hummed in delight. Her tongue flicked out to catch a smear of frosting on the fork.

"You're fucking with me," he growled.

She grinned, unable to hold a straight face. "You deserve it."

He dropped the easygoing façade and stepped into her space. She had to lock her muscles against the instinctive urge to retreat. He was so close that she could smell his cologne. Clean, fresh, inviting. It didn't match the man who wore it. He should be wearing something spicy, musky, with bite.

His eye contact was so direct that it felt like a physical touch. She stared into dark, fathomless blue. His beast was in his eyes. Being around Gavin for over a decade, she should have been immune to Angel's brand of badassery and sex appeal. He was his own brand of psycho in a pretty package. On the surface, he appeared as affable as Marcus, but she knew better. He had a cruel streak that made him the perfect candidate to bring Las Vegas to heel.

"You wanted what I gave that slut."

His coarse words matched the dark hunger in his eyes.

She gave a one-shoulder shrug. "I'm not into group sex."

"What are you into?"

"You'll never know now, will you?"

They stared at one another, a silent battle of wills. She refused to walk away. She wasn't a weakling, and she wouldn't bow down to him because of his title.

"I was letting off steam after a few kills," he said in a goaded tone.

That explained his pathological behavior that night. "Well, I hope that got you off."

"It didn't."

The implication was obvious. He was still hungry. She felt warmer than she had a minute ago. "What a shame."

"Yes," he drawled as his eyes traveled over her face and landed on her lips. "You made your point at Lux."

"So did you. You can't have everything you want, Roman."

"Fletcher can't handle you."

"He's handling me just fine." His energy cloyed the air and made the sweet cream of her dessert taste like dirt. She took a step back. "Well, I better get—"

"Not up to the challenge, Carmen?"

He was baiting her. Again. He thought he could provoke her into a night of angry, dirty sex? "I don't see a reward worth fighting for," she said tartly.

He clutched his chest. "Not nice, Carmen."

"You aren't either."

"No, I'm not nice, but you already know that." He lowered his voice. "Come with me."

Goose bumps traveled over her skin. "I'm with Marcus."

"You said you're friends."

"Yes. Friends with benefits."

"Then what does it matter?"

"We're exclusive... friends," she said lamely.

Angel raised a brow. "Exclusive friends? He doesn't even have the balls to claim you for himself? Why are you wasting your time?"

"You think every woman wants you because you're the bad boy? That I would give up what I have so you can do me dirty and leave me when you're bored?"

"What makes you think I'd get bored?"

"Because I'm a hunter too," she said quietly. "I understand the chase and the disappointment when it's over."

"Then why are you with Fletcher?"

"Because he's the unattainable." Marcus didn't give himself freely, and because of that, he was a prize. He was too good for the likes of her, but she would steep herself in him as long as he allowed it.

"You're taking the safe route." His eyes roved over her face. "How disappointing. We could have helped each other out."

"I'm getting mine. And I'm sure you have a plethora of volunteers to do whatever you want in bed."

"Yes, I've made my way through some of the best-looking women the town has to offer. A good selection." His eyes slid down her body. "But not quite what I'm looking for. He won't be able to give you what you need. You know that, right?"

"He already is."

"For now," Angel allowed. "But your need for more will come back, and when it does, he won't be able to satisfy you. Wild doesn't go away, Carmen. You're with a guy who's more focused on business than you."

"Marcus is responsible for thousands of jobs and billions in revenue."

Angel shook his head. "You think you're safe because you're with him, but you can still get burned."

"What are you talking about?" She saw movement over his shoulder and spotted Marcus watching them. "My ride's here."

"When you're ready, you know where I live."

His words drifted to her as she walked toward Marcus.

"Everything all right?" Marcus asked, but his gaze wasn't on her.

"Yes, are you hungry?"

"Lyla made me something to take home."

"Great. You ready to leave?" She took his arm and pulled him toward the house, but he didn't move. She turned back and saw he was staring at Angel. She yanked on his arm. "Marcus."

He glanced at her, his face hard and so unlike the easygoing man she'd come to know. He glanced once more at Angel before he followed her in the house. What the fuck was that? She came here to chill, not for drama. She dropped the plate with the half-eaten cake on the counter and towed Marcus through the living room where Gavin and Lyla sat on the couch. Gavin had his arm around her while she leaned into him. They weren't talking; they were soaking each other in. She missed that—the familiarity one had after being together for years. God, she had to get out of here.

"Thanks for dinner," she said as she kissed Lyla on her head and completely ignored Gavin. "Call me if you need anything before you leave for Bora Bora."

She didn't release Marcus until she walked out of the house. Mickey broke off from some guards and headed to the SUV.

"She'll ride with me," Marcus said.

She didn't argue. She slid into the Audi while he placed his takeout bag in the back seat. It smelled delicious. It wasn't until they were on the open road with the city tiny lights in the distance that he spoke.

"What were you and Angel talking about?"

Fucking Gavin and Angel ruined her perfect night. "Nothing. He was just being an ass."

"About what?"

She reached for his free hand and laced their fingers together. "Nothing important. I'm glad you made it."

"I tried to leave earlier, but some things came up."

"Well, I didn't give you much notice ..." *But Gavin made it*. She pushed that petty thought away. Marcus wasn't obligated to attend unplanned dinner parties she sprung on him without warning.

"I have a business dinner coming up in a few days," Marcus said, interrupting her thoughts. "You remember that businessman from Dubai? Khalid?"

"Yes."

"He's interested in buying one of the towers we're building for homeowners."

She pondered that for a moment. "It's still under construction."

"Yes."

"He wants it badly enough to buy without seeing it completed?"

"Yes."

"Why?"

"He wants to start doing business in Las Vegas, and there's very limited real estate on The Strip."

"What does Gavin think about that?"

His mouth curved. "The towers were my idea in the first place, and now that it's drawing people like Khalid, he's pissed at me."

"He's allowing you to negotiate this deal?"

"We haven't talked hard numbers yet. Khalid has a lot of connections in the business world and may be an excellent partner in future, which is why we're willing to talk to him."

"Good luck."

"I want you to come with me to the dinner we're having with his associates."

She glanced at him. "Really?"

"Yes. You don't mind, do you?"

"Of course, not."

He squeezed her hand. "Great. I've been following Khalid's career for years. It's an honor to talk to him and potentially do business with him in future."

Marcus spoke of Khalid's many accomplishments for the rest of the drive. She listened with half an ear as Gavin and Angel's words needled her. When they reached home, he went to the office while she got ready for bed. The night didn't exactly end on a high note. She felt uncomfortable and restless. Even the TV show Psych couldn't improve her mood.

She lay curled around a pillow on the edge of the bed, lost in her head. No one believed she and Marcus were compatible. She hadn't either, but with each passing week, she'd begun to believe that he might be the only other man on the planet capable of handling her. So what if they weren't technically dating? Their foundation was better than what most married couples had. It was companionship at its best, and it worked for them.

She was happy and satisfied... or had been before Gavin and Angel attacked their arrangement. Angel was so sure her restlessness would return. Angel had changed in the short amount of time he had been in Las Vegas. He arrived with an eager cockiness that had faded to something much darker. The underworld was taking its toll on him. That's why his craving was so bad. He was insatiable. Nothing was keeping him topped up.

Marcus entered the bedroom. Her eyes followed him into the bathroom where he stripped. She liked that he was dedicated to his job. Work was an intrinsic part of him. He had no guidance in his life, yet he showed such compassion and patience. He made something of himself, and that should be celebrated. Knowing how little he had in his past, she went out of her way to do little things for him. She hung photos of travel destinations to tempt him to see the rest of the world. She appreciated his fashion sense, so she bought him ties and shirts, which he could never have enough of. Every time she gave him something, he got the strangest look on his face. At first, she thought she had overstepped, but he had worn everything she got him, so she continued to give him presents.

Marcus walked into the bedroom in just his boxer briefs. She shifted to make room and laughed when he hopped on the bed and tucked her close. He buried his face in her hair.

"I like the way you smell," he said. "Candy and sex."

"Well, you know I love classy sin."

He tipped her on her back while he rested on his side, looking down at her. She reached up and traced his features with her finger.

"Did you buy the necklace you showed me earlier today?" he asked.

Her hand paused. "No, I decided not to."

"Why?"

She continued her exploration. "I don't know."

"You must have loved it if you took a picture of it."

He's not Vinny. She flinched as Gavin's words drifted through her mind. "Maybe I'll get it in the future."

As she stroked his face, his eyes closed. She ran her hands through his hair and then cupped his neck. She massaged, and he dropped his head forward to give her better access. Her hands moved to his shoulders. When he lay heavily on her, breathing slow and easy, she stopped. She wrapped her arms around him and soaked in his scent, weight, and warmth. This was all she needed—a partner who understood and accepted her. He had made the weeks since she awakened more than bearable; he had made them sweet and light. She'd done what Mom said. She found things that made her happy and spent as much time as possible doing them. The pain was still there, but it was beaten back by Marcus's warm generosity.

"What were you talking to Angel about?" he murmured.

"What?"

He lifted his head. "Angel."

His voice was calm, but his eyes were moody. He wasn't confrontational. If she learned anything about him, it was that he was the calm voice of reason in every situation. She was shocked he was bringing this up.

"You were angry, and he was standing very close to you," he continued when she didn't speak.

"It wasn't anything," she said.

"Tell me what he said."

"I asked him about the Black Vipers," she said slowly, trying to come up with an answer that wouldn't offend him.

"And?"

Her eyes flicked away as she tried to buy time. He cupped her chin in a firm but gentle grip. His thumb slid over her bottom lip.

"Tell me."

"He doesn't think we'll last." His eyes narrowed, and she tacked on, "To be fair, Gavin doesn't think so either."

"Gavin's extra hostile toward you. Why?"

The last time she and Gavin had been civil to one another was when Vinny was alive. After Vinny died, their relationship disintegrated. He blamed her for Vinny's death and rightly so. He'd never said it out loud, but he didn't have to. He also blamed her for taking Lyla from him the first time. He believed they could have worked it out after she discovered his infidelity. Maybe, but her loyalty was to her cousin, not him.

"Bad history," she said.

"So, Angel said he doesn't think we'll last and you got in his face?"

"Kind of. I said I was happy." She waited for a comment. When she got none, she shifted restlessly beneath him, but he didn't budge. "He was just being an ass. He wants what he can't have."

"He made a play for you." His tone was flat.

"I told him we were exclusive, that I wasn't interested." When he said nothing, she added, "It's mostly the chase."

"Is it?"

"What else could it be?"

He brushed her hair back from her face. "Any man would covet you. It has nothing to do with the chase. That's just a bonus."

She stared up at him. "You didn't chase me."

He raised a brow. "Every opening I had, I took it."

She blinked. "But you... you were just at the right place at the right time."

His expression eased, and he grinned. "You're so cute."

He kissed her on the nose, and she scowled.

"I'm not cute. I'm a killer!"

"You're adorable," he murmured as he cradled her face between his hands and brushed kisses over her face. "I told you I wanted you before I met you."

"But..." she said weakly and tried to hang onto the conversation when he was drowning her in affection. "You didn't make any moves! I made all of them!"

He smiled. "Yes, you did."

She shoved against his shoulders. "I can't believe this! You—"

He covered her mouth with his and pinned her arms above her head. She jerked her head to the side, and his mouth moved to her neck and sucked.

"You needed time, so I gave it to you," he said quietly. "But I always intended to be right here."

"That's not possible!"

"It is." He raised his head and looked down at her. "And it was worth the wait."

Her chest locked. "I didn't want to like you."

"I know." He rested his forehead on hers. "But you do."

She closed her eyes as conflicting emotions tumbled through her. "I don't know how I would have done this without you."

"You would have found a way, but I'm glad to be a part of it."

"You don't think I'm too much?"

"You are, but I like it," he murmured as he lifted her nightgown. "Roman can look all he wants as long as he doesn't touch."

24

Carmen stepped back from the vanity and posed in black lingerie and high heels. All she had to do was slip into her slinky black dress and she would be ready for the business dinner with Marcus. It had been a long week, and she was in the mood to let loose. Maybe she could seduce him in his suite after this business dinner. The fact that Lyla wasn't in town niggled at the back of her mind. She would have visited her mother, but she was on her cabin trip in the woods. Maddie was elbow deep in college homework, and Marcus had been busy all week. She kept herself busy by working out, visiting Cormac at the gym, having dinner with Janice and Alice, and volunteering at the dog shelter. These things distracted her but didn't cancel out her growing anxiety.

The beginning strains of her restlessness were coming back. Ever since her confrontation with Angel, she couldn't get his words out of her mind. It was almost as if he was deliberately summoning her old demons to wreak hell on her. The best remedy was to go on a trip. She made a reservation at a gorgeous resort in Laguna Beach. She and Marcus were going to sit in the sun, get massages, and swim in the ocean. She couldn't wait.

"If you wear that, no one will be able to concentrate."

She jumped and saw Marcus standing in the bathroom doorway.

"I didn't know you were coming by!" she shouted as she rushed to him and lifted her face for a kiss. He planted a deep one on her with enough heat to make her nails dig into his back.

"You're almost ready?" he asked gruffly when he raised his head.

"Yup! Just need to put on my dress."

"Great." He gave her another kiss and stepped back. "I have a surprise for you. I wanted to make sure you wear it tonight."

Her heart skipped. "Surprise?"

"You're always surprising me with gifts." He reached down and picked up a gift bag she hadn't noticed and handed it to her. "I think you'll like it."

She pulled a large velvet box out of the bag and stared at him. "What's this?"

He took it from her and opened it. Nestled on black velvet was the magnificent diamond necklace fit for a royal. She backed up with her hands over her mouth. She stared at him, astounded and slightly horrified.

"You bought this for me?" she whispered.

"Of course."

She shook her head. "You can't!"

"But I did." He pulled the necklace from the box and came toward her.

She backed up until the mermaid statue forced her to stop. "You must have paid a fortune."

"I'm a rich man, Carmen."

She put her hands on her hips. "And I'm a rich woman. I could have bought this for myself."

"Then why didn't you?"

Her mouth opened and closed without uttering a word. He reached her, and despite her bid to avoid him, he slid the necklace around her throat. The heavy weight immobilized her. He fastened it and stepped back with a smile.

"You look beautiful."

She was afraid to look in the mirror. She stared at him. "Why?"

"Because you wanted it."

"I wanted this house, and you didn't sell it to me!"

He laughed and wrapped her close. "Still harping on that, Carmen?"

"It's true! And this necklace cost more than the house! You can't—"

"What are friends for?"

"Friends don't buy friends expensive jewelry!" she snapped and tried to push him away.

"How much did it cost for you to do the mural in my office?"

"That's not nearly as much—"

"How much do the paintings on the walls cost? How much would it have cost to furnish the house? To hire the people who made this place into a home?"

"That was a gift!"

"And so is this."

He turned her toward the mirror. The necklace winked and shimmered around her neck. It was the most elegant piece she owned.

He wrapped his arms around her middle. "It's perfect."

She lifted her hand to touch the diamonds and stopped just shy of caressing them. "This is too much." She couldn't resist for long. She touched the diamonds, which should have been cold, but they were warm, alive. "I didn't send you the picture because I expected you to buy it."

"I know, but you love it, right?"

Tears stung her eyes. He had no idea how much this touched her. Without even knowing, he finished Vinny's part of the game.

"Carmen?" he pushed. "It's what you wanted, right?"

She couldn't speak, so she nodded. Her heart felt full. She closed her eyes for a moment to get a hold of herself. "You really shouldn't have."

He kissed her cheek as his hand stroked her abdomen and then slid down. She stiffened as he stroked her over her underwear.

"Now I know why men buy women jewelry."

She stared at their reflection, her in black lingerie and he in his suit. "Why?"

His hand slipped into her underwear. "Because they like knowing what she's wearing is from him."

She clutched the countertop. "Are you branding me?"

He wrapped her hair around his fist and pulled until her head tipped back.

"Do I need to?" he murmured in her ear.

She arched into his hand. "No."

He met her eyes in the mirror. "You can thank me properly later."

His dark tone made her stomach flutter. He would do her rough and dirty. Her legs quivered just thinking about it. She was so down. "Whatever you want."

He smacked her ass. "Good. Get dressed. We're going to be late."

She rushed into the closet and slipped into the black mini lace dress with a sweetheart neckline she had been planning to wear. It was the perfect outfit to show off her new present. She went back into the bathroom and stared at herself in the mirror. The brilliant necklace matched her insides, which were buoyant and full of light. Marcus was her anchor. Just being in his presence banished her dark restlessness.

He stood beside her as he shrugged into a tux that made her mouth water. "When Gavin and Lyla come back from Bora Bora, we're going on a trip," she announced.

His eyes roved over her. "Trip?" he echoed in a distracted tone.

She bounced on her toes. "I already made reservations at this resort on the beach. It's gonna be fab."

"I don't have time to go anywhere."

"Don't worry about it. I already talked to Gavin. He'll take care of your projects."

He slipped his hands into his pockets. "You talked to Gavin about this?"

"Yes. He knows you need a break. He said you can do what you want."

"I don't need a break."

His steely tone caught her off guard. "What do you mean?"

"It's not his job to cover for me."

"Of course, it is."

He held up a hand. "Carmen, I appreciate you putting this together, but I don't have time for a trip."

"It's just a weekend—"

"And I don't want you talking to Gavin on my behalf either."

Her excitement dimmed. He was upset, which was so unlike him. "It's not a big deal, Marcus."

"It is to me," he said quietly. "I can't just take off for the weekend. I'm working on a huge deal, and I have to be on my A game."

"You can't even take off for a day?"

"No."

They stared at one another. She didn't know what to say. She assumed he would fall in with her plan. She hadn't expected him to decline or reprimand her for a weekend trip.

"I thought you understood how important my job is to me," he said.

"Of course, I know how important it is."

He shook his head. "It's not just a job for me; it's who I am. You know why."

He was talking about his background, which so few knew about. "I get that, but the job will still be here when you get back."

"I wasn't born into it like Vinny. I have to work to keep my position."

She went cold. "You think Vinny didn't work to be COO?"

He frowned and then ran a hand down his face. "That's not what I meant. It's just... All my life, I've been working to be where I am today. I don't want anything to jeopardize that. I like everything just the way it is, and I don't want anything to interfere with my career."

She felt as if she walked into an invisible wall. He liked everything the way it was, including their convenient relationship, which apparently didn't include trips together.

"Gotcha," she said and ignored the mortification twisting her stomach into knots. "Will do."

She leaned toward the mirror to apply more lipstick. He stood behind her, watching silently. She hoped he didn't notice her shaking hand. When she headed toward the bedroom, he stepped in front of her. When his hand cupped her face, she resisted the urge to pull away. She confused his affection with something deeper and more meaningful. She wouldn't make that mistake again.

"You understand, right?" he said gently. "Work is all I have."

Everything in her turned to ice. He couldn't have said anything to hurt her more. He just put her in her place. They agreed to friends with benefits. He was keeping his end of the deal, and she wasn't. She was doing that stupid girly thing, complicating their relationship with emotions and vacations, and even went so far as to talk to his boss, and he didn't like it.

"Carmen?"

She could hear the worry in his voice.

"I thought we understood one another," he said.

There was something in his eyes, a wary concern that made her feel even worse.

Humiliation consumed her. What he once healed, ripped, and bled, but she didn't acknowledge it. She steeled herself and gave him an over bright smile.

"We understand each other perfectly. We're going to be late." She went up on tiptoes to give him a kiss on the cheek. "Come on, let's do this."

He moved aside, and she slipped past. She grabbed her clutch and walked through the house. She slipped into the Aston and tensed when Marcus knocked on the window.

"I thought we could ride together," he said.

"I know this meeting will go long, and I haven't driven in a while. I'll follow you." She kept her voice light even though she was dying inside. He had no choice but to let her go as she reversed out of the garage.

Mickey started up the SUV and followed as she put the Aston through its paces. Her chest was so tight she could barely breathe. Sex didn't mean anything. She, of all people, should know that. What the hell was she doing? She was treating him like a boyfriend, and he wasn't. He had made that abundantly clear, despite living together, his possessiveness, and his gift, which now felt like a noose around her neck. That expression on his face—confusion and a hint of pity—made her insides writhe with shame.

She wasn't sure how she made it to the casino because she didn't remember a thing about the drive. She handed her keys to the valet and rushed in as if it was a hospital and she was there to check on a loved one. She needed to get herself under control ASAP.

"Carmen?"

She turned from the bar to find Mickey and Marcus standing behind her. She downed her Cosmopolitan and took a deep breath.

"Sorry, I was thirsty." She slipped her arm through his. "Let's go."

Marcus led her through the casino. She didn't feel anything. Not the brush of bodies or the liquor running through her. She'd taken a crippling emotional blow and didn't have time to get herself together.

"Carmen, you remember Khalid?" Marcus asked.

She'd been so in her head that she didn't register Marcus leading her into a private dining room in an exclusive restaurant in the casino. The room was dimly lit. There were about twenty men in the space, most lounging near the private bar. Servers circulated with appetizers on gold platters. In the middle of the room was a table set for dinner with over-the-top arrangements and the finest china.

"Yes," she said and gave Khalid her hand.

He grasped her chilled fingers. "You're more beautiful than I remember."

Neither the smoldering looks he cast nor the compliment penetrated. Oh, God, she didn't want to be here. The last thing she wanted to do was mingle and be polite when her insides were bleeding. She felt as if her chest had been raked with razor sharp claws. She needed time to pack her wounds.

"Thank you."

Khalid registered her dismissive tone, and his eyes narrowed. Marcus gripped her waist.

"Come, let's get a drink," Marcus said, and they trooped to the bar. He leaned in close. "Can you handle this?"

Pride saved her. She straightened her spine and buried her pain. Marcus didn't mean to hurt her. She was the one who forgot the rules. Casual sex and they were supposed to remain friends. He kept up his end, and she would do the same even if it killed her.

"Yes," she said and patted his hand. "I'm fine."

She was introduced to every man present. They were all tied to Khalid in some way and most from Dubai. Marcus sat at the head of the table with she and Khalid on either side of him. Khalid's companions spoke in multiple languages. The man next to her didn't bother to engage her in conversation, which suited her just fine since she wouldn't have been able to feign interest. Instead, she focused on the food, kept her expression polite, and occasionally contributed to Marcus and Khalid's talk of the city. She sensed a distinct sexist undertone in the air, which wasn't surprising. Her attire could be a factor in their opinion of her, but if they wanted to do business in Sin City, they better get used to women who owned companies and dressed like her.

When the first man rose from the table, she was the next on her feet. The men passed around cigars and planned to visit the tower tomorrow. She gravitated to the bar and asked for a shot of tequila, which made the bartender's brows rise, but he didn't question her. She was knocking it back when she felt someone come up behind her.

"You didn't call me."

She so wasn't in the mood to be nice to the billionaire Marcus admired. The loaded glances he cast her throughout dinner made her want to stab him in the eye with her fork. She didn't have the capacity to be civil or flirty, which left only blunt honesty.

She turned to face him and saw Marcus in the middle of a huddle of Khalid's cronies. The room was filled with servers clearing the table, and a haze of smoke hovered in the air. Khalid was handsome, urbane, and rich. That was enough for most women but not her.

"I'm not interested," she said.

She felt a spark of satisfaction when his eyes flared. Apparently, he wasn't used to honesty. Well, they were both experiencing a novel experience tonight. He was having a woman turn him down, and she was being told she needed to stay in the friend zone. Perfect.

"Excuse me?"

She raised a brow. "I think you speak enough English to know what that means."

He took a step closer. With her heels, they were the same height. She was itching for a fight, and it seemed Khalid was willing to oblige.

"Do you know who I am?" he hissed.

"No, and I don't care. You should step back."

"You should know your place."

"My place…" She tasted the words and cocked her head to the side. "Exactly where is my place?"

"At my feet."

Rage made everything else fade away. "I don't know who told you American women bow at men's feet, but here, we carry guns, asshole."

"I heard you're sleeping with the new and improved COO." His dark eyes were filled with lust and malice. "You never fail to make sure you're screwing the most powerful men in the city. I'm next."

Carmen kneed him in the balls. As he sank to his knees, she belted him across the face with all her might. He reeled backward and knocked into a waiter carrying a tray full of drinks. Both of them crashed to the ground. She wasn't aware of anything but making sure he suffered. She was about to stomp his head with her stiletto when an arm locked around her waist and lifted her off her feet. She screamed in rage at being denied her prey. Marcus hauled her kicking and screaming into a hallway off the private dining room and dropped her so hard, her heel nearly snapped. She opened her mouth to shout, but he beat her to it.

"What the hell do you think you're doing?" Marcus roared.

He was angrier than she had ever seen him, but she didn't care.

"Do you know what he said to me?" she shouted back.

Marcus crowded her against the wall. "I brought you here tonight for support, and this is what you do? Assault a potential business partner?"

"He said—"

He slammed his hand against the wall inches away from her face. "This isn't the place for your antics! These are civilized people. You don't assault people, especially not a man as powerful as Khalid." He ran his hands through his hair. "You need to leave, and I have to do damage control."

He started toward the private room. She stared at his rigid back.

"Marcus, he said—"

He whirled back to face her. "I don't care what he said! Nothing justifies you humiliating him in front of everyone. I don't know what world you live in but using your fists and causing a scene isn't the way most things are handled. You've embarrassed me enough tonight. Get out of here."

She stood there, trembling with rage and pain as the servers carried out platters and averted their eyes. He would tend to that asshole and leave her standing here like she was nothing? Tears pricked her eyes, but she'd be damned if she let them fall. She walked into the kitchen, which went silent when she entered. Apparently, word already spread. She was being introduced to an all new level of humiliation tonight. Fantastic. Eyes followed her as she slipped into the bustling restaurant filled with candlelight, live piano music, and tiny food portions.

She was almost out of the restaurant when a hand grabbed her arm and pulled her backward. She whirled with an angry yell and swung her fist. The punch was deflected by Mickey, who wrapped his arms around her to stop her from beating him up.

"Hey, hey. It's okay," he said.

"Let me go," she hissed.

He obeyed, and she continued to the exit, aware that she was now making another scene. No doubt Marcus would never speak to her again after this, but she didn't give a fuck. She started off at a fast trot.

By the time she reached the casino, she was practically running. She elbowed her way through the throng until she reached fresh air.

"I-I need my keys," she said to Mickey who appeared at her side.

He produced her clutch and handed both of their tickets to the valet.

"Carmen, what—" he began.

"Don't talk to me." She wrapped her arms around herself as she trembled. Khalid accomplished an amazing feat—he made her feel cheap and sullied in less than five minutes. She knew what everyone thought—that she was an expensive whore—but they didn't dare say it when she married Vinny. Of course, now that Vinny was gone, they saw her relationship with Marcus as her trying to nab another wealthy man. She was a fucking millionaire in her own right! Fucking sexist bastard.

This was the moment everyone had been waiting for. When Marcus, the straitlaced businessman, had enough of her antics. If he thought she wouldn't attack someone who slandered her, he didn't know her at all. She killed to defend Vinny's memory. Her mother and Angel expected no less, but Marcus expected her to turn the other cheek. Fat chance. She had always let emotion lead. It had never steered her wrong until she convinced Gavin to allow Vinny to take his place. After that, it seemed she had been wrong about everything. She sucked in a breath as pain spread so deep her bones ached.

Her car pulled up, and she started forward.

"Carmen, let me drive. You're upset," Mickey said.

"I'll drive myself." When he tried to grab her arm, she wrenched away. "Stop, Mickey!"

Valets and guests turned to stare. Mickey stepped back, and she climbed into her car. She threw her clutch in the passenger seat and slammed her foot on the gas. She narrowly missed running over a pedestrian who dashed across the street without looking. Her tires screeched as she slammed on the brakes and screamed at the top of her lungs. She navigated through traffic, even riding the sidewalk at one point because she didn't have the patience to wait for the fucking light to change. She ignored the blare of horns as she drove.

Civilized. The word knocked around in her brain. No, she wasn't civilized. She was a daughter of the underworld. She was taught to take what was hers and defend at all costs. She didn't fight fire with fire. She fought fire with explosives that would leave craters in her wake. After Steven Vega, she wouldn't hesitate to shoot first and ask questions later. They lived in an uncivilized world, so a certain level of savage was necessary to survive.

The restlessness she had been trying to ignore reared its ugly head. She wanted to race, to tear something apart with her bare hands. Needs tumbled around in her chest and whispered dark temptations in her ear.

She stopped at a light. She opened her mouth to scream, to let her emotions go, but nothing emerged. The scream was internal and full of a sorrow so deep that if she released it, she would never recover. Loneliness and misery flooded her. The thought of going back to his house was unbearable.

Angel's words drifted through her mind. *I recognize another restless soul when I see one.*

The urge to throw herself into the deep end, to clash with someone who was as primitive and raw as she was drummed through her. If anyone could match her dark recklessness, it was Angel Roman. One wild, dark soul recognized another.

Even as her conscience told her this was a bad idea, she slammed her foot on the gas. She and Marcus were just friends. He made that abundantly clear. It was time to move on.

She pulled up to Angel's property and pressed the buzzer at the gate. There were at least ten cars in the front drive. Mickey pulled up behind her and flashed his lights. She was impressed he'd been able to keep up. The video monitor lit up, and Eli Stark stared at her with his cop gaze.

"What are you doing here?" Eli asked brusquely.

"I'm looking for Angel."

"How do you know where he lives?"

"He brought me here before."

Eli stared at her for a long minute. She wasn't in the mood to wait around.

"Is he here or not?" she snapped.

The video cut out, and a moment later, the gate began to swing open.

"Hallelujah," she said and pulled up beside the fountain.

Mickey pulled up behind her and was at her door before she could close it. He had his gun out and reached for her arm but stopped when she gave him that look.

"What are you doing?" he demanded.

Eli opened the front door, and Mickey cursed.

"Carmen," he said in a low voice, but she ignored him.

She walked toward the front door and would have sailed past Eli, but he pulled her to a stop.

"How well do you know Angel?" Eli asked.

"What do you mean?"

"How. Well," he bit out.

She scowled. "Better than most. Why?"

Eli released her. "I hope you know what to do."

She was too deep in her own drama to decipher his meaning. The mansion was no less breathtaking at night. The grand chandeliers gave off a soft, welcoming glow. She glanced at herself in one of the mirrors in the grand entryway and was relieved to see that her inner turmoil didn't show on her face.

She followed Eli between the double curving staircases to the massive living area, which was filled with men. Something was wrong with the massive backlit waterfall, but she couldn't put her finger on it. She registered the silence and a small army of silent guards before she spotted a naked man pinned to the wall by two swords through his abdomen. His body was coated with blood, which trickled across the floor to the pool, which explained the salmon-colored waterfall. She thought he was dead until a dagger embedded into his pelvis. He screamed and jerked against the swords. There was the nauseating sound of wet flesh tearing as he tried to get free.

Angel stood about ten feet away holding eight knives, each about a foot long. He was back to being badass James Dean in black jeans and T-shirt. He shook his hand, which was dripping red. His gaze was on Eli, and he didn't look happy.

"Didn't the police academy teach you how to guard a door?" Angel asked.

"I thought you'd be happy to see this visitor," Eli said.

She spotted five bodies floating in the pool. A quick glance around the room told her that Angel had been at this for a while. There were spectacular red splatters around the room that she was sure hadn't been done by an artist. What the hell was going on?

"You think she's going to stop me? I've been waiting for this," Angel said with relish.

To punctuate his point, he tossed another dagger without looking at his target. The dagger landed in the man's shoulder. His piercing cry made the hairs on the nape of her hair rise.

"I'm sorry, Carmen." Angel spread his arms wide. "As you can see, I'm entertaining tonight. You should have called."

"What did he do?" She was proud that she sounded calm despite the circumstances. Maybe her upbringing in the underworld was good for something after all.

"Does it matter?" Angel asked.

"Yes." She knew Angel was dangerous. He was a Roman, but nothing could have prepared her for this. She felt as if she was coming out of her own skin. Everything in her demanded she turn around, walk out of the house, and act as if she never saw anything. Instead, she stood there like an idiot, waiting to hear his reason for torturing a man to death.

"This is Theodore," Angel said politely. "Say hello to Carmen, Theodore."

When the man didn't speak, Angel threw another dagger. This one skimmed his calf. Despite the fact that the blade cut to the bone, the man didn't move. Apparently, he was beyond feeling anything at this point. She felt a burst of relief before Angel threw another dagger. This one landed right over his belly button. The man jumped, maiming his body even more as he struggled against the swords holding him in place. Rivulets of blood ran down his body before he sagged dejectedly against the swords, which shuddered under his weight.

"Hi."

Theodore's resigned greeting sent chills down her spine. She fought the compulsion to rush to the man's aid. She wanted to believe that Angel wasn't a psychopath, so she waited.

"Theodore here likes to drug, rape and mutilate girls," Angel said as he flipped a dagger through the air. "His father is a powerful drug lord who manipulates the police and judicial system. He's gotten Theodore out of a lot of charges. No one can stick anything to him. Yesterday, another body turned up. I decided to save the cops the trouble and take care of Theodore."

Angel indicated a camera on a tripod she hadn't noticed until then.

"I'm taking some shots for his father to remember him by. He's the one who taught Theodore how it's done. It appears the apple doesn't fall far from the tree." Angel shrugged. "They're into torture porn. I thought it would be poetic justice for him to go out the way his victims have. Our families go way back. Unfortunately for Theodore, his father's in a maximum prison right now, so he won't be able to able to help."

Angel walked up to Theodore, who began to whimper. He placed his elbow on the hilt of one of the swords protruding from Theo's chest. The man let out a god-awful scream that covered her body in goose bumps.

"I think Lucifer's onto something with ancient weapons. Gavin ran Steven Vega through with swords. It inspired me, so I got some of my own." He scanned her. "You look fancy. Hot date?"

She swallowed hard. "Not anymore."

He shook his head ruefully. "You took your sweet time coming to me. It's been almost a week."

Angel called to one of his men who had a camera. Angel directed the shots from different angles and asked Theodore to turn his head this way and that for lighting and effect. The sound of Theodore's whimpers made her feel sick. Theodore was a rapist and killer who was getting his just desserts, but... but it wasn't right. She shivered and found Eli watching her. She remembered his comment when she entered—*I hope you know what to do.* He didn't agree with what Angel was doing, but he didn't stop it. Did he think she could?

"Angel!" Carmen snapped.

"What?"

His dagger landed in Theo's eye socket, which knocked his head into the wall with a sickening thud. Theo's head flopped forward. Blood slid from his mouth and pooled on the floor in front of him.

"I'm sure he'll die any second now. I have some other guests, but I can postpone it if you want to do something?"

She averted her face. "End it, Angel."

"Why?"

"Because you've made your point."

She turned back to see that he had even more daggers.

"Finish it and we can do whatever you want."

Angel paused with the cluster of knives in his hand like a steel bouquet of death. "Whatever I want?"

"Yes."

The only sound in the room was of the soothing waterfall. Her legs quivered as she waited for Angel to decide. She imagined that Theodore was praying for death since it was clear that Angel wanted to draw this out.

Angel didn't drop eye contact as he pulled a gun from the small of his back and shot Theodore without hesitation. Out of the corner of her eye, she saw Theodore go limp and swallowed bile. Angel tossed his daggers on a white couch and strode toward her.

"Take the final pictures," he ordered his men before he jerked his head at her. "Upstairs."

She hesitated before she turned to follow. Mickey looked horrified, but he didn't intervene. Angel jogged up the ostentatious staircase while she followed more slowly. Her mind was suspended in numb disbelief over what she just witnessed. As she reached the top of the stairs, she saw a hallway extending in each direction. She wandered down a hallway of closed doors and paused in the doorway to a massive master bedroom. She could hear the shower running. She sat on the bed and stared straight ahead.

The water shut off, and a minute later, Angel walked out of the bathroom with a towel around his waist. The whiplash he got from Hell left a dark scar on his otherwise unblemished body. He stopped in front of her and skimmed the back of his knuckles down her cheek. She didn't react. The fingers slipped under her chin and tilted her face up. She focused on a water droplet that slipped from his hair and traveled down his face.

"Carmen."

Their eyes collided. The cold began to fade as his manic energy reached for her, rousing her own. He kissed her. He went deep and opened his mouth. She copied, and his tongue stroked hers. She expected him to taste bitter with the metallic bite of blood. Instead, chocolate and mint filled her senses, seducing and enticing her. Contradictory, like everything else about him. He pushed her on her back without losing her lips. Water dampened her thin lace dress as his naked body imprinted on hers. His skin was hot, almost feverish. His hands were greedy and rough as they moved over her.

She felt as if she was in free fall. Her mind whirled with need and fear. She couldn't get her bearings or think straight as the feel of him seeped into her starved soul. She raked her nails down his naked back. He grunted in approval and dragged her dress over her hips. She felt her thong snap and then a thick dick burrowed between her legs. Her eyes flew open, and she ripped her mouth from his.

"Angel!"

"I don't want to hear it," he growled as he tugged on the cups of her dress, freeing her breast, which he took in his mouth.

"I..." she gasped as he sucked hard, sending a thunderbolt to her pussy. "Angel, no!"

His head snapped up. "What?"

"We're not doing this." She tried to wriggle out from under him, which wasn't happening without his permission. She could feel his cock pulsing between her legs. She came here knowing that he would fuck her silly, but she couldn't follow through, not after witnessing Theodore's death.

His eyes were narrow slits of heavenly blue. "You said we could do whatever I want."

"Yes, but I have to agree."

"What the fuck are you playing at?" he demanded.

"You're high on the kill, and you want to fuck." She couldn't suppress her shudder. "You can get another girl. I just needed you to end it." She tried to wriggle out from under him, but he wasn't moving.

"You played me."

She stilled. The lack of inflection made her heart race. Stripped of the façade, Angel was just as imposing as Gavin. Even more so because she didn't know his limits.

"Get off, Angel." Her voice wavered, betraying her nerves.

Like a predator sniffing out easy prey, he planted his fists on either side of her head, caging her.

"What are you going to do if I don't?" he whispered.

"Scream."

"You think any of my men would help you?"

Probably not. She glared at him. "You're not so butt ugly that you couldn't get another woman."

"We put this off long enough."

His face was hard and carnal as he stared down at her. He held her gaze as his hand skated down her body. She bucked as his hand slipped between her legs. She gasped and reached down to grab his thick wrist.

"Wet, but not enough," he said.

He stuck his fingers in his mouth. Her breath left her lungs as she watched his eyes close. When they opened, they were a shade darker.

"You're perfect."

He sat up. She panted beneath him as his penis rested against her stomach. The towel was gone, and he looked like the warrior he was, ripped and ready to fuck. His body was rigid, veins pulsing and muscles rippling. The killing urge was still on him. His mood saturated the room, flooding her body with a fight or flight response. Her mind was full of a strange buzzing noise that interfered with her ability to think. Her body was electrified while she was intimidated and confused as hell.

"You came here for this," he stated.

She opened and closed her mouth.

He leaned down until his face was inches from hers. His good looks could deceive anyone into believing he had a heart of gold instead of one dark as sin.

"The moment I saw you, I knew we would end up here," he said, his lips brushing hers as he spoke.

She quivered beneath him.

"You came here so I could give you this." He rubbed his cock against her pussy. "What's the problem? I know you're not squeamish about blood or kills."

His head dipped, and he kissed the corner of her lip and then trailed his mouth to her neck. Carmen stared up at the ceiling and tried to block out the physical pleasure. His hips moved against hers. The urge to spread her legs and take him warred with the urge to protect herself. If she fucked him, it would be over. But… something in her knew if she did that, it would change something fundamental in her. Something Lyla mentioned about Gavin cheating, about him pouring his darkness into whores slipped through her mind. If she played the whore and absorbed Angel's darkness, would she come to crave it even more? Would she become an addict for what only he could give her?

He nuzzled her throat. "This necklace is in the way."

Her eyes opened as he tossed the necklace on the mattress. She stared at it as he stroked her.

"What do you want, Carmen?"

The tidal wave of emotion she'd been trying to hold at bay swamped her. "I want to be happy," she whispered.

"What will make you happy?"

"I want my life back."

The sob caught both of them off guard. Grief gripped her heart and squeezed with a vengeance. She was dimly aware of Angel's cheek brushing hers as he lifted his head.

"Carmen."

She frantically flapped her hands in front of her face, but that didn't help one bit. "I-I don't know what's wrong with me."

"Fuck." Angel rolled off and settled on his back beside her.

"I-I—" she stammered and tried to get a hold of herself. "I want..."

She didn't know what the fuck she wanted, not anymore. She didn't expect to be lucky enough to have two great loves in her life, but with Marcus, she'd begun to believe she found someone who understood her eccentricities. That belief had been destroyed tonight, and when she visited the one person she thought would understand her, she realized she wasn't ready for his level of dark. Her instincts had been right all along. She didn't want to get involved with a crime lord. A part of her still wanted the white picket fence and a little Nora of her own. She wanted a man to go on the road with, a man to laze on the beach with. That wasn't Angel, which left her with nothing. No safe place, nowhere to lick her wounds. Tonight had shattered her delusions and made her face cold, hard facts. She was well and truly alone.

"Why did you come here tonight?"

The calm tone made her peek at him. He lay beside her, as naked as the day he was born, hands folded on his stomach. She wanted to get the hell out of here, but that might incite him to chase, so she settled beside him, her shoulder touching his.

"I came to have raw, dirty sex," she said.

"And you cried instead."

"I wasn't expecting you to be playing with a human for target practice," she grumbled as she swiped at her eyes.

"He broke it off?"

The words raked at her. "Pretty much."

"Bound to happen."

She blew out a breath. "Yeah."

"How'd he do it?"

She sat up. "I don't want to talk about it."

He grabbed her arm. "That's the least you could do for crying in my bed."

She glared at him. "I kneed a potential business partner in the nuts."

He stared at her for a few beats of silence and then, "Why?"

"Apparently, he's going to be the next powerful man in the city, and since that's what I go for, I should know my place, which is at his feet."

There was a lot of activity going on in his eyes, but he didn't speak.

"Marcus told me to leave."

His grip tightened. "He didn't beat that guy's ass?"

"He didn't care what he said." She let out a shaky breath and stared at his ripped body. "Maybe we should still fuck."

"I'm not into women with blotchy faces."

She let out a weak laugh. Somehow, the laugh transitioned into sobbing.

"Fuck." Angel pulled her down beside him and tipped her against his side.

She buried her face against his chest and cried her heart out. She was lost in a sea of emotion. The feel of his skin and his steady heartbeat were the only things that kept her from losing touch with reality. She clutched him while his fingers moved through her hair. When the tears ceased, she lay slumped against him with her head throbbing.

"There's nothing worse than a woman's tears," he said.

"I'm sorry." She shouldn't be apologizing since it defused him. "I don't know what got into me."

"I do. Did you tell that fuck you love him?"

She stiffened. "I don't love him."

"Women don't cry like that for men they don't love."

"I'm just having a bad week," she said hoarsely.

"When you're over your bad week, we'll fuck each other's brains out. You're not into it tonight, so I'm going to get back to work. You done with the crying jag?"

"Yeah."

He rolled away and disappeared into the bathroom. She took in his beautiful body before it disappeared. Crisis averted by tears. Who knew that would work on Angel Roman? She took a deep breath and scooted to the edge of the bed. She stuffed her boobs back into her dress and then pulled the short skirt down. Her thong was ruined and no longer wearable. The necklace sparkled in the midst of rumpled bedsheets. She hesitated before she grabbed it.

Angel came out of the bathroom wearing a pair of jeans and a white tee. "What are you going to do?"

"I don't know."

He tipped his head to the side as he surveyed her. "I haven't known you long, but I like what I see. If Fletcher isn't giving you what you need, don't waste your time."

"I don't think that's going to be an issue anymore." The look on his face when he told her to leave was burned into her mind.

They left the bedroom and started downstairs. Mickey was waiting for them. She could only imagine what she looked like since he sent Angel a murderous glance. When they reached the bottom of the stairs, she instinctively looked back at the living area, but Angel grabbed her arm and escorted her through the entrance hall. She glanced at her reflection and saw that she had mascara smeared over her right eye and her eyeshadow was completely gone. She looked pathetic and lost.

Angel walked her to her car and opened the door. She stared at him, unsure how to feel over what happened.

"What are you going to do?" she asked.

"I'm going to keep entertaining."

"But he's dead."

"I have some friends in the basement."

She shuddered. "Be careful."

"Always."

She went on tiptoe and kissed his cheek. "I'm sorry."

He cupped her nape. “I can still taste you.”

“You shouldn’t have done that,” she whispered.

He searched her face. “You can still change your mind.”

“I need to get my head straight.”

He smoothed his hand over her back. “You could be my one. You know that, right?”

She wanted to deny it, but she wasn’t into lying to herself. “We would make each other crazy.”

A spark of humor lit his grim eyes. “That’s how life is supposed to be, right?”

They were two halves of the same puzzle piece, which wouldn’t make a whole. She needed a yin to her yang, and although he might be a fun alternative, Angel Roman wasn’t it.

“We would make each other miserable,” she predicted and gave him a hug. “But thanks.”

He slapped her ass as she got into the car and leaned into her window when she rolled it down. “Call me if you’re feeling suicidal or want to fuck, yeah?”

She shoved his face out of her car and drove off the property with Mickey on her tail. She wasn’t going back to Marcus’s house. She wasn’t in the mood to be berated, and she was too fragile right now for a knock-down, drag-out fight. She needed time to build up her walls. Maybe she wasn’t ready for a full-on fuck, but she still needed to be around her type of people.

25

Carmen parked in the back parking lot of the Red Diamond.

"What the hell is going on?" Mickey demanded as he materialized at her side.

"Girl stuff," she said as she tucked the necklace and her clutch in the glove compartment.

"Maybe I should call for reinforcements," Mickey said as he pulled out his phone. "Marcus is calling."

She slapped the phone out of his hand. "Don't you dare answer that!" She stooped to pick it up before he could and turned it off. "I just need some time. No big deal."

"No big deal," he repeated slowly. "We're at a strip club."

"Gentlemen's club," she corrected automatically and tossed his phone in the car before she locked it.

"You slept with Angel."

"I tried, but it didn't work so…" she said as she knocked on the back door, and Phil opened it, "I need my girls."

Mickey hesitated, but she dragged him in with her. A group of women in different states of dress chatted idly, but when they caught sight of her, they screamed and rushed to her. She was suddenly surrounded by bare breasts, big hair, and perfumed skin.

"What's up, chickie?" Mercedes, the woman she shared a kiss with on stage, slapped her ass in welcome.

"Boy problems," she said.

"Well, you came to the right place. Have a seat." Cherry Bomb settled her on a seat in front of the vanity and scrubbed her face with a makeup wipe. "I'm going to make you look like a million dollars, and then we'll dance."

"I don't know if I'm in the mood," Carmen said.

"We'll get you in the mood," she said. "I heard when you were on stage a couple of month's back, the tips were insane."

"They were," Mercedes confirmed. "She's still got it."

A petite blonde with large eyes bustled forward. She got the nickname Baby Doll from the customers. It suited her, especially since she had the bubbly personality of a child.

"Hey, Carmen!" she exclaimed and clapped her hands together. "You want to double team a pole?"

"We'll see, Baby Doll," she said and cupped one of her bulging breasts. "You went bigger?"

Baby Doll beamed in her iridescent bikini. "Yup! And I got my nipples pierced. I swear, my tips doubled. Good thing too since my husband left. I have to take care of the kids on my own now."

"You have two?"

"Four. I had twins on the last go."

"Damn, girl."

"I know, but I'm making it work. Now, tell me about this asshole."

Carmen let them fuss over her while Mickey stood in the corner. He should have been ecstatic to be in the dressing room, but he looked tense and worried instead.

The girls decided to give her a goth vibe. One of the girls offered a cheap crucifix with red rhinestones, which she humbly accepted. Baby Doll slapped a Katy Perry blue wig on her head, and Cherry Bomb took care of her face. When the girls backed off so she could examine the results, she had to admit that her new vibe matched her dark mood. She had a heavy smoky eye with a dark lip and fake eyelashes that made her baby blues pop.

While the girls went on stage, she slipped into the club with Mickey at her side. It was busy as usual. The lights flashed, and the women danced as if their lives depended on it. Scantily dressed servers carried food on sizzling platters. Smoke, liquor, and lust permeated the air.

She found an empty table. A server fetched drinks while Mickey stood guard and cock-blocked anyone who tried to approach her. The server brought her a dirty martini and Mickey a bottle of water. She yanked Mickey down beside her since he was blocking her view.

She watched Cherry Bomb, Mercedes, and the others lay it all on the stage. They were on fire tonight. It seemed like a year ago that she writhed on stage without a care in the world. She hoped just walking into the club would perk her up, but it wasn't working. She ordered another martini.

"What happened tonight?" Mickey asked.

"A reality check."

"Marcus gave me your clutch and told me to get you home."

"Fuck Marcus." She watched a man lick Cherry Bomb's feet. "Know your place," she muttered in disgust.

She should have broken Khalid's nose. At least he would bear her mark for a while and be embarrassed when people asked him what happened. Beat up by a whore. Ha! She had to be satisfied with the fact that he would waddle around for a couple of hours while his balls recovered from her hit. Served him right. She hoped every woman he propositioned gave him what he deserved. Marcus didn't realize how much grief she saved him. If Khalid talked to all women like that, and Pyre Casinos was connected to them, women would flip. She entertained herself by imagining Janice's reaction to a prick like Khalid.

I like things the way they are. She shifted uncomfortably as an invisible hand used her heart as a stress ball. She thought Marcus was safe, and that a good guy wouldn't hurt her. Wrong. *So* fucking wrong. She'd never had the "let's just be friends" talk with any man. That was her line.

She thought she had something good with him, but he didn't feel the same… and that stung. Maybe she was just a piece of ass to him. So why the necklace? What kind of man bought a gift like that for a booty call? He gave her mixed signals, but what came out of his mouth was the real deal. He didn't want to be in a relationship. He wanted to work till he died and never venture out of the desert. Fine.

Would he ask her to get out of the house? She should go on that trip to the beach. Why not? She glanced at her watch. It was midnight. She would arrive in the wee hours of the morning and watch the moonlight reflect on the ocean.

The hard stare from a man sitting several rows in front ruined her fantasy. He was turned in his seat and leering at her. She raised a brow. His eyes flicked to Mickey, and he rose. She tensed and was about to alert Mickey, but he walked out of the club. She shouldn't have left her gun in the car…

"I need to go to the restroom." When Mickey rose to accompany her, she put a hand on his shoulder. "There's never a line for the women's bathroom. I'll be right back."

After she did her business, she glanced in the mirror. She was really feeling this goth look with the electric blue hair. Maybe that should be her next hair color. She went red after Marcus because he made her feel vibrant and alive. Now who was she going to remake herself into? What was her next phase?

She exited the bathroom and heard a faint scream that was quickly cut off. For a moment, she wondered if she was hearing things, but the faint echo of men's raucous laughter sent a chill down her spine. She turned in the opposite direction of the club, walked down a dimly hallway, and turned the corner. In front of the janitor's closet was a group of men. She could only see their backs because they were all watching something. Her skin prickled. She shoved her way through the crowd and was stopped by two men, but not before she saw what held their attention.

Baby Doll was on her knees, being brutally mouth fucked by a man in a suit. Carmen registered that the man looked vaguely familiar before she lunged. The men holding her laughed and hauled her back. The rapist noticed the commotion and smiled at her.

"Carmen Pyre. Of course." He shoved balls deep in Baby Doll's mouth. She slapped his thighs in protest as she gagged. "Come to join the party?"

It was one of George Wotherton's sick son-in-law's. She thought of screaming, but there was no way anyone would hear over the pulsing music. Baby Doll choked, and her vision went red. The fucker pulled out, and Baby Doll puked on herself.

Carmen slammed her stiletto down. The man on her left screeched and released her arm. She turned to the other man and slammed her fist into his ear with as much force as she could. He howled and staggered back. Another man grabbed her shoulder. She grabbed his thumb and wrenched his wrist, so he folded in the perfect position for her to knee him in the face. He fell on his back, revealing a gun on his belt. She grabbed it and turned on the remaining men who put their hands up. There were no smiles or manly chuckles now.

She turned on Wotherton's son-in-law who still had his dick out. Baby Doll curled up in a ball at his feet. He stood over like a hunter would over a kill, proud and cocky.

"What are you going to do with that?" he taunted.

She shot him in the leg. He dropped, and one of his men lunged for her, but she turned the gun on him.

"Back off!" she snapped.

"Are you fucking crazy?" The rapist sounded astounded. "Don't you know who I am?"

She stomped over to him and kicked him in the thigh over his wound. He screamed and curled into a ball.

"I am so fucking sick of you men telling me who you are!" She kicked him in the middle of his back. He recoiled and tried to grab her foot. She kicked his hand and then ground her stiletto into his fleshy palm. He screamed and tried to dislodge her, but she wasn't having it. She put all her weight on his hand and crouched so he could get close to his face. "Do you know who *I* am? I'm Carmen motherfucking Pyre. You think you're the only one with money and connections, bitch? Unlike you, I don't prey on the weak. I try to help people in my city. People like you should be annihilated like the weak pieces of shit that you are."

Out of the corner of her eye, she saw movement and turned the gun in that direction. The man immediately froze.

"You're making a mistake," he wheezed.

"I don't think so. I'd kill your worthless father-in-law if I had the chance," she hissed through clenched teeth.

"When I tell Roman about this, he'll kill you!"

"I don't think so."

"You may be his new fuck toy, but Roman can't afford to lose allies. He's drowning in enemies. Besides, you're just Pyre's leftovers."

She placed the gun on his limp penis and had the satisfaction of seeing his eyes bulge. "How long do you think you'll survive if I blow your dick off?"

"He'll bleed out from his thigh wound first."

The placid tone cut through her rage. She swung her head around. Behind the rapist's men was a well-dressed hulk leaning against the wall. He stood mostly in the shadow so she couldn't see his face. He hadn't been there when she arrived.

"Blowing his dick off would be like cutting off an ear or finger. Painful, but he'll survive," the stranger continued casually.

His mild tone knocked some sense into her. She was about to commit murder in a public place in front of witnesses. She wasn't Angel, who could kill and get away with it. She tried to rein in her wrath and glanced at Baby Doll who huddled in the corner, her eyes flicking from Carmen to her rapist, to the watching crowd.

"Call the cops," Carmen said hoarsely.

"What for?" the man in the shadows asked.

"H-he was—" She couldn't think past the haze. "Just do it! Call the cops."

"Please don't," Baby Doll whispered as she used her soiled bikini top to mop up her face.

"Why?"

"I don't need any trouble. I just want to go home."

"Baby Doll, if you don't press charges—"

"I don't want to. I want to go home." Baby Doll's eyes welled up with tears. "I want my babies."

Carmen turned back to the asshole who thought he got away with this. He didn't see the blow coming. She used the butt of the gun and swung with all her might, catching him on the temple. He slumped to the ground.

"That could kill him," observed the man in the shadows.

"I'll take my fucking chances." She tried to help Baby Doll to her feet, but the woman backed away as if she were contaminated.

"I'm fine," Baby Doll whispered.

Carmen held up the gun and the men parted to let Baby Doll pass, leaving her with George Wotherton's unconscious son-in-law and a handful of witnesses.

"Get him the fuck out of here. If I see any of you in here again, I'll consider it a challenge to find a creative way to end you," she said.

The men glanced at each other before they edged forward. They picked up their wounded leader and retreated. She leaned against the wall as she trembled with rage.

"You move very well."

She tightened her hold on the gun as the stranger spoke. She hadn't realized he was still here. "What?"

"Your training is obvious."

She tensed. "How much did you see?"

"Most of it. You're quite impressive."

"You watched? Why didn't you help?" she demanded.

"Looks like you had it in hand."

"I didn't!"

"You did."

"Show's over. You can run along now." So she could collapse. God, men fucking sucked. Baby Doll was so sweet. She didn't deserve that. She needed to talk to Kiki, make sure the girls weren't left alone when they were on the floor. Maybe they needed a guard over here...

"Do you take jujitsu?"

She turned her head to stare at the stranger. "Seriously?"

"I can't help but be curious. That was some bloodthirsty rage you dished out."

"He was forcing her."

"And you're a trained bodyguard?"

She let out a rusty laugh. After being put in her place by Marcus and almost screwing Angel, this was the icing on the cake. Beating the hell out of that fucking asshole felt good, but it wasn't enough. If this guy hadn't said anything, she would have pulled the trigger. Wotherton's son-in-law would have been her third kill. She shook with the effort it took to stop from murdering him in cold blood.

"I'm from out of town. I heard this was the best place for action in the city. I don't think I dressed right for this establishment."

The stranger stepped into the light. At a glance, she pegged him as a middle-aged businessman. He wore a black pinstriped suit with his hair slicked back and a neatly trimmed thick beard.

"You're overdressed," she agreed.

He shifted in his suit as if it was too tight even though it fit him perfectly. "Some acquaintances of mine dress like this, and I thought I'd try it. It's not comfortable."

"You're not a businessman?"

"No. I don't know how they wear this every day."

"What do you normally wear?"

"Much less."

"You're a nudist?" This mundane and slightly bizarre conversation was keeping her from losing her shit.

He threw back his head and laughed. She examined him more closely. He had a slick braid down his back. The beard made him appear older than he was. He was probably in his early or mid-thirties, and when one got past his size, he was quite handsome in a rugged sort of way. He could be a basketball player with his height, but his width made him a better fit for rugby or football. When he wiped his eyes, she noticed his black fingernail polish.

"You're a rock star?"

He grinned. "You could say that."

"What's your name?"

"John."

There was a slight hesitation before he answered, which told her he was lying, but that wasn't unusual. Most men who frequented clubs lied through their teeth, but she continued anyway.

"What's your last name?"

Another pause and then, "Smith."

As soon as the words were out of his mouth, a shit-eating grin spread over his lips. He didn't even bother to hide the fact that he was amused by his bad improv.

"Really? That's the best you could come up with?" she asked.

He gave a halfhearted shrug. "Yeah."

"Why the hell is Pocahontas on your mind in a gentlemen's club?"

"I have no idea. I heard him call you Pyre. You're related to Gavin?"

She tightened her grip on the gun. "Who wants to know?"

"I ran into him a few months ago. He left an impression."

She tried to decipher what that meant. Friend? Enemy? She had no idea.

"Are you Angel Roman's whore?"

"Excuse me?"

"He called you Angel's fuck toy, which makes you his whore, right?" When her gun hand shifted he asked, "What else do you call a woman you fuck?"

She glared at him. "Lover, girlfriend, friend, wife."

"Are you his wife?"

She bared her teeth. "Don't push me, John." Then she registered what he said. "You know Angel and Gavin?"

He didn't look like he was from the underworld. He didn't have the edge that Gavin and Angel had. He was huge, but he wore fucking nail polish and had the social awkwardness of a geeky weatherman.

"I ran into both of them. I was hoping they frequented a place like this," John said.

"Angel has. Gavin doesn't."

John nodded. "Right. He's committed now."

She relaxed a little. "Yes."

"I really enjoyed that," he said and gestured to the blood and puke on the floor. "Very entertaining."

Before she could come up with a response, a figure turned the corner. She relaxed when she saw Mickey. He had his gun out, and when he spotted John the behemoth, he raised it. John gave Mickey a friendly grin, which made him blink. John was definitely an odd one.

"That's my cue," she said and made sure she gave the giant a wide berth as she joined Mickey. "You have a great night, John."

"I will. I enjoyed your fight," he said and gave her a thumbs up.

She stared at him for a moment before she walked down the hallway with Mickey. She stopped in the bathroom to wash the blood off her hands, which were already bruised from beating up Khalid.

"What the hell happened?" Mickey hissed. "I've been looking for you everywhere."

"One of the girls was attacked by Wotherton's son-in-law."

Mickey cursed. "I saw them carry him out. I was hoping you had nothing to do with it."

"I need to talk to Kiki."

An hour later, she left Kiki with four security guards who would stop her from hunting down the rapist. They'd taken away her weapons and extracted a promise from her to check on Baby Doll tomorrow. Fucking rich pricks thought every woman was fair game...

Carmen embraced the slap of cold air as they walked out the back door of the club. It was almost three in the morning. She debated whether to give Angel a heads-up. What if he sided with the Wotherton's? She couldn't handle another disappointment tonight. If Marcus heard about this, he would really think she was uncivilized. She was barbaric, vengeful, savage—all the emotions he was too refined to feel. She clung to anger because it was easier to handle.

"Let's get you home," Mickey said as they weaved between the cars.

She glanced at him over the top of a BMW. "I'm driving to California."

Baby Doll getting mouth raped was the final straw. She needed to get out of town and regroup. She needed the sun, sand, and ocean.

"Come on, Carmen. I'm sure you can figure it out with Marcus."

"I don't want to figure it out with Marcus," she snapped as she rounded a vintage Mustang. They had been forced to park in the last row, and the light wasn't good. She could still hear the deafening beat emanating from the club. She should install some lights out here.

"Whatever happened, you guys can—"

There was an all-too-familiar popping sound. Mickey dropped even as someone grabbed her hair from behind and yanked viciously. Blade and her father's training took over. She trapped the man's hand on her head and tipped forward to break his hold and put him in an arm lock. She managed to dislocate his shoulder before someone bear hugged her from behind and lifted her into the air. She kicked off an SUV and launched them both backward. The man lost his breath as they crashed into a car. She broke his grip and rolled under a truck. Motorcycle boots jostled for position. Fuck. There were too many of them, and she had no weapon.

A man ducked to look under the truck. She threw a handful of gravel in his face before she rolled out the other side and ran toward the Red Diamond. A body slammed into her before she could reach the circle of red lights surrounding the club. Her ribs protested as she was crushed beneath a heavy body.

"Payback's a bitch," a man panted in her hair.

"No shit."

He flipped her on her back. The punch knocked her head against the pavement. White stars flashed behind her eyes, and her ears began to ring. Through watery eyes, she recognized the man from the club who had been glaring at her.

"Roman's not going to recognize you when we're through with you," he said and hit her again.

The cheap metal crucifix nestled between her breasts cut into her skin. When he drew back his fist again, she grasped the cross between her fingers and struck. A metal point sliced the fragile skin of his throat. He lurched back and made a choking sound. She slashed again and was rewarded with a gush of warm blood. She shoved him off and scrambled toward the lights, but she didn't make it. A man barreled into her, and she tumbled across concrete. Before she could get her bearings, another man was on her. A boot in her abdomen made her retch before she was shoved on her back. A biker sat on her stomach and gripped her by the throat. The man choked her while another stomped on her wrist.

"Hurry up before somebody comes!" a man said.

She clawed and kicked, all to no avail. Through the panic, she felt a prick in her arm. Oh, God. A needle. What were they shooting her up with? It could be anything. Maybe it was Clorox or a lethal dose of...

Her cold, desperate, terrifying world disappeared. The hand disappeared from her throat, and she took a deep breath. Her heart soared as euphoria chased away every other emotion. She felt as if she was flying even though she could feel the unforgiving pavement beneath her. The behemoth sitting on top of her disappeared. The shadows that gathered around her didn't matter. Nothing did because there was no pain, only happiness and freedom. One of the men with blurred faces pulled something out of his jacket. She grinned at him and spread her arms wide, ready to receive sweet relief.

"Now that's a foul," a familiar voice said. "Ten against one is just bad sportsmanship."

There was a strange popping sound as her assailant's head whipped to the side at a strange angle that made her giggle. There were shouts and a series of muted gunshots. From her position, she watched a pair of shiny gentleman's shoes dance with biker and combat boots. It was a mesmerizing sight. Men began to hit the ground with stunning force, so much so that she felt as if the ground was rocking beneath her. Bodies lay in odd, almost poetic angles that her buzzing brain wanted to investigate more thoroughly. She heard grunts, wheezing, and screaming, which were quickly cut off. She was very aware of a rock digging into her spine, but she didn't have the strength to shift an inch to the left.

The fancy shoes, now covered in blood, came in her direction. The shoes were taking too long to reach her, so she stared up at the inky black sky as she waited. She wished she could fall into it. A man knelt beside her. She tried to focus on his face, which slid in and out of focus. Her body began to shake uncontrollably. Her pulse was racing out of control. She reached for him as her world pitched from side to side. Her body flushed with heat one moment and was chased by an icy cold that made her teeth chatter in the next.

John Smith's face appeared for a second before her eyes dilated, and his face turned back into a blob of color. Above him, the Aurora Borealis ripped across the sky. She opened her mouth to tell John to look, but she couldn't get her tongue to work.

John said something, but she couldn't hear anything over the sound of her own heartbeat. He lifted her. She flapped her arms, so she wouldn't drown. She landed on something soft and slippery. Familiar scents she couldn't place teased her nostrils. She heard a roar and whatever she was lying on shifted. She fell off the soft thing and landed on something hard that didn't smell nice. She flailed and tried to find something to hold, but her eyes wouldn't focus, and her body wasn't listening to her. After an eternity, she decided to give in and float.

Light invaded her dreamlike state. She raised her arm to shield sensitive eyes. Something pulled on her ankles. She kicked, but the hold on her didn't disappear. She was dragged backward and then cradled in two bearlike arms. She reached up and brushed her fingers against a bristly vine. She tugged on the vine and heard someone chuckle. She blinked furiously and realized it was a beard.

Music assaulted her ears, and she moaned and burrowed against the bear. She began to shiver and moan as invisible knives were shoved into her skull. She struggled to get away to no avail. The man had been carrying her for days. Where were they going? She hoped he was taking her somewhere nice. Male voices rumbled around her along with the cheer of a massive crowd. Maybe it was the Super Bowl. Whoever had the hottest players should win. Why didn't they make shirtless calendars for football players like they did for firemen?

An unpleasant smell reached her, a sterile one that made her curl her toes and clamp a hand over her face before she realized she was suffocating herself. She breathed in something metallic that made her want to gag. Lights disappeared, and she was placed on something hard and unforgiving. She tried to focus, but her head was spinning. What was happening to her?

"You have spirit and guts, which is rare enough to make me intervene."

She turned her head toward the pleasant voice. She knew that voice, right? It belonged to a friend? She tried to remember and came up with an image of a unicorn prancing majestically across a moonlit beach. She panted as her body tried to fight off whatever was attacking her insides. Her limbs jerked as lava slid through her veins and started little fires in her brain. She curled into a ball and rocked. What was happening to her?

"I've heard of you. You killed the leader of the Black Vipers. I was intrigued but not terribly impressed since you used a gun, but tonight, you showed how resourceful you can be. I'm impressed."

When a hand brushed over her hair, she edged away. She couldn't bear to be touched right now, not when her skin felt as if it would fall off her bones.

"If you survive, maybe your presence will bring Gavin back to Hell. Maybe Angel too if you really are his whore. It would be titillating to get them in the pit again. I'm trying to save my annual visit, so I have to find other ways to entertain myself until then. Tonight was a pleasant surprise. I hope you don't die. I think you have potential, and you're quite amusing to boot."

She lurched forward and retched. Oh, God. She was going to die. Something was terribly wrong.

"I'll check on you in the morning. Good luck."

She retched again and opened her mouth to ask for help, but the man was gone.

26

Her body was trying to destroy itself. She tried to outrun the pain and rammed into a wall. She explored her surroundings with tingling fingertips since her eyes weren't working. It took her several rounds to make out that she was in a room made of stone, an eight-foot square with a drain, a stone bench, and a bowl of water. She sipped water before she used the drain and then huddled in the corner. Her body was a throbbing mass. She could feel every single cut and bruise on her body. It felt as if someone was pouring acid on them. Her face vibrated as chemicals crept beneath her skin. She turned on her belly and pressed her face against stone. It smelled like a sewer, so she flipped onto her back and tried to keep her face still by squeezing it between her hands.

Time stood still. Her quick, ragged breaths filled the room. She wasn't sure if her eyes were open or closed, and it didn't matter anyway. She shivered as cold seeped into her bones. Slivers of fire slipped through her veins, making her cry out and claw her own skin to get it out. The crusty crucifix dug into her skin, so she slipped it off and tossed it. She didn't care about defending herself. Hopefully, someone would put her out of her misery. She was so fucking tired of fighting.

Time passed. She vomited, drank water, and vomited again. She tried to find a spot in the room that wasn't soiled. She was chilled to the bone and in so much pain, she couldn't stand it. She thought of slamming her head against the stone until she knocked herself unconscious, but she didn't have the strength. She collapsed in a corner, pressed her forehead against the stone, and willed herself to die.

All feeling began to fade as her body went numb. She wasn't sure if she was freezing to death or if the drugs were killing her. Either was fine with her. Now that her body wasn't trying to destroy itself, her mind was surprisingly clear. Mickey. Was he dead? She whimpered. He couldn't be. He was too young, and he was just doing his job. Obviously, the loser in the club was a member of the Black Vipers and called his cronies. They had been waiting for her. She was stupid to let down her guard. No one forgot a slight. It didn't matter how much time passed. This was her just desserts. One couldn't take a life without consequences. Well, she'd pay the price. It was worth it. She'd kill Maddog again with pleasure. Did she kill someone with a crucifix? If she had the capacity to feel, she would have been impressed with herself. Maybe Blade would have given her credit for that kill. Blade… He needed to get laid before he turned into a human statue.

All those times Lyla had been attacked, she'd convinced herself the outcome would be different if she'd been present. Well, she had her moment, and she had been beaten and drugged and was now locked in a cell in God knew where. And unlike Lyla, she didn't have a Gavin to move heaven and earth to save her. She didn't have anyone. Everyone would be fine without her. Mom had Marv, Lyla had Gavin, Honey had Beau, and Marcus had work.

Just when she thought she was getting her life together, everything fell apart. With death imminent, she could admit that Angel was right. She fell for Marcus. He broke through her shields the moment they met in Incognito, which is why his condolences made an impression on her. Her soul recognized something different about him; it just took her mind a couple of years to catch up. His position as Vinny's replacement was a good reason to keep him at a distance. She reinforced her prejudices by holding onto her suspicions about his motivations. There was no doubt that Marcus was still hiding something, but it held no threat to the Pyre clan, and he was entitled to his privacy. He was the one-in-a-million guy. He was driven, successful, considerate, loving... He just didn't want to be in love with her. She'd heard it before. She was too wild, too impulsive, too clingy, too crazy. She needed too much, and after losing Vinny, her demands had a dark edge to it that most men wouldn't want to deal with, especially one with a pristine reputation. She wasn't lucky enough to snag two great men in one lifetime. She expected too much. She always had.

His promise the night Gavin and Lyla were in Hell echoed in her mind. *No matter what happens, we'll get through this together.* Even though she felt no emotions, a tear slipped down her face. Marcus helped her through some of her worst moments. She thought she could depend on him, that they might have a future together, but it was all in her head.

You're my fantasy.

She shook her head to dislodge his words. The way he lost himself in her meant nothing. It was just sex. She was new and interesting, and he had needs. Simple. An exchange of mutual pleasure, that's all.

Her heart labored in her chest. She touched her face to make sure her eyes were closed and relaxed. It was time.

She sprawled on top of Vinny. They were naked in bed, post orgasm, with the gentle flow of air conditioning drifting over their sweaty bodies. She rested her face on his chest and listened to his heart gradually settle into a normal rhythm. She didn't want or need anything else in life, just this. This man loved her, worshipped her. Everything would fall into place as long as they had each other.

"Why do you love me?" she whispered.

"What?" Vinny rumbled.

She folded her hands on his chest and eyed him. He looked wrecked and sated. "Why do you love me?"

He grinned. "Why wouldn't I love you?"

"I'm serious."

"I love you because you're smoking hot."

"Vinny," she said in a warning voice.

"I love you because you're the horniest woman I've ever met."

"Vinny!"

"I love you because you make me want to sing a cappella in bed."

Carmen bit his nipple, and he yelped.

"Okay, okay. I love your smile."

"You're talking about sex and my looks."

"That's the most important."

She was about to yank his balls when his next words stopped her.

"I love you because you bring out the best in me. I love you because you know exactly who I am and remind me when I forget." He stroked damp strands of hair back from her face. "You love with everything in you. I knew if I could hook you, you would never leave me. You'd be here by my side no matter what. Your love made me into the man I'm supposed to be." He searched her eyes. "You get me?"

She blinked back tears. "Yes."

"Why do you love me?"

She laughed. "I should have seen that coming." She sat up and surveyed him in all his masculine glory. She splayed her hand over his heart. "I love you because of this. It's the most beautiful part about you." She ran her hands through his thick, soft hair. "I love you because you love me for who I am. You're so patient with me. You listen to me." She leaned down and rested her forehead against his. "You made me believe I'm perfect. That's why I love you."

He cupped her face. "Forever, Carmen?"

"Forever. No matter what comes," she murmured.

"That's my girl."

27

Carmen opened her eyes and squinted against the dim light. Her eyelids, like the rest of her body, felt bruised and swollen. Her throat was raw, and the awful taste of bile lingered on her tongue. She opened her eyes and grunted at the pain that simple task caused.

"You're alive."

She dropped her head sideways in the direction of that voice. She stared at her surroundings for a full minute before she registered what she was seeing. John Smith stood in front of a massive canvas finger-painting red mountains. He had nixed the suit and now wore the loose pants people wore in karate classes. His shirt was skintight and showed off his muscles. Her weary brain didn't want to move past his bare feet, but eventually her gaze tracked around the room. The walls and floor were made of smooth white stone. There were intricate designs carved into the stone, but she couldn't make out what it was. Maybe she was in a Greek castle. Arched doorways led into other rooms also made of the same stone.

"Where am I?" she croaked.

"You don't know?"

He didn't turn from his painting. He tilted his head, and his braid swished to the side.

"Who are you?"

"You haven't figured that out either?"

She glanced around the room for a weapon. He had saved her life, but he also hadn't called for help. Instead, he put her in a dark cell where she almost froze to death. Somehow, she found the strength to lift her head. There was a wooden cup with colored pencils and a compass on a stand. She wriggled up the cot she was on and reached out. Her hand trembled as it hovered in midair. She glanced at John Smith who slapped more red paint onto the canvas. She gripped the compass and carefully lifted it without jostling the pencils and slipped it beneath the thin sheet covering her body. It took her a few seconds to realize she was buck naked.

"What did you do to me?" Her voice was pathetically weak. She tried to muster up a healthy dose of anger or fear that would give her strength, but her emotions and motor skills were sluggish and not yet back to normal.

"A Black Viper injected you with a drug cocktail. That's all I managed to get out of them before they died." He glanced at her over his shoulder. "You don't remember?"

"You put me in a cell."

"Yes." He turned back to the canvas. "I didn't think you would survive. It was touch and go on for a while. After I realized you were going to live, Augustus cleaned you up."

"Augustus," she repeated flatly.

"A submissive eunuch," John said distractedly and flicked his hand, sending dots of red over the paint splattered floor. "If anyone else tended to you, you wouldn't be breathing right now."

"Who are you?"

John turned and spread his arms. "Come on. I know you know."

Her temples throbbed. "I don't know."

"You're underground." He slapped the wall, leaving a red handprint behind. "You're in my *lair*..." He rolled his hand as if beckoning the right answer. "You know, Carmen."

She glanced around the majestic room that, despite its beauty, was really a fancy cave. Underground… She stared at John Smith and then shook her head. "No."

He grinned. "Yes."

"You can't be Lucifer!"

He gave a mock bow. "In the flesh. Welcome to Hell."

"But… but…" Lucifer was said to be more vicious than his father, the most feared man on the continent… and he was finger-painting in a yoga outfit. Maybe she was still high. "That's not possible."

"Why not?"

"You don't leave Hell."

"I rarely leave Hell," he corrected as he smudged the base of his mountain to give it more shading. "But it's come to my attention that maybe things above ground aren't as boring as I thought they would be."

"You mean since Gavin and Lyla were here?"

Lucifer jabbed a rust colored finger in her direction. "You got it. I have terrible ennui."

"Poor you," she muttered.

"Life has become so predictable. Kill, kill, kill." He waved his hand, sprinkling more paint over the floor. "I don't know why I keep expecting to find something different in someone's entrails. Humans are all the same."

She tried to banish the image of a person digging through another's human's organs.

"But Steven brought Gavin back to me, and I realized…" He braced his elbow on the wall and leaned into his dirty hand, getting paint in his hair. "I've been looking in the wrong place for entertainment."

Her muscles protested when she tensed.

"Most humans are predictable. They all want the same things. Sex, money, power, and purpose."

She blinked. "Purpose?" She was definitely still drugged. Lucifer, the king of Hell, couldn't be a finger-painting philosopher. No fucking way.

"The weak need someone to give them purpose." He spread one hand on his tunic, marring the white fabric with garish scarlet. "Which is where I come in. I enslave them, hence, giving them purpose."

His smile was wide and guileless. If she didn't know his reputation, she might be fooled into letting down her guard. He seemed as open and friendly as a Bible salesman, which couldn't be further from the truth. She imagined Lucifer with crazed eyes, foaming at the mouth, more demon than man, but his appearance was throwing her off. She desperately tried to reconcile the tales of the king of Hell with the man before her.

"Then there are those who want power. They come here to gain notoriety by battling it out in the pit… and that's where they go wrong. Most die, as they should. Power isn't for everyone, but for men like Gavin and me, it's what we were destined for."

"What do you want from me?"

He turned back to his canvas. "The same thing I want from Gavin."

She had no fucking idea what Gavin gave Lucifer in exchange for Lyla's life. She wished she died in the cell. Anything Lucifer planned for her would end in blood and torture. She gripped the compass pressed against her thigh.

"Good entertainment is so hard to find," Lucifer said.

A chill ran down her spine. Entertainment in the pit?

Lucifer stepped back from the painting. "What do you think?"

She couldn't focus on the painting, not when her life was at stake. "Beautiful."

"There's nothing better than painting with fresh blood."

That got her attention. Her stomach dipped as she stared at his dripping hand. "Fresh blood?"

He nodded to a wooden bowl full of what she assumed was red paint. "It has the best consistency when it's still warm."

She retched, and he laughed.

"I wouldn't think a woman who fights like you has a weak stomach."

Kill to survive? Yes. Play with blood and organs or dead bodies? Hell fucking no.

Lucifer approached. Her eyes were riveted to his hands. Why didn't he wash it off? How could he stand to have someone's lifeblood staining his hands? How could he stand to paint with it? This was a new level of morbid.

"What's your story, Carmen?"

"Story?" On his forearm, the blood had already dried and was starting to flake. Her stomach rocked.

"You fight like someone with nothing to lose."

Because she had nothing to lose. He stood over her. She tried to zero in on the best place to hit, but all the best parts were higher up where she couldn't reach. If he was telling the truth, piercing his dick with the compass wouldn't incapacitate him for long, and besides, he was built like a tree. Everything about him was supersized. Crap.

"I didn't realize so many of you above ground have such a penchant for violence. Or is it just the women around Gavin? You're quite skilled in hand-to-hand combat, and I appreciate your creativity during an attack. If I hadn't seen you in action, my first night above ground would have been a waste of time."

What was she supposed to say? You're welcome?

"Where's the rage coming from?"

She jerked. "What?"

He knelt beside the bed, braced his elbows on the mattress, and stared at her as if she would start reading a bedtime story.

"That chip on your shoulder is what intrigues me the most. It's what's driving you, what gives you strength. It's common in men, not so much in women." He paused. "So what is it? Abuse? Rape? Infidelity?"

"I don't know what you're talking about."

"You shouldn't tease me. I'm not a patient man."

He didn't move, but the hairs on the nape of her neck rose. He still had that smile on his face, but his eyes were frighteningly clinical. He wasn't looking at her as a woman or even a human being, but a toy. And if that toy didn't perform... "I lost my husband. He was murdered by Steven Vega."

"Years ago."

His dismissive tone made her feel homicidal. She tightened her hold on the compass. "It doesn't matter how long ago it was."

Lucifer shook his head. "Humans."

She couldn't tell if he was disgusted or amused. "You act like you're not one. Oh, wait. You're right. That explains a lot."

He shrugged. "I don't possess the emotions others have."

"No shit."

"I'm fascinated by one person's attachment to another like Gavin's for Lyla and yours to this husband who has been dead for years. I don't get it."

Of course, he didn't get it. He was a sociopath.

"We live in a world full of selfish monsters, yet you all naïvely choose to trust each other and be continually let down again and again. It's baffling. Down here, we continue the old ways."

"Old ways?"

"I want, I take. If someone covets, we fight. Whoever wins, gets to keep it. That's the way it should be, right?"

In her addled state, he was making far too much sense. It was beginning to scare her. "What does this have to do with anything?"

"Gavin's changed," he grumbled.

"Yes."

"Why?"

He was genuinely confused. She considered the big brute and recalled Lyla's tone of voice the night she was in Hell. Lyla sounded more exasperated and annoyed by Lucifer than afraid. She could relate. Lucifer was a murderer with a child's curiosity. It was appealing and terrifying at the same time. She clutched the compass and waited for the right moment.

"Because Gavin fell in love," she said.

"I don't believe in love."

"No surprise," she muttered.

"Everyone thinks they love someone else, but in the end, they always choose themselves. Humans are intrinsically selfish. Do you believe in love?"

"Of course."

"Why?"

"Why?" she echoed incredulously.

"Yes, why do you believe in it?"

"Because I've felt it. I don't have a choice. Love just is. My parents love me. Vinny loved me."

"And these people would do anything for you? Die for you?"

"Yes."

"Then who's Marcus?"

His name was a trigger that ripped through her lethargy. The volatile mix of heartache and misery detonated in her chest. She swung and aimed for his neck. She imagined the compass piercing his throat as effectively as the crucifix sliced her attacker. Her wrist was caught in a firm grip. Lucifer ground her fragile bones together, which caused her to drop the compass into his waiting hand.

"You need to control your energy before you strike," he said calmly as he placed the compass back in the cup. "You need to harness your emotions. Emotions give you strength, but they're also a liability. I sense your energy, and therefore, I can anticipate your moves. Your energy is all over the place right now." He snapped his fingers like a gay man talking about Lady Gaga. "Very easy to predict. Everyone thinks body language is the giveaway. It isn't. What you sense is more important than what your eyes tell you."

He released her and she stared at the red smears on her wrist. She could smell that familiar metallic stink. Knowing this was fresh and that Lucifer had probably gathered it... She wiped as much of it on the bedsheet as she could and tried to control her gag reflex.

"You called out his name many times," Lucifer continued. "You didn't call for your husband or Angel."

She froze.

He cocked his head to the side. "I thought you were Angel's whore."

"Shut up," she said through clenched teeth.

"There you go with the emotions again." He clucked his tongue. "I liked you better when you were stone cold. It was beautiful."

Fantasies of strangling him played through her mind. "Did you bring me here to talk me to death?"

"I brought you here, so Gavin would come to play, but he's not even in town. So disappointing."

"He's in Bora Bora," she said numbly. So, no rescue for her.

"I just got off the phone with him. I assume he'll tell Angel that you're here, so I have time to kill. Who's Marcus?"

"Kiss my ass."

"So vulnerable and weak as a kitten, yet you still spit at me. Love him, do you?" He caught her first in his hand. "I'm going to teach Gavin's daughter how to fight. You should attend, so I can teach you to control your energy."

"Fuck you, *John*."

He grinned and released her. "I quite liked that name. I can pass for a John, right?"

She stared at the ceiling. This so wasn't happening. She was literally in Hell being emotionally flayed by the devil.

"You've replaced Vinny," Lucifer said.

She ground her teeth. "You can't replace one person with another."

"Humans do it all the time, especially the weak ones. Why are you so mad? Marcus doesn't love you back?"

For someone who didn't have emotions, his insight was uncanny.

"That must be hard," he mused. "Loving two men who never loved you back."

She whipped her head around. "What?"

He held up two fingers. "Your ex-husband and now this lover. You're mad because neither of them loved you."

"Vinny loved me!"

Lucifer cocked his head. "Then why isn't he here?"

"Because he took Gavin's place. You know that."

"Yes, but why did he take Gavin's place?"

"Because—" She stopped abruptly. Everything in her turned to ice. Lucifer and the cave disappeared as the truth struck her with such force that everything in her shattered. She thought bearing the weight of sorrow and guilt all these years was unbearable, but this… This ripped her soul in two.

She stared into Lucifer's dark eyes and he nodded.

"You see it now, don't you?" he murmured almost gently. "If he loved you, he would still be here. He took the position to make a point because he cared more about himself than you."

She went numb with shock. She clung to her relationship with Vinny, idolizing it and comparing every other man to him, but… Vinny hadn't loved her more than he loved Gavin. If he loved her, he wouldn't have tried to be crime lord. He would have been content with her, with their marriage, with her love. She hadn't been enough, and that was why he wasn't here. Because she wasn't enough to make him feel complete. He needed more than she could offer.

"Come, you must be hungry," Lucifer said.

He walked through an arched doorway. She didn't attempt to escape. She lay there, wondering if one could die from having their soul destroyed. There was the sound of running water and then Lucifer reappeared with clean hands, damp hair, and an identical pair of shirts and pants. He grabbed her and settled her on the side of the bed. The bedsheet fell away. She was so far gone that she didn't even notice.

"This is all I have," Lucifer said as he dropped the shirt over her head.

She didn't have the strength to dress herself, so he did it, pulling her arms through the sleeves as if she was a child. He even rolled up the sleeves with tiny, precise folds. She didn't realize she was crying until he traced a tear down her cheek.

"I don't understand this either," he said quietly. "Fascinating."

He thought heartbreak was fascinating. Of course, he did. He knelt and slid his monstrous pants over each leg.

"Mickey?" she whispered as he made her stand. She had to grip his waist to keep from falling over. She felt dizzy, weak, and nauseated.

"Mickey?" he echoed as he pulled the pants up and cinched the drawstring on the waist as tight as possible.

"Mickey, my guard. Is he...?"

"Dead as a doornail. Shot in the back of the head."

His callous response made her dig her nails into his skin. He didn't seem to notice. He fussed with her attire. She felt as if she was wearing a parachute and stood there like a mannequin, allowing a man she didn't know to dress her. This was all just a bad dream. She stared at his painting, which was actually quite beautiful. Rocky mountains cast in red that was darkening to rust as the blood dried. She looked away.

"You battle wounds have created a beautiful palette," he said.

"What?"

His finger brushed over her cheekbone, which had its own heartbeat. The physical pain paled in comparison to what was happening inside her.

"Purple, rose, indigo," he said before he raised her shirt and prodded the huge bruise on her side she hadn't noticed until now. She slapped his hand away. "The patterns of violence have always intrigued me. In your case, it's a cream base broken by black, violet, and more indigo. No broken bones according to Augustus. I love the way skin changes color when it's damaged."

Fucking freak.

He grabbed her hands and held them in front of her nose. Her knuckles were bruised and cut up to hell. Her hands were so swollen that she couldn't extend her fingers.

"Congratulations," Lucifer said and inclined his head. "You put up a decent fight. Using your crucifix was a beautiful move."

"You killed the Black Vipers?" she asked.

"It didn't take long."

"Why?" As far as she knew, Lucifer wasn't on any side, so why save her life?

"You have spirit and guts and a connection to Gavin. If you survived, he would fetch you, and I'd get another face to face. If you died, he'd come to fetch your body and possibly feel compelled to fight me. Win, win."

She couldn't comprehend his logic and didn't even try.

"Besides, I don't like when an opponent is outnumbered. You put up a good fight and would have won against a handful, but not in a fight ten to one, and they played dirty." He moved through an archway into another room. "Come."

It took a concentrated effort to move. Every step felt as if there were needles jabbing into her feet. She was chilled, sick, sore, and thirsty.

Lucifer stepped out of his chambers into a wide, dark hallway. The sound of their steps was absorbed by the cold, rough stone beneath her bare feet. Even with the high cathedral-like ceilings, she felt the beginning pangs of claustrophobia.

Lucifer pressed the button for an elevator with a red door. "You're lucky to be alive."

She didn't feel lucky. With a few well-placed questions, Lucifer destroyed the memory of her marriage and all hope for the future. She clasped Vinny's memory to her like a lucky talisman and now realized it was a poisoned apple.

"I knew you were a fighter." He clapped her on the back with enough force to make her stagger into the wall. "I'm sure Angel will be here soon."

The elevator dinged a moment before the door opened. She peered into the car and saw that it was surprisingly sterile and shiny. What the hell?

"You're related to Gavin through marriage?" Lucifer asked genially.

"Lyla and I are first cousins," she said warily as she stepped in.

"Lyla was a surprise," he said as the elevator rose with nauseating speed. "I lost faith in women long ago, but she's renewed my interest in the opposite sex. She brought some much-needed excitement into Hell."

The elevator opened onto another poorly lit hallway. Lucifer stepped out and strolled away with his hands in pockets. He didn't look back at her. For a moment, she debated whether she should make a run for it, but she didn't have the energy. Technically, he hadn't tried to kill her yet, so she followed.

As she neared the end of the hallway, she shielded her eyes against the harsh light. Had she stepped outside? She gave her eyes time to adjust before she dropped her hand. She touched her ear, wondering if she had fallen deaf. Despite the crowd walking in every direction, no one made a sound. To the left was a sports bar with a bartender, tables, and TVs mounted on the wall. Straight ahead, the landing dropped off into nothing.

She took tiny steps forward with one hand out for balance and stopped six feet from the drop-off. Wide, obsidian stairs led down to the infamous pit of Hell. The auditorium held enough seats for a Las Vegas headliner. An arena of spectators watched as two men battled on the sand. It was so quiet, the sound of their fists making contact with flesh sounded sharp and clear in her ears.

"From Japan," Lucifer said quietly as he stopped beside her. "Amazing technique. Shall we?"

He gestured to the bar. She followed slowly in his wake. She could feel what little strength she had ebbing away. She sat heavily at the table he indicated. There was a handful of men in the bar area, and every one of them was staring at her. She kept her eyes on the table. She had no weapons and no fight left. If this was the part when Lucifer tossed her to the dogs, there was nothing she could do to defend herself.

"Here." Lucifer slapped a can of Coke in front of her.

"Water, please."

He rolled his eyes and went to the bartender and returned shortly with water. She fumbled with the cap and tipped it to her mouth. Her mouth was so dry, she felt as if she had a dozen cuts in her mouth, but that didn't stop her from drinking. She set the empty bottle on the table and fought the urge to vomit.

Lucifer tapped his fingers on the table. "Roman's taking his time." He glanced at her. "You want chicken wings?"

"You're kidding."

"No, we make the best chicken wings on The Strip."

Just the thought of eating something made her feel sick. "No, thank you."

"Ah, this is unexpected."

She was about to ask what he was talking about when she saw movement out of the corner of her eye. She turned her head and saw Marcus walking toward her. He was dressed in a black on black suit, no tie. The sight of him sent a shockwave of agony through her entire being. He shouldn't be here.

A man rose from a table. She saw a flash of steel and opened her mouth to yell, but there was no need. Marcus did some fancy move and slammed the knife into the man's shoulder. He screeched and fell to his knees. The man's table companion leaped to his feet and rushed Marcus who managed to keep his feet during the tackle. His attacker reached for his leg, but Marcus grabbed the man's head and twisted savagely. There was a sharp snap and the man went limp and dropped.

"Friend of yours?" Lucifer asked.

She couldn't speak. It was Marcus as she had never seen him before. He might look like Pyre Casino's COO with his hair perfectly styled, but the man approaching her held no resemblance to the man she thought she knew. His face was expressionless, green eyes glittering and cold. His fighting technique was quick, practical, brutal. She didn't even know he knew how to fight. It was just another side of him she didn't know existed. He rounded the table to reach her but stopped when Lucifer held up a hand.

"Brave of a fancy pants like yourself to come into my territory," Lucifer said.

"I've been here before," Marcus said.

He sounded completely in control, which shouldn't surprise her. No matter the situation, one could always count on him to keep a cool head. She averted her eyes because the sight of him hurt more than anything she had been through since she last saw him.

Lucifer laughed. "I doubt that. You wouldn't last ten minutes in Hell dressed like that."

"The last time I was here, I left with Emmanuel Pyre."

Lucifer's tapping fingers stopped. She glanced at his face and saw the smile fade. She didn't know what was going on, but Marcus's words had a profound effect on Lucifer's demeanor. His expression became inscrutable, and he examined Marcus with calculated interest rather than amusement.

"So you made it."

She didn't understand Lucifer's quiet tone or the reason behind it.

"What brings you back to Hell?" Lucifer asked.

"You have something of mine."

Marcus's words made her jerk, but she didn't acknowledge him.

"You must be Marcus," Lucifer said and draped his arm on the back of her chair. "How fascinating. Carmen's been annoyingly mum about you." He gestured between them. "How do you two know each other?"

"I work with Gavin."

Lucifer clapped twice. "Bravo, Marcus. Made something of yourself, have you? And with Gavin, no less. Impressive." He glanced at Carmen before he clucked his tongue. "I sense trouble in paradise. I was expecting Roman, actually."

"She's mine."

"Is that so?" Lucifer asked as a scream split the silence.

Angel rounded the corner in jeans and a white shirt flecked with blood. He had a stained six-inch knife at his side. He spotted them and started forward. Relief calmed her nausea. Angel would get her out of this mess and give her the time she needed to shore up her defenses before she had to deal with life again.

"You have two suitors?" Lucifer asked cattily and nudged her with his elbow. "Which one are you going to choose?"

"I'm going to kill you," she hissed, and he grinned.

"You can try. I love challenges."

"Carmen, are you all right?" Angel asked.

She nodded and focused on him instead of Marcus. "Yes."

"Lucifer," Angel growled. "What the fuck?"

"This isn't my fault. You should be thanking me. I saved her," Lucifer said.

"Thanks," Marcus said in a voice that sounded like crushed glass. "Now give her to me."

"Not without payment. I was hoping for Gavin, but I got you two instead."

"What do you want?" Marcus asked.

Lucifer waved a vague hand. "Did either of you bring a present? No? How rude. I saved your princess's life. The least you could do is bring me a fruit basket or a head or something."

"Lucifer." Marcus sounded like he was speaking through clenched teeth.

"If Gavin came to fetch her, I would have renegotiated more than an annual visit, so what do you two have to offer?"

"What do you want?" Angel asked.

"Presents, a good fight...?"

"Whatever you want, consider it done," Marcus said.

"You didn't come the night Lyla was here. Why not?"

"I wasn't invited."

"But you can fight." Lucifer stroked his beard. "You're trained, probably by Gavin himself. I'd like to see you in a match."

She went rigid. "No." Marcus had never killed anyone in his life and only one winner emerged from the pit.

"Done," Marcus said.

"No, Marcus!" He could die and for what?

"And what about you?" Lucifer asked Angel.

"Going in the pit suits me just fine," Angel said with a shrug.

Lucifer winked at him. "Bitten by the bug, eh? I hear you're practicing. Gavin used to be a regular patron. You're welcome anytime."

"Lucifer," she began, but he put a massive paw over her mouth and squeezed.

"How about you two battle each other and then Carmen won't have to choose?"

She gripped his thumb and twisted his wrist so that his arm bent at an odd angle, but she didn't have the strength to hold him.

Lucifer laughed while Marcus and Angel watched from several feet away.

"I'd rather stay here with you than let them battle in the pit," she snapped.

He sighed and rolled his eyes. "Fine."

Lucifer uncoiled with ease and then tossed an arm over her shoulders. He leaned in close. Marcus took a step forward, but Angel grabbed his arm.

She stared straight ahead as the devil nuzzled her bruised cheek. She suppressed a flinch as he whispered, "I've killed men for looking at me the wrong way. Don't think I can't end you five different ways with one finger. I'm tempted to kill you just to see the looks on their faces when I pull your little heart from your chest and eat it in front of them."

Her heart skipped. Duly noted. He wasn't the king of Hell for nothing.

"Hmm." Lucifer rested his chin on her shoulder as he regarded Angel and Marcus. "You both care for her, which is interesting. I have to admit, she's entertaining." He pressed his cheek to hers as if they were BFFs. "What say you, Carmen? What's your life worth?"

"Nothing," she whispered.

He clucked his tongue. "Don't be so dreary. Two men came to your rescue."

The silence stretched. None of them moved.

"I like favors," Lucifer said quietly. "Marcus obviously doesn't know the art of a bloody fight so maybe a favor is more appropriate in this case. You too," he said to Angel. "I'll call on you when I'm ready."

"Fine," Angel said and looked at her. "Let's go."

"I'll see you soon," Lucifer murmured and to Angel and Marcus, "She's all yours. May the best man win."

She shrugged his arm off and got shakily to her feet. Marcus was in front of her before she could take a step. When he tried to take her arm, she jerked back, but he wouldn't be denied. He grabbed a handful of her outfit and yanked her against him.

She shoved against his chest. "Let me go."

He ignored her and picked her up in his arms. He moved swiftly, weaving through the tables. He was getting her out of here. She dropped her face on his shoulder, closed her eyes, and tried to ignore his familiar scent. His grip didn't slacken as he climbed stairs. She heard a familiar beat and opened one eye. She caught a glimpse of a familiar bar. Before she could place it, he shouldered through a door into the night. She shuddered as cold air penetrated through Lucifer's thin clothes.

Marcus set her down beside his Audi. She glanced around and saw the unlit sign for The Pussycat, the bar where she killed the leader of the Black Vipers.

Marcus cupped her cheek. "Carmen, did he do anything to you?"

She jerked away. "Don't touch me." She wrapped her arms around herself. "I want my mom."

"She's not here, remember? You told me she's in Utah. We didn't want to call her until we knew..." His voice trailed off, and then he said with more force, "Gavin and Lyla are on their way back from Bora Bora. Are you hurt?"

The physical pain was nothing compared to the emotional destruction Lucifer wrought. She was hanging on by a thread. She needed somewhere quiet and safe to recoup, and it wasn't with Marcus. His presence wreaked havoc on her control, which was paper thin and getting more tenuous by the second. There was a maelstrom of emotions inside her, trying to break free. She needed to get away from him. Over his shoulder, she spotted Angel leaning against the Bugatti, watching them. The knife was nowhere in sight.

"One of the employees at the Red Diamond found Mickey's body in the parking lot," Angel said, and Marcus tensed. "Kiki reviewed the footage, saw you were attacked and drugged and called me. Lucifer made sure to stay out of frame, so we couldn't identify him. We didn't know if you had been taken by another gang." Angel's eyes were piercing as he asked, "Did Lucifer touch you, baby?"

His gentle voice made her eyes burn with tears. She shook her head and held herself more tightly. The one time she was in a really bad bind, Mom and Lyla were out of town. Her life fucking sucked.

Angel pushed off the Bugatti and held out a hand. “You want to come with me?”

Marcus caged her against the car. “She’s coming with me,” he said without turning around.

She shook her head and pushed against his chest. She tried to talk, but her throat was closing up as panic swelled in her chest.

“She doesn’t want you, Fletcher,” Angel said.

“We had a misunderstanding,” Marcus countered.

Angel sneered. “A misunderstanding that caused her to go to the strip club where she was attacked?” His eyes gleamed. “A misunderstanding that led to her being in my bed?”

28

Marcus disappeared. One second, he was pinning her against the car, and the next, she was staring at his back, and Angel was on the ground at his feet. Angel leaped up and slammed his fist into his jaw. Marcus staggered back and then rammed him into the Bugatti and kneed him in the abdomen.

"Stop it!" she shouted.

Angel elbowed his face, which didn't faze him at all. She reached them as Marcus knocked Angel's head against the car. She slapped his back.

"Marcus, stop!"

He paused long enough for Angel to get in another blow. Marcus shook himself, turned, and picked her up. He carried her to his car and placed her in the passenger seat. He slammed the door and walked around to the driver's side. She looked out the window at Angel who sat in his car, watching her as he wiped blood from his lip. Holy shit.

She stared straight ahead as Marcus drove. The only sound in the car was his harsh breathing. What the fuck was that? What did he care if she hopped in Angel's bed?

"I'm taking you to the hospital," he said.

His voice was back to being cool and emotionless.

"I'm fine."

"You're not fine. You were drugged, and you're shaking, pale, and bruised. You need to go to the hospital."

"I don't have any broken bones."

"How do you know?"

"Lucifer had someone examine me."

"He didn't touch you?"

"Only to admire my bruises," she said tonelessly. She wanted to believe it was just a bad dream, but it was all frighteningly real. "You shouldn't have come for me."

He marched into Hell and now owed Lucifer a fucking favor. Did he know what that meant? Lucifer could make him do anything.

"You think I would wait around after I heard you were in Hell?" His voice began to shred, allowing some emotion to come through.

"You should've let Angel handle it."

The tension in the car was palpable. She turned her face away and shut him out. She was so drained, she could barely think straight. She was riding headlong toward a breakdown, and there was no safe place in sight.

When the car slowed, she opened her eyes as Marcus pulled into his driveway.

"Take me to a hotel," she said.

"We're going to talk."

"What for? We're done."

She was relieved to see her Aston in the garage. She shuffled to her car and stopped when Marcus leaned against it.

"Get in the house," he said.

She stood there for a full minute, gauging how much energy she had before she gave in. She walked into the living room and stopped. Being here reignited the pain that sent her into destruction mode last night. The recycled pieces from her old life taunted her from every corner of the room. She poured her heart and soul into decorating this house in the hopes of recreating what she had with Vinny, and it had been an epic fail. She needed to get out of here. She started for the front door. She looked like an escapee from an asylum but walking down the street and getting help from a stranger was preferable to facing Marcus. She might not survive it.

"Carmen."

She ignored him and focused on the exit until he blocked her. She stumbled to a halt. "Get out of my way."

"We're going to talk."

He reached for her, and she backed away.

"Don't touch me."

"Look at me."

She couldn't. The sight of him hurt so fucking bad, she felt nauseous. She could handle being beaten and drugged. She could handle Lyla and her PTSD, her mother grieving her father, and the possibility of becoming Nora's sole guardian if Lyla and Gavin died in Hell. She could handle anything except being rejected by someone she loved. The pain was unbearable.

"You're hurt. Let me help you," he said.

No, she wouldn't let him do anything else for her. It was time to stop looking to men to fix her. Lucifer was right. In the end, everyone chose themselves, and she had to do the same. She didn't have much left.

"Tell me what you need," he said.

"I need you to let me go."

"I can't."

She let out a harsh, slightly hysterical laugh. "You already have."

"I know you're angry. The bartender told me what Khalid said. I should have listened to you before I—"

Her shaky control snapped. Something raw and searing and deadly spread through her. She'd taken so many hits in the past twenty-four hours, emotional and physical, and she was done. The life she'd been rebuilding had been ripped away as surely as the illusion of the great love she had shared with Vinny. If Marcus wanted a showdown, she would give him one. She would prove him right and show him what a fucking savage she was.

She grabbed the closest object, a delicate vase, and hurled it at the wall. It shattered, just like her heart.

"This is what you don't need in your perfect, orderly life, isn't it?" She grabbed a picture frame and threw it. The sound of breaking glass was immensely satisfying.

"What are you doing?"

"I'm a crazy bitch! Everyone warned you about me; you should have listened!"

She couldn't stand seeing everything looking so perfect. She grabbed an abstract wooden sculpture and tossed that too. It didn't break, which pissed her off. She kicked over a mirror end table to compensate and was pleased by the loud smash. She was about to upend a vase of flowers she bought earlier in the week when Marcus grabbed her by the shoulders.

"Carmen, stop."

She struggled like a wild thing. He didn't want to hurt her, which she used to her advantage. She didn't fight fair, and when his grip loosened, she broke free. She stumbled into his office and faced an ocean painting she had commissioned for him. She had decorated his office with her dreams for their future. She had to destroy the evidence of her naiveté. She snatched a pair of scissors from the desk and turned back to the painting.

"Carmen!"

Marcus stopped her inches from the swirling blue waters. Her swollen hands couldn't get a good grip on the scissors as he fought her for them. She wasn't deterred. She released her weapon and went for the canvas with her fists. He picked her up. She managed to land a solid kick that made the painting shudder, but it stayed mounted on the wall.

"Fuck!" she bellowed.

He carried her kicking and screaming into the bedroom. He pinned her arms to her sides and pulled her back against his chest. She fought him with all she had, kicking his shins, stomping his feet, but he didn't release her.

"Let me go!"

"Listen to me."

"Fuck you! Let go of me!"

She cursed, threatened, and struggled, but it made no difference. When she had nothing left, she went limp and dropped her head forward. She panted as tears filled her eyes, but she refused to let them fall.

"I can fix this," he said.

She couldn't let him do that. Khalid was the catalyst that brought the hammer down, but their arrangement began to unravel when he revealed that he liked things the way they were. He didn't want things to advance. He had everything he needed, but she needed more.

"When I found out what Khalid said, I lost control. I choked him." He dropped his face into her hair. "When I couldn't get in touch with Mickey, I called Gavin. He told me what happened at the Red Diamond, that Angel was trying to figure out who'd taken you." His warm breath seeped through her hair and caressed her nape. "I didn't know what to do. Janice banished me from the office. I've been waiting here all day and then Gavin called."

"They were waiting for their shot, and I was dumb enough to give them one," she whispered.

"Tell me what you need."

"I need you to let me go."

His arms flexed before he released her. She took several steps away and took a deep breath. Her control wavered, but this had to be done. She wished she had the time to shore up her defenses and face him weeks from now when she could act cool and indifferent. Instead, she was forced to face him without any shields, when the pain was so great that she had no hope of hiding it from him.

She turned to face him. He didn't look like his suave, collected self. His clothes were in disarray, his hair was mussed, and he had a bruise forming on his jaw. Love and sorrow twisted her heart into knots. He was everything she needed, but he wasn't for her.

"I don't know how I would have made it through the past couple of months without you. You were there when I needed you. I overstepped yesterday." She clenched her hands into fists as she began to tremble. "Everything that happened after made me realize something."

She opened her mouth to go on, but her voice dried up. Marcus stepped forward with his hand outstretched, but she stepped back and shook her head wildly.

"No, you can't touch me. Let me... I need to say this. You need to understand," she said raggedly.

The only sound in the room was her hitched breaths as she tried to control herself and get through this.

"I get too attached to people. I hold on too tight. I need too much. That's why I never recovered from Vinny. I let myself go too deep and you..." She shook her head. "You woke me up, you brought me back to life, and..." Her last bit of self-control ebbed away, and a tear slid down her cheek. "I won't survive you either."

Nothing showed on his face, but she felt the atmosphere in the room shift.

"Vinny's need to prove himself to Gavin killed him. You feel indebted to Gavin for giving you a chance. That's why you work so hard, why you'll do anything for him. You're trying to prove that you deserve your position, but no one is questioning it but you." She tried to breathe past the pain. "I'm going to keep my promise. We're going to be friends. I just... I just need some time..."

Oh, God, the silence was awful.

"I already know how this goes. I can't love another man who needs work or someone else's approval more than he needs me. I wasn't enough for Vinny." She spread her hand across her aching chest. "And I won't be enough for you either. I don't have much left so... I can't do this."

The dam holding her emotions in check fragmented. Emotional overload. Too much in too little time. One event chased by another more traumatizing than the last. Her illusions shattered, another home that was no longer a home, and another man who couldn't give her what she needed. She dropped to her knees, hands over her face, and bowed her head as heart-wrenching sobs shook her.

Marcus wrapped his arms around her. She didn't have the

strength to push him away. She cried for everything she had lost, and everything that was still slipping through her fingers. Life put her through the wringer, and she was tapping out. All her fire and zeal had been beaten out of her. She had nothing left.

Marcus picked her up and placed her on the bed. She buried her face in the bedsheets and grabbed handfuls of it as she let go of her delusions and fantasies. His hand rested at the base of spine. When the tears ceased and she was empty, he lay beside her and tipped her against his chest.

"No! I don't want—" she said hoarsely.

"Shh," he murmured.

He pressed her face against his throat, and she was wreathed in classy sin. Even though she didn't want to, her body responded to his familiar scent and she relaxed. The only sound in the room was the occasional hitch in her breath as she tried to get herself under control. She was grateful for the darkness that hid the tears that slid down her face and soaked his shirt. She was too tired to battle for space, for privacy. Instead, she lay tucked against him with his hand tunneling through her hair, gently massaging her scalp. Her face rode the steady rise and fall of his chest. She trembled with fatigue, pain, shock, and heartache. She willed herself to sleep, but her mind wouldn't allow it. Time passed.

"My mother sold me to Lucifer's father when I was five years old," Marcus said quietly. "He used me."

She stopped breathing.

"He forced Lucifer to watch. I wasn't the only one. There were others."

There was no inflection in his voice, but his body was tense against hers.

"One day, Lucifer let it slip to a visitor about us. He saved my life." His fingers played with her hair as he spoke. "We were taken to a hospital. The man who saved us thought we were broken. He said if we survived, to look him up when we got older and he would help us."

He stopped. Even in her exhausted state, she had to know the rest.

"Who...?" she croaked.

"Emmanuel Pyre."

The final puzzle piece fell into place.

"He gave me my name. I went into the foster system and had years of therapy. Out of the group of kids saved that day, I'm the only one still alive."

Her broken heart bled for him. She reached up and cupped his cheek. His hand covered hers, holding her palm against his jaw.

"That image of Emmanuel is embedded in my mind. He's my hero. When I made it to college, I contacted him, and he told Gavin about me. He knew the challenges I faced and gave me a chance. I don't want to let him down."

It all made sense now. All his life, he strived to be a Pyre. He clung to the goal of success to get through the hard times. He was living his dream, a dream he fought for tooth and nail. He made it and didn't want anyone getting in his way.

"My whole life I've been trying to reach this pinnacle. That's what kept me going and now... I don't know anything about relationships. I've never had one. I don't know what's beyond this, but I like what we have. I don't want things to change. I don't—"

She put her hand over his mouth and shook her head. She didn't want to hear the end of that sentence. He owed her no explanations, and he had actually come after her in Hell. She made him step into a place he hadn't been to since he left. She closed her eyes against the burn of tears. Again, her fault. Now he owed Lucifer a favor because of her.

"I'm sorry," she whispered.

"What?"

"You shouldn't have come there. I didn't know—"

His hand fisted in her hair. "I spent hours thinking you were dead. Hearing you were alive, I didn't care that I had to go into Hell to fetch you."

"You owe him a favor because of me."

"I can handle it."

"You don't know what he'll ask for."

"Doesn't matter."

It did. Lucifer was twisted and maniacal. His favor could have deadly consequences and would no doubt twist Marcus's scruples. More blame on her head. *She'll ruin your life.* Gavin's voice echoed in her head, and she flinched. Marcus should be proud of the man he was. He had survived Hell and come out the victor. She couldn't say the same.

"I understand," she murmured.

He pressed his lips against her temple. "I care, Carmen."

She rested her forehead against his throat as another tear slipped down her cheek. Caring wasn't enough.

A ringing phone woke her. Marcus rolled away and picked it up.

"Yes?" He rose from the bed and headed to the closet. "The police are there?"

A casino emergency. She heard the rustle of clothing. She kept her eyes closed and breathing even. Her body felt heavy and unresponsive.

"Carmen, wake up."

She played dead. She didn't want to face him.

He cupped her face. "Come on, baby, wake up."

She allowed her eyes to open. It hurt to look at him. It hurt to smell him. Yes, she was a sucker for a good guy who fucked like a bad boy, had a chip on his shoulder, and would never love her back as much as she loved him.

"My head of security's dead. Witnesses say the assailants left on motorcycles."

The Black Vipers were making hits on Pyre Casino employees? More death and drama that could be traced back to her.

"I'll be gone three hours tops." He stroked her hair back from her face. "Gavin comes back today. Once he takes over, we can figure this out."

Figure out what? She understood his reservations. Knowing his background, his ambition and drive made sense. It meant he was Vinny on steroids. He would never stop, would never fill that well. If work made him happy, he attained a level of happiness and contentment very few people reached.

"Just give me some time," he said.

Give him time to figure out how he felt about her? They already knew the answer. When he didn't move, she nodded.

"Once I get back, I'll take you to the doctor. I want to make sure you're okay. There are guards outside. You're safe here."

He straightened and walked toward the door. He paused, looked back, and stared at her for a long minute. He opened his mouth, shook his head, and then disappeared.

She listened to him leave and stared straight ahead. Sunlight streamed through the windows. Her body felt as if it weighed one thousand pounds. She slid her legs over the side of the bed and sat there for a few minutes before she found the strength to move. She staggered to the window. There were two SUVs in the driveway full of Gavin's guards. Fuck.

She hobbled to the garage and fetched her clutch from her car. The diamond necklace winked at her. She left it in the console and nabbed her phone, which beeped with messages she ignored. She stared at the damaged living room as she dialed and put the phone to her ear.

"Carmen?"

"Angel, I need a ride."

AUTHOR'S NOTE

Hi All,

Yes, there is going to be another book for Carmen! I said each character after Gavin and Lyla would only get one book and broke my rule on the first try. Ugh! The characters have a mind of their own and I've stopped trying to control them. We're going to indulge them and tag along for the ride.

I hope you enjoyed Awakened by Sin. This book took me over a year to write and is the most emotionally complex story I've written. When Vinny was murdered in Crime Lord's Captive I didn't know that Carmen would get a story or that one day, I would have to deal with her grief. She ripped my heart out. This has been a very trying year for me. It's insane how my life paralleled a lot of the psychological struggles in this book. I had my first huge loss this year so writing this book was cathartic and gave new meaning to writing in your own blood. Carmen made me laugh, cry, cheer, and helped me through my darkest moments.

Thank you for giving the Crime Lord Series a chance and coming on this ride with me! I couldn't do this without you. If you have a chance, please leave a review and recommend to a friend. It helps me out a lot!

Also, I've written a bonus scene from Angel's POV during his debut as crime lord in The Pussycat. Join my email list and have it sent to your inbox!

Love,

Mia

BOOKS BY MIA KNIGHT

CRIME LORD SERIES

Crime Lord's Captive

Recaptured by the Crime Lord

Once A Crime Lord

Awakened by Sin

ABOUT THE AUTHOR

Mia is the author of the Crime Lord Series and writes dark, contemporary romances. She currently lives in Sin City where she is shadowed by her dogs who don't judge when she cries and laughs with the characters in her head. She loves road trips, fast food, lakes and rivers, trains, and daydreaming.

Stalk Mia
Website
Email
Mia Knight's Captives (Facebook Group)

facebook.com/miaknightbooks
twitter.com/authormiaknight
instagram.com/authormiaknight
goodreads.com/authormiaknight
bookbub.com/profile/mia-knight

Made in the USA
Columbia, SC
17 July 2018